Collier's *Junior* Classics

Series Editor
Margaret E. Martignoni

Series Titles	*Volume Editors*
A, B, C: GO!	**Rosemary E. Livsey**
ONCE UPON A TIME	**Elizabeth H. Gross**
MAGIC IN THE AIR	**Mary V. Gaver**
JUST AROUND THE CORNER	**Alice Brooks McGuire**
IN YOUR OWN BACKYARD	**Marian C. Young**
GIFTS FROM THE PAST	**Elenora Alexander**
LEGENDS OF LONG AGO	**Jane Darrah**
ROADS TO GREATNESS	**Louise Galloway**
CALL OF ADVENTURE	**Charlemae Rollins**
HARVEST OF HOLIDAYS	**Ruth Weeden Stewart**

just around
the
corner

A completely new selection of outstanding children's stories and poems compiled for enrichment reading by a distinguished editorial board of children's librarians.

Series Editor
MARGARET E. MARTIGNONI
Former Superintendent
Work with Children
Brooklyn Public Library

Editor-in-Chief
DR. LOUIS SHORES
Dean, Library School
Florida State University

Managing Editor
HARRY R. SNOWDEN, JR.

Volume Editor
ALICE BROOKS McGUIRE
Librarian,
Casis Elementary School
Austin, Texas

Collier's *Junior* Classics Series

THE CROWELL-COLLIER PUBLISHING COMPANY • NEW YORK

Just Around the Corner

Introduction

Collier's Junior Classics Series

We are children only once, and then only for a few brief years. But these are the most impressionable years of a lifetime. Never again will the world and everything in it be so eternally new, so filled with wonder. Never again will physical, mental, spiritual growth be so natural and unavoidable. During these years, habits become ingrained, tastes are developed, personality takes form. The child's whole being is geared toward learning. He instinctively reaches out for truth and, having no prejudices, seizes upon that which is good, just, beautiful. For these reasons, a child deserves what Walter de la Mare has called "only the rarest kind of best."

What do we mean by "best" in a book for children? Best books reflect universal truths with clarity and artistry. Such books reveal that man is essentially good and that life is infinitely worth living. They do not deny the existence of evil, but rather emphasize man's thrilling struggle against evil through faith, courage, and perseverance. They awaken the young reader's imagination, call forth his laughter as well as his tears, help him to understand and to love his fellow man. The reading of such books constitutes a rich heritage of experience which is every child's birthright.

The librarian-editors of *Collier's Junior Classics* have combed the best children's books of the past and present to assemble in a single series a sampling of the finest literature for boys and girls. High standards have been maintained for the art work also, which in most instances has been taken from the original book. No attempt has been made to cover all fields of knowledge or to include factual material for its own sake. The emphasis here is on good literature, chiefly fiction and biography, folk lore and legend, and some poetry. Special attention is given to the American scene and American democratic ideals, but many selections cover other cultures, geographical areas, and historical periods.

The purpose of *Collier's Junior Classics* is to introduce boys and girls to some of the best books ever written for children, to stimulate young readers to seek for themselves the books from which the selections have been drawn as well as other good books of similar appeal, and to encourage children to become discriminating, thoughtful, life-time readers. Author, title, and publisher are given at the foot of the page on which each selection opens. This enables readers to ask for the complete book at a library or bookstore. When necessary, brief introductions set the scene for the selection, while follow-up recommendations, complete with publishers' names, appear at the end of most stories.

Collier's Junior Classics is a series of ten individually indexed volumes. A, B, C: GO! has been lovingly compiled for the youngest, and consists of nursery rhymes, favorite folk tales, best-loved poems, and stories for reading aloud. Four volumes have been assembled for the intermediate group: ONCE UPON A TIME, a wonderous collection of fables, world folk tales, and modern fairy tales; MAGIC IN THE AIR, selections from great masterpieces of fantasy; JUST AROUND THE CORNER, excerpts from warm-hearted stories of other lands; and IN YOUR OWN BACKYARD, selections from stirring books about our own country. Four additional volumes cater to the interests of more mature boys and girls: GIFTS FROM THE PAST, memorable selections from world classics; LEGENDS OF LONG AGO, selections from great myths, epics, and American tall tales; ROADS TO GREATNESS, excerpts from biographies of some of the greatest men and women of the world; and CALL OF ADVENTURE, selections from action and suspense stories of today and yesterday. Finally, and most unusual of all, is the volume entitled HARVEST OF HOLIDAYS, a feast of stories, poems, documents, and factual material about twenty-two American national and religious holidays. Although perhaps of greatest interest to the intermediate group, HARVEST OF HOLIDAYS will intrigue and delight all ages.

The tables of contents for the ten volumes read like an all-time Who's Who of distinguished writers. A brief mention of only a few of these authors would include such names as Lewis Carroll, Kenneth Grahame, Charles Dickens, Mark Twain, Louisa May Alcott, Pearl Buck, Laura Ingalls Wilder, Eleanor Estes, Genevieve Foster, Robert Louis Stevenson, Robert McCloskey, Valenti Angelo, Carl Sandburg, A. A. Milne, Eleanor Farjeon, Elizabeth Enright, and Margaret Wise Brown. Among the illustrators, many of whom are also authors, are to be found the Petershams, the d'Aulaires, Wanda Gág, Louis Slobodkin, Helen Sewell, Lois Lenski, Roger Duvoisin, Maurice Sendak, Kurt Wiese, Marguerite de Angeli, Steele Savage, Howard Pyle, Lynd Ward, James Daugherty, Arthur Rackham, Fritz Kredel, and Gustave Dore.

Collier's Junior Classics is intended primarily for the home, although libraries will find the series valuable for browsing as well as for introducing children to many different books. Because each book is an individual volume, complete with its own index, it can be shelved where the librarian believes it will be most useful to the children.

No pains have been spared to make the individual volumes a series of stepping stones to all that is best in the magic world of children's books.

Margaret E. Martignoni
SERIES EDITOR

Contents

Just Around the Corner

"I wanted to share a bit of my life with the rest of the world," wrote Hilda von Stockum, author of *The Cottage at Bantry Bay*. The same wish inspired the many other authors represented in this volume. They have written about young people from eighteen different countries—eighteen countries that were once very far away from the United States, but are, today, JUST AROUND THE CORNER.

The backgrounds of the stories are startingly different—snow-capped hills in war-torn Norway, violent jungles in Burma, treeless pampas in Argentina, busy Venetian canals.

The costumes are vastly contrasting—Eskimo furs that bury the body in warmth, sparse clothes that leave the native Africans free to bound through forests.

The characters are worlds apart—some are black, some are white, some are Oriental. Some live in mansions, others in huts. Some are rich, others are poor.

Yet, when we look closely at the people, when we forget their clothes, their homes, the colors of their skins, when we block out the backgrounds and look at the people themselves, we discover they are all the same. They all think and feel and love and fear. They all laugh, they all cry. Heidi in Switzerland, Li Lun in China, Nomusa in Africa are as different as people can be . . . but at the same time, they are all brothers and sisters who share the joys and the fears, the fun and the problems of growing up.

ALICE BROOKS McGUIRE
*Librarian, Casis Elementary School,
Austin, Texas*

Ajax, the Golden Dog

BY MARY ELWYN PATCHETT

Illustrations by Eric Tansley

> *In the isolated back country of Australia, young people very often find themselves without friends their own age. Animals are their constant companions. Ajax, the great golden warrior dog, and the young girl with whom he lives, have many thrilling adventures together in this story of the land "down under."*

AUSTRALIA is a land of violent contrasts. Sometimes the country suffers from a drought, and sometimes from rolling floods that carry away animals and houses, fences and even people. If you look at a map of Australia, you will see where a river makes part of the border line between New South Wales and Queensland, and halfway along this the river takes a sudden hairpin bend. The river has many names. Sometimes it's called the Severn, sometimes the Sovereign, and sometimes the Dumeresque. My home was right on a bend. Its name Gunyan was an aboriginal word for "running water." At times there was far too much running water, for the homestead stood with the river curving round it on two sides, and in a really great flood the water overflowed the banks and poured down on the house, like someone taking a diagonal short cut across a street corner.

I remember only one such flood, and while it was frightening and terrible, drowning animals and causing thousands of dollars worth of damage, I could not help finding it exciting, and it did give me the most wonderful dog I have ever known—my golden giant, Ajax.

It had been raining for weeks, both at my home and far upriver where the small streams poured their rain-fed waters into the main channel of the river, swelling it into a great, thundering mass of water that broke its banks and spread into a swiftly running torrent seven miles wide. My father got news of the approaching flood by telephone, and so we had time to make preparations to leave the homestead and move to higher land.

When my father said we must get ready to move, the dogs and I were very excited. We were to take tents and to go up to a hill about three miles from the homestead, where we would be above the water however much it should rise. First of all, everything possible had to be put away, so we helped stack furniture up in the big loft; then the car was driven up a ramp onto a high veranda and chained there. It was no use to us then, because the water in the small gullies lying between us and the hill was already too deep to cross in the car.

We had to make our trek in buggies and sulkies and drays. Of course the station hands and their families were coming too, and everybody rushed about, loading drays, packing blankets and tents and food. My mother and Nessie, who was our housekeeper now that I was too big to have a nurse, packed cans of food and cut sandwiches, gathered together changes of shoes and clothes, and finally said they were ready.

I'd packed most of my toys and staggered up to the loft with them; then I put the bridle on Buck, my bay pony, to lead him by, for I was going in the sulky with Lewis, who was a wonderful bushman, full of the sort of stories that children love to listen to. I was to lead

Buck because Algy and Ben would not stay in the sulky without me, and Algy was afraid of water and would have to be carried over the streams, while Benny was really too small to follow if I rode Buck over the water-covered bush roads, full of rubbish and nasty deep potholes.

Finally we were ready, and the oddest-looking caval-cade you ever saw set off for the hilltop, which looked down on the muddy, rushing yellow torrent. Poor drowned animals floated and bobbed on the current. Great trees, uprooted as the water softened their earth-bound roots and toppled them into the flood, turned and twisted and bumped into tangles of fence posts and torn wires and jams of planks, where houses had been washed away and broken up in the fury of the waters, to be carried perhaps hundreds of miles downstream before being stranded by the receding river.

We reached the hilltop and the men began setting up the tents. The dogs and I seemed to be in everyone's way, so we walked down the hill to the edge of the river. It was a frightening sight, with water as far as my eyes could see, and once a small wooden cottage, all in one piece, went skimming by, twisting and turning in the current.

The dogs and I stayed for a long time at the edge of the water, watching it creep up on the stick my father had driven into the mud to test the rate the river was rising. Once we saw a huge gum tree, its twisted roots still earth-filled, towering above the water, hurtling along, twisting and turning and bumping other trees and logs. As the current swept it toward us I saw a long, evil head reared above the roots, like the carved figure on the prow of a ship. Thick coils twined about the roots, patterned as perfectly as if woven by a Persian carpet-maker, and I knew it was a very big carpet snake, a constrictor of the python type that sometimes grows

to fifteen feet and more in length. It is harmless, but a great eater of hens and their eggs, and I knew that somebody was going to have an unwelcome visitor when the water finally left the tree stranded. However, that might be after a trip of hundreds of miles.

The dogs and I would have been quite happy to sit for hours by the water and watch the strange flotsam that went rushing by. But suddenly I became aware that not all the movement was on the water—the land around me was simply alive with creatures that had come out of their haunts to find high land out of reach of the river. There were frogs and spiders, centipedes and scorpions, lizards and snakes and goodness knows what else—all traveling up the hill toward our tents!

Algy and Ben were more fascinated than I was by all the creepy-crawlies, and barked madly at the frogs, trying to anticipate which way they would jump. That was all right, but I was afraid they might pounce on one of the more deadly creatures, so we went back up the hill. It wasn't much better up there, as the tents seemed to be carpeted with spiders already, as well as other oddities, but fortunately all these disturbed creatures seemed more interested in finding somewhere to hide than in rushing about or attacking animals. I felt that a great big dog like Algy should protect *me* from the creeping things, but he didn't like them himself. If he was having a doze and woke with one crawling over him, he would twitch his hide and whimper for me until I came along and knocked it off. Ben, who wasn't much bigger than a good-sized lizard himself, was much braver and had to be restrained from snapping at scorpions and spiders and those horrible, ghost-white centipedes that you never see until something like a flood has chased them from the rotten logs they live in, where apparently they never see the sun.

Most of the station livestock had been moved back into the hills several days before. Cattle are hopeless in floods; horses, even sheep, will try to swim, but cattle simply stand there until the water rises high enough to lift them off their hoofs, turn them over and drown them. So all the cattle in the river paddocks had been moved to higher lands, and the Hereford studs had their stablemen with them, well out of the reach of flood waters.

We had a campfire supper, and I was sent to bed almost as soon as it was dark. Algy and Ben lay on saddlecloths on the end of my camp stretcher. The whole place was wet and smelly and I was afraid of the whispering, rustling things that crawled about me in the dark, so I let Algy and Ben creep up on my bed and lie beside me, which in the ordinary way was strictly forbidden.

In the morning the water had fallen a few inches, and the dogs and I set out to explore. The small, teeming life did not seem so bad in the sunlight. The ground was squashy with wet, but the sun shone down with a cheerful warmth. We had gone out of sight of the camp and were walking among a lot of felled trees that had been chopped down in the summer. I walked cautiously around these, because I could not tell what might be lurking on the other side if I jumped over them.

I was just running round one when I heard a whining, scratching sound in it. I listened and heard it again, and so did the dogs, and Benny began to dig violently at one end of the log. I pulled him away because I was afraid of what he might find in there. Then I marked the log, called the dogs and we raced back to the camp to find Lewis.

Lewis brought an ax and began to chop carefully at the waterlogged bark. There was no sound from inside it, and I think Lewis thought that I had imagined the noise; then a chip of wood came away, and underneath it we could see a bright, golden gleam. Lewis made the opening wider, put in his hand and pulled out a long, yellow puppy, quite dead.

"Well, there you are," Lewis said. "I'm afraid we are too late—the little chap's dead."

"Oh, Lewis, how awful! But how long has he been dead?"

"About a day—perhaps more, I should think."

"You mean he hasn't just died this minute?"

"No, he's quite cold. He's been dead some time."

"Then he can't be the one I heard!" I shouted excitedly. "There must be another one in there!"

So Lewis began his careful chopping again, and sure enough another bright golden gleam appeared. He tore the soft wood away with his hands and my heart sank. There was no movement at all—apparently this little chap was as dead as his brother.

Lewis put his hand in to lift the pup and pulled it back, saying, "Ouch! He bit me, the little demon!"

"Oh, he's alive! He's alive!"

"He's alive all right, and he's got a mighty fine set of milk teeth."

Lewis put his hand back in the log more cautiously and lifted out another yellow pup, so nearly dead that it made little difference, but still with enough spirit to draw back his tiny upper lip and snarl at the big man holding him.

Lewis handed him to me, saying, "Here you are. I don't think he'll live—he seems all in—so you mustn't be upset if you lose him. Take him back to camp and get some warm milk from your mother, and wrap him up warmly."

The dogs were leaping up like mad things, each trying to look at the pup, sniffing and yelping until I had to scold them and make them keep down. Once the little fellow made a feeble snap at my hand; his teeth closed on the skin, but he hadn't enough strength in his jaws to break it. After that he seemed to lose consciousness, and his yellow head, small and babyish yet somehow full of character, lolled against my arm, and his yellow eyes stayed closed.

I walked back as quickly as I could and wrapped the baby in an old jersey, warmed some milk and forced it between his jaws. He swallowed a little and I lay down on my bed, holding him close to me for warmth and making the dogs stay at the foot, which annoyed them very much. All that day I fed the pup on milk every hour. If he wasn't any stronger, he certainly hadn't lost strength, and then I fed him every two hours all through the night. My mother wanted to help me, but I wanted to care for him all myself, so she let me.

The next morning the pup was brighter, and I was half dead with sleepiness! Once he tried to struggle up, and snarled and gave quite a brisk snap at my hand. I left him asleep on my bed when I went to get my breakfast, and rushed into the tent again when I heard a violent yelp from Benny. I discovered that Master Ben, taking advantage of my absence, had been nosing around the pup, and had had his black button of a nose well nipped for his pains.

That afternoon I was very sleepy, so after I had fed the pup I lay down beside him and went off to sleep. I must have slept very soundly, for when I woke the pup was not there, and the jumper I had rolled round him trailed from the bed to the ground. I jumped up and hurried to the tent flap, pushed it aside, and there I saw a sight I shall never forget.

Outside on the wet ground I saw a circle of dogs. In it were Algy and Ben and the sheep and cattle dogs belonging to the stockmen. In the center of the ring stood my tiny, savage, golden pup. He swayed on his legs, but a faint, ominous growl came from the small golden chest. As he grew older this faint ghost of a growl turned into the deep, shuddering thunder of the fighter. His lips were drawn back, and his brilliant yellow eyes were filled with flickering pink lightnings. This wee, starved pup was defying a dozen full-grown dogs in his lonely, friendless world. My heart went out to him as I watched; his hind legs gave way and he sat down, but he still kept his head high and rumbled his tiny defiance of the crowd.

I couldn't bear it any longer, he was so alone. I stepped forward and picked him up. His sharp eyeteeth broke the skin on my hand and drops of blood welled out. I left my hand in his jaws, and he looked up at me uncertainly. I stroked his head with my other hand, and he opened his jaws. I kept on stroking him and presently he licked the salty blood off my hand, with a wondering expression in his eyes.

Then I held him against my face and whispered to him, "Do you know that you're *my* dog—that you're my Ajax, the bravest of the brave?"

He licked my cheek and that ended our first battle of wills. I had won—he was my dog, my Ajax, forever.

Once the flood began to go down, the river and the little creeks that fed it dropped rapidly. Actually I had had Ajax for only two days when my father decided that it would be safe to begin the trek home. So we packed up everything once again and started off home, I holding Ajax on my knee and the other two dogs sitting jealously —Algy at my feet, Benny on the seat between Lewis and me.

It wasn't at all a pleasant drive. There were only patches of dry road, and all sorts of things were hidden in the watery holes and pools, logs and washed-away earth. I had my work cut out trying to hold on to all three dogs as we went bumping along.

When we reached the homestead we found it in a horrible mess of mud and rubbish, but safe. An appalling smell hung over everything. The river had risen to nearly two feet high in the house, and the floors were a foot deep in smelly mud and dead crawlies—but not all of them were dead either! Everyone worked at shovel-

ing the mud out until hoses could be put on. Finally it
was pretty clean, but it stayed damp and beastly for
days. And as for the garden, it was absolutely ruined.
In the end the river mud did it a lot of good, the way
that the overflowing Nile feeds the crops, but nearly
everything had to be replanted.

Ajax grew stronger every day, and soon he could lap
up his milk; then his yellow eyes would narrow to slits
of ecstasy as he drank. When he got a little larger and
stronger on his legs, Algy longed to play with him. He
would bowl the pup over and push him along with his
nose, while Ajax went on with frenzied snappings and
snarlings. Then Algy blinked at the ridiculous pup,
seemed to shrug his big shoulders and probably gave
up the effort. When Ajax snapped at Benny, Benny
snapped back at him, and then there were such squeal-
ings and yelpings of rage on both sides that I had to
separate them.

Ajax grew into a tremendous dog. He never played
with other dogs and he just tolerated humans. He seemed
to get the exercise his huge frame needed on long, nightly
hunting trips from which he would return and throw
himself down beside my bed until morning. I was the
one thing he loved, and he hardly took his deep yellow
eyes off me. I hated to go anywhere without him, for
when I went away he was filled with savage despair.

In a couple of years he grew nearly as big as a calf,
and his coat was a glorious orange-golden color. We
decided that his mother must have been a dingo—one
of those clever, savage Australian wild dogs—and his father, most likely, was a big kangaroo dog. Kangaroo dogs
are like giant greyhounds, very fast on their feet, with
great deep chests and bony, intelligent heads.

When Ajax was three, my family took a house at the
seaside for the summer. I was excited about this, but
miserable at the thought of leaving the dogs behind,

especially Ajax who would be so unhappy without me. Nevertheless I had to go.

When we arrived at a quiet cove below Sydney called Half-Moon Bay, I was delighted with the bungalow, which was built high above the ground with a sort of open-air playroom beneath with a table-tennis table and other joys, and all around it a big, high-fenced garden. The wire-netting fence was there to keep away marauding dogs. The house overlooked the beach and the splendid, wild waters of the Pacific, with waves like emerald galleons topped by wind-torn white sails.

The morning after we arrived, after spending nearly a week in Sydney on the way down, I was plunging about in the surf when a "dumper"—that's a big wave full of churning undertow—caught me, knocked me down and then landed me on the beach in a smother of sand and water. When I got my breath and opened my eyes, I was knocked down again—by Algy and Ben!

They scrabbled and yelped and smothered me. Algy, in moments of excitement, always imagined he was a tiny puppy again and wanted to sit on my knee. So there he was, knocking me down and trying to sit on me at the same time!

When I managed to look up, Lewis was standing behind me, his dark face creased with laughter.

I called out, "Oh, Lewis, how lovely—where's Ajax?"

"He's waiting in the garden. I didn't know how he'd take to the beach if there was a crowd here. I didn't realize it would be so quiet——"

"But how did you get here?"

"Well, I think you have to thank Ajax. I had an awful job with him after you left. He kept starting out to find you. So I wired to your father after a day of this, and got my orders to drive the truck down and bring all the boys along. We've covered about five hundred miles in the last four days. Look!"

He broke off and pointed to where, against the sky line on the edge of the sand, stood a colossal, orange-colored dog. The dog stood motionless for a second, and then I called "Ajax!" and he left the bank. He didn't seem to jump; he just launched himself into space, and the next instant I was knocked flat and Ajax stood over me, his feet planted on each side of my body, his serious, savage eyes gazing into mine. The wild light died out of them, and I put my hand up to his muzzle.

He gave a little whine, strange from such a great, gaunt creature, and I think the only whine I ever heard him give. Then he put his head down and licked my face. I put my arms around his neck and pulled myself up, then we all went home to breakfast.

Each of the dogs had a different approach to the surf that curled and hissed up the long crescent of coarse, golden sand. Benny rushed at it, biting the bubbles and wobbling ludicrously behind as he backed away from a wave, and he always thought the waves were chasing him up the beach.

Algy mumbled in his chops, then put his head on one side until his expression said quite plainly, "Somebody's fooling me. I *won't* go in that great big bath!" Finally he licked at the froth, paddled a little where the sand was wet from the spent waves, decided that it was quite harmless after all and settled down to enjoy himself. The small crabs fascinated him—he sniffed at them, then leaped back wildly as they nipped his nose. His chops flapped with slapping sounds that startled the crabs and always made me laugh.

Ajax looked neither to right nor left. He followed me a few steps into a rushing wave, breasted it with me, and calmly followed into the deep water and swam beside me as if he had done it all his life. I think that Ajax really loved the water apart from his wish to stay near to me. He was a very strong swimmer, and would tow me along whenever I put my hand on his neck. Sometimes he let me swim by myself, but he always lay on the sand and watched until I came out again.

One fine morning I woke early and decided to go for a swim. Ajax was off on one of his prowls, and I could hear Ben and Algy quarreling about something at the back of the house, so I decided to trick them and slip off alone. The sun was still below the horizon, but it made a track of light from the beach to the end of the sea-filled world. It was high tide and the sea looked oily and heavy, with no waves to speak of. I decided that there was probably a heavy undertow and that I must be careful. I kicked off my sandals and waded in. The sudden, crisp, cool shock of the water was wonderful, and I began swimming.

Presently I thought I was far enough from the shore and turned to swim in, but I couldn't. I could feel the strong grip of the water drawing me away from the beach. I knew I mustn't panic. I let myself float for a moment to regain my strength, and was alarmed to find that I was being carried seaward even more swiftly than I thought.

I was very afraid. I couldn't fight the undertow, and the sea was so deep and undisturbed that it was likely to attract the deadly gray nurse sharks. It was a nasty thought that those powerful, hungry fish might be cruising near to me quite unseen. I grew more and more afraid. I tried to control myself, but as the weakness of weariness crept over me the terror mounted. I turned my head toward the shore and called despairingly, "Ajax! Ajax!"

It seemed minutes afterward, but it could only have been seconds, when I heard feet thudding on the beach. I turned my head, and bounding across the pale gold of the early-morning sands was the darker golden shape of Ajax.

He sprang from the hard-packed sand at the edge of
the water like something launched from a catapult, and
then I could see his great head moving strongly toward
me across the terrifying waste of water. In a minute or
so the head came nearer to me, and as I put my arm
across his neck he turned toward the shore, and I saw
my father and Lewis there. They were struggling to
launch the little boat we kept dragged up on the dry
sand out of reach of the tide.

Even Ajax, strong swimmer though he was, could make no headway against the terrible pull of the undertow. He could barely hold his own with my added weight dragging at him. I was too exhausted to help, and could only hang on and try not to hamper the dog too much. I thought I could hear my father's voice shouting encouragement, but I felt that even Ajax's great strength was waning. His shoulders moved more slowly, though his gallant heart kept him trying.

I don't remember much more, although I became conscious that the boat was beside me, and I had only one idea fixed firmly in my mind: I must not let go of Ajax. My father told me afterward that they just could not pry my hands loose from Ajax's neck, and that they had to pull the great dog and me into the boat in one piece. At one stage they decided to tow us in, but they, too, thought of the sharks; so with a great struggle they finally hauled the dog in with me attached.

When we reached the beach my father rolled me in his coat, made a sand pillow for my head and told me to lie there quietly. For once in his life Ajax lost his aloofness. No human face could have expressed greater anxiety for a loved one. He padded softly round me, every now and again putting his big head down close to mine, licking my hand, and finally lying close beside me.

In a few minutes I felt better. Then my father told me that he and Lewis decided on an early-morning swim too, and as they were leaving the house they heard a rush of feet and saw Ajax tear down the garden and sail over the fence. They decided that this must mean that I was in some sort of danger, and they ran after the dog. When they reached the beach they could see Ajax's head far out in the path of sunlight, and beyond it a small dot that they knew must be mine. They tore for the boat, and it was then that Ajax reached me and I saw them over his head.

The rest of the vacation was heavenly. Benny, especially, was fascinated by the life in the deep potholes
studding the rocks. These holes were round and quite
deep, for they are ground out by the tides swirling stones
round and round in the same places for years until the
holes are formed, and finally these become the homes
of all sorts of sea creatures.

Crabs were always fascinating mysteries to Ben as
well as to Algy. He would poke his nose into thick
bunches of seaweed, give a surprised yell as something
nipped him, then back away. Then he would creep
back cautiously, unable to control his curiosity, and
retire again with a shriek of surprise and a backward
bound, and sometimes he would have a small, outraged
crab fastened to his sharp nose! Then Benny would
squint down it, fill his lungs for a colossal yelp—and as
likely as not the crab would drop off. At that, Benny
staggered back on his haunches, looking for the back,
or non-nipping end of this strange creature—and the crab
scuttled off sideways!

Oh, it was fun! And even Ajax showed amazement
at one friend I made. I was gazing into a tiny rock pool,
when I noticed what I took to be a piece of strange,
speckled seaweed. I touched it gently with my finger
and it curled over the tip—I was holding hands with a
baby octopus! I peered into the pool and could see its
eight little arms waving about in the water, each one
just a few inches long. Its queer little face seemed merely
a pair of eyes and a strange sort of tiny beak. I put my
hand into the water and managed to detach it gently
from its rock. It wound its tentacles round my hand.
The dogs were wild with excitement, each wanting to
look, and I laughed when the dignified Ajax jerked his
head away in a far from dignified manner when the
baby touched his nose.

Algy was affectionate, as he was to all small creatures, and Benny belligerent, and he had to be scolded and kept in his place. The little octopus wasn't at all frightened, merely active. He untwined himself from my hand and ran up my arm and over my shoulder, perched there a minute and then ran down my back and dropped onto the rocks. Once on a rock he drew himself up high on his eight arms and bustled back into the pool, just like a Walt Disney octopus.

Those lazy, sun-filled days were full of unusual excitements for an inland-bred child, for even the finding of an old plank, washed up in the tide and covered with goose-necked barnacles, was thrilling. The dogs were madly excited over the barnacle-covered plank, and barked and bounded about it as the myriad heads waved about in their aimless manner, like the result of a badly done hair-do. I think the plank looked to the boys like one long and very peculiar animal!

The summer ended at last, and as our return road home meant going through Sydney we stayed a few days for my mother to do some shopping. It was not easy to manage the dogs in a town, for none of them had ever worn collars, and they had not a clue about traffic. So it meant that nearly all their exercise, in fact their whole life, was lived on the roof of the hotel. My family had always stayed in this particular hotel and they were very good about the dogs, so it really was not too difficult as it was only for a few days anyhow.

It was during this stay that we all acquired a new friend, so it was worth a little inconvenience.

During the few days we stayed at the Metropole with the dogs, my mother was busy interviewing possible governesses for me. I did not think much of this idea because I never had had regular lessons. And as I could read and write quite well by the time I was five I hated the idea of having to learn anything else! My father and I would spend hours at the zoo, Taronga Park, and as I loved the monkeys I used to get the keepers to let me follow them into the various cages so that I could nurse the gibbons, give the chimpanzees their milk and take the orangutans for walks.

It was while I was doing this that I made a wonderful friend, an old sea captain who loved monkeys too. He used to bring consignments of animals from the East for the Australian zoos, and when I met him he was visiting the last batch of monkeys he had brought. Usually these little tropical monkeys die on the voyage down, because the nights at sea are cold for monkeys born in the steamy, tropical forests of Malaya. The captain hated to see the poor little beasts huddled together and very miserable, for monkeys get seasick, and they develop pneumonia very easily.

So as soon as his ship put to sea, the captain made all his sailors sew little pajamas for the monkeys. The tough sailors were disgusted at being turned into monkeys' tailors, but the captain insisted. And then when the pajamas were finished the sailors had to catch the monkeys every evening and put them on, and then undress them every morning! The monkeys bit and scratched, but every evening the captain inspected the forty little monkeys in forty little suits of pajamas, and said good night to them. As a result of this care none of the monkeys died—but the sailors were very glad when the voyage was over.

The captain came to lunch at the hotel with us one day. Afterward I took him up to meet the dogs, and even the aloof Ajax could not help liking him. Then he and I went off to walk round the town. As we came out of the hotel we heard the sound of rollicking music in the street, and saw a young Italian turning the handle of a barrel organ. On it was the smallest, most miserable-looking monkey. It had a belt and heavy chain round its waist, and it wore a wisp of a dirty red coat and a silly cap above its pinched little face. It was shivering with cold, for it was May, and May in Sydney can be very cold indeed. The captain gave me a penny to give the little monkey, and it put out its little paw and ignored the penny, just clinging to my finger.

The Italian went on turning his hurdy-gurdy, and I lifted the monkey in my arms and it pressed its shivering body against me for warmth while it cheeped softly in the saddest way. It was one of the many varieties of capuchin monkey, the captain said. But it looked like a squirrel with its long tail, which should have been fluffy but which was very moth-eaten-looking. Most of the monkeys on barrel organs have rather wiry fur with a greenish tinge, and stand upright and have tails like whips. This one was small and soft and very miserable.

I was nearly in tears when I put the little thing on the top of the organ and it tried to creep back to me again. The captain gave the boy some money and told him to buy the monkey a warmer coat and we walked on.

We heard a voice calling us and turned to find the Italian walking after us, while in the distance the monkey crouched, trying to huddle itself together against the cold wind. The man wanted the captain to buy the monkey, but the captain refused. The Italian persisted, so I walked back and picked the monkey up again, and stood sheltering it from the cold wind.

Presently both men came back. The Italian spoke to me, smiling so that his teeth shone in the sunlight. But I did not care. I only wanted to keep the monkey warm.

He unfastened the heavy chain and put the end in my hand. "You taka da monk," he said, still grinning.

I looked toward the captain, who was smiling. "It's your monkey now," he said.

"But doesn't he want it any more?"

"He's going away——"

"The gentleman, he buya da monk," the man explained.

"Oh! Is it for *me*? Do you really mean it belongs to me?" I was too excited to believe it.

"It does—if your mother'll let you have it."

"Oh, thank you!" I said. "I do love it!"

I pulled my coat round the little monkey and we went back to the hotel and found my mother writing letters. She was rather horrified at my cuddling such a dirty little thing in its horrible rag of a coat, but I could see how upset she was at its neglected condition. She went upstairs and put on her hat and brought down a warm scarf to wrap around the little monkey. Then we got in a cab and set off for the vet's.

The vet said there was nothing wrong with my monkey except neglect. He took off the belt and chain and found its middle sore and raw, so he took the little thing away, and in about a quarter of an hour he returned with a much cleaner monkey, bandaged round the tum. We bought a light belt and chain, and then some grapes and bananas. As we could not buy a coat for the monkey we bought some soft flannel, and my mother said she would make one.

Then we went back to the hotel, wondering how we would smuggle the little fellow in, but pretty sure that the housemaid who did our rooms would not give us away. My father came in and said that finding a monkey did not surprise him—he always expected to find one new pet whenever he came back. The captain named my new pet Kiko, and we bought it a basket for a bed so that I could carry him about, onto the roof and into the parks.

I knew the dogs would not hurt him, although Master Ben, who was used to being the smallest pet, could be quite cross if I made a fuss over an even smaller gentleman. I certainly wondered how Kiko would take to them!

I was due for a big surprise, although I was right about Benny—he was a little jealous. Algy loved Kiko at once, but Ajax, who was so indifferent, was as nearly affectionate to Kiko as it was possible for him to be. It was to Ajax that Kiko always went whenever he was with the three dogs, and Ajax liked it. He would stretch out in the sunlight, pretending to doze and looking quite beautiful with his orange coat giving back the sunlight, and Kiko would creep between his big forelegs, right up under his chin, while Ajax nuzzled him as he never did any other creature.

We all enjoyed the long trip home, although I did not want to leave the captain. Kiko soon lost his sore middle and climbed about the car, slept on my lap, or played with the dogs quite happily through the long days of motoring over about five hundred miles of bad roads.

When we reached home Kiko took up residence in my nursery. He seldom climbed like other monkeys, but he would run about the floor with his bushy tail down between his hind legs and curling up in front of his chest like a tiny sleigh with a scroll-like prow. When he wore his belt and chain and it got in the way, he picked the chain up in one velvet-soft paw and lifted it around, as a lady might lift a train.

Kiko soon grew a beautiful, silky coat, and he would croon and cheep happily to himself all day long. He loved being made much of, and developed an enormous appetite for such a tiny creature. He had very nice table manners and would take a grape gently from your palm, patting it with his other paw as if to say thank you.

I believe he had a happy life. He was a busy little

fellow and had his own toy box. At night I would put his toys away; in the morning he would take them out again. His favorite toy was a scrap of carpet which he would tack down with thumbtacks, hammered in with a little hammer taken from my brother's tool chest. At night I would pull it up. In the morning he would start afresh. He never got tired of it and he never hit his thumb! When he got tired of playing, Ajax would lie down while Kiko crept over him until *he* got tired; then they both went to sleep.

For other exciting adventure stories read Mary Elwyn Patchett's Brumby, the Wild White Stallion, *and* The Great Barrier Reef, *both published by Bobbs-Merrill.*

Gift of the Forest

BY R. LAL SINGH and ELOISE LOWNSBERY

Illustrations by Anne Vaughan

> *Bim, a young Hindu boy, helps his mother to raise a tiger cub which she found abandoned in the Indian jungle. When Bim is old enough to make his first trip into the jungle alone, he is accompanied by Heera, the now half-grown Royal Bengal tiger that has become a member of the family.*

AFTER breakfast that morning, the boy and the tiger strolled out the gate to sit under the neem tree waiting for Grandfather.

"I will tell him that I don't like that sapling cage to sleep in any better than you do, Heera. As we get older, grow up, we need more space, not less."

Heera turned his head to lick Bim's face. It tickled. Bim laughed and rubbed his chin. All the same, he knew quite well, by this sign, that Heera understood him. He opened his palm-leaf book at the place where he had left off yesterday. But the words made a black blur and Heera didn't listen. They both, boy and tiger, looked longingly toward that high wall of dense green at the end of the dusty road. Bim threw an arm around Heera's neck.

"You are such a big fellow, Heera; more than half grown, my father says. Surely you would not run away

from me now. You have too much sense. How would
you like to take a walk with me today, right now, into
that big green jungle? Plenty of things to learn there!
More than in all the books of the world, my grandfather
says."

Heera lost no time in giving Bim's face a long lick.

"I thought so. Well, then, I'll have to go and tell my
mother. Want to come?"

They raced each other and Heera won, as always, now
that he had grown so big. Bim looked in at the kitchen
door.

"Mother, just to make up to Heera for that prison cage,
he and I thought of taking a walk to the forest. All right?"
he called. "We can both learn so much there; and I promise to take good care of him." Bim tried to sound casual.
"Today, I will study the jungle book. Grandfather will
be pleased."

"Why, why, I'm not sure you should go, son." Her voice
was full of doubt and anxiety, too. "You had best ask
your father. He is in the front room."

"Father, Heera is so big and so wise, now, that we are
thinking about a walk to the forest. I will show him the
way there, and he will show me the way home again."
Bim leaned against his father's desk, where he sat adding
up long rows of figures that stood for rents and prices of
rice and sacks of grain. He had to be a good agent for the
Maharajah.

"Why, why, you had best talk about that with your
mother; see what she has to say. You really think that
Heera is old enough not to run away? Have you forgotten that your grandfather is coming today?"

"Aie, no, sir; but we'll be back in plenty of time to greet
him," Bim said. So he laid down his book, caught up his
flute, and ran out of the house, with Heera bounding at
his heels. At the kitchen, Mother Lakshmi enticed them
both to an extra bowl of milk. So Bim sat down in the

doorway. His mother went to speak to his father through
the window.

"Bim is growing as nearly like the Bapu as two seeds
in a neempod," the boy heard his father say. "But we
can't help it."

His mother nodded, quoting a *sloka* from the sacred
books:

> *All beings follow their own natures;*
> *Of what use then, is restraint?*

"My mother's mother used to tell me that, as a boy,
Father would disappear for days in the forest, just to
learn the ways of the wild things there."

Quickly, Mother covered her mouth with her hand.
"Our son is a brave boy, but surely he is not big enough
to go alone to the jungle?"

"Yet how can we keep him from going when we have
tried to teach him to be fearless? He no longer feels like
a little boy."

"No, I feel very old and very big," Bim called to encourage them. "And, besides, I am never alone, you know. I have Sri Krishna in my heart, and Heera to protect me."

"Then mind you don't go too far in, Bim," cautioned his mother.

"Aie, Mother, we won't." Having drained the last drop of milk, boy and tiger ran, leaping and skipping for joy. From the wall, Bindi mewed while Danu chattered. Both came to join the party, but Bim waved them back. "Another day," he promised. "You both wait for us here." Danu scolded, and Bindi turned round and round to curl up for a nap.

So the two bounded out of the gate, out along the dusty road, away from the village, away to the jungle.

Every few paces, Heera stopped to sniff at a roadside thicket. Now on this side, now on that, a rabbit was startled from its hiding place, to run in confusion just ahead of them. Catching a strange scent, Heera gave chase, until the swift brown creature hopped off into the dense brush, just out of reach of the big clumsy paw.

Heera returned to look up into Bim's face, bewildered. What manner of creature might this be? Bim laughed and explained, "That's a rabbit, Heera; soft and furry and very much afraid of you. It doesn't know you only want to play."

Beyond the bend in the sunny road, where they entered the forest, they both blinked at the half twilight. Both quivered with delight as feet and paws sank into the moist cool green carpet. When they reached the place where a stream of clear water ran beside the road, they both bent down to drink. Heera sat down on his haunches while Bim played with the frogs that lived there. Splash! They plopped down off a rock into deeper pools.

Seeing them, Heera's amber eyes grew dark and

round. He thought he would like to play with frogs too. He pushed his big paw down into the stream and tried to catch one of the slippery green creatures. But it hopped away with a loud and indignant ga-lump! Heera jumped back and looked in astonishment at his paw. It was wet and cool. He hunched up his back and began jumping about in circles as Bindi did when he played with his own tail. When Bim shouted with laughter at him, Heera held his head to one side and drew back his upper lip.

"Heera," Bim told him, "this world is all very new and strange to you. Come along, old comical one, I'll take you to the places I know." Bim slipped his hand inside Heera's collar, and together they walked along the cart road till they came to the clearing.

Bim sighed in contentment. Though it was many months since he had been here, he felt the same joy in the familiar nearness of it all, in the dim coolness of the dense shade. He sat down on the old log, looking about carefully to make certain that Nag the cobra was not about. Heera sat beside him, sniffing, his nose twitching, his muscles rippling under the smooth silky fur. Bim

pointed out to him the bright darting birds and butterflies, the chattering and curious monkeys that soon
swung down, jibbering with shrill reedy voices.

"They can't think what manner of tiger you are, Heera.
They are half afraid of you; and yet not afraid, but surprised and very curious about you."

Heera crouched on his haunches, staring up at them.

"You are thinking how astonishing it is to be seeing
Danu's brothers up there; ten monkeys, twenty monkeys,
twenty hundred monkeys!"

Now feeling an impelling need for action, for play,
Heera bounded off toward the monkeys, only to find
that they leaped and scurried, back up the long creeper
ladders to safe branches, with a noisy clamor. Whereupon, the surprised tiger bounded back to Bim, round
and around the log, until stopped in his tracks by a fearful new sound.

"There!" said Bim. "Did that peacock screech startle
you, too?" Bim laughed. "Don't mind him. He's telling
the jungle people. 'Man and tiger have arrived. Beware!'
I was even a little frightened of him, too, the first time I

heard him. I suppose we are always a bit afraid of the creatures we don't know. But these peacocks are your real brothers, Heera; they came as a sign from Mother's name-goddess the time you first came to live with us— remember? If only I could catch two of them, I think they would make friends with you and Bindi and Danu and Rani and Meta; don't you think so too?"

But Heera did not reply. He sat as one stunned with sensations, hearing all these strange yet delightful sounds, his nose twitching with so many new yet delicious smells. His head moved furtively now to this side, now to that. So much to see all at once, so much to sniff, to hear, to feel. A whole new world full of ecstasy.

"You love it as much as I do," Bim told him. "I know how you must feel, because I feel the same way myself, free and—happy—here." Bim stroked Heera's ruff and rubbed his face against the clean soft fur. "And I love it all a thousand times more than ever before, because you are with me. Come."

The boy led the tiger in through a thicket of tangled vines. "Now I think this must be the very spot where you were born. You were lying just here, between the roots of this old stump, when my mother found you. Remember?"

Heera began sniffing about the old stump, stalking stealthily around it. "Do you smell your own mother tiger whom you never saw? Your father never knew where you were hidden, Heera. If he had known, my grandfather says he would have eaten you. And then I would never have known you."

For answer, Heera sniffed, lay down flat on his belly and buried his nose in that delicious damp coolness of ferns.

"And if the forest had not meant to give you to me, then your mother would have come in the night, in her fierce anger, to eat up someone in the village, or else Grandfather. But she never came!"

Heera lifted his head, sprang to Bim's shoulders, knocked him down, rolling him over and over, in the exuberance of his new-found joy at being here in this wonderful world. When both were tired, they lay looking up into the thick green canopy overhead. Both were unmindful of any danger of fang or tongue or tusk lurking in this jungle world.

They saw only the flashing colors of wings and blossoms: ruby and rose and white, amethyst and blue and yellow. They heard only the thin, twanging, immeasurable murmur, like the strings of a harp, from unseen millions of insects. They smelt only the mingled fragrance of leaf mould and incense trees, camphor and sandal, together with scarlet and white and yellow blossoms.

"Come," said Bim at last. "Now, I'll take you to the big tamarind tree. Come." He led the way along an animal trail, past trailing creepers, over fallen trunks, around great naked roots.

"Here we are. Here's the very tree where they bound our grandfather. Since he was willing to give his life for you, Heera, that makes him your grandfather, too."

Heera sniffed all around the big trunk, finding a scent that was familiar to him. He showed his delight by bounding up, reaching as high as he could to sharpen his long claws.

Bim was hot. He sat down, with his back to the big tree, and took out his flute. "Come, rest here beside me, Heera. We will try to pipe the birds to us; only, today, we are *not* inviting old Nag."

Bim began to play a gay little nameless tune, all trills and running quavers. First he ran up, then he ran down, stopping the six holes in turn with his finger tips. And though the song had neither melody nor words, yet it said things too, out of his heart: gratitude to Sri Krishna, to Aranyani, for the best playmate a boy could have; happiness for all the months together in the compound that was home; joy that they had come together now into this deep dark forest that was a larger, grander home.

Heera watched the birds flit close and closer, until they perched on the lowest branches overhead. At first, he kept as still as a statue. Then his head dropped to sniff the ground at his feet. New scents in the cleft track of a deer, in the stubby hoof of a wild hog, in the four-toed mark of a hyena. He had no one to tell him that these were scents of the common dinners enjoyed by his wild brothers of the tiger clan. Yet soon the scents became too tantalizing to resist. Noiselessly, he crept deeper into the shadows.

Bim played on, as softly as he could, so as not to disturb Heera who still disliked a shrill flute. Soon a frisky gray squirrel perched on the boy's brown foot, and his fur tickled Bim's toes. His quick movement sent the little creature scurrying and scolding. Instantly the birds fluttered up, and darted out of sight.

The boy laughed. "I wouldn't hurt a hair or a feather of any of you, any more than Heera would." He turned to his companion. He sprang up and ran around the tree. "Oh, I know, you are playing hide and seek," he called. "Heera, Hee-ra!"

"Hee-ra," he heard the faint echo.

"Where are you?" he shouted.

"Are you?" came back to him. Oh, that voice of Aranyani again. He felt desperate, bewildered. He couldn't lose Heera. Yet the forest was endless. It went on and on for miles, ten miles, twenty miles, twenty hundred miles, for all he knew.

So he tried running forward, then backward, now to the right, now to the left. He tripped over vine ropes, brushing them from his path; he dodged giant tree trunks; he ducked under great-leaved ferns; he stumbled over roots; he followed one animal trail after another; he fell in and out of thorn bushes, frantic at losing his pet.

Yet as often as he called, there came back only the faint echo of his own voice. "That forest nymph is mocking me." He threw himself down at last, to quiet his racing heart. There came to his mind the voice of his grandfather: "Never fear in the forest, son. The jungle is your friend, remember that."

"Well, then, he never told me how to find Heera," Bim told himself. He had to admit, however, before he heaped reproach on his grandfather, that perhaps he should not have come today, after all. Should he not run home now, to bring his father and Bukaru to help? But how could they find Heera if he, Bim, couldn't? That thought steadied him.

"Then if the forest gave him to me, the forest must find him for me, now." He said it aloud. "I will just wait for him here." Bim was hot and scratched and torn, breathless and miserable. But when he had grown calm, he lifted his flute to his lips. Heera will know where to find me by this, he thought. He knows the Vishnu hymn as well as I do.

Thou, seated in the heart of all,
Father of worlds, of all that moves and stands—

The familiar tune floated out into the quiet forest. Again the birds gathered. Again Danu's brothers swung down close and closer. "Go tell Heera I am waiting for him, *O bander-log.* Pass the word along the treetop road, too."

Bim listened. Out of the purple shadows he heard a sharp, pitiful cry, an animal in pain. Bim sped through the forest, following the cry. Then silence. But as he parted the heavy fern fronds blocking his path, he came upon a water hole. Here, he saw that two animals had fought. One, a young doe, lay fallen and bleeding; the other, somewhat like a wolf, with a striped coat of dusty brown, was crunching bones with savage growls and snorts.

"You've killed it, you low-born thing, you," Bim said to himself. "I think you're a hyena: that's what you must be." The boy opened his mouth wide and yelled, a high terrifying human yell that startled the silence as well as the beast. It sprang back into the jungle, and yelled in reply, a terrifying animal yell with a laugh at the end of it that quite turned Bim's hair on end.

He crept forward and bent over the doe. So little and young! He stroked the velvety head. "If I could, I would bring you back to life," he whispered. It was his first experience of seeing the jungle law, "a life for a life." He knew well that some animals must kill that they might live. "But they are cowards to kill you, who live on leaves!"

Some instinct made Bim turn. The hyena had slunk back. In that instant, Bim made a lunge toward the creature, yelling again. Then he caught hold of a dangling, stout creeper vine and climbed, monkey-fashion up beyond reach of the creature's leaps. The hyena returned to his feeding.

When Bim had swung himself to a tree and had gained a safe foothold on a branch, he called down, "You'd run fast enough if only Heera were with me. He would teach you not to kill a beautiful little doe." He lifted up his voice in a pleading cry, "Hee-ra."

"Hee-ra," came only the echo.

The boy bit his lips. He could see how dark were the shadows around the forest pool. Night would be coming; other beasts might come here to drink. If he stayed up in the tree, what would his mother think? And his father and grandfather, too? Only that morning he had gaily told his mother that he was unafraid because he had Sri Krishna in his heart and a tiger to protect him!

Well, then, there was one thing he could do to muster

up his courage. Bim settled himself firmly in the crotch of a big limb, lifted his flute to his lips and began to play again. Then he felt, rather than heard, a movement below him. Looking down, he saw a tiger crouch for an instant, and spring upon the hyena still feeding on the doe. With one swift powerful cuff of the big paw, the brown creature was sent spinning into the brush with a scream of pain where the claws had pricked deep.

"Good," shouted Bim in delight, as he slid down the tree trunk. "Serves him right, Heera, for eating up that little doe." The boy caught a firm hold on the leather collar as the tiger sniffed curiously at the lifeless deer.

Bim cuffed his broad nose, and then hugged him. "Take that, for running away from me, but I'm glad you found me again and drove off that old scavenger." The boy's foot touched something soft. He stooped down. "Look, Heera, it's her fawn!"

Heera sniffed and licked the tiny creature that gave a feeble cry. Then the tiger licked the boy's face, bent down over the spotted coat.

"Yes, she was defending her baby. We'll take the little thing home with us." Bim gathered it into his arms, the small painted face, the dangling slender legs. Heera looked up into Bim's face, excited, his hair rising, his mouth watering. If only his master would let him go free, to return to that tantalizing odor beside the pool! But Bim had taken again a firm grip on the leather collar, that had been three times enlarged. "You stayed too long away from me, Heera; you bad, bad striped cat! Grandfather will be wondering where we are, and Mother will be anxious."

They started forward into the darkening jungle. But which way was home? Searching, Bim had run about heedless of direction. Now he was quite turned round. However could he find the way out to the road again, he wondered?

"Heera, we are lost! And we must start home now, this minute, before they get so worried they call the whole village to find us. Don't you know the way?"

Heera sniffed at Bim's feet and started forward. Frisky and gay as a colt he would have bounded ahead. But Bim could not think of their being separated again. Laying down for a moment his small warm bundle of the fawn, he caught up a broken length of vine rope, fastened one end to Heera's collar, and grasped the other.

"Now, you lead the way!"

And most willingly Heera led the way; and the way was long and hot and it was nearly dark before they came at last to the rutted cart road, and so out from the twilight to the glare of a setting sun. At last they arrived at their own compound gate.

Danu was watching, and leaped down to ride in on Heera's back. Bindi, too, come running to rub against Bim's legs. Heera rushed first to the kitchen, to find his own water jar and drink it dry.

"We've come back home," Bim announced to his mother. "And see what the forest gave us today!"

When she looked at him, his mother dropped her dish and ran out to him. "Bim! your legs are bleeding, and your arms and body are covered with scratches. What has happened to you? Why did you stay away so long?" She reached out to gather the fawn into her arms. "Oh, it's nothing, Mother. Heera and I were playing in the forest, and the thorn bushes reached out to keep us there," he said.

"But you've been gone for hours, Bim, since morning! I have been anxious about you. Your father was forced to make a journey, but your grandfather is waiting for you under the lime tree. Wash and go to him."

Bim hid his hot face against her. "I suppose I do deserve a scolding, Mother; I suppose both of us do. But—but we did bring you the little spotted fawn!"

"Another baby to nurse." She sighed. "But next time, I shall beg your father not to let you go to that jungle."

Bim doused himself with water, put on a fresh *dhoti* and ran to the singing tree. He hugged the Bapu. "We've had a long day in the jungle, Grandfather," he announced as if it were fresh news.

"And who did you see there, my son's son?"

"We saw lots of the free people: Heera played with them; and we found a little new baby deer to bring home." He sighed. He did not want to confess how frightened he had been. Nor was he ready to speak of the hyena.

The Bapu smiled, his eyes kindling, his face crinkling. He patted the broad striped head as Heera fawned at his feet.

"As the twig is bent," he murmured happily. "Surely you are one of us."

"One of—whom?"

"One of us who belong—there in the great jungle—" He nodded toward the green wall of the forest, the treetops turned to gold now by the setting sun.

"Aie, and Heera is one of us, too, Grandfather."

"Look over there," said the Bapu, pointing to the banyan tree.

"Oh, Grandfather! No more prison cage for Heera. I knew what you would say."

"Your father meant it for the best, son; but nature will take care of Heera's future housekeeping. So Bukaru has taken it away."

"Good! Bukaru may have it! Now I will carry the fawn home to Kamala; it can live in the cage."

R. Lal Singh and Eloise Lownsbery have collaborated to produce a superb tale of life in rural India, one that displays real knowledge and sympathetic understanding of the people. For a story of North India during a time of famine, read Jean Bothwell's The Little Flute Player, *published by Morrow.*

Damasi's Party

BY REBA PAEFF MIRSKY

Illustrations by W. T. Mars

> *Children the world over love a party. Ten-year-old Nomusa, daughter of a Zulu chief, is no exception.*

THE distance to Damasi's kraal was quite far, but it did not seem so to Nomusa or to her brothers and sisters as they walked toward it, single file. Far off, they saw a thin line of children coming in their direction. They, too, were on their way to the party. Nomusa wondered how many children would be at Damasi's party. Maybe a hundred.

Kangata was terribly excited about going to a party in a neighboring kraal. It was his first one.

"We are near now, Nomusa, are we not?" he asked.

"Yes," she answered. She began to laugh as she looked at her small brother's face, for it was marked and painted in such a curious and grotesque manner that his nose looked as if it had been divided in two.

Kangata looked offended and put his grubby hand up to his face to discover the cause of Nomusa's mirth. Nomusa quickly reassured him. "You have certainly made a design like that of no other. Perhaps you will win a prize."

When the children neared the thorn fence surrounding Damasi's kraal, Zabala walked forward quickly to lead the line of twenty brothers and sisters, all children of Nomusa's father. Zabala, whose mother was called Great Wife because she was Zitu's first wife, would be chief of Nomusa's kraal some day, because he was Zitu's eldest son.

Standing just within the entrance of the kraal to greet the guests as they entered were Damasi's father and uncle and their wives. They pointed out the huts that had been reserved for the party.

Nomusa found Kangata close at her side, his eyes wide with curiosity, trying to see everything in the strange kraal at once. Delicious smells of food cooking filled the air and made Kangata's mouth water.

Nomusa began straightening the halo of beads around her head, adjusting some of the bangles that had got twisted on the way. Most of her sisters were arranging their short grass skirts and bead kilts, too.

Zabala walked up to the entrance of Damasi's hut, followed by his nineteen brothers and sisters. He stood tall before the hut, legs apart, arms by his side, and loudly cleared his throat. "A-hem!" But there was so much noise in the hut, and such excitement, that no one, it seemed, had heard his announcement of their arrival. Again he cleared his throat, this time more loudly, with a reinforcement of "A-hems" from behind him. Zabala glowered at those who had given him this unwanted help.

This time they were heard. There was a sudden hush within. Almost immediately a fantastic-looking head, stuck full of small birds' feathers, green, blue, yellow, and red, appeared in the entrance. It was Damasi. "*Sakubona! Sakubona!*" he said, smiling.

"*Usaphila! Usaphila!*" called the guests from Nomusa's kraal.

Chief for the day, Damasi was in charge of everything. He quickly beckoned to everyone to enter. First went Zabala. Then, one by one, all the brothers and sisters crawled in after him on hands and knees.

At first the children from Nomusa's kraal were shy, but soon they began to mingle freely with the other guests. Waves of noise surged up in the hut. More guests arrived, making the hut hotter and noisier than ever. The boys wandered over to one side of the hut, and the girls stayed on the other.

Nomusa went to look at a calf that was tied in a corner of the hut. It was only a few days old and still too young to be taken to pasture. Together with a young goat, it was being kept as a pet. Girls did not often have a chance to be with cows and calves, and Nomusa enjoyed petting the calf.

Several dogs which had followed some of the children to the party ran in and out, between and over the legs of the smaller guests, looking for pieces of food that had been dropped on the floor. Every little while there was a fight between two dogs when both snatched at the same morsel.

Their barking, snapping, and growling frightened the chickens that had wandered in. Flapping their wings in terror, they crowed and cackled, one or two flying onto the backs of the shrieking children.

This caused more excitement, laughter, and screech-

ing, until the poor little calf began to strain at its grass rope in an effort to get away. Nomusa patted her. "Do not be afraid, little calf. I will not let anyone hurt you."

While she was talking to the calf, Damasi's sister Intombi, a year older than Nomusa, came up to her and said, "It is a fine calf. Do you like it?"

"Who would not?" answered Nomusa. "She will be a beautiful cow." Then, seeing Intombi's bulging neck-pocket, she pointed to it. "What have you in there?"

"I will gladly show you," said Intombi. "But you must show me what is in your pocket, too."

Nomusa opened her neck-pocket and drew from it a red and green feather, now somewhat bent—the one she had found at the stream.

"M-m-m-m!" said Intombi, admiringly. "What else have you?"

Nomusa's fingers probed the depths of her pocket. She brought out a lovely bead of clay, brown, with a red and yellow border. The bead was no bigger than a small grape. "I made it myself," explained Nomusa. "I found a very special kind of clay, mixed the colors, and then baked it in the sun. Do you like it?"

"I do," said Intombi. "If you will part with it, I will give you this." She quickly loosened her bulging neck-pocket and took out something brown, spotted with white. It looked very soft and furry.

"Why, it's a deer mouse!" cried Nomusa. "Where did you get it?"

"I found it nibbling in my mother's garden. If you like it, you may have it in exchange for the bead."

"Be careful not to drop the bead, for it may break," Nomusa said, handing it to Intombi and taking the deer mouse.

"It's not alive, you know," Intombi said, as she saw Nomusa carefully examining her new treasure.

"Is it still good to eat?" Nomusa asked.

"That I do not know, but the fur can be used."

Intombi opened her neck-pocket wide and showed Nomusa all the bits of stone, feathers, bangles, and other trinkets that she carried around with her. Suddenly Intombi sprang up. "Oh, they are starting another game. Let us play, too, Nomusa."

"What are they playing?"

"Husbands and wives. It's lots of fun. I hope Zabala chooses me." Intombi moved closer to the line of boys so that Zabala would not fail to see her. She looked smilingly at him until he caught her eye.

How tiresome to play such a game, thought Nomusa. I should much prefer going outside.

She was standing apart, watching the good-natured scramble of the boys picking their girls, not once thinking about a partner for herself. Suddenly she felt someone tapping her shoulder insistently. "You are my wife for this game," Damasi said. "Now let me see if you are a good one."

"And let me see if you are a good husband," replied Nomusa.

The girls picked up little grass mats and baskets and filled them with food for themselves and their "husbands."

Damasi said to Nomusa, "I hear you can do all the things that a boy can do. Are you a good cook, too? That is more important."

"You shall see," answered Nomusa. "But you must promise to go outside with me afterwards to shoot at targets." She set to work to prepare a dish that would not take very long. Soon she gave Damasi a mixture of chicken, corn, pumpkin, goat meat, and fried locust.

"Very good," said Damasi. "Now pass me the *amasi*." These were the delicious curds of clotted milk that Nomusa liked so much. They were excellent for cooling and for quenching one's thirst. When Damasi had finished, he belched and said, "Soon we'll see if you are as good a hunter as you are a cook."

"Let us go outside now," Nomusa suggested, "if you have finished eating."

Together they left the hut. Damasi went into one of the other huts and brought out two bows and some arrows. One bow he handed to Nomusa.

"See if you can hit that branch," he said, pointing.

Nomusa stood straight and drew her right arm back with a quick pull. Off sped the arrow, straight into the middle of the thick branch.

"Good!" shouted Damasi. "We'll each take five turns and see how many hits we make."

As Damasi took a shot, Nomusa saw a bird flying about a hundred yards away. Quickly she let the arrow go, and down went the bird.

"Not many boys your age can shoot a bird on the wing," said Damasi admiringly. "Where did you practice shooting?"

"In my mother's garden," answered Nomusa.

Just then Mdingi appeared. "Let me shoot," he said.

"Let us take turns shooting," said Nomusa. "You first, Damasi. Then Mdingi, then I."

Damasi let his arrows fly swiftly, one after the other. "Three out of five," announced Nomusa, running to pick up the fallen arrows.

"Your turn, Mdingi," said Damasi.

Taking careful aim, Mdingi shot his five arrows. "Four out of five!" he shouted.

Nomusa aimed and shot. "Three out of five, like me, Nomusa," Damasi said.

By now the younger children had grown tired of being husbands and wives—especially the girls, since they had to do all the work for the boys. The smaller girls

began to play with clay dolls, and the little boys ran out-doors to play horse.

Sisiwe came up to Nomusa. "What will everyone think of you, playing with boys, shooting at a mark," she scolded. "You make us ridiculous with your tomboy ways! What good will it do you to know how to trap and shoot? You will never be allowed to go on a hunt. It is better for you to know how to be a good wife."

Nomusa left Damasi and went to sit with the girls from neighboring kraals. Bored, she listened to stories about things that had been going on in their kraals since the last time they had seen each other: about new babies, accidents to brothers or sisters, what vegetables were growing in their mothers' gardens, and such things. Body designs were compared and discussed, grass skirts felt, beads admired, and new teeth examined.

There was no special hour for eating. Children wandered in and out of the hut to get what they wanted. It was a never-ending feast.

Reba Paeff Mirsky received the 1952 Charles W. Follett Award for Thirty-One Brothers and Sisters. *There are more stories about Nomusa in the author's other book,* Seven Grandmothers, *also published by Follett.*

The Saucepan Journey

BY EDITH UNNERSTAD

Illustrations by Louis Slobodkin

When the Larsson family inherited the horses Laban and Lotta, they decided to make up a two-wagon caravan and set out from Stockholm into the countryside. Of course, they took along "Peep," the wonderful saucepan which Papa had invented and which he hoped would make his fortune. Eleven-year-old Lars tells the story.

W HEN Laban and Lotta turned into our street the next morning, I was hanging out of the window, waiting for Mama to finish sewing up a tear in the seat of my pants which she hadn't seen, of course, until the last minute.

"Plop, plop, plop." I heard a sound from the stairs where the last bundles of bedclothes had obviously slipped out of Mirre's hands and were going downstairs alone. Knutte went out the door of the room, with his favorite airplane in one hand and four airplane books in the other, and Little O lay on Mama's bed, all bundled up, and sang and kicked and peeped at me between her fingers. It was a sort of game she sometimes played. The others were on their way downstairs with all our things.

I remember thinking that our old gray street seemed to come to life at the sound of the horses' hooves on the asphalt. From my place at the window, four flights up, it looked as if a whole toy store had spread its wares out down below. The Larsson family and Mrs. Palm, with striped mattresses and colored blankets, came out of the building. Lotta's and Laban's backs shone copper red in the morning sun. Rosalind was sitting on the driver's box and waved her hat when she saw me in the window. It was red and from the distance looked like one of those "Danger: High Explosives" flags. Under the light-green wagons I caught a glimpse of their black chassis, shiny as patent leather shoes in a store window; and the ground-glass lenses, in the newly polished lanterns on both sides of the driver's seat, sparkled. The whole caravan looked great from up there. And perched on top of the wagons were Dessi's lemon-yellow signs with their large black letters.

Papa came in and said: "Well, they're here. Is everything ready?" And he took Little O and her mattress and went out. Mama went around the apartment once more while I put on my trousers. And then the door closed behind us.

"Get ready for something funny," Papa said on the way downstairs. "Try to take it as a kind of trial by fire."

At first I couldn't understand what he meant. You never did see such a handsome caravan. But then I heard Mama gasp, and I noticed that she stared at the sign on the parlor wagon and that Papa whispered something soothingly to her.

First there was a Peep saucepan. I almost said it was as big as life. It was a little bigger. It was so well painted that I thought I could reach up and take it down and begin to cook in it. And then there was Peep—no, what in the world was it? PEEP-LARSSONS. Yes, "Peep-Larssons" was what the sign said; nothing else. I ran back to the sleeper and looked at the sign there. On it was a saucepan just like on the first, and then PATENT-ED SAUCEPAN. I went across the street to look at the

other sides—the signs were put up lengthwise with the wagons. On the back side of the sleeper sign was another saucepan and PEEP-LARSSONS, and on the back of the parlor sign was a saucepan and PATENTED COOKER.

I heard Dessi explaining to Mama. "Yes, but there wasn't room for everything on just one sign. And this is just as good."

"And we are the Peep-Larssons?" asked Mama and had a hard time because the corners of her mouth were dancing up and down.

"Yes, it is silly," Dessi said. "But there wasn't room for more space between Peep and Larssons, so I put a mark in to separate the words."

"That's what I mean," Mama said. "It looks like a hyphen. And you've left out the apostrophe."

"Well, people can think a little, can't they?" Dessi asked.

"They certainly can," Mama said and succeeded in looking serious.

"Peep-Larssons . . ." I began.

And then Mrs. Palm came up. She was going to clean the apartment after us and take care of the new tenants—a family with children, who had rented the apartment for the time we were away.

"Well, good heavens, isn't that nice," she said and waved her head at the signs. "What a smart little girl you are, Dessi. Tell me, is that the play you're going to be doing? Or is that the name of your troupe?"

"Well, it's the name of the troupe," Mama said politely. "It's just a kind of a joke, Mrs. Palm." Then she went in back of one of the wagons and laughed good and hard all by herself.

"I didn't mean . . ." Dessi began. "Oh, now I see how silly it is. I didn't notice it before. Papa, we can't go until I've painted them over. I can make the letters smaller and push them closer together so there'll be more room. PEEP, LARSSON'S PATENTED SAUCEPAN it ought to be."

"We don't have time now," Papa answered. "The new tenants are moving in this afternoon, so we have no place to stay while we wait for them to dry."

Dessi looked away very sad and disturbed. She had expected praise and not what was happening.

"Then we'll have to take them right down," she said desperately and started to try to climb on the parlor roof.

"Whoa, whoa, Dessi," Papa shouted. "Let them alone. If we go without signs, we'll lose the whole point of the saucepan journey. And what's wrong with them, anyway? Peep-Larsson is as good as Pop Larsson. Peep Larsson was my nickname all the time I was in school. I couldn't get rid of it even when my voice changed. So I'm used to it and I don't mind at all."

"Yes, but the rest of us," Dessi said bitterly.

"I think it's funny," said Mirre. "What are you fussing about?"

Rosalind said she didn't think it was *so* funny. Anyway it was time to start, she thought, and why should everybody stand around and talk?

Then Mama came back, and even though she had straightened her face out, it was all red. "You know, I think Peep-Larssons is very clever. I mean from the advertising point of view," she said.

"I think so, too," Mrs. Palm said earnestly. "A remarkable idea."

"Peep-Larssons are traveling around with Peep," Mama went on. "And people come and look and try to figure it out, and half the game is won. For Peep, I mean. And it certainly doesn't bother me any to be called Mrs. Peep Larsson."

"I've always said that the nice thing about you, Mrs. Larsson, was that you have a sense of humor," Mrs. Palm said.

Then I said that I was already thinking of changing my name to Lars Larsson Peep when I grew up. Because I thought it was a noble name—and different, too.

We took in the clothes and the other things. We rushed around and made the beds, and Mama cleaned the new kitchen and put it in order. This took a short while.

"Lars," Dessi called from the roof, "come and help me

tie the hay racks a little higher—maybe they'll cover up more of these horrible signs."

We tried it, but it didn't work. Just then an old man, an early morning bird, with a red face all wrinkled up, came along. He stopped and looked at us and read the signs.

"PEEP-LARSSONS," he spelled out. "What kind of a parade is this?"

"It's one of them theatre troupes," Mrs. Palm said.

"Excuse me," he said. "I thought they were making a movie."

Right after that, we left. Mrs. Palm waved at us for a long time. And this time I was the one who sat beside Papa on the driver's box.

We turned into Flemming Street. There still weren't many people around. But the ones we did meet stopped and gaped at us. The little door in back of me opened and Dessi stuck her head out.

"They're laughing at us," she said pitifully.

"So much the better," Papa said. "There's nothing that does the human being more good than a laugh early in the morning. It makes you feel good the whole day. And anyway—the idea in having signs is to make people stare at us."

We went out over the West Bridge. The sun shone and the water was glittering blue, and a flock of silver-white gulls flapped around up in the air, a very pretty picture.

"Adjö,* old Stockholm," I said. "We're on our way to Norrköping."

"But we're not there yet," Papa said and laughed.

"How is it back there?" I shouted and turned around.

"Noble," came a lot of voices.

Noble was a word I had introduced to the family. Mama said that it was like a nightmare epidemic, but nobody could stop using it.

* Good-by.

Laban and Lotta trotted ahead very nicely. We met three or four streetcars before we were out of town. But otherwise the traffic wasn't very bad. One or two trucks passed us, and the drivers always slowed down and looked at us carefully before they smiled and resumed speed. Right in the middle of Liljeholm Bridge we heard Mama yell.

"The coffeepot. I forgot the coffeepot."

"Hurry up and remember all the other things you forgot," Papa shouted back at her, "and we'll make one trip do it."

"That's awful," said Mama. "But we're not going to turn around. If we do it'll be that way the whole trip. We'll stop at a hardware store and sell a Peep and buy a new coffeepot."

"That sounds just fine," Papa said. "Is that the way you had planned on making money?"

"Not exactly," Mama said. "But there was a hole in the old one anyway, which I had repaired with enamel, and you know that doesn't last. It was only a matter of time before we had to get a new one."

"Are you sure you've got everything else?" Papa asked.

"By the way you haven't forgotten anything, have you?" Mama answered. "I just thought I'd ask since I don't see your sample cases anywhere."

"Phooey," he spluttered. "You're right. I'll have to take the next bus back to town and get them. That's just fine!"

"There's a man for you every time," Mama purred and looked pleased.

"We'll stop at a bus stop," Papa said. "What a nuisance!"

"No, wait a minute," Mama said. "If we drive a little further and stop at the next village, the youngsters and I can try to sell some Peeps while you're gone."

Papa said this wasn't the time of day people usually went out and bought saucepans. But Mama isn't the sort who gives in easily. She said she would try anyway, because why had they come on this trip? Papa said he was beginning to wonder.

Mirre finally opened her mouth.

"Papa's sample cases are under his bunk," she said. "I carried them down myself and stuffed them in."

"Now there's a child after my own heart. Tack, pet," Papa said gratefully.

We all breathed easier. The thought of our performance, or debut, you might say, as salesmen had frightened us a little. It isn't so easy the first time.

I had been on the Södertälje road before, since we knew a man there who had a car, and sometimes he came and took us for a ride. He was a traveling salesman, too. I had never before thought it was as beautiful as it looked from my place above Laban's and Lotta's brown backs. The sky was as blue as a Stockholm streetcar. The leaves weren't dark green yet, and the fir trees looked as if they had just been washed. There were still wood anemones and cowslips growing along the side of the road, and Rosalind said that she wanted to get off and pick some. Papa said that we didn't have time for that sort of thing, that we could pick flowers during our regular rest stop.

We were going along fine when we came to a big hill. Papa said that we'd all have to get out of the wagons to spare the horses and not wear them out. We did, and while we walked up the hillside, Rosalind and I tried to tear up as much grass from the sides of the road as we could, to give to Laban and Lotta. But Papa said that we didn't have time to be always feeding the horses, and that we'd have to keep it until we stopped somewhere. And he said that it might be the same with horses as with people—too many between-meals is not so good.

As soon as we heard Papa say "between meals" we all felt suddenly very hungry. So Papa promised to hunt for a good place where we could drive off the road and let the horses stand in grass, and where we could maybe unharness them for a bit. But it was important that this place was just right so that we could get back on the road again. You can't back a whole caravan. You have to make sure you have a place to turn around, and that means a big space.

I told Papa that when he was tired driving, he only had to say the word, but he felt we should wait a bit before letting any of us children drive.

"The traffic gets worse," he said, "and busses come along all the time, and wobbly bicyclers are all over this highway. It would be too bad if we ran over a bicycle, now wouldn't it? But after you're a little more used to what goes on, some of you may give it a try."

Then I told Papa that Rosalind and I already knew how to drive and that the brewery driver had said that we were really good at it. He hadn't any idea we had learned so he was very glad. He said that Mirre had better driver's hands than we had and could certainly handle the reins, once she got used to it. So Mirre looked very pleased, too.

When we got to the top of the hill, we all got in again. Mama went into the sleeper with Little O. We went down the other side of the hill with great speed. Papa had to use the brakes hard—there were brakes on our wagon just like on a car. They didn't look like car brakes; there was a sort of big crank, like the kind they had on old railroad cars.

It was late enough in the morning for things to look more normal. The stores along the road were open, and the service stations were busy. We talked about where we would stop, but we didn't find a convenient place. We didn't want to stop at a service station; we wanted the horses to have a nice soft place to stand.

"What's all the racket in there?" Papa asked.

I looked. It was Knutte, playing with his airplane, with

which he was about to poke out everybody's eyes. Papa
told him that if he didn't stop at once, the airplane would
be hung up in the ceiling where it would stay for the
whole trip. That quieted Knutte down for a while.

"Mama is knocking at the window in the sleeper," Dessi
shouted. "She wants something."

Papa stopped the horses.

"We're going to have to install a telephone between the
wagons," he said.

When Mama finally got the window open—I guess it
must have stuck a bit—she shouted: "It's time we were
beginning. Didn't any of you see that big store we drove
past back there? We're way past it now. What a fine
bunch of salesmen you are. You must keep your eyes
open in this business."

We all promised to be more careful. After that we
watched for everything. We were going through beautiful country now. There was a little church right near the
road. It looked very old. Then we went downhill. Dessi
yelled: "This is where I'd like to stop. Look! It's pretty
here."

"Whoa," shouted Papa.

We saw right away that it was a good place to stop.
In between the white trunks of some birch trees we saw
the blue shimmer of a lake. The grass-covered earth tipped
slightly down toward the lake, and an almost overgrown
road went down to the water. There was a pasture down
there big enough to turn the whole caravan around in
a circle.

"I want to go swimming," Rosalind yelled.

"Me, too," and "me, too," came from everywhere.

Papa took up the reins.

"Well, Lotta and Laban, you're going to have a chance
to rest right soon," he said as he turned off into the old
road.

Everything rocked and wobbled, and Mama appeared at the window again. She probably thought we were going to turn over.

But when we stopped, she got out and said that everything had gone just fine, and that we couldn't have found a better place.

Mirre and I helped unharness the horses. Rosalind looked through all her things, hunting for her bathing suit, and as soon as she found it, she was off to the lake.

We tied Laban and Lotta with long ropes to a couple of birch trees and got water for them from the lake. They started eating the grass at once. Mama was already well under way with the food, and Papa went around and gave the wagons a good close inspection to see how they had stood the first stage of the trip. He wasn't exactly pleased with the wagon coupling, so he fussed with it a bit.

Then the rest of us went in swimming. The water was cold, but after all it was early in June, so you could hardly expect it to be hot. Rosalind was already a long way out in the lake. She was a regular Olympic swimming champion. She'd rather live in water during the summer than on land.

Mama called out after us, "See if you can find some plants for your collection, I mean something you haven't already."

Oh, dear! The press! We had promised Mama and Papa to take the flower press with us and collect specimens during the entire trip. And now we had left it at home. Personally, I thought it was a bad thing well forgotten. But I knew what would happen when Papa and Mama found out. Here we were, probably gone for the whole summer, and we couldn't press a single flower for our collection.

I decided not to say anything yet. They'd find out soon

enough. And our energetic Mama would be sure to find some way so that we could get those blooming plants pressed!

I found a stone and skipped it off into the lake. Mirre snorted into the water like a hippopotamus. Dessi sat on a stone, looking at the lake and the birch trees and everything, until I yelled at her. Then she slowly got up and walked into the water.

I swam out and played with Rosalind. She was as slippery as a piece of soap and much quicker than I. On land, though, it's different.

Knutte just dipped himself quickly. Then he came out and played with his airplane. It flew beautifully until it got caught in a tree, and he had to climb up and get it. Its nose was dented a little, so he didn't dare fly it any more. There isn't anybody so careful of his things as Knutte.

Mama wouldn't let Pysen go swimming. It was too early in the summer. He went crawling around on all fours, and raced Laban and Lotta to see who could eat the most grass.

Then Mama called to us, "Come on and get out now or you'll all of you be frozen blue!"

Rosalind pretended not to hear until Papa came and called her.

"I never want to go home again," she said, as we lay and sunned ourselves. "I just want to live like this always. I'm going to swim in every lake I see."

"Then you'd better get moving," Papa said, "because Sörmland is full of lakes, and we don't have time to wait for you."

Rosalind and I raced each other to get warm, and then Knutte wanted to run, too, so we made him lean over and played leapfrog. Dessi and Mirre went back to the wagons to help Mama set the table. Dessi wanted us to sit out in the grass among the cowslips for lunch, but we booed at that idea because we wanted to try our new dining room table.

Suddenly there was quite a commotion up on the highway. A crowd of people had collected, and they were standing looking at us and watching what we were doing. We couldn't help noticing that they laughed and pointed at the signs.

"We have an audience," Mama said, as they started coming toward us. "I wish we could have eaten in peace first. The food's about ready. I'm glad we set the table inside!"

There were two boys, who had parked their bicycles beside the road, and an old woman with a couple of milk bottles, and a middle-aged man in shorts with a rucksack. He looked as if he had never been out on a walking tour before but that he would show the world he was quite a man. And once those four had decided to pay a visit, more people followed. Cars, bicycles, and wagons stopped on the highway, so that it began to look like a traffic tie-up.

"Peep-Larssons! What's that supposed to be?" one of the boys asked and grinned.

Just then the food finished cooking, and Peep gave its signal. It began with a peep and got louder and louder until it was a scream. Mama was in the parlor, so it was about a minute before she got to the kitchen to take the saucepan off the fire. I had always thought it was a little noisy, but now, out-of-doors, it sounded hair-raising. The old woman with the milk bottles dropped one of them and couldn't collect wits enough to pick it up until half the milk had poured out onto the grass. The man with the rucksack jumped and got gooseflesh on his skinny, white legs.

"Police!" he yelled. "They're whistling for the police! They're trying to murder someone in the wagon!"

"Police!" someone else shouted. "Someone get the police!"

"Hey, Gosta," one of the boys said, "get going. Run to the store down the road and call the police!"

"Run yourself!" the other one answered and went closer to the wagon. "I want to see what happens."

People were now running toward us from all directions. But Mama got a good grip on the handle and

turned happily and proudly to her audience with the screaming saucepan held high in the air. The noise began to fade, became a peep, and then died with a sigh.

Everybody stared with amazement at Peep. Little O, who lay sprawled out half-naked on her blanket among the cowslips, imitated the racket.

"Ee-eee-eee-ee!" she shrilled. "Eee-eee-eee!"

The only creatures who seemed completely undisturbed were Laban and Lotta. They had flapped their ears at the noise and then continued calmly to eat. And that was good, because they were going to hear that sound rather often. If it had made them nervous, they might sometime run away with the whole caravan.

"What on earth is that?" asked the milk woman.

Mama had just cleared her throat and opened her mouth to begin her first lecture demonstration on Peep's

remarkable qualities, when someone said, "The police!"

A motorcycle with a sidecar had stopped up on the highway, and two policemen came striding down at us with giant steps. If Rosalind hadn't grabbed Little O out of the way, she might have been trampled.

"What's the meaning of this?" one of them asked and looked around. "Let me see your driver's license—well, I mean—no—that is—ahem! Who was doing all that whistling?"

"Ha, ha!" laughed one of the boys. "Driver's license! The police thought this was a car!"

Everyone started snickering.

"This is all a mistake, officer," Papa began.

Mama interrupted him.

"You see, Captain, it was this," she said and held up the saucepan.

"That thing!" the policeman said gruffly. "You trying to put something over on me?"

"I assure you it was this," Mama said and beamed at him.

We pushed up to the wagon and gathered in a little clump at Mama's feet.

"That's right," we said. "It was our pan that whistled."

The audience burst out laughing. The other policeman took hold of the gruff one's arm and pointed at the wagon and the signs. And they began to laugh a little, too, although they looked as if it were against regulations.

"Yes," Mama said, "this is Peep. And we're the Larssons. How do you do? We were only getting a little lunch ready. And Peep always lets us know when the food is cooked, Captain."

"It certainly lets you know in a loud voice," one of them said.

"Doesn't it though?" Mama sounded happy.

Several of the audience looked disappointed.

"Was that all it was?" they said. "We thought they'd murdered someone."

Mirre heard this and decided to give our fallen reputation some help.

"But we've got an uncle who's dead," she said.

"What did she say?" someone asked from the back of the crowd.

"She said they've got the body of an old man there," someone answered.

"Where? In the wagon?"

"Guess so."

"Well, well," said one of the policemen as he pulled out his notebook. He sounded gruff again. "What did he die of?"

"He was run over," I said.

"They've run over someone with those wagons." It was the same voice that had said we had the body of an old man. It sounded pleased.

"Horrible! Just horrible!" said the man with the rucksack. "And so, of course, they hid the body in the wagon. Isn't that so, officer?"

Everybody rushed up to the parlor wagon to look in the windows. They looked disappointed when they saw only a table set for lunch.

"He's probably in the other," said the boy. "It looks more mysterious."

Papa tore after the people who wanted to climb up on the coupling to look in the sleeper window.

"Let me explain the whole thing," he yelled.

The policemen said, "Everyone stand back so we can clear this matter up. All right. Now then. Your name is Larsson, you said. First names?"

Mama set Peep down and picked up the frying pan and spoon and pounded so that the birch trees rattled. She announced loudly that she had something to say. And the policemen were so stunned that anyone should dare interrupt a cross-examination, they didn't even protest.

Mama then delivered the greatest speech of her life,

as Papa said afterwards. She stood there in front of the
silver curtain and told the audience exactly what the
whole story was and how we happened to be on the road.
She showed them Peep and told them what a remarkable
invention it was. She took off the lid and let them see the
three pans where our lunch lay steaming: potatoes and
pork sausages and Little O's cereal. She asked if there
were a law against getting your own lunch in your own
wagon.

"And Peep is made in three sizes," she added, "and this
one is the largest, because as you can see, we're a large
family." And then she told them the price of each size
and that a "Directions for Using" came with each one.

She finished by saying that she thought they were an
enchanting audience and that she was convinced that
both the friendly captains and the audience now understood that everything was all right. And if anyone wanted
to see how we lived, they were welcome to come up one
at a time and go through the wagons. And while they
were doing that they could see for themselves that we
didn't have the body of an old man anywhere. Uncle
Enok was run over right near Katrina Hissen in Stockholm on April 19, she added.

Well let me tell you, everybody laughed. Some of the
audience paraded into the wagons and said they thought
we had the perfect solution to the perfect way to live—
if only they could come along! And some others asked
Mama to explain the wonderful Peep all over again, and
she was only too glad to do so.

You could see that the policemen were trying very
hard to maintain a serious expression, but it didn't work
out too well. So they said that they had to go make sure
there wasn't a traffic jam up on the highway, and they
added loudly that anyone who had a car or bicycle,
would they please be so kind as to move them? They
went back up the hill to the road, and I could see how

their shoulders shook once they had turned their backs to us and thought we weren't watching.

The old lady with the milk bottles said that Peep was just the kind of saucepan she needed. She only had to go home to get the money, because she didn't have any with her.

After she'd gone, Mama asked Papa if they could cut the price a little for the old lady, since maybe she didn't have so much.

But one of the boys who happened to hear said: "She's the owner of all those big farms over there."

A couple of men who had driven their car down the little road and had been very anxious to peer into the wagons said that they were from a newspaper and were out on a reporting trip. They asked if they couldn't photograph the whole Peep-Larsson family and Laban and Lotta and the wagons. Mama said that it would be silly to refuse because it was such good publicity for Peep. So we hitched up the horses again—although not too well because it wouldn't show—and then we all stood up, and they took pictures and asked a million questions.

Mama said that Dessi painted, and Dessi looked horrified and said: "Oh, Mama!"

But Mama felt they might as well know that our family had artistic talents, since it wouldn't hurt the Peep business a bit. Quite the contrary.

Then one of the men asked me what my name was and what my talents were.

"Lars Larsson Peep," I answered, "and I haven't any talents at all, so I'll probably be a newspaper reporter and drive around and take pictures."

"Lars!" Mama said, a little shocked, but the men laughed.

Then one of the men told me that if I were going to be a reporter, I'd have to begin young.

"You can begin by writing about your adventures on this trip."

I didn't think that was such a bad idea. Later I even thought a lot about it. So I guess you could say that it was that newspaperman who gave me the idea for this book.

We unhitched the horses again, and one of the men bought the smallest Peep to take to his wife. And the milk woman came back and bought another small Peep.

We were all about to die of hunger, so Papa finally told everybody who stood around that they'd have to excuse us. The food had naturally grown stone-cold, because so many had looked to see if the potatoes were really done and whether the cereal had been scorched. But it all tasted good anyway.

Mama boiled coffee in an enamel pitcher and served rusks with it. Then one of the policemen came back and wondered how large the middle-size Peep was, and if there would be room for it in the sidecar. He was thinking of giving it to his fiancée as a little kitchen present. The little one wasn't large enough, because he liked potatoes so well that a lot had to be boiled at one time. He bought the saucepan and looked quite pleased with it, except he seemed also to be a little embarrassed.

"Good luck with the Peep business!" he said when he left.

"Oh!" Mirre said, "I'm going to be a policewoman. I thought he was awfully sweet!"

"Oh, you and your crushes!" I said. "Here all of us were about to go to jail just because of what you said. You would have loved that, of course."

Papa started to laugh at the whole incident, and the first thing we knew we were having one of the Larsson-double-special family laughs. We don't just giggle when we once get started. Mirre laughs louder than the rest of us, but we're almost as good.

Papa said that now it was all over, we did have to admit it had been wonderful fun, every bit of it, and that Mama had done magnificently.

"Yes," Mama said and wiped away laugh-tears from her eyes, "this was a real nice première, and thus far everything has gone the way I'd—we'd planned. We've already sold three saucepans, and that's only the beginning. Speaking for myself, I think I'm going to like this life very much. Time was when I went on the road in Shakespeare. And I really don't think the saucepan journey is a bit harder."

"You're smart, Mama," I said.

"Noble, you mean," she said and laughed. And she gave us all second cups of coffee—for once.

"What do you have principles for, if you can't abandon them sometimes?" she said.

"The man with the rucksack is still standing outside," Dessi piped up. "He looks very unhappy about us somehow. Look at the way he's staring!"

"Shall we offer him a cup of coffee?" asked Mama while she poured herself a third cup. "It might cheer him up; might make him as cheerful as we are!"

I went out and asked. He looked me up and down. Then he raised his eyebrows and said very pointedly: "Nej tack,* Mr. Peep-Larsson!"

"My name's Larsson Peep," I said because I thought it sounded better.

"I don't drink poison," he said.

"We weren't planning on offering you any," I said.

"Coffee is a poison," he said. "Coffee in small doses induces an anxiety neurosis and heart flutterings. Coffee in large doses induces grave disorders in the heart and ultimately death."

"We don't drink coffee in doses," I said. "We drink coffee in plastic mugs from the five-and-ten."

*No, thank you.

He left, looking puzzled as he walked off.

After each of us had washed his own plate and mug in the lake, we began to break camp.

Laban and Lotta each got several lumps of sugar before we drove off. They seemed very willing to get back into the traces, just as if it were a great honor for them.

Little O went to bed again, and Pysen went to sleep because it was time for his nap. He fell asleep the minute his head hit the pillow. Since he usually slept a couple of hours, Mama decided she might as well sit with us in the parlor for a while and knit. Mirre and Rosalind quarreled about whose turn it was to sit on the driver's box, so Papa said that, for the sake of keeping a little order, we'd have to take it by age. So Mirre won.

There were a number of people standing around and looking at us, but we were already so used to it that we hardly noticed. We got back to the highway without any particular difficulty.

Dessi looked back and said that we must remember that place for some other time.

In Sweden, in 1958, The Saucepan Journey *was judged the best book for children. There is more about the irrepressible Larssons in two sequels entitled* Pysen *and* Little O. *The author's* Spettecake Holiday *won the Nils Holgersson Medal, awarded annually by Swedish children's librarians.*

Tomas Is Lost

BY ELIZABETH KENT TARSHIS

Illustrations by Harold Haydon

> Now that the Mexican village of Benito
> Juarez has a school and a schoolteacher,
> everyone wants to learn to read. Everyone,
> that is, except the mayor's son, Pedro Lopez.

BEFORE the sun was up on Sunday people were streaming into Benito Juarez from all directions. Some rode on donkeys, sitting far back toward the tail because the rest of the back was covered with bundles. There were rope nets packed with red bowls and jars and dishes carefully wrapped in hay; round blocks of charcoal that the charcoal burners brought down from the hills; baskets crowded with unhappy chickens poking their heads out and squawking all down the road. Underneath all these loads the patient burros walked.

Many men and women walked too. They carried huge piles of baskets on their backs, or rolls of straw matting; they balanced large flat trays on their heads, filled with fruit—the golden yellow of oranges, the sharp green of limes, and the rich dark green of avocados. A constant stream of them moved through the streets of Benito Juarez in the cool dawn. Many had walked all night to get there and would have to walk all night to get home. They

moved easily in spite of their burdens, shuffling quickly
along with knees that were always bent and feet that
barely left the ground.

The market-place was the space under the arched roof
that ran around three sides of the plaza and the streets
that led out of it. In it each kind of merchant had his own
area. The pottery-sellers, the serape-makers, the fruit-
merchants, the grain-sellers, all gathered in the same
places week after week, as probably they and their families had done for many tens, even hundreds, of years.

As soon as they arrived they undid their bundles and
set out their wares. Some, like Señora Lopez, had little
wooden stalls—a board on trestles, with perhaps a canvas
awning on four poles if it were in the sun. But many
spread their goods on a piece of cloth laid on the pave-
ment, or even on the ground itself, and sat or knelt beside
them, ready for business.

The women wore full blue or brown skirts and white
blouses. Many of them brought their children, and it was
often hard to tell whether it was a baby or a chicken that
was kicking in the *rebozo* slung across a woman's back.
Most of them had bare hard-soled feet. Others wore
sandals cut from old rubber tires. They were Indians,

most of them, come down from the hill villages or up
from the valleys to sell the goods they had made so that
they might have enough to eat for the next week. The
soil on the steep hillsides could not grow enough to feed
them.

The men went barefoot too, though more of them
than of the women rode on burros. Some came from the
towns, bringing cheap cottons, combs, and stockings that
would hardly last till the next week.

As the sun rose and blue shadows took shape under the
eaves of the pink-and-cream houses, the noise grew. Each
man and woman tried to get people to buy, each shouting
louder than the next.

Pedro had set up his mother's stall just where she
wanted it—at the corner of the Avenida Zapata and the
plaza, under the arched roof. She had quickly laid out
her embroideries and woollens. She stitched birds and
animals on tablecloths in blue and red; she wove belts
with fringed ends in blue and red and green angular
designs. When she could get wool she wove serapes—the
long woollen blanket with the slit in the center that almost
every man of the central plateau wore to keep out the
cool night air and the winter winds. The serapes were

brown or blue with white patterns, sometimes with a touch of red.

Maria came along with Tomas on her back and a blue-and-purple-striped shopping bag on her arm.

"Come with me, Pedro," she said. "I have so many things to get that I can't possibly carry them all by myself."

Pedro was glad of an excuse to walk around the market; and he liked to watch Maria bargain, looking as firm and serious as her mother.

"First I need some vegetables," she began.

Pedro groaned. "Haven't we got enough food? What was all that cooking for that we did yesterday?"

"You don't know much," said Maria, as she picked her way along the crowded cobblestones. "That was just a beginning. We're going to have *guacamole,* so I have to get avocados and peppers and tomatoes and onions. They have to be fresh."

"You're always right, aren't you?" said Pedro.

"Oh," said Maria, pulling his ear, "not always. Just about five times out of five, though. I forgot, you don't know what that means."

"I do too," began Pedro; then he began to laugh. "All right. You can tease me if you want, but I have such a good temper that I don't really mind."

Maria stopped in front of a fruit and vegetable stall piled so high that they could just see the dark unsmiling face of the woman who tended it. Oranges were in the middle, then a ring of limes and bunchs of bananas outside them. Down one side were all kinds of peppers, from small fiery red ones to large green mild ones. On the other side were the shiny green avocados, and along the top hung braided strings of silver-white and gold-brown onions and white garlic pods. Round red tomatoes were piled at the back. Mangoes, papayas, and prickly pears were beside them, some sliced open to show the sweet

dripping pulp, and still farther on deep yellow and orange yams.

Pedro did not see how Maria could possibly choose
among so many good things, but she began to pinch and
poke everything, and at last took a string of white onions,
six avocados, soft and ripe, eight tomatoes, and four of
the sweet green peppers. She also got an orange for
Tomas, who began at once to suck it loudly. The shopping bag was quite heavy now.

"Some eggs now," and she pattered along to another

corner of the market-place. "The hens didn't lay enough yesterday."

"Don't they cost a lot?" asked Pedro as he caught up to her.

"Of course—that's why we're having them today. Don't you remember that company is coming?" She found the egg stall and chose six large satiny brown eggs. "Keep them at the top—it would be dreadful to have them broken."

"I'll put them in my sombrero," said Pedro, taking it off.

"That reminds me," added Maria. "Mother said to buy a hat for Tomas. Come with me while we do that, and then you can take him back to mother while I carry the vegetables home."

They passed a section where women were selling steaming meats and vegetables in sauces hot with red pepper, and then the live-animal district, with tiny pigs fastened by a thin cord round one hind foot to trip them up when they tried to run away, and chickens squawking as loudly as ever in their wicker baskets.

The man who sold hats seemed to sell every other kind of thing made of straw and reed and fiber. His stand was hung with rows of hats—tall, flat, white, yellow, bordered with red and blue, round, pointed, deep, and shallow. There were brooms, bird-cages, coils of rope and balls of string, *petates*—reed mats—of all sizes.

Maria looked carefully at the hats.

"I want a small one," she said, "for my little brother here."

"Try that one," said Pedro, and pointed to one with a bright red border. The hat-seller handed it to him and he tried it on Tomas. It came almost down to his chin.

"Here's a smaller one of the same kind," said the man.

The second one fitted well, resting on Tomas' ears. Maria paid for it and the three went off, the red-brimmed hat bobbing along on Maria's back.

As the morning passed the heat and noise in the market-place grew steadily. The smell of ripe fruit mixed with that of cooking meat, of leather and pepper and garlic, in one rich strong smell that seemed to hang like a cloud over the stalls and streets. Pedro sniffed it with pleasure as he walked slowly toward Juanita's house to call for the teacher.

Juan Mendez was waiting for him in the doorway.

"Good morning, Pedro," he called.

Pedro said good morning politely.

"It is kind of your mother to ask me to eat with you," remarked the teacher as they walked through the crowded plaza, where most of the merchants were having their lunch in what shade they could find.

"Well," replied Pedro, "it is nice for us too. We shall get such a good dinner."

Juan Mendez laughed. "I hadn't thought of that side of it. But don't you always get good dinners?"

"When the harvest is good—then we do."

"And is it good this year?"

"Better than last year. My father says that if all the peasants knew more about what to plant and how to get water for the fields and things like that, they wouldn't have to worry so much about the harvests and the rainfall."

"He is right"—Juan Mendez looked thoughtful. "Perhaps that is something in which the school can help."

Pedro did not understand. "I thought the school was just for learning to read, and——" He was going to say "and that kind of nonsense."

"Oh, no," said the teacher. "A school is ever so much more than that—at least it should be. It should teach all sorts of things: sewing and cooking and farming, music and dancing and making things with one's hands. And it should be for everyone, not just for the children. In many places the school is called 'The House of the People.'"

This was a very new idea for Pedro.

"I don't see——" he began; but by this time they had come to his house, and his mother was rushing out of the door to shake hands with the teacher.

The dinner was even better than Pedro had expected. First they had soup: the soup that Tomas had so nearly fallen into the night before. Then came rice, fried first and then boiled with tomatoes. In the middle of each helping of rice was a fried egg and over it all a hot sauce, full of chile. Next came the best part of the dinner —*mole*—slices of turkey covered with a sauce so rich and dark with spices that it looked almost black, full of twelve different kinds of peppers and even chocolate. It was Señor Lopez' favorite dish, and he ate a great deal of it and drank a lot of the pineapple juice that went with it. Pedro was more interested in the fried bananas and the *guacamole*—mashed avocado with minced tomato, onion, and green pepper, all well seasoned. Afterward came salad and a dessert of tiny pears preserved in a thick syrup.

After such a meal everyone was glad to sit in the patio and say nothing for a while.

"I have a question, Señor Lopez," said Juan Mendez at last. "Would it be possible for the school to get a blackboard and some chalk?"

Señor Lopez blew a long curl of smoke from his cigarette.

"It might be done," he answered cautiously.

"That is not the only thing we need," went on the teacher, "but it is the most important right now."

"I have to ask the council," said Señor Lopez. "But you know we have no money."

"I do know that—and I want to tell you of a plan that has been tried in other villages. The council can set aside a piece of land for the school, to be cultivated by everyone in turn—children too. The money that comes from selling its crops is used to pay for books and pencils and repairs for the school. And it is also useful in teaching the children the best ways of farming."

Señor Lopez thought this over. "I see no reason why we could not do it. In fact it sounds very sensible. It helps the school to pay for itself."

"Then," went on Juan Mendez eagerly, "I wonder what you will think of another plan of mine. I was talking to your son about it just before dinner. I feel that the school should do more than simply teach reading and writing— though it must do that well. I feel that a good teacher should teach anything that a child or his parents want to learn."

"What kinds of things do you mean, Señor Mendez?" asked Señor Lopez.

"Almost everything: what crops are best to plant and how best to grow them; how to cure sickness and to keep well; how to make clothes for the children and to cook; how to paint pictures and make music—there is no end to the list." Señor Mendez' eyes were glowing.

Señor Lopez too was excited. "I was right," he declared, "when I told those who doubted the need for a school that it would help not only the children but the whole village. I will give you all the help I can with your plans."

As he listened to his father and the teacher, Pedro was thinking hard. If all these things came true the school might not be such a waste of time as he had thought. But as yet there was only talk. He would wait a little longer before he learned to read.

"Perhaps," said Señor Lopez slowly, "you will be able to interest my son in what you are doing. He does not yet think that school is a good thing."

Pedro did not like to have his thoughts read so neatly.

"I never said that," he began. "I just meant that it may be all right for some people—but what good does it do me?"

"If you are mayor of a village, like your father," answered Juan Mendez, "you should be able to read the newspapers to know what is going on in the world, and to understand figures. A peasant can get better crops from his land if he can read what the government prints about farming. When something is wrong in his village he can write a letter to ask the government to set it right."

"And supposing—well, what about bullfighters?" Pedro looked up quickly through his thick lashes and down again, and did not see his father and the teacher smile.

"Even a bullfighter should know how to read, or he might get cheated out of his pay. Besides, he might some day want to become something else—a doctor, or even a teacher."

"Oh, no!" cried Pedro. "To be a bullfighter is the most

exciting thing in the world. I'll never want to be anything else."

But all the way back to the market-place, carrying Tomas, who was heavy from much dinner, he kept thinking about what his father and Juan Mendez had been saying.

Señora Lopez had asked him to watch her stall while she cleaned the kitchen.

"What shall I do with you, Tomas?" he asked. "I wish I had time to make my invention. I'd better tie you to something that will stand still instead of to my ankle the way I did at the *fiesta*."

Tomas looked up at him from under the shadow of the red-brimmed hat and gurgled. Pedro fastened a cord around the place where Tomas' waist should have been and tied the other end to one of the legs of the stand. Then he set Tomas down beneath the table on an empty bag and gave him some spools to play with.

"There," he said. "That ought to keep you quiet."

As people came back slowly from their siesta the chattering and shouting began to rise again as it had in the morning. Pedro felt very drowsy. No one came to buy serapes or embroidered tablecloths. He leaned against the wall and shut his eyes for a moment. The waves of sound swept around him with the low roar of a storm, and then seemed to die away. The heat of the sun reflected from the rough stones rose around him. His head dropped lower and lower on his chest. Pedro was asleep.

He was awakened by someone shaking his arm roughly and jerking him from side to side. He opened his eyes, blinking in the sunlight. It was his mother who was holding him by the arm, and she looked more frightened than he had ever seen her.

"Where is Tomas?" she cried. "What have you done with him? Answer me. Are you deaf?"

Pedro rubbed his eyes. Then he looked under the table. There was no one there, not even a rope. Pedro felt as though a large hole had opened inside him. He shivered and his teeth chattered.

"I—I don't know," he stammered. "He was here—just a few minutes ago. I tied him to the leg of the stand. With a rope. The rope's gone too!"

"That's plain to everyone," said his mother bitterly. "What I want to know is—where is he now?"

"I don't know, I tell you." Pedro was almost in tears.

Señora Lopez let go his arm. "I didn't mean to be angry," she said sadly, "but we must find him. Where in the world could he be?" Large tears began to follow each other down her round cheeks.

"Don't cry," Pedro told her, forgetting to weep himself. "We'll get him back. He can't have gone far. I'll ask everyone in the plaza whether he's been seen."

By this time a crowd had gathered round the stall. As soon as Pedro asked his first question the word was passed around, and in no time at all almost everyone in the market-place knew that the mayor's youngest child had disappeared, no one knew how or where. But no one was very helpful until the woman whose stall was next to Señora Lopez' pointed out that the basket-maker who had set up his wares on the other side, around the corner on the Avenida Zapata, had moved out early and taken all his goods with him. She had noticed Tomas before the man left, and not afterward, but she couldn't say for sure that he had taken him. Still, it was a clue.

Pedro asked more questions. No one seemed to know much about the basket-seller. Some thought that he came from the north, probably from the mountain villages. He had a donkey, they were certain of that, and a boy who helped him, a tall boy with a dark face.

Pedro turned to his mother.

"I'll take Rosa," he whispered, "and ride out the north road a little way and see whether anyone has seen Tomas go by. They ought to know him by his red hat."

"Yes, yes—go," said Señora Lopez, wringing her hands. "Please do something. All this talking does no good. And tell your father and Maria," she called after him.

As Pedro started to cross the plaza someone called his name. It was Carlotta. She was out of breath and excited.

"I just heard about your brother," she said, "and I want to tell you something."

"I'm busy," answered Pedro shortly. He did not feel like listening to girls' secrets just then.

"But this is important," went on Carlotta firmly. "Do you remember the boy who pushed you and Rosa in the race on Friday?"

"Of course; but what has that got to do with Tomas?"

"Everything," said Carlotta proudly. "That boy is the one whose father has the basket stall beside your mother's!"

"How do you know?" asked Pedro in surprise.

"I noticed that big silver buckle he wears. I saw him when he was packing up to go this afternoon, when you were asleep."

"Did you see Tomas too?" Pedro grabbed her arm so tightly that it hurt.

"No," said the girl sadly. "I expect I'm really not much help."

"Never mind—it's something to know who those people are, even if we don't know whether they really took Tomas, or where they have gone." Pedro was very excited.

"Carlotta," he went on, still holding her arm. "Let's go and look for him right away. Will you come?"

Carlotta nodded.

"Then come home with me and we'll get Rosa."

Carlotta followed Pedro into the Lopez' house. Maria was putting the dinner dishes away on the shelves. When Pedro told her what had happened to Tomas she almost dropped one of the best plates.

"I'm going out to look for him," continued Pedro hurriedly. "You go over and tell father, Maria. Carlotta and I are going up the north road on Rosa."

While Maria set out to look for her father, Pedro and Carlotta led Rosa out of the stable-yard, climbed on her back, and started for the north road through back streets.

Whenever they met someone leaving the market they asked him if he had seen a child in a red-brimmed hat. But no one had seen Tomas, or even heard a child cry out. They felt sadder and sadder as Rosa plodded through the maguey plantations. Bulging white thunderclouds were rising on the horizon, full of rain and lightning, but neither Pedro nor Carlotta noticed them. They were too busy thinking of Tomas and what might be happening to him.

After they had ridden for nearly a mile, without meeting anyone who could give them any news of Tomas, Rosa stopped with a jerk.

"What is it?" said Carlotta. "Has she hurt herself?"

"I don't know," answered Pedro as he swung himself down from her back.

But Rosa had not picked up a stone or stumbled in a rut. What Pedro saw lying on the ground where a narrow hill path met the road was a small red-brimmed hat.

Pedro and Carlotta looked at the red-brimmed hat for a moment without saying anything.

"Well," said Carlotta at last, "are you sure it's his?"

"Yes," replied Pedro slowly; "and Rosa seems to think so too. I'm just wondering what we ought to do next."

Carlotta looked surprised. "Aren't you going to follow the path? That must be the way they went."

Pedro did not like to admit to a girl that he felt a little frightened. Who could tell what kind of people these might be who would take a baby like Tomas?

"I was only thinking that perhaps we ought to go back and tell my father."

"Let's go up a little way," suggested Carlotta. "It isn't late—and it would be wonderful if we could find him ourselves."

"All right," said Pedro, and climbed on again. Carlotta held the hat tightly.

The path rose gently at first, a faint track in the dusty gray earth. Only the tapping of Rosa's hoofs broke the hot silence among the maguey plants. Then the ground grew steeper, and first Carlotta and then Pedro slid off Rosa's back as she climbed steadily upward. They walked through tall cool pine woods instead of through the spiky maguey with its broad pointed leaves.

The path zigzagged, sometimes dipping into a little valley or coming out on an open height so that they could look down and see the whole village laid out like neat toy blocks on the valley floor. Rosa went steadily on as though she knew the way. Whenever Pedro and Carlotta stopped for breath she pushed them ahead.

Suddenly she stopped and pricked her ears forward as though she heard something on the path above. Pedro and Carlotta listened hard, but could hear nothing.

"Go on, Rosa," urged Pedro. "We're not nearly at the top." But Rosa stood stock-still with her feet planted firmly in the path.

"There's no moving her when she acts that way," said Pedro.

"I'm just as glad," answered Carlotta. "It's so hot—and I'm so tired."

They sat down on the roots of a pine tree that stretched across the path.

"Listen," said Pedro suddenly. Carlotta held her breath. Far up the mountain she heard a sound as though something were moving with faint footsteps down the path. Sometimes the noise died away entirely and then came back a little louder.

"That must be what Rosa heard," whispered Pedro.

"Shall we go on?" asked Carlotta.

"No. Let's wait and find out who it is. Perhaps he can help us find where those people live."

They sat still while the footsteps grew steadily louder. Carlotta wanted to ask Pedro about his plan, but he made her keep quiet.

At last they could see a figure moving through the trees, bounding down the mountain with light springy steps and carrying a large basket on its back. There was a sharp turn in the path just above them and they watched eagerly for the man to appear.

It was Carlotta who cried out, "Why, it's that boy!"

So it was. Pedro noticed the big silver eagle on his belt buckle. His black head was bent low under the strap that held the basket, and he did not see the children until he almost stumbled over them. He would have passed by if Carlotta had not reached up and caught his ragged trouser.

"Wait," she said. "We want to ask you something."

The boy looked at them for the first time. He had a dark, unsmiling face, with thick straight brows and a thin mouth. His black eyes stared at them, but he said nothing.

Carlotta did not know how to begin.

Pedro felt that it was important to be polite.

"Please, Señor," he began, "we want to ask if you have seen anything of a small boy, just a baby, in a red hat."

At last the dark boy opened his mouth.

"Why?" he said in a low voice.

"He's lost," answered Carlotta. "And—and we thought you might help us to find him."

"Why?" he asked again.

"Weren't you at the market in Benito Juarez today?" demanded Pedro.

"Why?" he said a third time.

This made Pedro very angry. "Can't you answer polite questions?" he shouted.

"Sh-sh!" whispered Carlotta. "If you make him angry he won't tell us anything." To the boy she explained: "This is why, Señor. Pedro's brother, Tomas—this is Pedro—got lost today from the market-place. He had a red hat on—Pedro found the hat down at the foot of the hill. And you *were* at the market today. I saw you there. And you had your stall next to where Pedro and Tomas were sitting. We just wanted to ask you if you had seen him—before you left the market."

This long speech left Carlotta out of breath. She and Pedro waited eagerly for the boy to answer, but for a long time he said nothing, and they could not tell from his face what he was thinking.

At last he answered, very slowly: "Yes. I saw him. I saw the red hat. But I did not see him go away—and I did not see anyone take him."

Pedro's hopes rose and sank again.

"Well," he said sadly, "I suppose we'll have to go back without him." He had counted so much on the dark-faced boy, and now he turned his head away and looked out through the trees. All the branches were blurred as though it were raining. He swallowed several times and sniffed hard.

"Come on, Carlotta," he said at last, and pulled at Rosa's

bridle. But Rosa still would not move. She had her nose close to the basket on the boy's back.

"Wait," said the boy.

Both children looked at him in surprise.

"Would you like to see what I have in my basket?" he went on.

Pedro could not see what good that would do.

"No, thank you," he said politely. "We really have to go." And he tried again to lead Rosa down the path—and again she would not move.

"Your burro is smarter than you are," said the boy, and for the first time they saw what might be a smile on his face. "Even though she can't always win races," he added.

He swung the basket down from his shoulders. It was a tall one, closely woven, with a tight cover. Rosa seemed to be very excited. She managed to nose the cover off. Pedro decided that after all there must be something interesting in there. He walked up and looked in. What he saw made him call to Carlotta.

When Carlotta peered in she saw at the bottom of the basket a faded blue serape, and on the serape, curled like a kitten, fast asleep, lay Tomas Lopez.

The pine woods were filled with shouts.

"Hurrah!" cried Pedro, and threw his arms around Rosa and then around Carlotta and very nearly around the dark-faced boy.

Then he thought of something.

"What were you going to do with him?" he said sternly to the boy.

"Take him back to his home, of course." The boy nearly smiled again. "Don't you think we have enough babies up there?" He pointed up the mountain.

"Well, then," went on Pedro, "why did you take him?"

"I didn't—"

"Let me hold him," interrupted Carlotta, and she

reached down into the basket and picked up Tomas, who was beginning to wake up. His black eyes flew open all at once, and he made loud contented noises when he saw Rosa and Pedro. He did not seem to be any the worse for his adventure. Carlotta sat down on the path and held him tightly.

"Go on," she said. "Tell us how you happen to have him."

"I saw him tied up under the stall at the market. But when we left I didn't see him. I told you the truth. When we got home, far above this place, there he lay in one of the baskets! He must have untied his rope and crawled in when no one was watching him." At this Pedro looked at the ground.

"That's all there is to tell. I brought him down as soon as I could because I knew people would be looking for him."

"What about his hat?" asked Carlotta.

"My father must have put it with the rest of his when

he packed up his goods, and then it must have rolled away as we turned up the path."

"Lucky it did," remarked Pedro.

The boy looked a little surprised.

"I was bringing him back anyway," he said gently.

"One more thing," went on Pedro. "Why didn't you tell us right away that you had him?"

The boy *really* smiled this time. "Do you think I would give him to the first person who came along? I had to make sure that he really belonged to you. And if you want to know, it was your burro that made me sure."

"Thank you—what is your name, anyway?" Pedro held out his hand as he spoke.

"My name is Pablo," said the boy, and shook Pedro's hand firmly. "But you should thank your burro." He shook hands with Carlotta too.

"If you like," went on Pablo, "I'll carry him down the path for a while, until it isn't so steep. You might drop him."

"Would you?" said Pedro. "That would be fine."

So Tomas was put back into the basket, only this time he pushed away the cover and stood up, holding on to the edge and bouncing up and down as Pablo jogged along the path. Pedro and Carlotta tried breathlessly to keep up with him.

After about ten minutes they came to one of the clearings and found Pablo looking down into the valley.

"I want to ask you, Pablo," said Pedro, coming up behind him. "Why did you go away so quickly after the race on Friday?"

"I'm sorry my burro pushed yours," answered Pablo. "He has a bad temper, but there's nothing I can do about it. The reason I went away so fast is that you looked so fierce—and I didn't want to have the trouble of fighting you!"

"Pooh!" exclaimed Pedro. "You weren't really scared of me. Why, you're almost twice as big."

"Well, I didn't want to get into trouble. If I beat you, people would think badly of me; and if you beat me, they would laugh. So I went home."

Toward the south the rainclouds were crowding up the sky and thin sheets of rain were moving toward the village.

"Soon the plaza will be wet," said Carlotta, "and the school."

"Do you go to the school?" asked Pablo.

"Of course," answered Carlotta. "Everybody does."

"But you don't, Pablo," said Pedro. "Why?"

"For one thing, it's too far away. For another, I have to work with my father or we should not have enough to eat. But I want to go."

This surprised Pedro very much. "I have to go," he said. "And I don't like it at all. I wish we could change places. I'd like to live up in the mountains."

"You don't know when you're lucky," said Pablo. "If I could just go to the school for one year, I'd always be thankful."

"Perhaps you can sometime," said Carlotta.

Pablo shook his head. "Not until we have our own school up on the mountain, and that probably won't be for a long time. Too many people up here think that a school is no good. Besides, they have no money at all."

"That's true in lots of places," said Carlotta. "And yet the schools come all the same."

"Perhaps—but let's go on down. I'll have to leave you soon."

After another fifteen minutes of walking Pablo swung his basket to the ground, and Pedro lifted Tomas out.

"You lead Rosa," he said to Carlotta. "I'll carry Tomas."

"Better tie him more tightly next time," smiled Pablo.

"I was going to make a kind of cage for him—on wheels,"

said Pedro, lifting Tomas onto his back. "But he ran away."

Pablo shook hands all round for the second time. "Good-bye," he said. "I'm glad we met on the mountain. You saved me a trip to the village. Also—well, perhaps we shall see each other again. Good-bye, Carlotta—and Tomas—and Rosa."

"When market day comes we shall look for you. And thank you for bringing Tomas back," said Pedro.

Pablo watched them move down the path, Carlotta in front, leading Rosa, and Pedro behind with Tomas' black head bobbing on his back. When they were out of sight in the pines he turned and climbed quickly up the mountainside.

To Pedro and Carlotta it seemed a long way home. They were tired, and Tomas was heavy. But when they were nearly home the excitement of having found Tomas made them forget their aching feet. Rosa began to trot faster through the plaza, and Pedro ran too. Señor and Señora Lopez were sitting silently with Maria in the kitchen when he burst in.

"Surprise, surprise!" he shouted, and put his hands over his mother's eyes. When Carlotta came in, holding Tomas on Rosa's back, he took his hands away. Señora Lopez could not believe her eyes. She began crying all over again, but this time from happiness. She did not even notice that Rosa, who was never allowed in the kitchen, was tracking dirt onto her clean floor.

Tomas did not understand what all the noise was about. He threw his arms around his mother's neck and held her as tightly as she was squeezing him.

Señor Lopez could not believe his eyes either. As soon as Maria had told him Tomas was lost, he had got his friends together. They had ridden up and down the roads and across the fields, asking everyone they met whether they had seen a child in a red-brimmed hat. Everywhere they had had the same answer. No such child had been seen, or even heard of, either yesterday or today. They had returned sadly to the village, not knowing what to do next. To see the child suddenly appear, safe and well, was almost a miracle.

While Pedro told of their adventures, Maria bustled round the kitchen, beating up chocolate and setting out *pan dulce*—sweet bread—for supper. Señora Lopez persuaded Carlotta to stay to have supper with them.

"I can't believe it," she repeated over and over again. She held Tomas in her lap while she was eating, afraid to let him out of her arms for a second now that she had got him back. It was hard to eat that way, because Tomas was always reaching for a cake just as she began to drink her chocolate.

"I'd better get that thing done that I was planning last night," said Pedro between bites.

"What's that?" asked Maria, whose mouth was also full.

"A cage to keep Tomas in."

"Would it be like a bird-cage?" asked Carlotta.

"Much bigger, and it would have a door and wheels and a little awning for the sun."

"I think it might be better," suggested Señor Lopez gently, "if boys who were asked to look after their little brothers did so, instead of going to sleep. After all, if Tomas could untie a rope, he might easily get out of such a cage."

Pedro wriggled. "But I did find him, father," he said in a small voice.

"I know that—and I am glad. Though if what you say is right, the boy from the mountain—Pablo, you said his name was—would have brought him back anyway."

Pedro hung his head still farther.

"And so," went on his father, "I really think that if any-one is to get a prize it should be Pablo."

"I wonder what he would like," said Maria.

"He's very poor," answered Carlotta softly; "and what he wants most is to go to school."

"Does he indeed?" Señor Lopez looked up quickly. "He must be quite different from some people we know. Per-haps something can be done about that."

Pedro walked home with Carlotta. Most of the people with goods to sell had left the market, but they found a pottery-seller just packing his wares into straw-lined nets.

Among the bowls and plates, enormous mixing-bowls, jars, and jugs, all of red-brown earthenware, he found a water jar exactly like the one he had lost down the well.

"I almost forgot about it," he said to Carlotta. "Shall we fill it?"

"No," answered Carlotta. "It's late enough already."

It was dark in the village streets and the moon was not yet up. They walked along in silence for a little way, past the plaza with its heavy stone benches and neat gravel paths and beds of petunias, and into the narrow alleyways by the river.

"Do you think your father will really do something to help Pablo go to school?" asked Carlotta as they turned the corner by the well.

"He might," answered Pedro. "When he makes up his mind about something he usually does it."

"Like you?"

"More than me, even."

"And you don't think you'll ever decide that you want to learn to read?" inquired Carlotta anxiously.

"Never. So don't talk about it any more. I am getting tired of people asking me such questions."

"Oh, dear!" cried Carlotta. "I didn't mean to make you angry."

"You didn't," said Pedro, and sounded more friendly. "At least, I'm not angry with you. Only, all I hear is school, school, school all day long—from the teacher and my father and mother and Maria, and Pablo this afternoon, and now from you. Next thing I know Rosa will be telling me to learn to read."

They had come by this time to the corner of the street on which Carlotta lived. It was the poorest part of the whole village—no paving-stones in the streets, no clean white houses like Pedro's. Carlotta's house, and all the others, were brown and dingy, of rough adobe crumbling at the corners, with roofs of palm-leaf thatch or maguey leaves that could not keep out the rain as well as the Lopez' trim tiles.

"You don't need to come any farther," said Carlotta. She felt ashamed of her house.

"All right," replied Pedro at last. "I'll see you tomorrow. And thank you for coming with me today." He turned and ran home quickly through the starlit dark, back to a house that was happy again.

Pedro eventually changes his mind about learning to read, but not before he has many more exciting adventures, all of which may be followed in The Village that Learned to Read, *the book from which this story is taken.*

Anne's Confession

BY L. M. MONTGOMERY

Illustrations by Emil Weiss

> Marilla and Matthew had expected to adopt
> a boy orphan, when Anne appeared and
> captured them both—especially Matthew.

I T'S time Anne was in to do her sewing," said Marilla, glancing at the clock and then into the yellow August afternoon where everything drowsed in the heat. "She stayed playing with Diana more than half an hour more'n I gave her leave to; and now she's perched out there on the woodpile talking to Matthew, nineteen to the dozen, when she knows perfectly well she ought to be at her work. And of course he's listening to her like a perfect ninny. I never saw such an infatuated man. The more she talks and the odder the things she says, the more he's delighted evidently. Anne Shirley, you come right in here this minute, do you hear me!"

A series of staccato taps on the west window brought Anne flying in from the yard, eyes shining, cheeks faintly flushed with pink, unbraided hair streaming behind her in a torrent of brightness.

"Oh, Marilla," she exclaimed breathlessly, "there's going to be a Sunday-school picnic next week—in Mr. Harmon Andrews's field, right near the Lake of Shining Waters. And Mrs. Superintendent Bell and Mrs. Rachel

Lynde are going to make ice cream—think of it, Marilla
—*ice cream!* And oh, Marilla, can I go to it?"

"Just look at the clock, if you please, Anne. What time
did I tell you to come in?"

"Two o'clock—but isn't it splendid about the picnic,
Marilla? Please can I go? Oh, I've never been to a picnic
—I've dreamed of picnics, but I've never—"

"Yes, I told you to come at two o'clock. And it's a
quarter to three. I'd like to know why you didn't obey
me, Anne."

"Why, I meant to, Marilla, as much as could be. But
you have no idea how fascinating Idlewild is. And
then, of course, I had to tell Matthew about the picnic.
Matthew is such a sympathetic listener. Please can I go?"

"You'll have to learn to resist the fascination of Idle-
whatever-you-call-it. When I tell you to come in at a
certain time I mean that time and not half an hour later.
And you needn't stop to discourse with sympathetic
listeners on your way, either. As for the picnic, of course
you can go. You're a Sunday-school scholar, and it's not
likely I'd refuse to let you go when all the other little
girls are going."

"But—but," faltered Anne, "Diana says that everybody
must take a basket of things to eat. I can't cook, as you
know, Marilla, and—and—I don't mind going to a picnic
without puffed sleeves so much, but I'd feel terribly
humiliated if I had to go without a basket. It's been
preying on my mind ever since Diana told me."

"Well, it needn't prey any longer. I'll bake you a basket."

"Oh, you dear good Marilla. Oh, you are so kind to me.
Oh, I'm so much obliged to you."

Getting through with her "ohs" Anne cast herself into
Marilla's arms and rapturously kissed her sallow cheek.
It was the first time in her whole life that childish lips
had voluntarily touched Marilla's face. Again that sud-

den sensation of startling sweetness thrilled her. She was secretly vastly pleased at Anne's impulsive caress, which was probably the reason why she said brusquely:

"There, there, never mind your kissing nonsense. I'd sooner see you doing strictly as you're told. As for cooking, I mean to begin giving you lessons in that some of these days. But you're so featherbrained, Anne, I've been waiting to see if you'd sober down a little and learn to be steady before I begin. You've got to keep your wits about you in cooking and not stop in the middle of things to let your thoughts rove all over creation. Now, get out your patchwork and have your square done before tea-time."

"I do *not* like patchwork," said Anne dolefully, hunting out her workbasket and sitting down before a little heap of red and white diamonds with a sigh. "I think some kinds of sewing would be nice; but there's no scope for imagination in patchwork. It's just one little seam after another and you never seem to be getting anywhere. But of course I'd rather be Anne of Green Gables sewing patchwork than Anne of any other place with nothing to do but play. I wish time went as quick sewing patches as it does when I'm playing with Diana, though. Oh, we do have such elegant times, Marilla. I have to furnish most of the imagination, but I'm well able to do that. Diana is simply perfect in every other way. You know that little piece of land across the brook that runs up between our farm and Mr. Barry's. It belongs to Mr. William Bell, and right in the corner there is a little ring of white birch trees—the most romantic spot, Marilla. Diana and I have our playhouse there. We call it Idle-wild. Isn't that a poetical name? I assure you it took me some time to think it out. I stayed awake nearly a whole night before I invented it. Then, just as I was dropping off to sleep, it came like an inspiration. Diana

was *enraptured* when she heard it. We have got our
house fixed up elegantly. You must come and see it,
Marilla—won't you? We have great big stones, all covered with moss, for seats, and boards from tree to tree
for shelves. And we have all our dishes on them. Of
course, they're all broken but it's the easiest thing in
the world to imagine that they are whole. There's a piece
of a plate with a spray of red and yellow ivy on it that
is especially beautiful. We keep it in the parlor and we
have the fairy glass there, too. The fairy glass is as lovely
as a dream. Diana found it out in the woods behind
their chicken house. It's all full of rainbows—just little
young rainbows that haven't grown big yet—and Diana's
mother told her it was broken off a hanging lamp they
once had. But it's nicer to imagine the fairies lost it one
night when they had a ball, so we call it the fairy glass.
Matthew is going to make us a table. Oh, we have named
that little round pool over in Mr. Barry's field Willow-
mere. I got that name out of the book Diana lent me.
That was a thrilling book, Marilla. The heroine had
five lovers. I'd be satisfied with one, wouldn't you? She
was very handsome and she went through great tribula-
tions. She could faint as easy as anything. I'd love to be
able to faint, wouldn't you, Marilla? It's so romantic.
But I'm really very healthy for all I'm so thin. I believe
I'm getting fatter, though. Don't you think I am? I look
at my elbows every morning when I get up to see if
any dimples are coming. Diana is having a new dress
made with elbow sleeves. She is going to wear it to the
picnic. Oh, I do hope it will be fine next Wednesday.
I don't feel that I could endure the disappointment if
anything happened to prevent me from getting to the
picnic. I suppose I'd live through it, but I'm certain it
would be a lifelong sorrow. It wouldn't matter if I got
to a hundred picnics in after years; they wouldn't make

up for missing this one. They're going to have boats on the Lake of Shining Waters—and ice cream, as I told you. I have never tasted ice cream. Diana tried to explain what it was like, but I guess ice cream is one of those things that are beyond imagination."

"Anne, you have talked even on for ten minutes by the clock," said Marilla. "Now, just for curiosity's sake, see if you can hold your tongue for the same length of time."

Anne held her tongue as desired. But for the rest of the week she talked picnic and thought picnic and dreamed picnic. On Saturday it rained and she worked herself up into such a frantic state lest it should keep on raining until and over Wednesday that Marilla made her sew an extra patchwork square by way of steadying her nerves.

On Sunday Anne confided to Marilla on the way home from church that she grew actually cold all over with excitement when the minister announced the picnic from the pulpit.

"Such a thrill as went up and down my back, Marilla! I don't think I'd ever really believed until then that there was honestly going to be a picnic. I couldn't help fearing I'd only imagined it. But when a minister says a thing in the pulpit you just have to believe it."

"You set your heart too much on things, Anne," said Marilla, with a sigh. "I'm afraid there'll be a great many disappointments in store for you through life."

"Oh, Marilla, looking forward to things is half the pleasure of them," exclaimed Anne. "You mayn't get the things themselves; but nothing can prevent you from having the fun of looking forward to them. Mrs. Lynde says, 'Blessed are they who expect nothing for they shall not be disappointed.' But I think it would be worse to expect nothing than to be disappointed."

Marilla wore her amethyst brooch to church that day
as usual. Marilla always wore her amethyst brooch to
church. She would have thought it rather sacrilegious
to leave it off—as bad as forgetting her Bible or her collection dime. That amethyst brooch was Marilla's most
treasured possession. A seafaring uncle had given it to
her mother who in turn had bequeathed it to Marilla.
It was an old-fashioned oval, containing a braid of her
mother's hair, surrounded by a border of very fine
amethysts. Marilla knew too little about precious stones
to realize how fine the amethysts actually were; but she
thought them very beautiful and was always pleasantly
conscious of their violet shimmer at her throat, above
her good brown satin dress, even although she could
not see it.

Anne had been smitten with delighted admiration
when she first saw that brooch.

"Oh, Marilla, it's a perfectly elegant brooch. I don't
know how you can pay attention to the sermon or the
prayers when you have it on. *I* couldn't, I know. I think
amethysts are just sweet. They are what I used to think
diamonds were like. Long ago, before I had ever seen
a diamond, I read about them and I tried to imagine
what they would be like. I thought they would be lovely
glimmering purple stones. When I saw a real diamond
in a lady's ring one day I was so disappointed I cried.
Of course, it was very lovely but it wasn't my idea of
a diamond. Will you let me hold the brooch for one
minute, Marilla? Do you think amethysts can be the
souls of good violets?"

On the Monday evening before the picnic Marilla
came down from her room with a troubled face.

"Anne," she said to that small personage, who was
shelling peas by the spotless table and singing "Nelly
of the Hazel Dell" with a vigor and expression that did

credit to Diana's teaching, "did you see anything of my amethyst brooch? I thought I stuck it in my pincushion when I came home from church yesterday evening, but I can't find it anywhere."

"I—I saw it this afternoon when you were away at the Aid Society," said Anne, a little slowly. "I was passing your door when I saw it on the cushion, so I went in to look at it."

"Did you touch it?" said Marilla sternly.

"Y-e-e-s," admitted Anne, "I took it up and I pinned it on my breast just to see how it would look."

"You had no business to do anything of the sort. It's very wrong in a little girl to meddle. You shouldn't have gone into my room in the first place and you shouldn't have touched a brooch that didn't belong to you in the second. Where did you put it?"

"Oh, I put it back on the bureau. I hadn't it on a minute. Truly, I didn't mean to meddle, Marilla. I didn't think about its being wrong to go in and try on the brooch; but I see now that it was and I'll never do it again. That's one good thing about me. I never do the same naughty thing twice."

"You didn't put it back," said Marilla. "That brooch isn't anywhere on the bureau. You've taken it out or something, Anne."

"I *did* put it back," said Anne quickly—pertly, Marilla thought. "I don't just remember whether I stuck it on the pincushion or laid it in the china tray. But I'm perfectly certain I put it back."

"I'll go and have another look," said Marilla, determining to be just. "If you put that brooch back it's there still. If it isn't I'll know you didn't, that's all!"

Marilla went to her room and made a thorough search, not only over the bureau but in every other place she thought the brooch might possibly be. It was not to be found and she returned to the kitchen.

"Anne, the brooch is gone. By your own admission you were the last person to handle it. Now, what have you done with it? Tell me the truth at once. Did you take it out and lose it?"

"No, I didn't," said Anne solemnly, meeting Marilla's angry gaze squarely. "I never took the brooch out of your room and that is the truth, if I was to be led to the block for it—although I'm not very certain what a block is. So there, Marilla."

Anne's "so there" was only intended to emphasize her assertion, but Marilla took it as a display of defiance.

"I believe you are telling me a falsehood, Anne," she said sharply. "I know you are. There now, don't say anything more unless you are prepared to tell the whole truth. Go to your room and stay there until you are ready to confess."

"Will I take the peas with me?" said Anne meekly.

"No, I'll finish shelling them myself. Do as I bid you."

When Anne had gone Marilla went about her evening tasks in a very disturbed state of mind. She was worried about her valuable brooch. What if Anne had lost it? And how wicked of the child to deny having taken it, when anybody could see she must have! With such an innocent face, too!

"I don't know what I wouldn't sooner have had happen," thought Marilla, as she nervously shelled the peas. "Of course, I don't suppose she meant to steal it or anything like that. She's just taken it to play with or help along that imagination of hers. She must have taken it, that's clear, for there hasn't been a soul in that room since she was in it, by her own story, until I went up tonight. And the brooch is gone, there's nothing surer. I suppose she has lost it and is afraid to own up for fear

she'll be punished. It's a dreadful thing to think she tells falsehoods. It's a far worse thing than her fit of temper. It's a fearful responsibility to have a child in your house you can't trust. Slyness and untruthfulness—that's what she has displayed. I declare I feel worse about that than about the brooch. If she'd only have told the truth about it I wouldn't mind so much."

Marilla went to her room at intervals all through the evening and searched for the brooch, without finding it. A bedtime visit to the east gable produced no result. Anne persisted in denying that she knew anything about the brooch but Marilla was only the more firmly convinced that she did.

She told Matthew the story the next morning. Matthew was confounded and puzzled; he could not so quickly lose faith in Anne but he had to admit that circumstances were against her.

"You're sure it hasn't fell down behind the bureau?" was the only suggestion he could offer.

"I've moved the bureau and I've taken out the drawers and I've looked in every crack and cranny," was Marilla's positive answer. "The brooch is gone and that child has taken it and lied about it. That's the plain, ugly truth, Matthew Cuthbert, and we might as well look it in the face."

"Well now, what are you going to do about it?" Matthew asked forlornly, feeling secretly thankful that Marilla and not he had to deal with the situation. He felt no desire to put his oar in this time.

"She'll stay in her room until she confesses," said Marilla grimly, remembering the success of this method in the former case. "Then we'll see. Perhaps we'll be able to find the brooch if she'll only tell where she took it; but in any case she'll have to be severely punished, Matthew."

"Well now, you'll have to punish her," said Matthew, reaching for his hat. "I've nothing to do with it, remember. You warned me off yourself."

Marilla felt deserted by everyone. She could not even go to Mrs. Lynde for advice. She went up to the east gable with a very serious face and left it with a face more serious still. Anne steadfastly refused to confess. She persisted in asserting that she had not taken the brooch. The child had evidently been crying and Marilla felt a pang of pity which she sternly repressed. By night she was, as she expressed it, "beat out."

"You'll stay in this room until you confess, Anne. You can make up your mind to that," she said firmly.

"But the picnic is tomorrow, Marilla," cried Anne. "You won't keep me from going to that, will you? You'll just let me out for the afternoon, won't you? Then I'll stay here as long as you like afterwards *cheerfully*. But I *must* go to the picnic."

"You'll not go to picnics nor anywhere else until you've confessed, Anne."

"Oh, Marilla," gasped Anne.

But Marilla had gone out and shut the door.

Wednesday morning dawned as bright and fair as if expressly made to order for the picnic. Birds sang around Green Gables; the Madonna lilies in the garden sent out whiffs of perfume that entered in on viewless winds at every door and window, and wandered through halls and rooms like spirits of benediction. The birches in the hollow waved joyful hands as if watching for Anne's usual morning greeting from the east gable. But Anne was not at her window. When Marilla took her breakfast up to her she found the child sitting primly on her bed, pale and resolute, with tight-shut lips and gleaming eyes.

"Marilla, I'm ready to confess."

"Ah!" Marilla laid down her tray. Once again her method had succeeded; but her success was very bitter to her. "Let me hear what you have to say then, Anne."

"I took the amethyst brooch," said Anne, as if repeating a lesson she had learned. "I took it just as you said. I didn't mean to take it when I went in. But it did look so beautiful, Marilla, when I pinned it on my breast that I was overcome by an irresistible temptation. I imagined how perfectly thrilling it would be to take it to Idlewild

and play I was the Lady Cordelia Fitzgerald. It would be so much easier to imagine I was the Lady Cordelia if I had a real amethyst brooch on. Diana and I make necklaces of roseberries but what are roseberries compared to amethysts? So I took the brooch. I thought I could put it back before you came home. I went all the way around by the road to lengthen out the time. When I was going

over the bridge across the Lake of Shining Waters I took
the brooch off to have another look at it. Oh, how it did
shine in the sunlight! And then, when I was leaning over
the bridge, it just slipped through my fingers—so—and
went down—down—down, all purply-sparkling, and sank
forevermore beneath the Lake of Shining Waters. And
that's the best I can do at confessing, Marilla."

Marilla felt hot anger surge up into her heart again.
This child had taken and lost her treasured amethyst
brooch and now sat there calmly reciting the details
thereof without the least apparent compunction or re-
pentance.

"Anne, this is terrible," she said, trying to speak calmly.
"You are the very wickedest girl I ever heard of."

"Yes, I suppose I am," agreed Anne tranquilly. "And I
know I'll have to be punished. It'll be your duty to punish
me, Marilla. Won't you please get it over right off because I'd like to go to the picnic with nothing on my
mind."

"Picnic, indeed! You'll go to no picnic today, Anne
Shirley. That shall be your punishment. And it isn't half
severe enough either for what you've done!"

"Not go to the picnic!" Anne sprang to her feet and
clutched Marilla's hand. "But you *promised* me I might!
Oh, Marilla, I must go to the picnic. That was why I confessed. Punish me any way you like but that. Oh, Marilla,
please, please, let me go to the picnic. Think of the ice
cream! For anything you know I may never have a
chance to taste ice cream again."

Marilla disengaged Anne's clinging hands stonily.

"You needn't plead, Anne. You are not going to the
picnic and that's final. No, not a word."

Anne realized that Marilla was not to be moved. She
clasped her hands together, gave a piercing shriek, and
then flung herself face downward on the bed, crying and

writhing in an utter abandonment of disappointment and despair.

"For the land's sake!" gasped Marilla, hastening from the room. "I believe the child is crazy. No child in her senses would behave as she does. If she isn't she's utterly bad. Oh dear, I'm afraid Rachel was right from the first. But I've put my hand to the plow and I won't look back."

That was a dismal morning. Marilla worked fiercely and scrubbed the porch floor and the dairy shelves when she could find nothing else to do. Neither the shelves nor the porch needed it—but Marilla did. Then she went out and raked the yard.

When dinner was ready she went to the stairs and called Anne. A tear-stained face appeared, looking tragically over the banisters.

"Come down to your dinner, Anne."

"I don't want any dinner, Marilla," said Anne, sobbingly. "I couldn't eat anything. My heart is broken. You'll feel remorse of conscience someday, I expect, for breaking it, Marilla, but I forgive you. Remember when the time comes that I forgive you. But please don't ask me to eat anything, especially boiled pork and greens. Boiled pork and greens are so unromantic when one is in affliction."

Exasperated, Marilla returned to the kitchen and poured out her tale of woe to Matthew, who, between his sense of justice and his unlawful sympathy with Anne, was a miserable man.

"Well now, she shouldn't have taken the brooch, Marilla, or told stories about it," he admitted, mournfully surveying his plateful of unromantic pork and greens as if he, like Anne, thought it a food unsuited to crises of feeling, "but she's such a little thing—such an interesting little thing. Don't you think it's pretty rough not to let her go to the picnic when she's so set on it?"

"Matthew Cuthbert, I'm amazed at you. I think I've let

her off entirely too easy. And she doesn't appear to realize how wicked she's been at all—that's what worries me most. If she'd really felt sorry it wouldn't be so bad. And you don't seem to realize it, neither; you're making excuses for her all the time to yourself—I can see that."

"Well now, she's such a little thing," feebly reiterated Matthew. "And there should be allowances made, Marilla. You know she's never had any bringing up."

"Well, she's having it now," retorted Marilla.

The retort silenced Matthew if it did not convince him. That dinner was a very dismal meal. The only cheerful thing about it was Jerry Buote, the hired boy, and Marilla resented his cheerfulness as a personal insult.

When her dishes were washed and her bread sponge set and her hens fed Marilla remembered that she had noticed a small rent in her best black lace shawl when she had taken it off on Monday afternoon on returning from the Ladies' Aid. She would go and mend it.

The shawl was in a box in her trunk. As Marilla lifted it out, the sunlight, falling through the vines that clustered thickly about the window, struck upon something caught in the shawl—something that glittered and sparkled in facets of violet light. Marilla snatched at it with a gasp. It was the amethyst brooch, hanging to a thread of the lace by its catch!

"Dear life and heart," said Marilla blankly, "what does this mean? Here's my brooch safe and sound that I thought was at the bottom of Barry's pond. Whatever did that girl mean by saying she took it and lost it? I declare I believe Green Gables is bewitched. I remember now that when I took off my shawl Monday afternoon I laid it on the bureau for a minute. I suppose the brooch got caught in it somehow. Well!"

Marilla betook herself to the east gable, brooch in hand. Anne had cried herself out and was sitting dejectedly by the window.

"Anne Shirley," said Marilla solemnly, "I've just found my brooch hanging to my black lace shawl. Now I want to know what that rigmarole you told me this morning meant."

"Why, you said you'd keep me here until I confessed," returned Anne wearily, "and so I decided to confess because I was bound to get to the picnic. I thought out a confession last night after I went to bed and made it as interesting as I could. And I said it over and over so that I wouldn't forget it. But you wouldn't let me go to the picnic after all, so all my trouble was wasted."

Marilla had to laugh in spite of herself. But her conscience pricked her.

"Anne, you do beat all! But I was wrong—I see that now. I shouldn't have doubted your word when I'd never known you to tell a story. Of course, it wasn't right for you to confess to a thing you hadn't done—it was very wrong to do so. But I drove you to it. So if you'll forgive me, Anne, I'll forgive you and we'll start square again. And now get yourself ready for the picnic."

Anne flew up like a rocket.

"Oh, Marilla, isn't it too late?"

"No, it's only two o'clock. They won't be more than well gathered yet and it'll be an hour before they have tea. Wash your face and comb your hair and put on your gingham. I'll fill a basket for you. There's plenty of stuff baked in the house. And I'll get Jerry to hitch up the sorrel and drive you down to the picnic ground."

"Oh, Marilla," exclaimed Anne, flying to the washstand. "Five minutes ago I was so miserable I was wishing I'd never been born and now I wouldn't change places with an angel!"

That night a thoroughly happy, completely tired-out Anne returned to Green Gables in a state of beatification impossible to describe.

"Oh, Marilla, I've had a perfectly scrumptious time.

Scrumptious is a new word I learned today. I heard Mary Alice Bell use it. Isn't it very expressive? Everything was lovely. We had a splendid tea and then Mr. Harmon Andrews took us all for a row on the Lake of Shining Waters—six of us at a time. And Jane Andrews nearly fell overboard. She was leaning out to pick water lilies and if Mr. Andrews hadn't caught her by her sash just in the nick of time she'd have fallen in and prob'ly been drowned. I wish it had been me. It would have been such a romantic experience to have been nearly drowned. It would be such a thrilling tale to tell. And we had the ice cream. Words fail me to describe that ice cream. Marilla, I assure you it was sublime."

That evening Marilla told the whole story to Matthew over her stocking basket.

"I'm willing to own up that I made a mistake," she concluded candidly, "but I've learned a lesson. I have to laugh when I think of Anne's 'confession,' although I suppose I shouldn't for it really was a falsehood. But it doesn't seem as bad as the other would have been, somehow, and anyhow I'm responsible for it. That child is hard to understand in some respects. But I believe she'll turn out all right yet. And there's one thing certain, no house will ever be dull that she's in."

Three other Anne books that you're sure to enjoy are Anne of Avonlea, Chronicles of Avonlea, *and* Anne of the Island, *all by L. M. Montgomery and published by Grosset & Dunlap.*

Chúcaro

BY FRANCIS KALNAY

Illustrations by Julian de Miskey

> A gaucho *is a cowboy of the Argentine* Pampa—*the rich prairie grassland sweeping from the Andes Mountains to the Atlantic Ocean;* a criollo *is a descendant of horses brought over by the early Spanish conquerors. This is the story of a gaucho, a* criollo, *and a boy.*

SOME growing corn has golden hair, some yellow, some red, some brown. But look, there is one stalk with locks as black as the night, and if you creep up close, you will find this hair is not growing out of corn. It belongs to Pedro, the twelve-year-old son of the *Vaquero.* He was hunting for the hiding place of the *perdiz,* which is like our partridge—a little more shy perhaps, for even Pedro's sharp eyes couldn't find it. He was near the edge of the cornfield, searching through the jungle of stalks, when he saw something strange, and he stopped, stock-still. Hidden in the tall, leafy corn, Pedro held his breath and stared.

There, ankle-deep in the luscious alfalfa a short distance from where Pedro stood, a wild pony was having his breakfast. Maybe because he was so terribly hungry, or maybe because it was his first taste of this forbidden food, the pony acted as though he had never in his life tasted grass so juicy and sweet. He grazed in keen delight. His mouth watered and foamed and formed bubbles, beautiful green like jade. Each time his mouth was full, he lifted his head and, while chewing, looked about him. The air, heavy with the sweet scent of corn, made his nostrils quiver with delight. Once or twice he stood still, hesitant. Quietly Pedro stepped a little closer and watched the pony's every movement. He expected the horse to leave the alfalfa for the corn, but no, the grass was too delicious.

Pedro had been born in the *estancia*, where horses were kept without number, and he had ridden ponies ever since he was five. But he had never seen anything like this one! Pink certainly is a most unusual color for a horse, and Pedro could hardly believe his eyes. The color of the pink geraniums in the owners' patio, he thought, and no doubt just as soft. He noticed that the pony's ankles were pure white and looked new, like the socks worn by the wealthy village boys on Sundays. The pony also had snow-white beauty spots, one on his left cheek, one on the right. They suited him exactly.

"If only I could lasso him," pondered the boy, but he decided this was far too big a prize to take a chance of losing. So instead, he crept back to the Vaquero's hut and brought his father along.

"*Qué maravilla!*" cried the old man. "You were right, son; there isn't another pony like it. But, no, no, I couldn't risk throwing the noose on him."

"You must; you have done it hundreds of times," begged Pedro. "Why couldn't you do it now?"

The old man spread his palms. "My hands are no longer the same, Pedrito," he said with a bitter smile. "When you get old, your hands shake, my boy, and are no longer safe for the lasso."

But there was something else, they both knew, beside

advancing age that made the Vaquero's hands unsteady. The boy had noticed for some time that his father no longer sipped the wine with his meals but gulped it down fast and furiously as if dying of thirst. When his mother died, Pedrito was barely a year old. People at the ranch said that after the burial the Vaquero was no longer himself. He used to be strong as an ox and always full of fun. With his strength went also his pride. He was usually in rags, to which nobody objected, and it was sad that he didn't seem to care.

"Do you want him badly, Pedrito?" asked the old man, bending down.

"I would give anything to have him, Papa," whispered the boy.

"Well, then there is only one man who can get him for you. You just sit quietly here, and I'll go back for Juan."

Not for a second did Pedro let the horse out of his sight. Lying on his stomach to have a clearer view between the rows of corn, and with his mouth wide open, he watched the slightest movement of the pony. It took hardly more than a few minutes for the gaucho to reach the place, but to Pedro it seemed hours.

"Please get him quick," begged Pedro before Juan was even near. "He may run off and I'll never see him any more!"

"Now, wait, wait; don't get so excited!" quieted the gaucho. "Let me look at him first."

"There, there," whispered the boy, his cheeks aflame.

"*Caramba!* What a perfect colt! A pure *criollo,* if I ever saw one! I wonder if it has been branded. Have you noticed any marks on him?"

"I don't see any, but what do we care?"

"We can't lasso him if he belongs to some other rancho, you silly boy."

"But we'll have to lasso him first to see the brand. You

can't notice it from here." The boy's voice was hoarse
with excitement.

"Now, there is something in that. Wait."

The Pampa is an enormous land, and there are some
mighty fine gauchos there. But there never was a man
more skillful with the rope than Juan. The usual method
with wild ponies was to herd them into the corral. But
Juan looked down upon that kind of sport. He preferred
to swing the noose, which he always prepared himself,
out in the open field. This was ordinarily considered a
risky chance, but not with Juan. His eagle eye measured
the distance to the inch, his timing was as exact as a fine
cuckoo clock.

You could hear a slight whistle as the lasso spun
through the air, and seconds later Juan gently pulled in
the rope. There stood the little horse right in front of
them, a bunch of alfalfa still hanging from his mouth.
His frightened eyes were wide open and wild. As the boy
quietly advanced, the horse reared frantically and made
a desperate effort to escape. He would have dragged an
ordinary man along, but not Juan—no fear! Juan held
the end of the rope tight—he was strong and obstinate,
like a bull.

His legs spread wide and his eyes filled with tears, the
pony was now a pitiful sight. Pedro could no longer
stand it. "Let him go; please let him free," he begged.

"What is the matter with you?" Juan stamped his foot,
indignant. "A moment ago you begged me to lasso him,
and now you want me to let him go. Some gaucho you
are! Now run back to the ranch and bring me a piece of
rope for a halter, and run quick!"

As soon as Pedro left, the gaucho slackened the rope
so that the pony would feel more at ease. Then they
looked each other straight in the eye—the pony in horror
and the man with a big, melting smile. "Now, now,"

he said. "Relax. I am not half as tough as I look, and some day, I bet, you and I will be real friends. You'll see."

The colt pricked up his ears. "Easy, easy," said the gaucho, advancing no more than a step, his voice soft and soothing. "Turn your head and look at me sideways; that's right! Now I can see that you are getting reasonable, except for those shiny eyes. Crying? What a shame! Here, try this alfalfa. There is nothing like it in the whole province!" He threw a bunch of fresh grass to the pony. "Now I know perfectly well that you won't touch it, not yet. I know how you feel. All I want is to show you the kind of food we grow here! What do you think? Why are you looking at my left hand? Would you like to know what's in it? It is a *rehenque,* my whip. I seldom use it. I see you don't like it. All right, I'll throw it away. There it goes, you see? Now what is worrying you? My little mustache? Sorry, I can't take that off so easily, not even for you. But you'll get used to it, like everybody else. May I come a step nearer now? Gently, gently. Don't shy away. I want to know your name. I am a fool to ask. You wouldn't know, even if you had one. When I was a young kid, I had a nice little pony, quite wild like you, and everybody called him Chúcaro. Chúcaro is just the right name for a good horse like you. You, too, seem to like it. You even seem to like me! If that's so, I'll pick you some corn. You don't have to eat it, just smell it. So."

When Pedro returned with the rope for the halter, he simply couldn't believe his eyes.

"The pony doesn't seem to be afraid of you, Juan. What did you do to him?"

"Nothing. We only had a little chat."

"You really think he understood what you said?"

"Every word of it, and perhaps even more."

"You don't say!"

"Well, you'll see."

"Did you find any brand on him?"

"Not a trace. Except those white spots on his cheeks, but he was born with them. Don't touch him yet, Pedro; just talk to him."

"I wonder what his name is?"

"Chúcaro."

"Chúcaro? How do you know that is his name?"

"Because it fits him perfectly," smiled the gaucho. "A name is like a *sombrero*. It must fit the owner."

When you are walking in a forest, you seldom notice a single tree. How different it is when you are riding over the flat, boundless Pampa, where for miles and miles you see nothing but grass. Then all of a sudden you sight a tree and exclaim, "Look there! A tree!" Yes, a real tree, and your heart goes out to it.

It is an *ombú*, the lonely tree of the Pampa. The trunk is fat, the branches widespread, with large, waxy leaves. And it has a big, soft heart. It will offer what you want most—shade!

Not far from the tree you will probably find a hut or a tiny house. The hut may be made of mud, mixed with cornstalks, or—don't be shocked—of horse-dung and mud.

You will see more and more of such huts as you look around—some close together, some far apart. Gauchos, shepherds, pigherds, *medianeros,* who farm on shares, live in them. Then if your eyes are very sharp or you have field glasses ready, you may see a green spot in the distance. It is a park around a beautiful mansion. This is where the *patrón,* the owner, lives. You will also see wide fields of wheat, oats, and corn, and vast grazing land for the cattle.

Now, all this that you have just seen, and miles beyond, belongs to the patrón. It is his estancia.

You may lie down under that ombú tree. Its shade is so inviting. But if you are not on speaking terms with

ants and crickets and other little creatures playing hide-and-seek in the grass, you may prefer to sit in a chair. If you are lucky, you may find a gaucho's chair. It is made of the hipbones of cows, firmly tied together, and the seat is of rawhide. You'll find it very comfortable—but beware! When the sun goes down, you'd better get up and move your chair away from the tree. It is bedtime for the chickens, and before long you will find them roosting all over the tree!

Between that old ombú tree and the tallest windmill of the ranch, there stood a little hut, which belonged to Juan. From the outside, this modest little *casita,* with its adobe walls and corrugated tin roof, did not seem to differ from the rest of the huts that were dotted like matchboxes around the ranch. But the moment you were inside the house, which had only one room, you would be sure that it belonged to Juan. The door hung from a single hinge so that it was conveniently half-closed, half-open. On the wall opposite the door, there was a small opening the size of two bricks. If it had been covered by glass, it might have been called a window. Juan referred to it as a "hole." Really it would have been difficult to get along without that hole. Whenever Juan needed something from the house, he would usually reach for it through the hole instead of bending down to go through

the doorway, which was four inches lower than he. Or if
Pedro was around, he would say to the boy, "Get me that
piece of wire from the house. You'll find it right near the
hole." True enough, Pedro always found it, for everything that did not belong in the chest could always be
found "around the hole."

There is nothing easier in the world than to drive a
good-sized nail into a wall built of mud. That may be
one reason why Juan had so many pictures hung on his
walls.

Now, take that photograph on the right side of the
window. An awful "mug" with a long dark beard, and
under it printed, "MURDERER WANTED—1000 pesos
Reward!" Why did he nail that on the wall? It was given
to him some ten years before by the village policeman,
who regarded him as the most capable gaucho on either
side of the Salados River. "Hold onto this picture, Juan,"
he had said. "Maybe some day this fellow will come
around the ranch, and if any gaucho can capture him,
you're the one to do it!" No use denying that Juan was
flattered by these words, but since he had a little prac-
tical sense, he risked the question: "And what are my
chances of capturing him?"

"Ten times better than winning the big prize in the
lottery," said the policeman with emphasis.

"And what does that mean?" asked Juan.

"Well, as a police official I don't like to commit myself.
I'd rather ask you this question: Did you ever win the
big prize in the lottery?"

"No, never."

"All right. Multiply that by ten. The results are your
chances. But you can easily figure this out for yourself."

He had never bothered to figure it out. Instead he
nailed the picture on the wall, just in case . . .

There are few rivers or streams on the Pampa proper,
and those flow quietly as if asleep. Maybe this explains

why Juan had picked a picture of the most spectacular body of water to decorate the left-hand side of the window: "The Waterfalls of the Iguazú."

Juan never bothered to read the papers. He considered that a pastime for city folks who had nothing better to do. There was, however, one paper, *La Prensa* of Buenos Aires, for which he had a great respect, although he had never read a single copy of it. It was in *La Prensa* that the beautiful full-page photograph of the waterfalls of the Iguazú had appeared. He was always grateful to the *estanciero's* servant who gave it to him.

For several days after the picture was hung, Juan did not send Pedro when he wanted something "around the hole." Instead, he himself went for it straight through the doorway. And he always lingered just to admire the picture of the marvelous falls. There was a little map boxed into one corner of it that showed the location of the falls between Argentina and Brazil. Sometimes Juan would take a nail and scratch lines on the wall, indicating the road he would follow someday to view this most wonderful spectacle in the world, which no one whom he had ever met had actually seen. . . . There is also Paraguay, he thought, so close, where the finest *maté* grows, that sweet and bitter tea the gaucho sucks through a silver tube from a hollow gourd—maybe five, maybe ten times a day!

More pictures hung above the rusty, old iron bed, which, by the way, was just the bare frame with not a stitch of bedding on it. It was pushed against the wall, and right in the center above it hung "The Good Shepherd"—Christ guiding a flock of golden sheep. The whole flock of sheep was painted gold. It was a beautiful picture, entirely worthy of the fancy leather frame around it. Juan had spent a whole week making it. The picture itself was the gift of a traveling missionary who was grateful to Juan for having shown him a short cut to the train.

Then there were above the door picture post cards from the biggest towns—Buenos Aires, Rosario, La Plata —but only one actually addressed to him. This was from a girl he had met many, many years before at a carnival. Oh, how eager he was to answer that card, how often he had sat down and begun to write! But what's the use of spoiling a pen, breaking your back—and your heart— for a girl who forgot to give her address!

There was no table in the room, nor any chairs. But there was something else, which was even more useful— a chest. In a pinch, you could use the top as a card table or to write on, but Juan never did either. He kept his personal things in the chest. Anyone allowed to lift the top would see a brown *poncho* with fine white stripes. Ponchos like that can't be found so easily nowadays. It was of llama wool, so firmly woven that neither heat, nor rain, nor cold could get through it. An Indian from the Andes had given it to him for one silver coin and a pair of boots. This poncho was reserved for Sundays, as was the black sombrero that lay next to it. In the folds of the poncho, he kept his guitar. Wrapped in an old *corralera*, a collarless gaucho blouse, were a pair of leather stirrups, heavily carved in a chain design. They had belonged to Juan's father, a half-breed Indian gaucho. After his father's death, his mother had sent him a package with these keepsakes. Besides the stirrups and the corralera, which had been his father's wedding shirt, there were two kerchiefs, a fancy silver tube for sipping maté, and a wide leather belt for gala occasions. The belt was very heavy, as it was studded with silver coins and buttons, and it had extra leather pockets for money, and straps for knife and quirt. It must have been very, very old, because the silver studs were almost black. It had a peculiar odor that reminded you, all at the same time, of a perspiring horse, fresh cabbage, and onion soup with Parmesan cheese. This strong, exotic perfume permeated every single article Juan wore, including his shirts, ker-

chiefs, and even his *vincha*, his special headdress. Now
don't make any mistake. Juan was usually clean and
neat. This particular odor really belonged to him. It
was a family aroma, handed down from father to son
through this remarkable belt. Both men and beasts became used to it and rather liked it. Pedro found it especially convenient, particularly on Sunday evenings when
more than the usual group were seated around the campfire. By means of it he could single out Juan in the dark
from quite a distance.

The two kerchiefs are worthy of special mention. After
all, a gaucho is not a gaucho without his kerchief! He
may give you his boots, his nice baggy trousers, or even
his last shirt, but he won't part with his kerchief. Without his kerchief around his neck, he would feel shy as if
he were naked. Now, Juan had a yellow kerchief for
everyday use, while the two in his chest were red and
blue. If Sunday happened to be nice and bright, he wore
the red, but when it rained, or the cold *pampero* blew
from the southwest, he tied the blue kerchief around his
neck. His friend Pedro could tell the weather just by
looking at him.

It's too bad he only had one red kerchief, for it really
was very becoming to him. It gave an additional strength
and light to his dark complexion, his long eagle nose,
and to those deep-set brown eyes, which were, at the
same time, sharp, intelligent, and kind. One thing he
missed pitifully—a beard. The little black mustache,
which curved and pointed toward his nostrils, seemed
so insignificant and lonely. Only when he smiled, the
little mustache began to feel fine, jumping up and down
on his wide, red lips. So whenever you saw the little
mustache jump, you could rest assured that all of them
were in high mood—Juan, the mustache, and Pedro.

Pedro really belonged to Juan. He was as much a part
of him as his kerchief. From early morning till nightfall,

the boy was always at Juan's heels. It was really Juan
and not the Vaquero who raised the child. He took
charge of him soon after Pedro's mother died. There was
an unwritten agreement between the two men, and both
knew that, for all concerned, it was for the best.

Juan didn't spoil the boy; nobody could accuse him of
that. There were two things he knew to perfection—the
training of horses and young cowboys.

It's true that every Sunday morning he would enter his
house, reach down into the chest, open the little pocket
in the old belt, and give Pedro a few pennies for that
long stick of hard candy with pink and green stripes in
it. But that certainly couldn't spoil a tough boy like
Pedro!

The big chest and the lovely things in it, the old iron
bed, and the beautiful pictures on the wall were the real
treasures of Juan's casita, his little house. But the truth
will surprise you—he never spent a night in his house!

His sleeping place was far out in the field. It consisted
of a cart with two high wheels. The top and the sides of
the cart were covered with leather. It was a convenient
bedroom, easy to move. Sometimes the cart stood near
the ombú tree; at other times it stood nearer to the cattle.
Inside it was cosy, although there was no furniture or
any sort of decoration. A thick, heavy mattress, filled
with straw, covered the entire floor. It was very easy to
keep in order. Once every year, shortly after the harvest,
he would fill the mattress with fresh straw. And once or
twice a year he would go to the big barrel standing at
the end of the trough under the windmill and wash his
blanket in cold water and spread it out on the grass. The
sun did the rest. The sides of the cart in warm weather
were always kept open, both for fresh air and because
when Juan went to bed, he liked to sit up for a while and
watch. He liked to watch the distant lights, and listen to
a strange music—the Pampa sounds. And so many things

to think about—but the moment he lay down, he fell asleep almost before he could finish his yawn.

Sometimes he dreamt about that picture card he had received and about the answer he had never written.

Juan led the pony, and Pedro walked at a safe distance behind. But when they reached Juan's house, the boy ran ahead.

"I think we ought to put Chúcaro in your casita for the night. Let's remove the door; it's only hanging by a thread anyway."

Juan was struck dumb. His right hand resting on his hip, he just stood silent for a while, his eyes measuring the house, the horse, and the boy.

"This is going a little bit too far, Pedro," he said at last with a smile. "If it were up to you, you would put the horse in the bed, give him a nightshirt and *La Prensa* to read."

"But I thought your house would be the safest place. Besides, you never sleep in the casita anyway."

"Well, if I can't sleep shut up in the casita, how could Chúcaro stand it? I know his feelings as well as mine."

"Just for a single night? I would feel better knowing he is safe."

"Safe? Why, if four walls make me jumpy, they would make him crazy with pain. He is a criollo pony. The finest, don't forget! You shouldn't hurt his feelings like that. . . . No, Pedrito, that wouldn't do! We'll fence him off in the corral for a few days. As long as he can feel the Pampa grass under his hoofs, some oats in his mouth, and see the sky above his head, he won't feel the place is a prison. But first bring me the currycomb. You'll find it around the hole."

When Chúcaro first caught sight of the currycomb, he was so frightened that you could see the whites of his eyes. And at the first touch of the brush, he jumped and trembled as if he were shell-shocked.

"If he acts like that, we'd better tie him to the kicking strap," said Juan for the benefit of both Chucaro and Pedro.

But the kicking strap was really not needed. When the

pony felt the gentle strokes of the brush, he relaxed and you could tell he was thrilled. No doubt it reminded him of certain fence posts and tree trunks he used to rub his neck against. But this seemed a hundred times more satisfying.

Now scratching, you will agree, is a very personal thing. Few of us practice it in company, and when we do, it is completely absent-minded. With animals, scratching is a serious business. It is as much a part of their toilet as washing our faces in the morning is for us. Our animal friends don't mind scratching even in high society. Observe that they practice two kinds of scratching. One is a quick act, as, for instance, the dog when trying to brush off an arrogant flea. This sort of thing is ordinary routine. The other type of scratching occurs only at certain times of the day or the night and is performed in leisure, ceremoniously. With some, it may take only half an hour, while with others it may last—like a double-feature program—half the afternoon. Some animals on this occasion will lie down and relax and have their colleagues do the work for them. Others prefer not to share the pleasure and do it all by themselves. Some do it with their claws, some with their tongue, their nose and teeth, or feet, and some, like the armadillo, prefer the tail to do the whole business from A to z.

Horses have a different technique, limited to one of these—rub against a tree trunk or telephone pole, or roll over on the grass. Whatever the method, it is a lot of fun. But, frankly, neither is entirely satisfactory. There are a few sheltered parts of a pony, like the tiny spot under his elbow, which he can never get at by rubbing against any kind of pole or rolling back and forth till doomsday.

Now you can understand how Chúcaro reacted to the sweet tickle of the currycomb. Never had he experienced such delights except when his mother used to rub her nose against his neck. Stroke after stroke, inch by inch, all over his body he felt the same amusing sensation. He knew that it wasn't the brush only but those kindly fingers that offered him joy and begged for friendship. Chúcaro was kept in the corral for about a week. Each morning, after the roundup of the cattle, Juan would visit him. But he couldn't get there early enough to be ahead of his friend Pedrito. Each would bring to the pony some delicacy, a piece of carrot, a handful of oats, or a little piece of sugar. And they would take turns in brushing his lovely coat, which really was like those geranium flowers—a shade between yellow, brown, and pink—growing in the patio of the estanciero. Sometimes Juan would tie the pony to a rope and let Pedro give him some exercise running around in circles.

The news traveled fast around the estancia; it passed from mouth to mouth. "Pedro has a new pony! You never saw anything like it! He has a pinkish coat like the geranium petals in the *patio* of Señor Muñez. He has four little white socks, like those you see on city children on Sundays. He is supposed to be a wild colt, and yet he eats out of your hand! You can't help petting him. Just go and see!"

And they all came, one after another—Carlos and José, gaucho friends; Mr. and Mrs. Pizetti, the medianeros who cultivated a stretch of the cornfield; all the "swallows" or harvest workers; the shepherds and pigherds; the overseers; the Italian, Hungarian, Polish, and Slovak immigrants and their children, who rented a piece of the land or worked for "half-and-half"; the blacksmith, the bookkeeper, the tractor-driver, the chauffeur, and even the veterinary came. On the Pampa, like any other place, some faces seem hard, others soft; some cold and others warm. There wasn't a face, though, that failed to light up when Chúcaro approached. Some

stroked Chúcaro's neck or kissed his cheek. Others just shook their heads enviously and said, "Why couldn't I have such luck?"

There was an Indian gaucho who offered Pedro two beautiful ponies broken in for riding, with saddle, stirrups, and all the proper fittings, if only he would give him Chúcaro. A young Italian farmer offered a pair of slightly worn black boots—just a little too big—twenty-five sacks of corn and a rehenque with a silver handle. And the assistant bookkeeper was ready to give him all his accumulated wealth, which he said amounted to thirty pesos and some change, plus a harmonica, highly polished and beautiful, which, however, didn't work.

Your guess is correct. Pedro politely refused every one of the offers. However, at the bookkeeper's bid, he became so excited one could almost see the blood rush to his cheeks.

"I know that thirty pesos is a lot of silver," he said, "but I wouldn't give up Chúcaro if you gave me a million and a million and, on the top of that, the whole world." So everybody saw there was no room to bargain.

Pedro got up earlier than usual one morning—long before Juan was up. In fact, he made quite certain that Juan was asleep. Then without the customary blindfold-

ing or the use of the kicking strap, he jumped on Chúcaro's back.

The first few days after that, to tell you the truth, were very trying to both of them.

Juan had expected that the pony would be ready for his first tryout with saddle about three weeks after his capture. So when he thought the time had come, and he and Pedro met in the corral, Juan threw sheepskin and a rough saddle on the pony. He was amazed that Chúcaro stood perfectly quiet.

"How strange," remarked the gaucho. "Chúcaro does not seem to mind it! I've never seen a wild colt carry the saddle without blindfolding. *Qué milagro!*" he cried. "No jumping, no kicking, no biting! Well, my friend, you might as well jump on him."

"You try him first," said Pedro with downcast eyes.

"What's the matter, Pedrito? Are you afraid?"

"No, Señor," and Pedro's eyes were still fixed on his own bare feet.

"I don't understand. There's something funny about this. I never heard of your refusing a first ride!"

The boy stepped back and sat down on the ground. It took some effort to answer, "I want you to have the pleasure now."

Juan stared at the horse, then at Pedro. Then he understood.

"You shouldn't have done it, you rascal! I told you to go easy with that horse. You don't appreciate a good pony when you have one. He should be treated gently, as you treat a friend." He threw his sombrero over the corral fence. He was angry.

"I'm sorry, Juan," said the boy, and his voice quavered. "Chúcaro didn't seem to mind it. It was so tempting . . ."

"Tempting, eh? Well, I give up! I can't be bothered with two pets at one time. Get out of my sight!! I'm through!"

Pedro got up. He felt his throat dry and swollen, and he could hardly drag his bare feet through the dust. He stumbled along and was just able to reach the corral gate when he burst into tears. He had to sit down, for his heart seemed too heavy and his legs too weak to go further. He turned toward the gatepost and buried his head in his hands. Now he was sobbing, but no sound was heard. As his fingers pressed his eyes, everything became terribly dark. It seemed as if a black, black cloud covered the whole world, and he, Pedro, all alone with no place to go, must face the oncoming storm.

Juan fussed with the straps, patted Chúcaro's neck, unlatched the stirrups, and fumbled with the saddle again. You could see that he was just killing time, absent-minded and miserable. "Why did I tell the boy to get out? And suppose someday he should really clear out —out of my life," he tortured himself. After all, no harm had been done. He stole a look at Pedro. "Why doesn't he cry out loud, at least?" He could see only the boy's high forehead and flat, funny nose. His hands ached to stroke that dark head, to lift him in his arms. He longed to say, "Don't cry, Pedrito. No harm has been done. Just jump on Chúcaro and everything will be all right. We are old friends; you ought to know that." But he was too clumsy to put all that into words, so instead he threw his yellow kerchief at Pedro's feet and said, "You'd better wipe your face with that and bring my red kerchief from the chest, you—touchy little lamb!"

The storm was over.

As if shot from a gun, the boy ran to the casita and in a jiffy ran back waving the kerchief in his hand.

For the first time in many years Juan lifted Pedro up into the saddle.

With his right hand holding the bridle rein, and with his left furtively wiping away a few stray tears, Pedrito sat up straight in the saddle, secure and proud. Suddenly he turned to the gaucho. "Why did you ask for your red kerchief? It isn't Sunday."

"Well . . . I don't know. . . . After all . . . when you think of it . . . Chúcaro and you riding out for the first time . . . and everything. Who says it isn't like Sunday?" and he quickly turned back to open the gate. He leaned against the gatepost and watched Chúcaro gallop by. Two graceful heads held high, Pedro and Chúcaro heading for the open fields—they seemed one. Thrilled by the sight and absorbed in his thoughts, Juan stood at the corral gate for a long, long time.

If you like horses and stories about them, you will also enjoy Marguerite Henry's King of the Wind, *published by Rand McNally, Inc.; Ann Nolan Clark's* Blue Canyon Horse, *published by The Viking Press, Inc.; and* Serilda's Star, *by Olive R. Cook, published by Longmans, Green & Co., Inc.*

Eskimo Boy

BY PIPALUK FREUCHEN

Illustrations by Ingrid Vang Nyman

When his father is killed by a walrus, young Ivik becomes the Man of the Family. After much bad luck and a period of semi-starvation, Ivik sets off on foot across the ice for help. On the way he is attacked by a polar bear.

T HAT night the sea finally freezes. In the morning there are big patches which haven't the brightness of water. Gradually the current pushes these patches together, and it looks as if the sea is frozen almost solid. There are still some big openings where little waves come splashing up over the edges of the ice, but they grow smaller and smaller. Unfortunately, heavy clouds come up from the southwest at the same time.

"That means the Nigerk wind," says Old Grandfather. "And the Nigerk, while it brings big game to the hunter, also brings bad weather and snow. Nature seems to be angry, and wants no smooth ice near our camp. Too bad men haven't strength enough to keep the snow clouds away."

When they wake the next morning, the ice covers everything. Unfortunately, some snow has fallen, and some drift-ice has floated in.

There will be no smooth-ice fishing. Worse still, the drift-ice that has packed around the island also prevents air-hole hunting for seals. Because seals are sly, they make their breathing holes in under the juts and edges of rough ice. That makes it hard for the hunter to stand over the hole and harpoon the creatures when they come to get air.

Ivik and Grandfather sit and talk about this. Ivik, young and without his full strength as yet, lacks the experience he needs to be the provider for his family. Grandfather Kriternerk is a storehouse of experience about game animals and hunting, but alas he is old and quite feeble. His knees betray him when he walks a long distance; gout bends his back and slows his arms.

So these two talk, the one who has passed the prime of life and the other who has not reached it.

"This camp is short of meat and blubber for lamp oil," says Kriternerk, "and the ice is still so thin that visiting sleds can't be expected here for a while. But how glad they are on the mainland for the new ice sheet! Now they'll drive off in light sleds to fetch home the summer catch. And even though they know how lonely we are and anxious to hear the news, they dare not venture out here yet. But they'll come, they'll come, the moment the ice will bear them."

Then they sit silent for a while. Ivik feels that Grandfather wants to say something, but does not like to say it.

"It may happen that one will have to try to walk across the ice," Ivik says finally.

Then there is silence again.

"My poor legs are too feeble to walk across," Grandfather says; "my strength would fail on the way; but no one reaches any camp without effort."

Ivik knows that Grandfather is grieving because he cannot fetch help, he who was always first man of his camp in the days of his strength.

"When we have slept once more, the ice will be thick enough," Ivik says; "walking fast will keep a person warm, and now there's some moonlight to see by after daylight goes."

They get up and go in to tell Ama that they have decided Ivik shall walk across the ice the next day and find help over at "The Sand," the mainland.

Ama says nothing. She knows how dangerous it is for her son, but she also realizes that it is necessary for him to go if they are to stay alive. The little ones are so thin, they cannot keep warm under the blanket skins. She herself no longer feels hunger, only an empty weariness. She sees how hollow-cheeked Old Grandfather is, and how ashen. But to look at Ivik is worst of all. The dear boy, the once laughing, round-cheeked, chubby Ivik, has a new expression on his face. He looks troubled as he stands there in clothes that should have been replaced this fall. The hair is gone from his furs: his bearskin trousers are worn in front and in the seat. She knows they only keep off the wind, not the chill.

But still Ama says nothing. She must let Ivik go. What provisions can they spare for Ivik to take on his long trip, she wonders. He cannot move fast. He must pick his way across the uncertain ice, and he has so little strength. How good it would be if she had something savory, something nourishing to give him!

No light burns in the hut, which makes it cold and dark the moment daylight is gone, so Ama asks Ivik to lie down on the bench for a few hours' sleep. She will mend his clothes meanwhile, and make them warm and comfortable for the trip. A mother is always able to work miracles. Somehow she manages to scare up a few pieces of good fur, and when Ivik gets up in the evening, there are beautiful bottoms on his boots, lovely fox skins to warm his feet in.

Kriternerk, meanwhile, has been out digging around

on the meat platform where he finds an old seal flipper. He chops it into bits with his ax and mixes it with scraps of dog harness.

"This is good to chew on," he says, "when one walks a long way and has nothing in his stomach. The juice runs down the gullet and gives warning that the empty space down there will soon be filled. And that gives strength!"

Ama wants Ivik to take the flensing knife, but he says it is too heavy to carry. But the others know he says that because he doesn't want to leave the family without a weapon.

At last Ivik is ready. They agree he should not take a harpoon with him. He must not waste time hunting, but concentrate on one thing: to reach his goal as quickly as possible. The weapon he finally chooses is his father's old spear. It has a short shaft and a strong walrus-tusk head, with a tip of well-sharpened iron. It had been used to take many animals when his father was alive. He can use it walking, partly to lean on and partly to try the ice, which, after all, is still dangerous.

Ivik sets out. His mother and grandfather go with him a little way from shore. They do not say good-bye or fill him full of frightening warnings. All three know it is a mortally dangerous trip. Besides, in the course of time, the grown-ups have taught him a good deal, so last minute advice would be useless. Good-byes are always dismal. Parting is easier when both sides pretend they'll meet again soon.

And so Ivik goes off. He walks and walks and walks.

New ice at sea is always tough and much safer than fresh-water ice, which breaks easily. Even so, if you have a spear like the one Ivik carries, you drop it on the ice in front of you, just to be sure. If the spear-handle doesn't punch through, then it's safe to walk on.

When Ivik comes to spots with no snow, it is easy for him to tell whether they are dangerous. Black ice is always dangerous. Only when it starts to turn white as if it had small clouds underneath is it firm and hard enough to carry a man.

It will not be difficult to keep a straight course for the mainland, Ivik sees, if he keeps the wind behind him and from the right. He notices, too, that the Nigerk wind has whipped the snow in piles in some places. With these

it is impossible to go wrong, because the snowdrifts always point in the same direction, and by keeping at a fixed angle to them, you are as sure of your course as if you had set it by the stars.

After walking for some time, long enough, Ivik thinks, for the sun to have made a quarter-turn around the earth, he feels tired. The little bag Grandfather gave him is hanging down his back. He pulls it around in front of him, and begins to stuff the contents into his mouth. There are pieces of bone and skin, a few sinews, and even a trace of fat. It is far more solid food than the skin scraps they had eaten at home. Without stopping to think, he eats all the food in the bag. And there is still a long way to go.

As he walks on, he thinks what fun it would be to meet some strangers. But then he remembers he would have to tell about his father's death. That in turn reminds him how badly off they are without his father. If his father were alive, they would all be at home now, fat and well fed. They would have dogs to take them visiting. He remembers riding on his father's sled one time when they had so much meat the dogs could not drag it up to the meat platform. He thinks of all his father taught him, of how wise and clever his father was, of how they had stood together and watched the game animals. He had known about useless creatures, too, like snow birds, wagtails and butterflies. His father really knew everything.

Then he begins to think how pleasant the summer has been. Somewhere he has heard that in the white men's country the sun comes up even in winter, and it is light by day. But this still seems strange to him, because, after all, anyone would know that the sun has to rest for part of the year. Anyhow, he thinks, one hears so many queer tales about the white men's country that it is impossible to know what to believe.

The tiny bit he has eaten has led his stomach to suspect that now there might be food again. He feels hunger gnawing at him, so he takes the food pouch, cuts it to pieces with his little knife, and eats them, too. The thin thong the pouch hung on makes good chewing. He puts it all in his mouth at once, and chews until it is soft and smooth and he can swallow it.

All this takes some time, and he is getting on across the ice, which is more firm. He no longer hears it cracking under him, and he forgets to be careful. He just pushes on.

He begins to feel thirsty. He knows it is no good eating snow. If a person begins that, his strength soon dwindles. There is nothing to do but change his course toward the ice crags that lie between the island and the mainland. There he can chop off a few splinters of fresh ice, warm them under his fur jacket so that he can put them in his mouth.

Darkness is falling, but his eyes grow used to it. The sky clouds over, and everything is so gray he can no longer see the separate mountains on the mainland. But he keeps his course by watching the snowdrifts.

He finds he is not very far from the first ice crag. It is a little one, some distance from the others. This is wonderful, because by now he is very thirsty. He feels he will be stronger and will walk faster if his throat is not so dry. Actually it is fat he needs, but there is no chance of getting that. He looks forward to the lovely sweet taste of the water he will suck from the ice splinters.

Involuntarily he quickens his pace, and he is less alert. It is too late when he sees something moving toward him —a strange unreal something he cannot quite make out in the dark. But it is something that seems to glide over the ice.

At first he thinks it is a fox, but it grows bigger and bigger. He realizes in a flash he is facing the biggest game animal in the Arctic—the biggest and the most dangerous —a polar bear.

He completely forgets how for years he has longed to meet a bear, just once, and drive the shaft of his spear between its ribs. He forgets his mother, grandfather, sisters and brother waiting anxiously at home for him to bring food. All he feels is that he is a small boy, alone, way out here far from people. He has no dogs to help him attack the bear by drawing away its attention. There is no hope of running away; the bear might pursue him. There is only one hope: that the bear is so full, it will not want to bother with him, but will go peacefully about its business.

The bear, however, comes closer and closer. To Ivik it looks monstrous, bigger than the biggest ice crag.

His first fear vanishes, and he remembers he is a hunter with his father's own spear in his hand, the spear that has so often been driven into game animals of all kinds, killing them surely and swiftly.

The bear comes closer. It is a middle-sized bear, but it is hungry. When polar bears have had good hunting in the fall, they take on a thick layer of fat under the skin

which keeps them warm all winter. This makes them so sluggish that they dig themselves into snowdrifts to sleep until the long days of light come back. Then they break out of their snow-covered holes, hungry and eager for the chase. But bears that are thin in the fall cannot sleep through the winter. They must roam the coast to find food, which is hard work in the dark days.

This bear had drifted far out to sea on a small ice-pan during the summer. It had gone hungry and is dangerous now that it is back on solid ice.

It sees something moving. It smells that it is edible, so

it makes straight for Ivik, ready to strike him down. A
bear's life is one long battle to live. It must kill and eat
what it kills. This does not look like a seal, which is the
prey a bear usually deals with, so the bear uses new
tactics. It pauses, surprised that its prey, instead of trying to escape, comes forward. The bear is almost doubt-
ful. Ought it perhaps to turn around and go the other
way? There is no way to tell if this is even fit to eat.

The bear stands still and sniffs. What is this? How can
the bear know that Ivik is an Eskimo, one of the polar
bear's most dangerous enemies? If it had known that he
was a boy, weak with hunger and stiff with cold, carrying
an unfamiliar weapon rather too heavy for his hand,
matters would have been different.

As it is, Ivik does not think much about his danger. He
has only one thought, now that he has conquered his
fear: there, in front of him, is food, *meat,* and beautiful
warm fur for trousers. If he can get the bear, all hardship
will be over in one blow. Besides, he will be known and
envied by his friends as the "bear-killer." When boys
went hunting with their fathers, the fathers always did
the spearing. It was not for the young lads to be ranked
as hunters.

Ivik had seen his father kill bears. He knows that you
brace the butt of the spear against your chest, and drive
the point with all your force between the bear's ribs. Of
course this is always done while the dogs leap and worry
the creature, so that it hasn't time to think about the pain.
It has enough to do to fight off the dogs swarming around
it, sinking their teeth into its back.

But Ivik is alone. He has no dogs, no help of any kind.
The chances are against him, but he does not think of
that. He sees the bear before him, and the hunter's pas-
sion, born in all his people, fills him. At that moment the
bear turns slowly to retreat. It is no coward, but it
suspects that this is not a usual enemy.

The next instant Ivik attacks it. The head of the spear almost touches the bear's fur as Ivik aims at a spot between the animal's ribs, but the bear jumps suddenly, and takes the spear behind its ribs, in its soft belly.

A fearful roar comes from the bear. Ivik himself yells in his excitement. The bear whirls around to lunge at him, but finds that the spear-shaft sticks fast. This is not a bite; it is something much worse. Again it turns a little only to discover that its mysterious foe is holding fast to the end of the weapon.

Ivik could never remember clearly afterwards what happened next. Actually, he tried to hold on to his spear, but the bear's motions were so violent that he was flung clear over the bear and spun around on the ice. Terrified though he was, he plainly heard the ice cracking under him. He tried to leap up, and did manage to get to his feet, expecting the bear to rush him. Strangely, it roared in a frenzy beside him. It struck at the spear-shaft, broke part of it off and chewed it to bits. At that instant Ivik took to his heels and ran as fast as he could.

After a few paces he sees he is not running in the direction of the ice crag, which he has suspected, so he changes his course. He turns his head for a look at the bear, who he sees is about to pursue him.

Fortunately, just then, the spear-shaft catches on a chunk of ice projecting through the snow. The bear yanks again at the spear, and stands up on its hind legs to trample on the broken piece of shaft. Its mad roars put

wings on Ivik's feet; and Ivik runs as he has never run in all his life until he reaches the little ice crag.

Only when he finds himself lying on his stomach on a ledge of ice does he begin to think.

"How did I get up here, anyway? Odd that a person could climb a sheer wall of ice like this."

When he has lain there for a while and his heart has stopped pounding violently, he takes some notice of his surroundings.

The bear's roars are now growls. Sometimes it trots a little; then Ivik hears its claws scraping the side of the ice crag.

"Now it's coming after me," he thinks. But he is not afraid. Pride drowns fear, and Ivik is still proud.

"One has driven his spear into a bear!" his inner voice whispers.

"It so happened that one came on a bear and struck it down," he will say to his companions when he meets them. He will be modest, so that they can ask questions and worm the story out of him.

But these happy thoughts do not last long.

He begins to feel the intense cold. His great fear, his excitement and the prodigious running make him sweat, and his poor worn-out body cannot stand the strain. He is exhausted. Perched on a narrow ledge of the ice crag, as high up as it is possible to climb, the thin, hairless seat of his trousers gives him no protection against the cold ice. He begins to shiver. Then he discovers he has lost his right mitten. Possibly it dropped when, clinging to the spear, he was flung over the bear; possibly he lost it when he was running. He does not know. All he does know is that his freezing fingers are now numb and stiff.

This fills him with terror, and he sticks his hand against his stomach to draw some warmth into his fingers. He shivers as the wind whips under his fur jacket. His emaciated body does not give much warmth, and it takes a long time to thaw out his fingers.

His boots are half frozen, too, from wandering over the wet ice. He trembles with fear. The simple fact is that the bear is alive. It is still down below, and in the darkness there is no way to tell whether the wound is fatal. Once in a while he hears the bear, but there are long stretches of complete silence.

How long he has waited there he cannot tell. Time and again he feels so weak and exhausted he is unable to move. What is he to do? There is no way out.

And then Ivik no longer knows what is happening. He hears no growls from the bear, the cold ceases, and the ice on which he lies is gone. Everything slides further and further from him. Perhaps he dreamt; he never knew; what he does know is that he slept for a long, long time. He can see that hours have passed, because it is growing light. He lies facing the mainland where he can plainly make out the juts of the headlands and the big ravine called Korkrut where he has often played. But he is so cold that he can barely move. When he tries to pull his legs up under him, his knees refuse to bend. Luckily, in his sleep, he pulled his arms out of his sleeves and put them against his bare body. But there is no warmth there now. His whole body aches, and his shoulder-blades hurt when he tries to put his arms back in his sleeves. He realizes how close to dying he had been when he slept and how it was only the pain caused by the cold which woke him up.

Suddenly he starts to cry. He does not know it is from exhaustion.

Must he die on this ice crag because he hasn't the strength to stand up? But he does rise and then he squats. The cold seat of his trousers sends a piercing pain through him. When he finds he can kick his legs, he stops thinking of the pain.

"If only I could get down off this crag, I'd go home to my mother and grandfather. All I want is to be with them," he tells himself.

But a little later he wakes up enough to realize that it would be useless to go home. There, too, he'd find nothing but hunger and cold, nothing to give him strength. He must get to "The Sand." He must save them all. He is dimly aware that there will be more suffering before he gets to the mainland, but it is still the only thing he can do.

Now it is light enough to see the ice. His eye is caught by a dark patch on it. Ah, now he sees: it is blood. And there, a little to one side, lies the bear he fought yesterday. A wave of warmth flows through him. His spear felled the bear. True, it is still alive. It sits up as much as it lies down, but it is unmistakably dying.

Ivik forgets his helplessness. Joy rises in him. "My bear is almost dead," he whispers. "Soon there will be fresh meat, fine slabs of fat, warm skins for clothes."

Yes, he will skin the bear, take what meat he can carry and go home. Then will his sisters and brother be big-eyed at their brother, a real hunter returned with a real catch. Grandfather will mean his words of praise; his mother will be proud. The lamp will burn and the pot will cook over the fire night and day.

He can already feel the warm soup thawing them all out, putting new strength into weak limbs.

Yes, Ivik is a hunter to be reckoned with. If only his father, who had been his hunting companion from the time he was small, had lived to see this. He would have taken delight in driving around to other camps to say to his friends: "It has come about that my son went out on the ice and drove his spear into a bear without any help from dogs. Those who care to come for a visit may have boiled meat from my son's first catch."

All these happy, proud thoughts run through his mind

as he lies there daydreaming, half dazed. Then he comes to. Why am I sitting here? Why don't I climb down off the ledge? He stares again at the bear. It is growing weaker and weaker. Its hind legs are paralyzed, and it is bleeding heavily. A knife would finish it off. But to do that means climbing down the ice crag, and before he can do that, he will have to get up. He does nothing because he is rigid in every limb. The only part of him he can still use is his brain, to think and to dream.

"I must get up," Ivik thinks. "I must go down to the bear I took."

But he continues to lie where he is.

"Yes, it's true," he thinks, "it's wiser not to rush. If I wait a while, the bear will be weaker and then it'll be easier to kill."

He remembers, too, that the blade of his little hunting knife had broken once, and Grandfather had re-pointed it. Now it is very short, not much longer than his thumb.

More time passes, but still he does not stir. He feels as if everything he dreamt had happened. He no longer feels the cold, and hunger does not gnaw at him. He knows he can go down the ice crag, put his lips to the bear's neck where he intends to stab it, and suck until the strength flows back into him. Then he will carry the meat back home.

High on the ice crag Ivik lies dreaming, and slowly consciousness slips away from him. Before his senses quite leave him, he suddenly lifts his head—why he does not know. Nothing has changed, but somehow the atmosphere around him seems different. He is aware of the pain in the back of his neck when he moves his head, so he lets it sink down again on the ice.

He gazes at the bear. It is still sitting there, or rather lying flatter than it has been. But Ivik no longer cares. He just wants terribly to rest. He is so tired, and he must gather strength enough for his final struggle with the bear, the struggle that will get him all the glorious things he dreams of.

But there it is again. This time he not only lifts his head, but raises his body. There is something there! He knows even if it hurts he will be able to move a little. His rest must have done him good.

Then he discovers a fox sitting near by, waiting for a share of the kill. Ivik laughs aloud. He knows that many great hunters are friendly with fox and are glad to have them follow the sleds because fox are wise. They know where great men go, there will be catches. They do not bother to follow unsuccessful hunters.

"They know me already," Ivik says to himself.

There it is again! It is something. He can plainly hear a sound far, far away. It is the howl of dogs, of dogs in the frenzy of pursuit.

Is he fully awake and does he really hear the dogs? Perhaps he is dreaming again. Then he hears not only the howl of dogs but the sound of men's voices.

"Yugit! Yugit!" comes the bear signal across the ice. "Terset, terset-huk-fo-o-r!"

Yes, there are men, big men with sleds, near by.

The word that Ivik had taken a bear must have spread. The men are coming to relieve him and haul his bear home. But in a moment he realizes that this is nonsense. How can people have heard about him and his bear? Never mind, they are here. Before Ivik is aware of it, he is standing up on the ledge. Far away he can see two sleds, two black specks on the ice, moving toward him. Halfway between him and the sleds he sees a bear running at full gallop pursued by the dogs the men have unleashed. The fastest dogs are now almost on the bear; those pulling the sled howl in fury because they cannot catch up.

From his high place Ivik sees that the men pull in the sled dogs, cut the traces, and turn them loose in full cry. The lead dog catches up with the bear, and sinks its teeth in the beast's rump. The bear, in a fury, turns as swiftly as a cat and slaps at the dog. The dog jumps aside, howling.

How exciting to hear the howls of dogs again! It is a long time since Ivik and his grandfather slaughtered their last dog.

The racing bear sees that its only chance of escape is to reach the ice crag where Ivik is. If it can climb up on that, it is safe from its pursuers. As it speeds along it tries to shake off the dogs at its back and heels. Now and again it strikes tremendous blows at them with its paws. Whenever it hits one, the dog flies far to the side, but the bear dares not stop to bite it. It must get away, so it bounds across the ice at great speed. First the forepaws swing forward with the hind paws right behind, then the forepaws again. It is gaining speed. But so are the sleds on the smooth ice. The men's whips crack as they yell and shout, and the dogs howl. More and more dogs are cut loose, and the bear is surrounded. It reaches the foot of the ice crag where the dogs stop it. They leap on its back. The bear fights back. It grabs a dog and throws it down to bite it, but before it can, the others leap at its neck and muzzle or tug at its ears. The bear jumps and whirls to free itself of its tormentors. They keep away from its jaws to keep their advantage in the fight, and there are too many of them for the bear to shake off.

Ivik hears its savage roars and the whines of the dogs. The sleds are moving slowly now. The last dogs are cut loose from the sleds, and the two hunters grab their spears to kill the bear before it cripples any of the dogs.

They rush into the fierce free-for-all. It is hard for them to distinguish the dogs from the bear as they stand on each side of the beast, ready to drive home their spears when there is an opening among the dogs. Finally one of them strikes, and the bear gives an unearthly roar. It turns on the man, but as it does, there is a tremendous thrust from the other side. The sharp spear is between the ribs. The creature rises on its hind legs in a final burst of strength, an awful, preternatural strength. It takes several leaps up the ice wall, and then collapses. It rolls like a snowball down the slope to the men's feet, dead.

Dogs at a bear hunt do a strange thing. While they fight, they are fierce and excited. They act as though they would never calm down. But the moment the bear is dead, they become friendly and peaceful. The fight is over, and they have won. There is no need to be ferocious. Only the youngest dogs rush for a last bite at the bear. With the hunters, it is quite different. This is their first sled trip to hunt for walruses. Quite by chance the dogs picked up the scent of a bear and trailed it. There was the wild chase, and now they have taken the season's first bear! What a joyful surprise to bring home. What an unexpected feast they will give their neighbors!

"Nanukrisugut, nanukrisugut!" they shout.

Ivik atop the ice crag remembers that triumphant shout, that message of joy after successful hunts with his father. They had shouted it in delight even when there was no one around to hear, for the catch meant fresh meat and fine bearskin. It also meant new respect for their bravery from the neighbors.

As if by magic these memories restore Ivik's strength. He, too, has taken a bear. In their excitement the two hunters have not yet discovered his catch, and Ivik, who is still a young boy, may not speak until the adults speak to him. Boasting, too, is bad manners. But he has been so close to freezing to death that now, with help at hand, he decides he had better do a little boasting:

"I got a bear. I, too, got a bear!" he shouts.

The men stop in their tracks, frightened. Who could be shouting? It is an eerie sound from high up. Perhaps the Inland-Dwellers have ventured out on the ice in search of human flesh! They look at each other in fear. Or perhaps some spirits are angry at their boasting about the bear they killed. Then they hear the same voice again. It sounds like the shout of a woman or a boy:

"Here I am. Help is needed!"

The men look up and see someone sitting on the ice crag—yes, it is a boy. But how did he get up there? They see no sled tracks. They look around in astonishment, and then they notice that there is a bear on the ice, not yet dead, but severely wounded and very weak. They had already pulled their spears from the first bear's body, and they hurry over to

the other. The dogs suddenly sense that something unusual is going on. There is another bear to fight. They
rush to attack the wounded bear, but the men are faster.
They finish off the bear with a quick thrust of the spear,
not a dangerous job since Ivik has done the real work.

How he managed to climb down the slippery ice crag
Ivik never knew. He forgets the pain that has wracked

his body. Now he approaches the two men who stand
gaping at him. At first they do not recognize him. Does
he belong to some tribe who lives across the sea?

Ivik knows he must wait for the men to speak to him,
but how happy he is to see these strangers! To him this
meeting means much more than it does to them. Why,
they're not strangers, they're Ehre and Krolugta, whom
he knows so well. They stare at him in a strange, unbelieving way, but Ivik in his joy bursts into speech:

"Sainak sunai! Sainak sunai! It's a great joy to meet
you!"

"Assukiak," the men answer. "It is mutual."

It is then that they recognize Ivik, the son of Maryark, one of their own relatives.

Ivik is on the verge of tears, he is so overwhelmed by this miraculous meeting. Now he and his family are saved. They have made contact with the mainland at last. But the six months of hunger and cold have toughened him, and he does not give way to tears. Very calmly he tells the men that it is good they came with their dogs and helped him kill his bear.

"You fought and killed it alone, single-handed?" they ask, unable to believe their eyes.

"There are only a few of us at our camp," says Ivik, "fewer than you expect."

The men understand what Ivik means, and no more is said about Maryark. They understand that some disaster has taken place. A glance at Ivik's clothes and his thin body tell them the whole tragic story.

"When did you come here?" they ask, as though they were not curious, but making conversation.

"One went on a trip to visit people on the mainland, and it happened that a bear got in one's way, and it was necessary to stick a spear into it to get past," Ivik says.

Nor does he need to say more. Both Ehre and Krolugta burst forth in loud praise of what Ivik has done. Here is a young boy, alone and without proper weapons, cut off with his family from the mainland, who has suffered great hunger. He set forth to get help, and, on his way, killed a bear!

One seemed to be hearing again the legend about Kagssassuk, the famous Eskimo hero, who as a boy saved a whole camp from starvation in winter by killing a bear. He strangled it with his bare hands. After the men talk for a while, they look at Ivik. Plainly he needs help. He is exhausted and near collapse.

They chase the dogs from his bear, and then they see his broken spear. Near by they find his mitten, and they can see from the tracks in the snow how he struggled with the beast and how it had tossed him on the ice while he tried to kill it. The whole story is there, written in the snow, and they can see it, as they read the tracks, as clearly as if they had been eyewitnesses.

New strength surges through Ivik's body, a strength he never believed he possessed. He takes his knife, drives it into the dead bear's neck, just as he had planned he would, and falls to drinking the blood in great, greedy gulps. This was his only desire. He feels strength and a warmth tingling in him from his fingertips down to his toes. As he lies there he is utterly happy to have real food again, happy that his family is saved.

Pipaluk Freuchen is the daughter of the famous Arctic explorer Peter Freuchen. She was born and grew up in Greenland, and knows firsthand the Arctic peoples of whom she writes.

Li Lun, Lad of Courage

BY CAROLYN TREFFINGER

Illustrations by Kurt Wiese

> *On Blue Shark Island off the coast of China, every boy who reaches the age of ten must go on a fishing voyage to prove he is a man. Li Lun refused, for he was afraid of the sea. As a punishment for this disobedience, Li Lun was commanded by his father to plant seven grains of rice on the top of Lao Shan, The Sorrow Mountain. He could not return until he had grown forty-nine grains. With the jeers of the boys ringing in his ears, Li Lun climbed the mountain and planted the rice.*

Anxiously Li Lun watched the grain heads as they developed. Besides the gulls and the rats, the sun also was now an enemy of the grain. It drank the water Li Lun poured upon the rice faster than the plants could drink it. And water was so hard to find! From sunrise to the hour of short shadows Li Lun worked to find sometimes only a half-dipperful. He searched until he was exhausted. Each day he had to travel farther. But there was also gain. On the longer trips he always came back with gulls' eggs in his shirt pockets.

The few shrubs and weeds on the mountainside were now seared brown. The rocks were hot to touch. Li Lun had to keep his sandals on his feet constantly during

163

the days. At night, when he curled up in his cave, it was a relief to take them off. He hung them carefully from the ledge so that the rats would not find them and chew them up. He had to guard against that, for he could not walk on the hot rocks without them, and he had nothing out of which he could make others.

The water in the special shadow rock hole where the

sun could not reach he saved for himself. Saved it against the time when the thirsty sun would have drunk all the water in the other rock holes.

One morning a great calm settled over the sea. Li Lun watched it from the rice rock as he fastened the blue shirt to the bamboo pole and set it up. The shirt hung tired and limp.

"I know how you feel, little shirt," Li Lun told the blue rag. "I feel tired, too. Almost I cannot breathe. It is so hot!" He wiped the trickling perspiration from his face. "But I must find some water. See, the plants are drooping their heads. The grains are getting ripe and heavy."

Li Lun looked around him. Not a gull was to be seen. "It is too hot even for gulls to be flying around," he said aloud. "Today I will get the water from the rock hole in the shadows. Then I will not be gone long."

He drank a little himself—hardly enough to quench his thirst. He wished that he could stay there where the sun could not torment him. But he must not. The gulls might return and get the rice grains.

He took enough in the dipper to water the remaining stalks. "Just a little drink for each of you," he whispered, "from my very own water supply."

Li Lun had been gone only a very little while. But when he returned, he stared at the rice rock unbelievingly. For there stood not two stalks of rice—but one. Only one stalk of rice! Even the husks were gone. No gulls were about.

"A rat!" gasped Li Lun numbly as the water dripped unheeded from his dipper. "It must have been a rat!"

Li Lun felt as if he were standing on his heart down in the bottom of his sandals. It could not be true. Perhaps it was a nightmare and he would waken from it!

After a time he climbed onto the rock and very carefully counted the seed husks on the one remaining plant. When he reached the seven times as many grains, he stopped counting, he was so relieved. There were more, many more. Li Lun breathed again.

Li Lun decided that he would sit beside the rice rock all day. He could still sleep through the dark hours, for nothing had ever disturbed the plants at night.

Four suns later, with the first streaks of dawn, Li Lun hurried to the shadow rock hole to get himself a drink.

"How thankful I am that Inner Spirit directed me to fill the shadow rock hole brimful during the rainy season! Now," pondered Li Lun seriously, "I must choose between guarding the rice from the gulls and the rats and carrying water for the plants."

Watching the gulls, he retraced his steps to the rice rock. "If I go far down the mountain to get water, my one precious rice plant will disappear also. I must guard it above everything!"

Content in his heart that he was doing what had to be done, Li Lun took a few rice kernels from the almost empty food bag and lingered near the rice plant.

From daylight to dusk Li Lun sat in the hot sun, guarding the single stalk of rice. As he watched, he gazed out over the sea. The water looked cool and green. It was not so hot out there as on the mountain, he knew. And there were no rats on the water. No, but there were spirits beneath it. Spirits that could pull a fisherboy out of the sampan and push him under the water. Li Lun shivered.

"I want to live on the land always," he told the sun. "I know how my grandfather felt. He would not go on the water either. I am like him. He grew rice. I will grow rice. I like to grow rice." He touched the plant gently to feel the aliveness of it.

The time for ripening seed must be near. Perhaps he would have to take the grains before they were wholly

ripe. He would count the stones of his rock calendar and set them in piles, one pile for each moon change.

While he watched the rice rock, Li Lun counted enough stones for one moon change. Enough for two moon changes. Three moon changes. Stones for half of the fourth moon change, and two stones more.

Li Lun whistled a wind song, he was so happy. It did not matter so much now if the grains dried for lack of water. The head was there with the seed grains in it, and harvest was near. To guard them—that was the important thing!

"I am a grower of rice!" Li Lun told himself proudly. And he repeated aloud what the priest had told him: "'The production of a grain of rice is as great a work as the creation of a mountain.'" He breathed deeply. It was good to be alive, good to be growing rice upon a mountaintop.

There was food for only two days more. Three days, if he ate less and went hungry to bed. On the third day, Li Lun decided, he must harvest the head of rice.

Early the third morning, before the gulls began circling the mountain on their never-ending search for food, Li Lun was beside his rice plant. It bowed its heads to the breezes, its seeds made heavy by mist and dew.

"I will not pick you until the sun has dried your heads," he murmured as he caressed the grains gently. "Then you can hold them up."

From the cave he took the twelve grains of rice which would be his breakfast and dinner on this last day of his aloneness on the mountain. There was a half-dipper of water, too. Warm water, but he drank it all. Then, taking one kernel of rice at a time, he champed and munched. "I am chewing long enough to be eating four pigs' feet," he chuckled.

He stretched himself on the rock before the cave. "Stomach," he patted it lightly, "do not get hungry today.

The new rice is not for us to eat. We have a long walk over rough stones to the North Temple. That is where we go first."

Li Lun was impatient to start for the Temple, yet he was reluctant to harvest his rice plant. He had watched time drag so many hours past it. Now he enjoyed seeing the heads gradually lift as the sun pulled the mists from their husks.

"Did you know that I came four times last night to see if you were all right?" Li Lun asked the rice stalk. "I could not sleep for thinking about taking you to the Temple today. I am going to take you, roots and all. The priest expected me to bring five plants. But he will understand if I bring only one. He has a knowing heart."

At first Li Lun thought he would carry the plant in his hands. Then he feared that some of the grains might fall out. "When it is time to take you, I shall put you into the deep pocket of my padded jacket," he decided.

Li Lun talked on and on as he chewed his rice-grain breakfast. He was overjoyed that it was the day of harvest for him. Happy, too, that he would be returning to his home.

He wondered how many fish the men had brought from the deep sea water. Would they have shrimp and squid, too? He looked down upon the village but it was still sleeping. A few older men—he could not tell who they were—were pulling seaweed to the drying racks.

Li Lun went about getting his belongings ready. He packed the birds' nests into the bag which had contained his food supply. His dirty clothing he rolled into a bundle. The bamboo poles he tied to the carrying pole.The gourd dippers he strung about his neck. As he took the small package of dragon bones from the ledge and stuck it into the deep pocket of his coat, he smiled. Not all the fears of the mountain had forced him to open it!

Then he went out to his rice patch. His heart was singing. Now that it was time to go, he could hardly wait to be home again. His mother would cook rice cakes seasoned with shrimp and seaweed. Li Lun's eyes shone brightly at the thought. And his father would be proud when he saw the rice his son had raised!

The long-awaited moment had come. Gently Li Lun pulled the rice plant from the soil. The dirt fell away easily from the roots. Almost, Li Lun thought, as if it were happy that the rice was going to the Temple. "I have told you so many times," he said to it.

Stooping, Li Lun put himself under the pole with its burdens. Then he picked up the rice plant and placed it carefully in his deep pocket. He turned for a last look at the familiar surroundings which for almost four moon changes had been home. How he wished the stone bench could be transported by loving thoughts to his father's door!

"I shall have to leave the bench for you," he told the gulls that circled above. "Good-by, gulls!" Li Lun waved to them. "I will not disturb you again."

He turned from his cave, glad that the long, dreary nights now belonged to the past. The rice repaid him for those nights. Days, he had been so busy caring for the rice plants that the time really had not seemed overlong. He turned and gazed back from the bend in the trail. A lump caught in his throat. The gulls were already claiming the bench and his old sleeping quarters.

With a joyous heart he followed the pathless trail down the mountain. Almost Li Lun had forgotten about the cliff which sloped into the sea. But it held no terrors for him now. He had crossed it too many times with a dipper of water. The green bushes which grew on its rocky surface were now bare scrawny twigs. He grasped them tightly and crossed safely with his full load.

As he picked his way over the rocks he considered how he would get to the Temple without going through the Village of Three Fir Trees. At the foot of the mountain one trail led directly to the village. Another path wound around back of the mountain, between Lao Shan and Lo Shan, and led at last to the Temple.

Li Lun thought that he could get to the Temple without being seen by any of the villagers. It was still early in the day, and few persons visited the Temple until late afternoon.

A few gulls followed him from the mountaintop, as if to keep him company on his homeward way. They flew ahead of him, then alighted to watch until he caught up. Li Lun wondered if they would miss him. Swiftlets darted from the camphorwood trees up the mountainside and flew to their cliff homes.

When he reached the foot of the mountain, Li Lun sat down on a rock to rest for a moment. Then he straightened up and, taking a deep breath, started on the trail which branched to the right.

Suddenly Li Lun heard voices from behind the mountain. Soon he saw a group of village boys. To his dismay he saw that some of them were boys who had been on the man-making fishing trip.

"Sea-water coward! Sea-water coward!" they jeered as they recognized Li Lun.

Li Lun flushed with anger. They had no right to taunt him. He had been sent to grow rice and he had done his work, just as they had done their fishing.

"Afraid of sea water! Afraid of sea water!"

Li Lun faced them bravely. "I am not a coward," he defended himself. "I have done what I was sent to do!"

By this time all six of them were sing-songing:

"Sea-water coward! Sea-water coward!
Afraid of sea water! Afraid of sea water!"

"Let's throw him into the sea!" one of the boys suggested. They made a dart at Li Lun.

But Li Lun was not entirely unprepared. Dropping the carrying pole from his shoulder, he started flaying the bamboo pole right and left, up and down.

The boys were taken completely by surprise. They scattered in all directions to avoid the sudden trouncing. Then, while they planned what to do next, Li Lun climbed under the yoke of the carrying pole and hurried on toward the Temple.

After he had gone a short distance, he glanced over his shoulder. He was dismayed to see that the boys were still following him. With no load to weight them down, they could run faster than he.

Li Lun grabbed the bamboo pole tightly and stumbled ahead. If only he could get around the next bend, he would be in sight of the Temple. He glanced swiftly back to gauge the speed of the boys. They were gaining on him.

Again the sing-song taunts began. Li Lun's heart quickened as he heard them. If they used their breath to hurl coward words, he reasoned, they would have that much less for running.

They had almost reached him when he stumbled through the little gate into the tea grove adjoining the Temple. There, on a stone bench beside the Temple steps, sat a priest. The same priest who had talked to Li Lun on the mountaintop. Gasping for breath, Li Lun stood before him.

"Mountaintop rice grower!" exclaimed the black-robed priest. "I am glad you have come!"

The village boys stopped short when they saw the priest. But they lingered outside the gate and hurled coward threats at Li Lun.

The Good One turned from Li Lun and walked over to them.

"Tell your people to come to the Temple with the long sun shadows today," he commanded. "Tell everyone in the village to come. There is something—" he turned to look at Li Lun crouched at the foot of the Temple steps—"there is something of importance to tell them."

Li Lun watched anxiously as the boys turned away from the gate. They hurled no more coward words, but they walked backward and sent ugly thoughts with their eyes.

The priest returned to his seat on the bench and beckoned Li Lun to sit beside him.

Li Lun did so gladly. He was weary from hunger and his feet were bruised where sharp stones had torn through his sandals.

"Tell me," asked the Good One, "how much rice did you bring?"

Li Lun reached into his deep pocket and drew from it the rice plant. He gave it to the priest. "Just this one, Good Father, was I able to save for the harvest."

Then, reaching again into his pocket, he pulled out all that remained of the other four plants. "The gulls pulled this one before it was ripe, and one they took that I could not find." Sadly he showed the priest the broken stalks. "I think that rats destroyed these three. See, the heads had already formed. This one was ripe, but the rats ate all the grains three suns ago."

"That was a severe disappointment, I know, to such a young heart," replied the Good One. "A young heart, but a big, brave heart."

"I brought the rice plant six suns before the time of harvest, Father. I—I could not wait, for there was no more food. And, the dipper and I could find no more water." He tucked the rice into the deep pocket.

The Good One rose. "Come with me to the Temple. While I attend to the tea gathering, do you improve your time with counting the rice grains. It is now the time of short shadows. You have until the time of closing of the flowers to complete the count. But first you must eat and bathe."

A servant appeared with a tray on which was a pot of tea and two small cups.

"That is good, Chang. The boy is tired and hungry."

Silently Chang set the tray on the bench and poured the tea, handing one cup to the priest, the other one to Li Lun.

Li Lun sipped and smacked his lips. "It is my first cup of tea in almost four moon changes! Thank you, most gracious Father." He drained the cup in several famished gulps.

"Give to Li Lun water for bathing and clean garments," the Keeper of the Temple commanded Chang. "Then give him food. He has had but little food in many days." The priest returned his cup.

Chang did not reply, but he refilled Li Lun's cup

before he picked up his poles and bundles and started up the Temple steps.

Li Lun gulped the second cup of tea hungrily. Then he set the cup on the tray, picked up his jacket and, with a bow to the priest, followed Chang.

"When Li Lun has bathed and eaten food," the priest called after Chang, "show him to the sunset room. I will meet him there."

Chang turned at the top of the steps and bowed to the priest.

Li Lun followed Chang down a red-and-black tiled hallway which smelled strongly of sandalwood. At the far end of the hall, Chang laid Li Lun's belongings on an open portico. Then he opened a sliding door and pointed to a red tile pool.

"The water is warm," Chang said as he placed soap and towels at the edge of the pool. "Soon I bring clean garments. Then food on the portico." Chang disappeared noiselessly through the sliding door.

Li Lun was speechless. He had never dreamed that there was on Blue Shark Island such a lovely place for bathing. He removed his dirty, tattered clothing and slipped into the sunken pool. The hot tea had relaxed him and the warm water tempted him to sleep. But he knew that he must not sleep. Too many things were waiting for him. Besides, he was starved, and Chang had said he would soon bring food.

Li Lun hurried through his bath. So quietly did Chang come in with clean clothing that Li Lun did not hear him. But when he was ready for them, a fresh white blouse and blue trousers were there on a bench, waiting for him.

When he was dressed, Li Lun pushed open the door which led to the portico. His poles and bundles were still there, with his jacket on top of them. Near them Chang had set a small black lacquered table and bamboo chair. On the table was a pot of tea.

Li Lun sat down and poured himself a cup of the steaming beverage. It tasted delicious!

As he drank, Chang came in with a tray and placed before him a plate with rice cakes and steamed seaweed.

Li Lun picked up the chopsticks and put some of the rice to his lips. "It is seasoned with shrimp," he breathed. "Ah, but it is good!" He sipped tea noisily between huge gulps of food.

Under a covered dish he found bamboo sprouts. "Bamboo sprouts I have never eaten," he murmured. His lips trembled. Almost the Good One and Chang were too good to him. Tears smarted his eyes as he glanced at the tray of fruit which Chang had set on the table before leaving.

When Li Lun finished his meal, Chang appeared and bowed. "The Father wishes you to come to the sunset room." He led the way through the hallway down which they had come.

Li Lun felt in the deep pocket of his jacket. Yes, the rice was still there. He followed Chang into a room with black tiled floor and cream-colored tiled walls. As Li Lun's eyes accustomed themselves to the change in colors, he saw several black chairs and two small tables. They stood beside a window which overlooked the sea where white waves splashed high over rocks.

"I can count my grains here," murmured Li Lun.

Chang left the room, and Li Lun was alone.

He pulled the rice plant from his deep pocket and sat on the floor where the rice grains showed against the black tiles. Then he began his counting.

He counted the grains by moon changes, as he had counted the stones on the mountain. The grain heads had separated into three blades. The shortest blade had two grains less than a moon change. The longest blade had a moon change and a half. The third blade had three grains more than a moon change.

When he had finished counting, Li Lun found that he had almost as many grains as he had spent days on the mountain. He had not thought one grain could grow so many kernels!

The hot tea and the well-cooked food made Li Lun drowsy. Tucking the empty grain head into the deep pocket, he folded his jacket and placed it on the floor for a pillow. He laid his head upon it and in an instant was sound asleep.

When Li Lun awoke, he was conscious of droning sounds. He turned toward the window on the side of the room opposite the sea. He could see that a crowd of people had collected in front of the Temple. Li Lun stood beside the window where he could see them without being seen. He stretched to his tiptoes to look for his most honorable father and his most beautiful mother. But he did not see them. When Teng Lun saw the rice, Li Lun wondered, would he still call his son a coward?

Now the Keeper of the Temple appeared, dressed in his long black robe and with the little round cap on his head.

"Have you counted the grains of rice?" he asked quietly.

Li Lun nodded.

"How many grains were there on the one plant?" the Good One asked, holding out his hand for the rice.

"Enough for three moon changes and for another half moon change," replied Li Lun happily. "Almost one grain for every day I was on Lao Shan."

"Good! Come, we shall tell your people."

The priest walked to the edge of the outer steps where the people were. Li Lun followed him.

Raising his hand, the priest waited for the people to grow quiet. Then he pulled Li Lun gently to his side and placed his hand on the boy's shoulder.

"This boy was called a coward," the Good One spoke.

"He was taunted because of his fear of deep sea water. He was sent to the top of Lao Shan to spend four moon changes alone. He was given seven small grains and commanded to grow rice from them—to grow rice on the top of Lao Shan."

A ripple of wonder ran through the crowd.

Li Lun's knees trembled. He shifted from one foot to another, so that the people would not see how he shook. "He has done what not one of you on this island has done," the priest went on. "He has grown rice. Grown it at the top of Lao Shan. Grown it from the seven grains given to him by his father. Two plants were carried away by gulls. Five plants he has brought back with him. The gulls and rats ate the four which you see in his hands."

Trembling, Li Lun held up the dried stalks.

"This plant—" the priest took the empty rice head from Li Lun and held it up—"this one plant grew ninety-nine grains. The boy was ordered to bring back seven times the number of grains he planted. He has brought back more than double that. During four long moon changes he has struggled and toiled. He had to carry up the mountain the soil in which to plant the rice. He had to drive away the gulls and the rats. He had to carry water to the plants with a small dipper, only to have the sun drink up the water before his eyes. He has toiled harder than the deep-sea fishermen. And now Li Lun has brought his harvest home."

A swell of happy murmurings passed through the crowd. Li Lun's knees knocked each other in their trembling. But the Keeper of the Temple had not finished his story.

"The wise men of old have said that 'the production of a grain of rice is as great a work as the creation of a mountain,'" he told the people.

"Ah, Li Lun did that!" came hums of approval for the boy who had refused to go on his man-making fishing trip.

"Li Lun has proved that it is possible to grow rice on Blue Shark Island," the priest continued. "No one has done this for many years. Not since the destruction of Mei Shan. . . . We are a fisher people. We have brought our rice from across the sea, over rough and treacherous waters. But now I shall ask Li Lun to teach other boys how to grow rice. Not on Lao Shan, but right here on our Temple grounds. From now on, the Island of the Blue Shark will have both fishermen and growers of rice."

"Ah!" Murmurs of pleased surprise swept the throng.

The priest turned to Li Lun and smiled.

Li Lun bowed low and mumbled, "Thank you, most honorable Keeper of the Temple."

Through the crowd a man and a woman came pushing until finally they stood at the bottom of the steps. Li Lun ran down to greet them.

"My most honorable father! My most beautiful mother!"

"My son!" greeted Wang Lun as she stooped to press her cheek to his. "You have grown the rice!"

Li Lun's father stood looking on coldly. His fellow fishermen watched to see how he would welcome the son who had disobeyed him.

Li Lun held out his hands. "Here, most honorable father, are the plants which the rats and the gulls destroyed. The rice heads are with the Keeper of the Temple."

Teng Lun made no effort to take the broken dried stalks. But his eyes met those of his son with a glint of pride. Wang Lun's hands quickly gathered in the broken stems to cherish.

Li Lun smiled at her gratefully through misty eyes. "And most beautiful mother—" his voice trembled—"here are the dragon bones which you gave me. I did not need them." He drew the small package from his deep pocket and placed it in her hands.

Wang Lun clasped the package tightly. "Li Lun," she whispered, "I am deeply proud of you. You are a lad of courage."

If you have enjoyed reading Li Lun's adventures, you may wish to read Armstrong Sperry's Call It Courage, *a similar story of bravery published by The Macmillan Company.* House of Sixty Fathers, *by Meindert De Jong, published by Harper & Brothers, is another story which takes place in China.*

The Wheel on the School

BY MEINDERT DeJONG

Illustrations by Maurice Sendak

> **All the children hoped that a wagon wheel
> on the school chimney might bring storks to
> the Dutch fishing village of Shora. It had
> been hard enough for the children to find a
> spare wheel, but now it looked as though a
> bad storm might prevent their fathers from
> hoisting the wheel up on the roof.**

ON Monday morning the storm hadn't stopped. It raged in fury against the dike. The sea was up-ended; the spume and roiled spindrift still flew high above the dike, landing in gray dirty flecks in the streets and on the roofs. If anything, the storm was more jerky and fitful, Odd sudden lulls seemed to fall momentarily between the high shrieks and moans of the wind, although behind the dike the sea thundered on. Enormous breakers hurled themselves up and washed in a last, thin, hissing line almost to the crest of the dike. Now and then the spent water of an unusually large wave managed to spill over the dike.

In the houses the fishermen sat loafing in the corners of their kitchens, behind the stoves if possible, to be out of the way of their busy wives and of their children getting ready for school. They were given no peace. In all

Shora the fisherman fathers were pestered by their children. The wheel had to go up on the school, storm or no storm.

"Just suppose some storks came through tomorrow," Lina argued with her father in the kitchen.

"Yes, just suppose and suppose," her father barked back. "Just suppose you let me be nice and quiet in my little corner. It feels good to be dry and warm and to do nothing for a change."

"Yes, but just suppose the storm ends, then you'll be going out to sea again, and we won't have a wheel up on the roof of the school. There's nobody else but Janus and old Douwa, and they can't get on roofs."

"They're lucky!" her father said impatiently. "It'll be a long storm, I've told you. There's plenty of time. That storm isn't just going to shut off like a faucet. Can't I wait at least for a quieter day?" He disappeared behind his week-old newspaper, which, since he had been at sea for weeks, was news to him—news and a refuge to hide behind.

He was given no chance to read it. Lina's little sister, Linda, at that moment insisted on climbing into his lap, and on the other side of the newspaper Lina still argued with him. "The teacher said Saturday that if the wheel could go up today, there'd be no school. So we can all help you," she said to the newspaper. "With all of us helping, it shouldn't take long."

"What does that teacher know about wind and storms? Let him get on that roof in a storm then! And it's off to school with you right now. There'll come a quieter day before we can take off for sea again, and then we'll see. But off with you, so I can have a quiet day today."

It was final. Lina indignantly shoved her feet into her wooden shoes. She knew better than to argue further. She had gone as far as she dared. She buttoned her jacket tightly up around her throat and stamped out of the house.

"Listen, Jella, how often do I have to tell you? I'm not stirring from this house today, and that's final. A man ought to have a couple days of rest after weeks out at sea without having to sit on top of a school. Now beat it! Get in that school and learn something instead of sitting on top of it."

"But the teacher said there'd be no school today if we put the wheel up."

"Well, you can't get the wheel up in this storm, so there is school, and I say so. Or do I have to take you there by the scruff of your neck and the seat of your pants?"

Jella shoved his feet disgustedly into his wooden shoes and slammed the door hard behind him.

"Listen, Pier and Dirk—that's the trouble with twins, a man gets a double dose of everything—one more yammer or argument out of the two of you, and I'll knock your two heads together so hard you'll be lucky if you have one head left between you. Even so, that ought to be enough—you don't use your two heads. The answer is: No, No, NO! NO wheel on NO school in NO storm!"

"But we'd help all you men. The teacher said no school if . . ."

"And I say there is school, and you two will be in it if only so I don't have to hear another word about storks. On your way!"

Pier and Dirk looked at each other. They glumly shoved their feet into their shoes and moved to the door, muttering dire things to each other. Behind his week-old newspaper their father sat grinning at their fuming threats. "Learn your lesson well today," he teased them. "I hear it's going to be about storks."

"Just so it isn't about lazy, stubborn fishermen," Pier said stormily. Afraid he'd said too much, he scooted to the door with Dirk close behind him. Their father rustled the newspaper. Dirk pushed Pier through the door and almost tumbled over him to get out as fast as he could. The door fell shut.

"Listen, Auka, don't you ever let up on me? If I hear another word about another stork, I'll . . . I'll take your neck and stretch it until you look like a stork. Then *you* can go and sit up on a wheel on top of a roof. Storks got more sense than to do that in a storm. How do you expect me to lug a wheel up that roof in a storm? I haven't got wings! And if I should slide down a slippery roof in this high wind and land on my head, who's going to earn the money so you can go to school and fool around with storks? You get to that school!"

"But there is no school if we put the wheel up."

"Well, nobody is going to put that wheel up today, so there is school. Bye, Auka."

There was nothing left for Auka to do but to put his shoes on and move off silently. His father watched him.

"If you stick that lower lip out much farther in your pout, you can put that wagon wheel on there instead of on the roof," he teased.

Auka said a few wicked things to himself and looked stonily at his father as he closed the door very slowly to let in as much wind and draft as possible.

Eelka's father, sitting cozily beside the stove in the kitchen, peered around his newspaper to watch Eelka slowly putting on his shoes, buttoning his jacket, and pulling up the collar. "Where do you think you're going, son?"

"To school," Eelka said. "It's Monday, you know, but it's much too stormy to put that wheel up on the roof of the school today. So I suppose it'll be school." He sighed. "I never did have much luck. Bye, Pop."

Eelka hunched himself to meet the wind that was driving down the street. Ahead of him were all the other school children, bent over, boring into the wind. Unwilling and angry and defeated, each one walked alone on the hard way to school. No one hurried to catch up with any of the others; each one hated to have to admit that he'd gone down in defeat. And Eelka was too slow and far behind and full of breakfast to make the effort.

It had been a scheme, hatched and planned after church yesterday. That was what Pier and Dirk had said to do about fathers—pester them until they gave in. If all the children worked at it, nagged and pleaded . . . Oh, your father would growl and act angry and make wisecracks, but that's the way men are, different from mothers. You didn't get to know your father very well—always out at sea—but that's the way it had to be done. Joke a little and tease and nag, and nag and tease. Wait and see! In spite of what your father said or growled, sooner or later he'd do what you wanted.

Some of the others had had their misgivings, Eelka especially. He'd said that *his* father would say, "Oh, sure, Eelka," and then not do it. But Pier and Dirk had knowingly assured them all that it was much easier than with mothers. You'd get a sound box on the ear from your mother if you kept on pestering her like that. But then your mother had you yapping around her all the time so she had less patience.

The others, all but Eelka, had been easily convinced, especially since the success of the scheme meant that not only would the wheel be put up on the school, but they'd also have the rest of the day free from lessons. It was worth a good try. But Eelka had said his father was just too good-natured, he wouldn't be pestered.

The scheme had failed miserably. Now each child on his way to school hated to admit to the others that he had failed, not knowing that the others had failed just as completely.

The storm was never going to stop. They knew it! There wouldn't be a stork left after this storm. Everything was hopeless and useless. Even if there should be one or two storks left over from the storm, what was the good of that? There'd be no wheel on the school anyway —just because of their fathers.

They had to face each other in the portal of the school. It was cold in the portal, but at least here they were sheltered from the vicious wind. They all made great pretense of blowing and stamping and beating their arms; they all breathed heavily. "Whew, what a wind!" somebody said. The others said nothing. They eyed each other while they flailed their arms across their chests in a great pretense of cold and chill.

Finally Jella turned on Dirk and Pier as the authors of the scheme. "Well," he demanded, "is your dad coming?"

Pier and Dirk looked at each other. "No-oo," Pier admitted slowly. "I guess not."

That cleared the air. "Mine isn't either. You should have heard him!"

"Neither is mine. He isn't coming at all. Said he'd just as soon try to sail the sea in a bushel basket in this storm as sit on the sharp roof of this school. Now maybe—he said—if we had a saddle, he might try it. But what good was a fisherman split in two on the ridge of a sharp roof in a high wind? The two halves of him—he didn't think —could go out fishing afterwards and catch double the amount of fish."

In spite of themselves they all laughed at the sally. Now that they'd all admitted failure, they tried to outdo each other in repeating what their fathers had said. Now they could laugh about it. And Eelka didn't say, "What did I tell you?" He was laughing too hard.

Jella summed it up for all of them. "Guess it *is* too windy for old men like our dads."

The teacher suddenly stood in the doorway.

Lina burst out with it for the group. "None of our fathers—not a single one—would come," she said. "Not a one would get from behind the stove. There they sit, baking!"

"So," the teacher said. "So is that the grievance? Wise men, I'd say. You'll have to learn that, too, sooner or later, that you can't defy a storm—that you can't hurt a wall with just your head. So let's go inside; let's start right in on our lessons to get our minds on other things. Your fathers will come through. You know that. If not today, the first possible day that the storm will let them. They'll put up the wheel before they set out to sea again."

"Did they tell you that?" Lina asked eagerly.

"No, they didn't tell me. I know that. And all of you ought to know it, too. Fathers always come through when it's possible. It's the way of fathers and mothers. You're just impatient, but the wheel can wait now. The storks will be waiting out the storm. Let's be just as patient and wise as the storks."

The lessons didn't go too well in spite of the teacher's reassurances. The wind, howling and shrieking around the corners of the exposed school, kept reminding them of the storm sweeping across the sea and the land. The wagon wheel leaning against the blackboard kept reminding them of storks. The howl of the wind made it difficult to understand the teacher and made it even more difficult to concentrate on answers. Who could think out arithmetic problems when hundreds of storks coming from Africa were maybe going down in the sea? How many storks would drown and never come to Shora? That was the outrageous arithmetic problem the wind seemed to be howling at them.

The teacher asked Auka how much sixteen times sixteen were. Auka had to jerk his attention away from the window where a tuft of hay was held against the glass by the relentless wind. "There won't be a single stork can come through a storm like this," Auka answered.

Nobody smiled at Auka's mistake. All eyes went anxiously to the window and from the window to the huge wagon wheel leaning against the front blackboard. Even the teacher looked somber.

"It's getting still worse," somebody in a back seat muttered.

"It only seems that way," the teacher said slowly, "because we feel so helpless. Because we're just sitting still and doing nothing about the wheel. Inaction is hard, and still, Auka, the only problem before us that we can do anything about is: How much are sixteen times sixteen?"

There was a long pause. Auka had to jerk his mind from his own inside woes, and then figure out the answer. He got it wrong.

"Oh," he said moodily to himself, "I thought he said sixteen times eighteen."

Nobody but Auka cared that his answer was wrong. Not even the teacher! The teacher himself was standing listening to the sounds outside. The wind seemed to be making new noises. Muttering, grumbling noises penetrated the classroom door. Outside the portal there was a sound as of something crashing down. Now there were stumbling noises in the portal. The wind must have blown something in and was rolling it around.

Everybody's head was cocked toward the classroom door. There came a hard knock. There were voices.

"Our dads!" Lina cried.

The teacher hurried to open the door. There stood the men of Shora. "It isn't sane. It's insane," one of the men said to the teacher. It sounded like Eelka's father. "First the kids nag you every waking minute, so you chase the kids off to school. What happens then? Their mothers start in on you! Nobody's got anything on the brain but those blasted storks on that wagon wheel. Well, they nagged us all out of our houses, so we got together and decided it was less grief putting up that wheel than facing a bunch of nagging women and children."

The teacher grinned at the men. "Solomon found that out a few thousand years before you. Didn't he in his Proverbs say that it was better to sit on the roof of a house than with a nagging woman inside the house?"

Auka's father turned to the men behind him. "Did you hear that? If his wives had even wise old Solomon up on a roof, what are a few dumb fishermen going to do?"

"Get on the roof with Solomon," somebody said in the portal. "He knew when he was licked."

The schoolroom tittered. The men were joking, and, in spite of the storm, they were going to try to put the wheel up. And they weren't unhappy about it—you could tell that—not if they were making wisecracks. That was always a good sign.

Jella's hefty father peered over the head of the teacher into the classroom. "It seems I was told," he boomed, "that part of the deal was that if we put that wheel on the roof, there'd be no school today. Was I correctly informed, or was that just Jella and his endless love for school?"

"No-oo," the whole room sang out. "No school. *He* promised!"

They did not wait for the teacher so much as to nod his head; they could see it in his face—anything went today. They streamed from the room and got into jackets and stocking caps and wooden shoes.

From the portal they saw that their fathers had even brought ladders and lumber and ropes. The stuff lay in a helter-skelter pile in the schoolyard where it had been dropped.

"Out of the way! Out of the way all you mortals," Jella came shouting. Jella alone had remembered. He had jumped to the front of the room to get the wagon wheel instead of just rushing out with the rest. Now he sent the

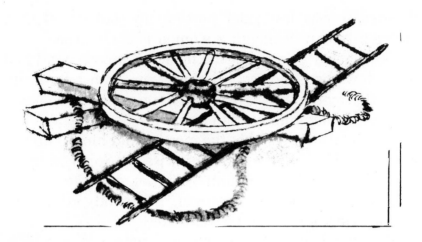

wheel rolling wildly into the portal. Everybody had to scatter. The wheel wobbled in an uncertain path, somehow found the outside doorway, plunged into the yard, and settled itself on the pile of beams and ropes and ladders.

"Well, it's all here now," a man shouted. "Now roll out your storks."

The men laughed, but not the children. Happy and relieved and eager as they were, now that their fathers were actually going to put up the wheel, it was not a good joke. The low, sweeping sky, scudding and racing with clouds that looked as angry as capped waves on the sea, threatened bad things. There was nothing in the sky but storm; there wasn't a bird anywhere, not even a sparrow. A rain squall slashed down. The wind hurled the rain into the portal.

"Will there be any storks left after a storm like this?" Dirk asked the group of men around the pile in the schoolyard.

The men looked up at the sky and shrugged. "Maybe, if the storm doesn't hang on too long," Lina's father said. "Maybe a couple of them will have sense enough to go bury their heads in sand until this blows over."

"That's ostriches!" Lina, standing right beside him, said

scornfully. She was half-ashamed of the ignorance of her father—and right before the teacher! "Ostriches are *supposed* to bury their heads in the sand, only they don't."

"I guess that takes care of you and your ostriches," Eelka's father said.

"Yeah," Lina's father said, nettled. "Maybe I'd better go bury my head in some sand. These modern-day school kids—they know everything, don't they? Me, all I know is fish." He grinned suddenly. "You kids wouldn't be satisfied with a couple of fish on the roof?" he asked plaintively. "Say a couple of sharks in a wash tub?"

The children hooted, and he grinned broadly. He sobered, stepped back, and eyed the sharp school roof. "Well, come on you Solomons," he said impatiently. "Let's get on the roof and get that wheel up."

The men stood studying the steep roof. "Wet and steep and windy, it'll be slipperier than a deckful of jellyfish," one of them said. "But up with a ladder, and we'll see what the climate is up there."

Two men raised the long ladder high and straight. As they carried it upright around a corner of the school, a blast of wind caught the high ladder. The two men struggled, but they couldn't hold it up. The ladder swayed and twisted and threatened to come crashing down.

Everybody stood anxiously watching the top of the ladder, expecting it to smash to pieces against the ground at any moment. "Watch it. Watch it," somebody yelled. "If you can't even set a ladder up, how do you expect to get a wheel up there? Get into it all of you; don't stand there staring at the top rung. Let it down! Let it down, I say. There. Now carry it flat around that windy corner. That isn't a flag you're carrying in a parade."

It was Janus! There he came in his wheel chair, forcing it ahead against the wind by sheer strength and at the same time loudly scolding everybody.

The men let the ladder down. Then they turned to face Janus, a bit peeved at being bawled out before their own children. But Janus was grinning broadly; he was having a fine time in spite of the wind and the struggle to move against it. He rolled up to the group in his wheel chair. "When it comes to doing anything on land, you guys are about as helpless as the fish are," he told them. He turned his chair so as to face the roof. "Now then, let's use our heads. Better yet, I'll use my head."

"So now we've got an overseer," one of the men said.

"All right, now lay that ladder down," Janus directed. "Place one end against the wall, then raise the other end. Get under it; walk your hands from spoke to spoke until it's up straight against the wall. Then all you have to do is pull out the bottom end. See, that way you don't fight the wind."

"Well, that worked," one of the men said.

When the ladder was up, the men automatically turned to Janus for further instruction. Janus looked at the pile of lumber and the one ladder beside it.

"Now the other ladder and push it up on the roof. But first tie a coil of rope on the top rung, so you can let the rope down the other side of the roof to fasten the ladder down. Then lash the second ladder to the first, otherwise the wind will just sweep it right off the roof. Meanwhile, you kids get me that wagon wheel."

While he waited for the children to roll the big wheel to him, Janus kept looking at the pile of beams and boards still lying in the schoolyard. "What's the big pile for?" he yelled up to the roof.

"To brace up the wheel. Got to have some brackets or braces or something to hold the wheel on the sharp ridge of this roof," Auka's father explained.

"Yeah, but you're just going to have storks up there, not elephants," Janus said scornfully. "The way I've doped it out—that wheel's got to be up there nice and simple.

With all your beams and boards and two-by-fours sticking in every direction, storks flying overhead will think
it's a trap, not a nest. But just get on with that ladder,
Janus will fix it nice and neat and simple."

"Yes, sir, yes, sir," Auka's father said. "Up with the second ladder, men, Janus says."

Jella, Auka, and Lina rolled the wagon wheel before
Janus. "Now where's that saw?" Janus said impatiently.
"Somewhere I hung a saw on this wheel chair contrap-
tion."

"There it is," Pier said behind him. "You brought a
hammer, too. You're sitting on it."

"The hammer, too," Janus said. "The hammer first."
Then paying no attention to the alarmed looks of the
children, he took the hammer and drove the steel rim off
the inner wooden rim of the wheel. After studying the
pitch of the roof and the ridge, he began sawing a deep
V into the side of the wooden rim. The children had to
hold the wheel steady for him while he sawed. "See, I'll
cut two deep V's; that way the rim will fit snug on the
ridge," he explained. "Then we'll fit the iron rim just

partly over the wooden one so it won't cover the V notches. The iron doesn't have to cover the whole wooden rim—this wheel isn't going rolling any place—it'll even be better that way. With the iron rim sticking up, it'll make a sort of pan of the wheel—storks are awfully sloppy nest builders. This may help them to hold all the stuff they'll lug up on this wheel."

The teacher came up. "Janus, don't you want to go inside? No sense in your sitting here in the wind when you can do your work just as well inside."

"If those men can sit on that windy roof, I can sit here where it's practically cozy," Janus said shortly, his whole grim attention on his sawing.

The teacher, realizing Janus wanted no favors, said no more. "Anything I can do?" he asked. "I feel sort of useless with everybody else busy."

"Well, I need a brace and bit—a long bit so it will go through the ridge boards on both sides of the roof."

"My dad's got a brace and all kinds of bits, all sizes," Jella said eagerly. "I'll go get them."

"Well, there goes Jella and the job you had for me," the teacher said.

"Hold it," Janus said. "I also need two heavy iron rods —long enough so the two edges of the wheel rim can rest on them. You see, we'll drill the holes through the ridge, shove the rods through them, and then rest the wheel on the rods. The two notches I cut in the wooden rim will fit snugly over the ridge. Then all we'll need to do is to wire the rim to the two supporting rods, and there'll be the wheel, steady and level and solid as a house. But I can't think of anybody in Shora who would have a couple of heavy rods like that."

"Hah!" the teacher said. "You're talking to the right man. It seems to me I've seen a couple of rods like that in the tower when I go there to ring the bell. I'm almost sure."

"Just so they're long enough," Janus said.

"I'll go look, and nobody can take this job away from me. As the official bellringer for the village, I'm the only one to have a key to the tower." The teacher pulled the big ancient key out of his pocket and held it up. He hurried off.

"Glad I found something for him to do," Janus said to Lina. "He makes me nervous watching so closely. He's just as jittery and excited as you kids." He had finished cutting the notches. Now came the job of fitting the iron rim partially over the wooden rim. The boys and Lina had all they could do to hold the wheel upright and steady as Janus struggled with the close-fitting rim.

Jella returned with the brace and all the bits. A few minutes later the teacher came back with two large, rusty rods. Janus studied the rods. "They should do. Good and thick and solid. Plenty long enough for the wheel. Good thing you remembered them," he said to the teacher. "It must be the only pair of loose rods in Shora. It was the only thing had me worried—me with my fine plans and no rods. I'd have been the laughing-stock around here."

Jella was sent up the ladder to carry the brace and bit to his father. The teacher was sent off to find some heavy wire that could be used to secure the wheel to the rods. "Got to keep him busy," Janus said with a sly wink at Lina.

At last the wheel was ready. The children rolled it to the ladder. The men began hoisting the huge wagon wheel up the ladder, while Jella's father drilled the two holes for the rods in the ridge of the roof.

It was a slow, hard struggle against the tugging of the wind. Two of the fishermen now straddled the ridge, ready to lift the wheel on to the rods when it reached them. A sudden hard hail and rain squall slashed down again. The men straddling the ridge had to press them-

selves flat; they lay with faces against the roof and clung
with one hand to the ladder. The men working the
wheel up the roof had to stop and be content just to hold
the wheel in place on the ladder. The squall passed as
suddenly as it had come, and the struggle went on again.

Janus watched every move with eagle eyes. He was
so intent he seemed unaware of the sweep of wind and
rain and hail. Yet from time to time Janus glanced down

the road to the village. Suddenly he bellowed out, "Look
at that, men! Look what's coming! The women! What do
you know? Wind or hail—here come the women. Pots of
hot coffee for you. This is going to turn into a picnic.
Hurray for women!"

All work stopped on the roof. Everybody sat looking
down the road; they called the women on. The women
came in a close group, trying to protect their steaming
coffee from the cold wind. Then a new blast of hail had
the men hanging on to the roof and the ladders again.

The moment the squall passed, they looked down the
road again. "No use looking," Janus shouted. "No hot
coffee, no nothing, until that wheel is up and secure."

"Janus, you're a slave driver," one of the men on the ridge complained. "All you need is a whip."

"Don't need a whip," Janus called back. "Got my tongue."

"Yeah," Pier and Dirk's father yelled down. "Too bad that shark didn't get your tongue instead of your legs."

Down below Janus flushed red and embarrassed. He looked away and then glowered up from under the peak of his cap to see how Pier's father had meant the joke. Pier's father saw the look; he gave Janus a good-natured grin. All of Janus eased in the chair. He let out his breath. "Well, all I can tell you is," he called out slowly, "that shark *was* eyeing my tongue. Got a good look at it, too— all I was telling him! But it looked too tough even for him, I guess. He must have decided my sea boots were tenderer. So he took my boots. How could that poor dumb fish know my legs were inside of them?"

Everybody laughed, and Janus sat back, relieved. He seemed to test the laugh, almost as if he were tasting it. Then he looked at Pier, hovering anxiously beside his chair. "Good kid," he said. "Don't think I don't know everybody's accepting that crazy story because it's good for me. And it is good!" he added fiercely. "Good."

The wheel was being fitted over the ridge. Janus riveted his whole attention on the operation. "It's got to work, my idea with just two rods," he muttered anxiously. "Otherwise my name is mud. They'll razz me out of Shora."

The teacher came hurrying up with a handful of wires. Janus picked out the heaviest and sent Pier up the ladder with them. "Nothing more for you to do," Janus told the teacher. "But the women have hot coffee on the stove in the schoolroom. Go get yourself a cup. You aren't used to being out in this kind of weather."

"Aye, aye, sir," the teacher said. He saluted smartly and trotted off.

Jella's father, lying full-length on the ladder on the roof, was twisting the wire around the rods and the rim of the wheel. It was awkward, slow, overhead work. The cold and the salt, stinging wind were numbing all the men and slowing their movements. The two men straddling the ridge were holding the wheel in place. One of them had to let go his hold to rest his numbed arm. He wearily rubbed a hand over his face to wipe away the icy wetness. He took a new hold, but now the wheel was tilted.

"Jan, hold that wheel straight," Janus said. "Those storks need a nest, not a chute."

"Look," Jan answered irritably, before he gave a thought to what he was saying, "if you think you can do it better, you come up here and hold it."

There was an awkward, stunned pause. Everybody looked at Janus. Lina, beside his chair, laid her hand on Janus' shoulder. But to her astonishment Janus was delighted. "Did you hear that?" he asked Lina. "He forgot I've got no legs. Bless his ornery old hide. That's the way it's got to be."

Now Jan, who had been preoccupied with the wheel and his precarious position, realized what he'd said. He looked down at Janus. A slow grin spread over his face. "Stay there," he said. "I'm not giving you a chance to come up here and show me up. I'll show you I'm as much a man as you are."

He hadn't apologized or even tried to cover it up. They were treating Janus man to man. He was one of them again. Janus bent low to straighten out the pin in his folded-over trousers leg. He fumbled with it. When he straightened up, his eyes were bright. "Bless his ornery old hide," he mumbled.

Lina took her hand off his shoulder. Even she mustn't baby Janus.

"Would you dare?" Janus asked suddenly. "We've got

to test that wheel, and you're the only one who is about the weight of two storks. I've got to know whether it'll hold their nest without tilting or wobbling. The men will hold you up on the wheel."

Janus wasn't babying her either. "Sure," Lina said stoutly.

On the ridge Jan held Lina's hand as she climbed on the wheel. Janus directed from down below. Lina walked along the rim of the wheel as far as Jan could reach and still keep his hold on her. Janus watched her closely. "You can come down now," he said. "It'll hold. It didn't so much as stir, even with you walking on the edge. Everybody down now! Take the ropes and ladders down and go get your coffee."

Lina made use of that moment of distraction to pull free from Jan's hand. She climbed up on the hub of the wheel. She flapped her arms. "I'm a stork, I'm a stork," she cried. The next moment a gust of wind caught her, and she had to let herself fall, clutching for the spokes of the wheel and grabbing wildly for Jan's outstretched hand. She hung on for dear life.

"Some stork!" the boys jeered up at her. "Let's see you fly down."

"Jan, come on down and bring that stork with you under your arms," Janus said, "before she tries to fly. I wouldn't put it past her."

It was a picnic—steaming coffee and cakes and fatballs. It was a feast! Hot chocolate milk for the boys and Lina! That was what made it really a picnic and a feast. You had hot chocolate milk only on the Queen's Birthday and fatballs only on Santa Claus Day. But now fatballs and chocolate all the same day! And the rest of the day free— it was a holiday.

The school room buzzed. Janus was in the midst of

it in his wheel chair. His voice carried above all the others. But everybody was in high spirits. They'd wrestled the wheel up on the roof in spite of the storm and cold and hail and squalls. It made it a holiday.

No school the rest of the day, and their fathers home with games to play. They'd all play dominoes with their dads. The five boys and Lina decided it among themselves as they sat in their seats, sipping hot chocolate while the grownups crowded around the warm stove.

It happened so seldom, having their fathers home. Always they were out at sea or, if home, busy with nets and sails and the readying of the boats. Now they'd have almost a whole day with their dads. The storm had made it a holiday for them, a chance for games and jokes with their fathers.

Everybody was talking, and Janus was in the midst of everything. Now he noticed the boys and Lina in their corner. "How is it?" he asked. "Is this a feast or isn't it?"

"Hot chocolate milk and hot fatballs!" Pier told him smartly. "Hey, Janus, all it lacks is some cherries."

Janus laughed. "To get them you'd have to go where the wind took them—over a couple of provinces or so, I think, or maybe into Germany. Well, there're a few under the tree, if you like salt cherries."

Lina hastily told the boys that she was going to ask Janus to play dominoes, too. He and Jana had no children. Janus ought to be invited, too. They all agreed eagerly; they all wanted Janus in their houses.

"Oh, no, you don't," Lina said. "I thought of it first!"

The American Library Association awarded the 1955 John Newbery Medal to Meindert DeJong for The Wheel on the School. *This author, who was born in the Netherlands, has given us another fine story about Holland in* Dirk's Dog, Bello.

The Big Wave

BY PEARL S. BUCK

Illustrations, authentic Japanese prints, by Hiroshige and Hokusai

> When a huge tidal wave washes away his home, a little Japanese boy proves that he has great courage.

K INO lived on a farm. The farm lay on the side of a mountain in Japan. The fields were terraced by walls of stone, each one of them like a broad step up the mountain. Centuries ago Kino's ancestors had built the stone walls that held up the fields.

Above all the fields stood the farmhouse that was Kino's home. Sometimes he felt the climb was a hard one, especially when he had been working in the lowest field and he wanted his supper. But after he had eaten at night and in the morning, he was glad that he lived so high up because he could look down on the broad blue ocean at the foot of the mountain.

The mountain rose so steeply out of the ocean that there was only a strip of sandy shore at its foot. Upon this strip was the small fishing village where Kino's father sold his vegetables and rice and bought his fish. From the window of his room Kino looked down upon the few thatched roofs of the village, running in two uneven lines on both sides of a cobbled street. These houses

faced one another, and those that stood beside the sea
did not have windows toward it. Since he enjoyed looking at the waves, Kino often wondered why the village
people did not, but he never knew until he came to know
Jiya, whose father was a fisherman.

Jiya lived in the last house in the row of houses toward
the ocean, and his house did not have a window toward
the sea either.

"Why not?" Kino asked him. "The sea is beautiful."

"The sea is our enemy," Jiya replied.

"How can you say that?" Kino asked. "Your father
catches fish from the sea and sells them and that is how
you live."

Jiya only shook his head. "The sea is our enemy," he
repeated. "We all know it."

It was very hard to believe this. On hot sunny days,
when he had finished his work, Kino ran down the path
that wound through the terraces and met Jiya on the
beach. They threw off their clothes and jumped into the
clear sea water and swam far out toward a small island
which they considered their own. Actually it belonged
to an old gentleman whom they had never seen, except
at a distance. Sometimes in the evening he came through
the castle gate and stood looking out to sea. Then they
could see him, leaning on his staff, his white beard blowing in the wind. He lived inside his castle behind a high
fence of woven bamboo, on a knoll outside the village.
Neither Kino or Jiya had ever been inside the gate, but
sometimes when it was left open they had peeped into
the garden. It was beautiful beyond anything they could
imagine. Instead of grass the ground was covered with
deep green moss shaded by pine trees and bamboos, and
every day gardeners swept the moss with bamboo
brooms until it was like a velvet carpet. They saw Old
Gentleman walking under distant trees in a silver-gray
robe, his hands clasped behind his back, his white head

bent. He had a kind, wrinkled face, but he never saw them.

"I wonder if it is right for us to use his island without asking?" Kino asked today when they reached its beach of smooth white sand.

"He never uses it himself," Jiya replied. "Only the sacred deer live here."

The island was full of sacred deer. They were not afraid, for no one hurt them. When they saw the two boys they came to them, nuzzling into their hands for food. Sometimes Kino tied a little tin can of cakes about his waist and brought them with him to feed the deer. But he seldom had a penny, and now he reached high and picked the tender shoots of the rushes for them. The deer liked these very much and they laid their soft heads against his arm in gratitude.

Kino longed to sleep on the island some night, but Jiya was never willing. Even when they spent only the afternoon there he looked often out over the sea.

"What are you looking for?" Kino asked.

"Only to see that the ocean is not angry," Jiya replied.

Kino laughed. "Silly," he said. "The ocean cannot be angry."

"Yes, it can," Jiya insisted. "Sometimes the old ocean god begins to roll in his ocean bed and to heave up his head and shoulders, and the waves run back and forth. Then he stands upright and roars and the earth shakes under the water. I don't want to be on the island then."

"But why should he be angry with us?" Kino asked. "We are only two boys, and we never do anything to him."

"No one knows why the ocean grows angry," Jiya said anxiously.

But certainly the ocean was not angry this day. The sun sparkled deep into the clear water, and the boys swam over the silvery surface of rippling waves. Beneath them the water was miles deep. Nobody knew how deep it was, for however long the ropes that fishermen let down, weighted with iron, no bottom was ever found. Deep the water was, and the land sloped swiftly down to that fathomless ocean bed. When Kino dived, he went down—down—down, until he struck icy still water. Today when he felt the cold grasp his body he

understood why Jiya was afraid, and he darted upward
to the waves and the sun.

On the beach he threw himself down and was happy
again, and he and Jiya searched for pebbles, blue and
emerald, red and gold. They had brought little baskets
woven like bags, which they had tied with string around
their waists, and these they filled with the pebbles. Jiya's
mother was making a pebble path in her rock garden,
and nowhere were the pebbles so bright as on Deer
Island.

When they were tired of the beach they went into the
pine forest behind it and looked for caves. There was one
cave that they always visited. They did not dare to go
too deep into it, for it stretched downward and under the
ocean. They knew this, and at the far end they could see
the ocean filling it like a great pool and the tides rose and
fell. The water was often phosphorescent and gleamed
as though lamps were lighted deep beneath the surface.
Once a bright fish lay dead on the rocky shore. In the
dark cave it glittered in their hands, but when they ran

with it into the sunshine, the colors were gone and it was gray. When they went back into the cave, it was bright again.

But however good a time they had on the island, Jiya looked often at the sun. Now he ran out on the beach and saw it sinking toward the west and he called to Kino.

"Come quickly—we must swim home."

Into the ocean, ruddy with sunset, they plunged together. The water was warm and soft and held them up, and they swam side by side across the broad channel. On the shore Jiya's father was waiting for them. They saw him standing, his hands shading his eyes against the bright sky, looking for them. When their two black heads bobbed out of the water he shouted to them and waded out to meet them. He gave a hand to each of them, pulling them out of the white surf.

"You have never been so late before, Jiya," he said anxiously.

"We were in the cave, Father," Jiya said.

But Jiya's father held him by the shoulders. "Do not be so late," he said, and Kino, wondering, looked at him and saw that even this strong fisherman was afraid of the anger of the sea.

He bade them good night and climbed the hill to his home and found his mother ready to set the supper on the table. The food smelled delicious—hot fragrant rice, chicken soup, brown fish.

No one was worried about Kino. His father was washing himself, pouring water over his face and head with a dipper, and his little sister, Setsu, was fetching the chopsticks.

In a few minutes they were all sitting on the clean mat around a low square table, and the parents were filling the children's bowls. Nobody spoke, for it is not polite to speak until the food is served and everybody has had something to eat.

But when the supper was over and Kino's father was drinking a little hot wine out of a very small cup, and his mother was gathering together the black lacquered wood rice bowls, Kino turned to his father.

"Father, why is Jiya afraid of the ocean?" he asked.

"The ocean is very big," Kino's father replied. "Nobody knows its beginning or its end."

"Jiya's father is afraid, too," Kino said.

"We do not understand the ocean," his father said.

"I am glad we live on the land," Kino went on. "There is nothing to be afraid of on our farm."

"But one can be afraid of the land, too," his father replied. "Do you remember the great volcano we visited last autumn?"

Kino did remember. Each autumn, after the harvest was in, the family took a holiday. They always walked, even little Setsu. They carried packs of food and bedding on their backs and in their hands tall staffs to help them up the mountainsides, and then forgetting all their daily tasks they walked to some famous spot. At home a kind neighbor tended the chickens and looked after the place. Last autumn they had gone to visit a great volcano twenty miles away. Kino had never seen it before, but he had heard of it often, and sometimes on a clear day, far to the edge of the sky, if he climbed the hill behind the farm, he could see a gray, fanlike cloud. It was the smoke from the volcano, his father had told him. Sometimes the earth trembled even under the farm. That was the volcano, too.

Yes, he could remember the great yawning mouth of the volcano. He had looked down into it and he had not liked it. Great curls of yellow and black smoke were rolling about in it, and a white stream of melted rock was crawling slowly from one corner. He had wanted to go away, and even now at night sometimes when he was warm in his soft cotton quilt in his bed on the matting floor he was glad the volcano was so far away and that there were at least three mountains between.

Now he looked at his father across the low table. "Must we always be afraid of something?" he asked.

His father looked back at him. He was a strong wiry thin man and the muscles on his arms and legs were corded with hard work. His hands were rough but he kept them clean, and he always went barefoot except for straw sandals. When he came into the house, he took even these off. No one wore shoes in the house. That was how the floors kept so clean.

"We must learn to live with danger," he now said to Kino.

"Do you mean the ocean and the volcano cannot hurt us if we are not afraid?" Kino asked.

"No," his father replied. "I did not say that. Ocean is there and volcano is there. It is true that on any day ocean may rise into storm and volcano may burst into flame. We must accept this fact, but without fear. We must say, 'Someday I shall die, and does it matter whether it is by ocean or volcano, or whether I grow old and weak?'"

"I don't want to think about such things," Kino said.

"It is right for you not to think about them," his father said. "Then do not be afraid. When you are afraid, you are thinking about them all the time. Enjoy life and do not fear death—that is the way of a good Japanese."

There was much in life to enjoy. Kino had a good time every day. In the winter he went to a school in the fishing village, and he and Jiya shared a seat. They studied reading and arithmetic and all the things that other children learn in school. But in the summer Kino had to work hard on the farm, for his father needed help. Even Setsu and the mother helped when the rice seedlings had to be planted in the flooded fields on the terraces, and they helped, too, when the grain was ripe and had to be cut

into sheaves and threshed. On those days Kino could not run down the mountainside to find Jiya. When the day was over he was so tired he fell asleep over his supper.

But there were days when Jiya also was too busy to play. Word came in from the fishermen up the coast that a school of fish was passing through the channels and then every fishing boat made haste to sail out of the bays and inlets into the main currents of the sea. Early in the morning, sometimes so early that the light was still that of the setting moon, Jiya and his father sailed their boat out across the silvery sea, to let down their nets at dawn. If they were lucky the nets came up so heavy with fish that it took all their strength to haul them up, and soon the bottom of the boat was flashing and sparkling with the wriggling fish.

Sometimes, if it were not seedtime or harvest, Kino went with Jiya and his father. It was an exciting thing to get up in the night and dress himself in his warm padded jacket tied around his waist. Even in summer the wind was cool over the sea at dawn. However early he got up, his mother always got up, too, and gave him a bowl of hot rice soup and some bean curd and hot tea before he started. Then she packed his lunch in a clean little wooden box, cold rice and fish and a bit of radish pickle.

Down the stone steps of the mountain path Kino ran straight to the narrow dock where the fishing boats bobbed up and down on the tide. Jiya and his father were already there, and in a few minutes the boat was nosing its way between the rocks out to the open sea. Sails set and filling with the wind, they sped straight into the dawn-lit sky. Kino crouched down on the floor behind the bow and felt his heart rise with joy and excitement. The shore fell far behind them and the boat took on the deep swell of the ocean. Soon they came to a whole fleet of fishing boats, and then together they flew after the schools of fish. It was like being a bird in a flock, flying into the sky. How exciting it was, too, to pull up the fish! At such times Kino felt Jiya was more lucky than he. Fish harvest was much easier than rice harvest.

"I wish my father were a fisherman," he would tell Jiya. "It is stupid to plow and plant and cut the sheaves, when I could just come out like this and reap fish from the sea."

Jiya shook his head. "But when the storms come, you wish yourself back upon the earth," he said. Then he laughed. "How would fish taste without rice? Think of eating only fish!"

"We need both farmers and fishermen," Jiya's father said.

On days when the sky was bright and the winds mild the ocean lay so calm and blue that it was hard to believe that it could be cruel and angry. Yet even Kino never quite forgot that under the warm blue surface the water

was cold and green. When the sun shone the deep water was still. But when the deep water moved and heaved and stirred, ah, then Kino was glad that his father was a farmer and not a fisherman.

And yet, one day, it was the earth that brought the big wave. Deep under the deepest part of the ocean, miles under the still green waters, fires raged in the heart of the earth. The icy cold of the water could not chill those fires. Rocks were melted and boiled under the crust of the ocean's bed, under the weight of the water, but they could not break through. At last the steam grew so strong that it forced its way through to the mouth of the volcano. That day, as he helped his father plant turnips, Kino saw the sky overcast halfway to the zenith.

"Look, Father!" he cried. "The volcano is burning again!"

His father stopped and gazed anxiously at the sky. "It looks very angry," he said. "I shall not sleep tonight."

All night while the others slept, Kino's father kept watch. When it was dark, the sky was lit with red and the earth trembled under the farmhouses. Down at the fishing village lights in the little houses showed that other fathers watched, too. For generations fathers had watched earth and sea.

Morning came, a strange fiery dawn. The sky was red and gray, and even here upon the farms cinders and ash fell from the volcano. Kino had a strange feeling, when he stepped barefoot upon the earth, that it was hot under his feet. In the house the mother had taken down everything from the walls that could fall or be broken, and her few good dishes she had packed into straw in a basket and set outside.

"Shall we have an earthquake, Father?" Kino asked as they ate breakfast.

"I cannot tell, my son," his father replied. "Earth and sea are struggling together against the fires inside the earth."

No fishing boats set sail that hot summer morning. There was no wind. The sea lay dead and calm, as though oil had been poured upon the waters. It was a purple gray, suave and beautiful, but when Kino looked at it he felt afraid.

"Why is the sea such a color?" he asked.

"Sea mirrors sky," his father replied. "Sea and earth and sky—if they work together against man, it will be dangerous indeed for us."

"Where are the gods at such a time?" Kino asked. "Will they not be mindful of us?"

"There are times when the gods leave man to take care of himself," his father replied. "They test us, to see how able we are to save ourselves."

"And if we are not able?" Kino asked.

"We must be able," his father replied. "Fear alone makes man weak. If you are afraid, your hands tremble, your feet falter, and your brain cannot tell hands and feet what to do."

No one stirred from home that day. Kino's father sat at the door, watching the sky and the oily sea, and Kino stayed near him. He did not know what Jiya was doing, but he imagined that Jiya, too, stayed by his father. So the hours passed until noon.

At noon his father pointed down the mountainside. "Look at Old Gentleman's castle," he said.

Halfway down the mountainside on the knoll where the castle stood, Kino now saw a red flag rise slowly to the top of a tall pole and hang limp against the gray sky.

"Old Gentleman is telling everyone to be ready," Kino's father went on. "Twice have I seen that flag go up, both times before you were born."

"Be ready for what?" Kino asked in a frightened voice.

"For whatever happens," Kino's father replied.

At two o'clock the sky began to grow black. The air was as hot as though a forest fire were burning, but there was no sign of such a fire. The glow of the volcano glared over the mountaintop, blood-red against the black. A deep-toned bell tolled over the hills.

"What is that bell?" Kino asked his father. "I never heard it before."

"It rang twice before you were born," his father replied. "It is the bell in the temple inside the walls of Old Gentleman's castle. He is calling the people to come up out of the village and shelter within his walls."

"Will they come?" Kino asked.

"Not all of them," his father replied. "Parents will try to make their children go, but the children will not want to leave their parents. Mothers will not want to leave fathers, and the fathers will stay by their boats. But some will want to be sure of life."

The bell kept on ringing urgently, and soon out of the village a trickling stream of people, nearly all of them children, began to climb toward the knoll.

"I wish Jiya would come," Kino said. "Do you think he

will see me if I stand on the edge of the terrace and wave my white girdle cloth?"

"Try it," his father said.

"Come with me," Kino begged.

So Kino and his father stood on the edge of the terrace and waved. Kino took off the strip of white cloth from about his waist that he wore instead of a belt, and he waved it, holding it in both hands, high above his head.

Far down the hill Jiya saw the two figures and the waving strip of white against the dark sky. He was crying as he climbed, and trying not to cry. He had not wanted to leave his father, but because he was the youngest one, his older brother and his father and mother had all told him that he must go up the mountain. "We must divide ourselves," Jiya's father said. "If the ocean yields to the fires you must live after us."

"I don't want to live alone," Jiya said.

"It is your duty to obey me, as a good Japanese son," his father told him.

Jiya had run out of the house, crying. Now when he saw Kino, he decided that he would go there instead of

to the castle, and he began to hurry up the hill to the
farm. Next to his own family he loved Kino's strong
father and kind mother. He had no sister of his own and
he thought Setsu was the prettiest girl he had ever seen.

Kino's father put out his hand to help Jiya up the stone
wall and Kino was just about to shout out his welcome
when suddenly a hurricane wind broke out of the ocean.
Kino and Jiya clung together and wrapped their arms
about the father's waist.

"Look—look—what is that?" Kino screamed.

The purple rim of the ocean seemed to lift and rise
against the clouds. A silver-green band of bright sky
appeared like a low dawn above the sea.

"May the gods save us," Kino heard his father mutter.
The castle bell began to toll again, deep and pleading.
Ah, but would the people hear it in the roaring wind?
Their houses had no windows toward the sea. Did they
know what was about to happen?

Under the deep waters of the ocean, miles down under
the cold, the earth had yielded at last to the fire. It
groaned and split open and the cold water fell into the
middle of the boiling rocks. Steam burst out and lifted
the ocean high into the sky in a big wave. It rushed
toward the shore, green and solid, frothing into white
at its edges. It rose, higher and higher, lifting up hands
and claws.

"I must tell my father!" Jiya screamed.

But Kino's father held him fast with both arms. "It
is too late," he said sternly.

And he would not let Jiya go.

In a few seconds, before their eyes the wave had grown
and come nearer and nearer, higher and higher. The air
was filled with its roar and shout. It rushed over the flat
still waters of the ocean and before Jiya could scream
again it reached the village and covered it fathoms deep
in swirling wild water, green laced with fierce white

THE METROPOLITAN MUSEUM OF ART. ROGERS FUND. 1914

foam. The wave ran up the mountainside, until the knoll where the castle stood was an island. All who were still climbing the path were swept away—black, tossing scraps in the wicked waters. The wave ran up the mountain until Kino and Jiya saw the wavelets curl at the terrace walls upon which they stood. Then with a great sucking sigh, the wave swept back again, ebbing into the ocean, dragging everything with it, trees and stones and houses. They stood, the man and the two boys, utterly silent, clinging together, facing the wave as it went away. It swept back over the village and returned slowly again to the ocean, subsiding, sinking into a great stillness.

Upon the beach where the village stood not a house remained, no wreckage of wood or fallen stone wall, no little street of shops, no docks, not a single boat. The beach was as clean of houses as if no human beings had ever lived there. All that had been was now no more.

Jiya gave a wild cry and Kino felt him slip to the

ground. He was unconscious. What he had seen was too much for him. What he knew, he could not bear. His family and his home were gone.

Kino began to cry and Kino's father did not stop him. He stooped and gathered Jiya into his arms and carried him into the house, and Kino's mother ran out of the kitchen and put down a mattress and Kino's father laid Jiya upon it.

"It is better that he is unconscious," he said gently. "Let him remain so until his own will wakes him. I will sit by him."

"I will rub his hands and feet," Kino's mother said sadly.

Kino could say nothing. He was still crying and his father let him cry for a while. Then he said to his wife:

"Heat a little rice soup for Kino and put some ginger in it. He feels cold."

Now Kino did not know until his father spoke that he did feel cold. He was shivering and he could not stop crying. Setsu came in. She had not seen the big wave, for her mother had closed the windows and drawn the curtains against the sea. But now she saw Jiya lying white-pale and still.

"Is Jiya dead?" she asked.

"No, Jiya is living," her father replied.

"Why doesn't he open his eyes?" she asked again.

"Soon he will open his eyes," the father replied.

"If Jiya is not dead, why does Kino cry?" Setsu asked.

"You are asking too many questions," her father told her. "Go back to the kitchen and help your mother."

So Setsu went back again, sucking her forefinger, and staring at Jiya and Kino as she went, and soon the mother came in with the hot rice soup and Kino drank it. He felt warm now and he could stop crying. But he was still frightened and sad.

"What will we say to Jiya when he wakes?" he asked his father.

"We will not talk," his father replied. "We will give him warm food and let him rest. We will help him to feel he still has a home."

"Here?" Kino asked.

"Yes," his father replied. "I have always wanted another son, and Jiya will be that son. As soon as he knows that this is his home, then we must help him to understand what has happened."

So they waited for Jiya to wake.

"I don't think Jiya can ever be happy again," Kino said sorrowfully.

"Yes, he will be happy someday," his father said, "for life is always stronger than death. Jiya will feel when he wakes that he can never be happy again. He will cry and cry and we must let him cry. But he cannot always cry. After a few days he will stop crying all the time. He will cry only part of the time. He will sit sad and quiet. We must allow him to be sad and we must not make him speak. But we will do our work and live as we always do. Then one day he will be hungry and he will eat something that our mother cooks, something special, and he will begin to feel better. He will not cry any more in the daytime but only at night. We must let him cry at night. But all the time his body will be renewing itself. His blood flowing in his veins, his growing bones, his mind beginning to think again, will make him live."

"He cannot forget his father and mother and his brother!" Kino exclaimed.

"He cannot and he should not forget them," Kino's father said. "Just as he lived with them alive, he will live with them dead. Someday he will accept their death as part of his life. He will weep no more. He will carry them in his memory and his thoughts. His flesh and blood are part of them. So long as he is alive, they, too, will live in him. The big wave came, but it went away. The sun

shines again, birds sing, and earth flowers. Look out over
the sea now!"

Kino looked out the open door, and he saw the ocean
sparkling and smooth. The sky was blue again, a few
clouds on the horizon were the only sign of what had
passed—except for the empty beach.

"How cruel it seems for the sky to be so clear and the
ocean so calm!" Kino said.

But his father shook his head. "No, it is wonderful that
after the storm the ocean grows calm, and the sky is blue
once more. It was not the ocean or the sky that made the
evil storm."

"Who made it?" Kino asked. He let tears roll down his
cheeks, because there was so much he could not understand. But only his father saw them and his father understood.

"Ah, no one knows who makes evil storms," his father
replied. "We only know that they come. When they come
we must live through them as bravely as we can, and
after they are gone, we must feel again how wonderful is
life. Every day of life is more valuable now than it was
before the storm."

"But Jiya's family—his father and mother and brother,
and all the other good fisherfolk, who are lost—" Kino
whispered. He could not forget the dead.

"Now we must think of Jiya," his father reminded him.
"He will open his eyes at any minute and we must be
there, you to be his brother, and I to be his father. Call
your mother, too, and little Setsu."

Now they heard something. Jiya's eyes were still
closed, but he was sobbing in his sleep. Kino ran to fetch
his mother and Setsu and they gathered about his bed,
kneeling on the floor so as to be near Jiya when he
opened his eyes.

In a few minutes, while they all watched, Jiya's eyelids
fluttered on his pale cheeks, and then he opened his eyes.

He did not know where he was. He looked from one face
to the other, as though they were strangers. Then he
looked up into the beams of the ceiling and around the
white walls of the room. He looked at the blue-flowered
quilt that covered him.

None of them said anything. They continued to kneel
about him, waiting. But Setsu could not keep quiet. She
clapped her hands and laughed. "Oh, Jiya has come
back!" she cried. "Jiya, did you have a good dream?"

The sound of her voice made him fully awake. "My
father—my mother—" he whispered.

Kino's mother took his hand. "I will be your mother
now, dear Jiya," she said.

"I will be your father," Kino's father said.

"I am your brother now, Jiya," Kino faltered.

"Oh, Jiya will live with us," Setsu said joyfully.

Then Jiya understood. He got up from the bed and
walked to the door that stood open to the sky and the sea.
He looked down the hillside to the beach where the fishing village had stood. There was only beach, and all that
remained of the twenty and more houses were a few
foundation posts and some big stones. The gentle little
waves of the ocean were playfully carrying the light
timber that had made the houses, and throwing it on
the sands and snatching it away again.

The family had followed Jiya and now they stood
about him. Kino did not know what to say, for his heart
ached for his friend-brother. Kino's mother was wiping
her eyes, and even little Setsu looked sad. She took Jiya's
hand and stroked it.

"Jiya, I will give you my pet duck," she said.

But Jiya could not speak. He kept on looking at the
ocean.

"Jiya, your rice broth is growing cold," Kino's father
said.

"We ought all to eat something," Kino's mother said.
"I have a fine chicken for dinner."

"I'm hungry!" Setsu cried.

"Come, my son," Kino's father said to Jiya.

They persuaded him gently, gathering around him, and they entered the house again. In the pleasant cosy room they all sat down about the table.

Jiya sat with the others. He was awake, he could hear the voices of Kino's family, and he knew that Kino sat beside him. But inside he still felt asleep. He was very tired, so tired that he did not want to speak. He knew that he would never see his father and mother any more, or his brother, or the neighbors and friends of the village. He tried not to think about them or to imagine their quiet bodies, floating under the swelling waves.

"Eat, Jiya," Kino whispered. "The chicken is good."

Jiya's bowl was before him, untouched. He was not hungry. But when Kino begged him he took up his porcelain spoon and drank a little of the soup. It was hot and good, and he smelled its fragrance in his nostrils. He drank more and then he took up his chopsticks and ate some of the meat and rice. His mind was still unable to think, but his body was young and strong and glad of the food.

When they had all finished, Kino said, "Shall we go up the hillside, Jiya?"

But Jiya shook his head. "I want to go to sleep again," he said.

Kino's father understood. "Sleep is good for you," he said. And he led Jiya to his bed, and when Jiya had laid himself down he covered him with the quilt and shut the sliding panels.

"Jiya is not ready yet to live," he told Kino. "We must wait."

The body began to heal first, and Kino's father, watching Jiya tenderly, knew that the body would heal the mind and the soul. "Life is stronger than death," he told Kino again and again.

But each day Jiya was still tired. He did not want to think or to remember—he only wanted to sleep. He woke to eat and then to sleep. And when Kino's mother saw this she led him to the bedroom, and Jiya sank each time into the soft mattress spread on the floor in the quiet, clean room. He fell asleep almost at once and Kino's mother covered him and went away.

All through these days Kino did not feel like playing. He worked hard beside his father in the fields. They did not talk much, and neither of them wanted to look at the sea. It was enough to look at the earth, dark and rich beneath their feet.

One evening, Kino climbed the hill behind the farm and looked toward the volcano. The heavy cloud of smoke had long gone away, and the sky was always clear now. He felt happier to know that the volcano was no longer angry, and he went down again to the house. On the threshold his father was smoking his usual evening pipe. In the house his mother was giving Setsu her evening bath.

"Is Jiya asleep already?" Kino asked his father.

"Yes, and it is a good thing for him," his father replied. "Sleep will strengthen him, and when he wakes he will be able to think and remember."

"But should he remember such sorrow?" Kino asked.

"Yes," his father replied. "Only when he dares to remember his parents will he be happy again."

They sat together, father and son, and Kino asked still another question. "Father, are we not very unfortunate people to live in Japan?"

"Why do you think so?" his father asked in reply.

"Because the volcano is behind our house and the ocean is in front, and when they work together for evil, to make the earthquake and the big wave, then we are helpless. Always many of us are lost."

"To live in the midst of danger is to know how good life is," his father replied.

"But if we are lost in the danger?" Kino asked anxiously.

"To live in the presence of death makes us brave and strong," Kino's father replied. "That is why our people never fear death. We see it too often and we do not fear it. To die a little later or a little sooner does not matter. But to live bravely, to love life, to see how beautiful the trees are and the mountains, yes, and even the sea, to enjoy work because it produces food for life—in these things we Japanese are a fortunate people. We love life because we live in danger. We do not fear death because we understand that life and death are necessary to each other."

"What is death?" Kino asked.

"Death is the great gateway," Kino's father said. His face was not at all sad. Instead, it was quiet and happy.

"The gateway—where?" Kino asked again.

Kino's father smiled. "Can you remember when you were born?"

Kino shook his head. "I was too small."

Kino's father laughed. "I remember very well. Oh, how hard you thought it was to be born! You cried and you screamed."

"Didn't I want to be born?" Kino asked. This was very interesting to him.

"You did not," his father told him smiling. "You wanted to stay just where you were in the warm, dark house of the unborn. But the time came to be born, and the gate of life opened."

"Did I know it was the gate of life?" Kino asked.

"You did not know anything about it and so you were afraid of it," his father replied. "But see how foolish you were! Here we were waiting for you, your parents, already loving you and eager to welcome you. And you have been very happy, haven't you?"

"Until the big wave came," Kino replied. "Now I am

afraid again because of the death that the big wave brought."

"You are only afraid because you don't know anything about death," his father replied. "But someday you will wonder why you were afraid, even as today you wonder why you feared to be born."

While they were talking the dusk had deepened, and now coming up the mountainside they saw a flickering light. The fireflies had come out, but this light was steadily climbing the pathway toward their house.

"I wonder who comes!" Kino exclaimed.

"A visitor," his father replied. "But who can it be?"

In a few minutes they saw the visitor was Old Gentleman, coming from the castle. His manservant carried the lantern, but Old Gentleman walked behind him very sturdily, with the help of a long staff. They heard Old Gentleman's voice in the dusk.

"Is this the house of Uchiyama the farmer?" Old Gentleman asked.

"It is," his servant replied, "and the farmer sits there at his door with his son."

At this Kino's father stood up, and so did Kino.

"Please, Honored Sir," Kino's father said, "what can I do for you?"

Old Gentleman came forward. "Do you have a lad here by the name of Jiya?"

"He lies sleeping inside my house," Kino's father said.

"I wish to see him," Old Gentleman said. Anyone could see that this old gentleman was one who expected to be obeyed. But Kino's father only smiled.

"Sir, the lad is asleep and I cannot wake him. He suffered the loss of his whole family when the big wave came. Now sleep heals him."

"I will not wake him," Old Gentleman said. "I only want to see him."

So Kino's father led Old Gentleman tiptoe into the

room where Jiya slept, and Kino went too. The servant held the light, shaded by his hand so it would not fall on Jiya's closed eyes. Old Gentleman looked down on the sleeping boy. Jiya was very beautiful even though so pale and weary. He was tall for his age and his body was strong, and his face showed intelligence as well as beauty.

Old Gentleman gazed at him and then motioned to the servant to lead him away. They went again to the dooryard and there Old Gentleman turned to Kino's father.

"It is my habit when the big wave comes to care for those who are orphaned. Three times the wave has come, and three times I have searched out the orphans and the widows and I have fed them and sheltered them. But I have heard of this boy Jiya and I wish to do more for him. If he is as good as he is handsome, I will make him my own son."

"But Jiya is ours!" Kino cried.

"Hush," his father cried. "We are only poor people. If Old Gentleman wants Jiya we cannot say we will not give him up."

"Exactly," Old Gentleman said. "I will educate him and give him fine clothes and send him to a good school and he may become a great man and an honor to our whole province and even to the nation."

"But if he lives in the castle we can't play together any more," Kino said.

"We must think of Jiya's good," Kino's father said. Then he turned to Old Gentleman. "Sir, it is very kind of you to propose this for Jiya. I had planned to take him for my own son, now that he has lost his birth parents, but I am only a poor farmer and I cannot pretend that my house is as good as yours, or that I can afford to send Jiya to a fine school. Tomorrow when he wakes, I will tell him of your kind offer. He will decide."

"Very well," Old Gentleman said. "But let him come

and tell me himself, so that I will know how he feels."

"Certainly," Kino's father replied proudly. "Jiya will speak for himself."

How unhappy Kino now was to think that Jiya might leave this house and go and live in the castle! "If Jiya goes away, I shan't have a brother," he told his father.

"You must not be so selfish, Kino," his father replied. "You must allow Jiya to make his own choice. It would be wrong to persuade him. Kino, I forbid you to speak to Jiya of this matter. When he wakes I shall speak to him myself."

When his father was so stern Kino did not dare to disobey, and so he went sadly to bed. He thought when he drew his quilt over him that he would not sleep all night, but being young and tired he slept almost at once.

Yet as soon as he woke in the morning he remembered Jiya and the choice he had to make. He got up and washed and dressed and folded his quilt and put it into the closet where it stayed during the day. His father was already out in the field, and there Kino went and found him. It was a beautiful mild morning, and a soft mist covered the ocean so that no water could be seen.

"Is Jiya awake yet?" Kino asked his father when they had exchanged morning greetings.

"No, but he will wake soon, I think," his father replied. He was weeding the cabbage bed carefully and Kino knelt down to help him.

"Must you tell him about Old Gentleman today?" Kino pleaded.

"I must tell him as soon as he wakes," his father replied. "It would not be fair to let Jiya grow used to thinking of this as his home. He must make the choice today, before he has time to put down his new roots."

"May I be there when you talk with him?" Kino asked next.

"No, my son," his father replied. "I shall talk to him alone and tell him all the benefits that a rich man like Old Gentleman can give him and how little we who are poor can give him."

Kino could not keep from wanting to cry. He thought his father was very hard. "But Jiya will certainly want to go away!" he sobbed.

"Then he must go," his father said.

They went into the house to have breakfast, but Kino could scarcely eat. After breakfast he went back to the field, for he did not want to play. His father stayed in the house, and they could hear Jiya getting up.

For a long time Kino stayed in the field working alone. The warm tears dropped from his eyes upon the earth, but he worked on, determined not to go to the house until he was called. Then when the sun was nearing the zenith, he heard his father's voice. He got up at once and walked along the path between the terraces until he reached the doorway. There his father stood with Jiya. Jiya's face was still pale and his eyes were red. He had been crying today, although until now he had not cried at all.

When he looked at Kino his tears began to flow again.

"Jiya, you must not mind it that you cry easily," Kino's father said kindly. "Until now you could not cry because you were not fully alive. You had been hurt too much. But today you are beginning to live, and so your tears flow. It is good for you. Let your tears come and do not stop them."

Then he turned to Kino. "I have told Jiya that he must not decide until he has seen the inside of the castle. I want him to see all that Old Gentleman can give him for a home. Jiya, you know how our house is—these four rooms and the kitchen, this little farm, upon which we have to work so hard for our food. We have only what our hands can earn for us."

Kino's father held out his two hard, work-worn hands. Then he went on, "Kino, you are to go with Jiya, and when you see the castle you must persuade him to stay there, for his own sake."

Kino heard this and felt the task laid upon him was very hard. But he only said, "I will go and wash myself, Father, and put on my good clothes."

"No," his father said. "Go as you are—you are a farmer's son."

So the two boys went down the mountainside, and avoiding the empty beach, they went to the castle. The gate was open and the garden was most beautiful. A gardener was sweeping the green moss.

When he saw them he came over to them. "What do you want?" he asked.

"My father sent us to see the honored Old Gentleman," Kino faltered.

"Are you the Uchiyama boy?" the gardener asked.

"Yes," Kino replied, "and this is Jiya, whom Old Gentleman wants to come and live here."

"Follow me, if you please," the gardener said. He bowed to Jiya and made his voice polite.

The two boys followed him along a wide, pebbled path. Over their heads the ancient pines leaned their crooked branches. In the distance beyond the forest the sun poured down upon a flower garden and a pool with a waterfall.

"How beautiful it is!" Kino whispered sadly.

Jiya did not answer. He walked along, his head held high. When they reached the house they took off their shoes and followed the gardener through a great door. Inside this the gardener paused, and a manservant came forward and asked what they wanted. The gardener whispered and the manservant nodded. "Follow me," he said to the boys.

So they followed him through wide passageways. The walls were of fine polished wood, unpainted, but smooth and silvery. Under their feet, fine woven, padded mats were softer than the moss beneath the trees. On both sides of this passageway panels slid back to show beautiful rooms, and in each room were a vase of flowers, an exquisite scroll, a few pieces of dark polished furniture. Neither Jiya nor Kino had ever seen such a house. Kino was speechless. How could he hope now that Jiya would not want to stay in the castle?

Then far in the distance they saw Old Gentleman sitting beside a small table. The table was set in front of the open sliding panels that looked into the garden, and Old Gentleman was writing. He held a brush upright in his right hand and he was carefully painting letters on a scroll, his silver-rimmed spectacles sliding down his nose.

When the two boys came near he looked up and took

off his spectacles and laid down his brush. "Would you like to know what I have been writing?" he asked.

Neither Kino nor Jiya could answer. The great house, the silence, the beauty, all of this fell into place as the background for Old Gentleman himself. He was tall and thin, and his hair and beard were white. His face and hands were beautiful. The bones were delicate and the skin was smooth and brown. He looked as proud as a king, but his dark eyes were wise as an old scholar's eyes are wise.

"It is not my own poem," he said. "It is the saying of a man of India, but I like it so much that I have painted it on this scroll to hang there in the alcove where I can see it every day." He took up the scroll and read these words: *"The Children of God are very dear, but very queer— Very nice, but very narrow."*

He looked at the boys. "What do you think of it?" he said.

They looked at one another. "We do not understand it, sir," Jiya said at last. Since he was a little older than Kino, he felt he should speak.

Old Gentleman shook his head and laughed softly. "Ah, we are all the children of God," he said. Then he put on his spectacles and looked hard at Jiya. "Well?" he said. "Will you be my son?"

Jiya turned very red. He had not expected to have the question put to him so suddenly and so directly.

Old Gentleman saw he found it hard to speak. "Say yes or no," he told Jiya. "Those are not hard words to say."

"I will say,—*no!*" Jiya said. Then he felt this was harsh. "I thank you but I have a home—on the farm," he added.

Ah, how Kino felt when he heard these words! He forgot entirely about the big wave and all the sorrow it had brought, and for a moment he was filled with pure joy. Then he remembered the small farmhouse, the four little rooms and the old kitchen.

"Jiya," he said solemnly, "remember how poor we are."

Old Gentleman was smiling a half-sad little smile. "They are certainly very poor," he said to Jiya. "And here, you know, you would have everything. You can even invite this farm boy to come and play sometimes, if you like. And I am quite willing for you to give the family some money. It would be suitable, as my son, for you to help the poor."

"Where are the others who were saved from the big wave?" Jiya asked suddenly.

"Some wanted to go away, and the ones who wanted to stay are out in the back yard with my servants," Old Gentleman replied.

"Why do you not invite them to come into this big house and be your sons and daughters?" Jiya asked.

"Because I don't want them for my sons and daughters," Old Gentleman replied rather crossly. "You are a bright, handsome boy, and they told me you were the best boy in the village."

Jiya looked about him. Then he shook his head again. "I am no better than the others," he said. "My father was a fisherman."

Old Gentleman took up his spectacles and his brush again. "Very well," he said. "I will do without a son."

The manservant motioned to them and they followed, and soon they were out in the garden again.

"How foolish you are!" the manservant said to Jiya. "Our Old Gentleman is very kind indeed. You would have everything here."

"Not everything," Jiya replied.

They went out of the gate and across the hillside again back to the farmhouse. Setsu was outside and she came running to meet them, the sleeves of her bright kimono flying behind her and her feet clattering in wooden sandals.

"Jiya has come back home!" she cried. "Jiya—Jiya—"

And Jiya, seeing her happy little face, opened his arms

and gave her a great hug. For the first time he felt comfort creep into his sad heart, and this comfort came from
Setsu, who was like life itself.

Their noonday meal was ready and Kino's father came
in from the fields, and when he had washed they all sat
down to eat.

"How happy you have made us!" he told Jiya.

"Happy indeed," Kino's mother said.

"Now I have my brother," Kino said.

Jiya only smiled. Happiness began to live in him
secretly, hidden inside him, in ways he did not understand or know. The good food warmed him and his body
welcomed it. Around him the love of the four people who
received him glowed like a warm and welcoming fire
upon the hearth.

Time passed. Jiya grew up in the farmhouse to be a
tall young man, and Kino grew at his side, solid and
strong, but never as tall as Jiya. Setsu grew, too, from
a mischievous, laughing little girl into a gay, willful,
pretty girl. But time, however long, was split in two
parts by the big wave. People spoke of "the time before"
and "the time after" the big wave. The big wave had
changed everyone's life.

For years no one returned to live on the empty beach.
The tides rose and fell, sweeping the sands clean every
day. Storms came and went, but there was never again
such a wave as the big one. Then people began to think
that perhaps there would never again be such a big
wave. The few fishermen who had listened to the tolling
bell from the castle and had been saved with their wives
and children had gone to other shores to fish, and they
had made new fishing boats.

But as time passed after the big wave, they began to
tell themselves that there was no beach quite so good as
the old one. There, they said, the water was deep and

great fish came close to the shore in schools. They did not need to go far out to sea to seek the booty. The channels between the islands were rich.

Now Kino and Jiya had not often gone to the beach again, either. Once or twice they had walked along the place where the street had been, and Jiya had searched for some keepsake from his home that the sea might have washed back to the shore. But nothing was ever found. The surf was too violent above deep waters, and even bodies had not returned. So the two boys, now young men, did not visit the deserted beach very often. When they went to swim in the sea, they walked across the farm and over another fold of the hill.

But Kino saw that Jiya always looked out of the door every morning and he looked at the empty beach, searching with his eyes as though something might one day come back. One day he did see something. Kino was at the door putting on his shoes and he heard Jiya cry out in a loud voice, "Kino, come here!" Quickly Kino went and Jiya pointed down the hillside. "Look—is someone building a house on the beach?"

Kino looked and saw that indeed it was so. Two men were pounding posts into the sand, and a woman and a child stood near, watching. "Can it be that they will build again on the beach?" he exclaimed.

But they could not rest with watching. They ran down the hill to the beach and went to the two men. "Are you building a house?" Jiya cried.

The men paused and the elder one nodded. "Our father used to live here and we with him. During these years we have lived in the outhouses of the castle and we have fished from other shores. Now we are tired of having no homes of our own. Besides, this is still the best of all beaches for fishing."

"But what if the big wave comes back?" Kino asked.

The men shrugged their shoulders. "There was a big wave in our great-grandfather's time. All the houses were swept away, but our grandfather came back. In our father's time the big wave came again, but now we come back."

"What of your children?" Kino asked anxiously.

"The big wave may never come back," the men said. And they began to pound the post into the sand again.

All this time Jiya had not said another word. He stood watching the work, his face musing and strange. The big wave and the sorrow it had brought had changed him forever. Never again would he laugh easily or talk carelessly. He had learned to live with his parents and his brother dead, as Kino's father had said he would, and he did not weep. He thought of them every day and he did not feel they were far from him or he from them. Their faces, their voices, the way his father talked and looked, his mother's smile, his brother's laughter, all were with him still and would be forever. But since the big wave he had been no longer a child. In school he had earnestly learned all that he could, and now he worked hard on the farm. He valued deeply everything that was good. Since the big wave had been so cruel, he could not bear cruelty, and he grew into the kindest and most gentle man that Kino had ever seen. Jiya never spoke of his loneliness. He did not want anyone to be sad because of his sadness. When he laughed at some trick of Setsu's, or when she teased him, his laughter was wonderful to hear because it was so whole and real.

Now as he stood watching the new house being made on the beach, he felt a strong delight. Could it be true that people would gather once more on this beach to make a village? Was it right that it be so?

At this moment there was a commotion on the hillside. They looked up and saw it was Old Gentleman, coming slowly down the rocky path. He was very old indeed now, and he walked with difficulty. Two menservants supported him.

The elder builder threw down his stone mallet. "Here comes our Old Gentleman," he told the others. "He is very angry or he wouldn't have left the castle."

Anyone could see that Old Gentleman was angry. He grasped his long staff, and when he came near them he pulled his beard and moved his eyebrows. His body was as thin as a bamboo, and with the wind blowing his white hair and long white beard, he looked like an ancient god out of the temple.

"You foolish children!" he cried in his high old voice. "You have left the safety of my walls and come back to this dangerous shore to make your home, as your fathers did before you. The big wave will come back and sweep you into the ocean again!"

"It may not come, Ancient Sir," the elder builder said mildly.

"It will come!" Old Gentleman insisted. "I have spent my whole life in trying to save foolish people from the big wave. But you will not be saved."

Suddenly Jiya spoke. "This is our home. Dangerous as it is, threatened by the volcano and by the sea, it is here we were born."

Old Gentleman looked at him. "Don't I know you?" he asked.

"Sir, I was once in your castle," Jiya replied.

Old Gentleman nodded. "Now I remember you. I wanted you for my son. Ah, you made a great mistake, young man! You could have lived in my castle safely forever and your children would have been safe there, too. The big wave never reaches me."

Jiya shook his head. "Your castle is not safe either," he told Old Gentleman. "If the earth shakes hard enough, your castle will crumble, too. There is no refuge for us who live on these islands. We are brave because we must be."

"Ha," the builders said, "you are right," and they went back to pounding the foundation posts.

Old Gentleman rolled his eyes a few times. "Don't ask me to save you next time the big wave comes," he told everybody.

"But you will save us," Jiya said gently, "because you are so good."

Old Gentleman shook his head at this and then smiled. "What a pity you would not be my son," he said and then he went back to the castle and shut the gates.

As for Kino and Jiya, they returned to the farmhouse, but the whole family could see that Jiya was restless from that day on. They had supposed that he would be a farmer, for he had learned everything about the land,

and Kino's father trusted him with much. But Jiya fell into a mood of forgetfulness, and one day Kino's father spoke to him when they were working in the fields.

"I know that you are too good a son to be forgetful on purpose," he said. "Tell us what is on your mind."

"I want a boat," Jiya said. "I want to go back to fishing."

Kino's father was shaping a furrow. "Life is stronger than death," he said quietly.

From that day on the family knew that someday Jiya would go back to the sea, and that he would build himself a house on the beach. One after another now seven houses had risen, the frail wooden houses of fisherfolk that the big wave could lift like toys and crush and throw away. But they sheltered families, men and women and children. And again they were built with no windows toward the sea. Each family had built on the bit of land that had belonged to it before the big wave came, and at the end was left a bare piece. It belonged to Jiya now, for it had belonged once to his father.

"When I have a boat, then I shall build my own house there," Jiya said one night to the farm family.

"I shall pay you wages from this day," Kino's father said. "You have become a man."

From that day Jiya saved his wages until he had enough to buy a boat. It was a fine boat, slender and strong, of seasoned wood, and the sails were new. The day he got it he and Kino sailed it far into the channel, and Jiya had not been so happy since before the big wave. Kino could not forget the deep still cold of the bottomless waters upon which they floated. But Jiya thought only of the joy of having a boat of his own, and Kino did not want to spoil his joy by any hint of fear.

"I knew all the time that I had to come back to the sea," he told Kino.

Then to Kino's surprise Jiya grew very red. "Do you think Setsu would be afraid to live on the beach?" he asked Kino.

Kino was surprised. "Why should Setsu live on the beach?" he asked.

Jiya grew redder still, but he held his head high. "Because that is where I shall build my home," he said firmly. "And I want Setsu to be my wife."

It was such astonishing news that Kino did not know what to say. Setsu was his little sister, and he could not believe that she was old enough to be anybody's wife. Nor, to tell the truth, could he imagine anybody wanting her for his wife. She was careless and teasing and mischievous and she still delighted to hide his things so that he could not find them.

"You would be very foolish to marry Setsu," he now told Jiya.

"I don't agree with you," Jiya said, smiling.

"But why do you want her?" Kino urged.

"Because she makes me laugh," Jiya said. "It is she who made me forget the big wave. For me—she is life."

"But she is not a good cook," Kino said. "Think how she burns the rice because she runs outside to look at something!"

"I don't mind burned rice," Jiya said, "and I will run out with her to see what she sees."

Kino said no more, but he kept looking at his friend. Jiya, wanting to build a house, to marry Setsu! He could not believe it.

When they got home he went to his father. "Do you know that Jiya wants to marry Setsu?" he asked.

His father was looking over his seeds, for it was springtime again. "I have seen some looks pass between them," he said, smiling.

"But Jiya is too good for Setsu," Kino said.

"Setsu is very pretty," his father said.

Kino was surprised. "With that silly nose she has?"

"I believe that Jiya admires her nose," his father said calmly.

"I don't understand that," Kino replied. "Besides, she

will hide his things and tease him and make him miserable."

"What makes you miserable will make him happy," his father said.

"I don't understand that, either," Kino said soberly.

"Someday you will understand," his father said, laughing. "Do you remember that I told you life is stronger than death? Jiya is ready to live."

On the day in the early summer that Jiya and Setsu were married, Kino still did not understand, for up to the very last day Setsu was naughty and mischievous, and indeed on the day of her own wedding she hid his hairbrush under his bed. "You are too silly to be married," he told her when he found it. "I feel sorry for Jiya."

Her big brown eyes laughed at him and she stuck out her small red tongue at him. "I will always be nice to Jiya," she said.

But when the wedding was over and the family took the newly married pair down the hill to the new house on the beach, Kino began to feel sad. The farmhouse would be very quiet without Setsu and he would miss her. Every day he would come to see Jiya and many times he would go fishing with him. But Setsu would not be in the farmhouse kitchen, in the rooms, or in the garden. He would miss even her teasing. He grew very grave indeed. What if the big wave came again?

There in the pretty little new house he turned to Jiya. "Jiya, what if the big wave comes again?" he asked.

"I have prepared for that," Jiya said. He led them through the little house to the room that faced the sea, the one big room in the house, where at night they would rest and where in the day they would eat and work.

All the family stood there, and as they watched, Jiya pushed back a panel in the wall. Before their eyes was the ocean, swelling and stirring under the evening wind. The sun was sinking into the water, in clouds of red and gold. They gazed out across the deep waters in silence.

"I have opened my house to the ocean," Jiya said. "If ever the big wave comes back, I shall be ready. I face it. I am not afraid."

"You are strong and brave," Kino's father said.

And they went back to the farm, and left Jiya and Setsu to make a new life in the new home on the old beach.

For The Big Wave, Pearl Buck received in 1949 the Children's Book Award of the Child Study Association of America. If you enjoyed this story you will want to read some of Pearl Buck's other books about children of other lands, especially The Chinese Children Next Door and The Water-Buffalo Children, both published by the John Day Company.

The Son of the Gondolier

BY ELSA STEINMANN

Illustrations by Johannes Grüger

> Twelve-year-old Gabriello wanted to be a gondolier, like his father. Not even his father's tragic death in an accident on Venice's Grand Canal could change that. But now, as the man of the house, he must earn enough to help support his mother and sisters. So he hires out as a helper to Uncle Beppe, a fisherman, until he becomes old enough to qualify as a gondolier's helper.

COLD ribbons of mist unrolled from the rio. The stone slabs of the little square shone with wetness, and the houses across the water loomed up like phantoms as Gabriello closed the door behind him in the pre-dawn of the following morning. He stretched and sniffed the air. If only there were no mist; in a mist Uncle Beppe would not venture far out into the lagoon. As he stamped off in his father's boots, he drew the sou'wester—which like the slicker was at least two sizes too big for him—down over his face. Here and there in the houses which towered above the darkness of the square, a dim light was burning. The entire square was deserted, except for the farther end, where a strapping fellow was washing himself at the fountain. As Gabriello approached, he straightened up, rubbed his face dry with his sleeve, and greeted him: "Hey, Gabriello! Where are you off to so early? You look neat in your slicker."

"Hi, Cesare!" Gabriello replied, clumping along toward the fountain. "I'm going fishing on the lagoon. With Uncle Beppe. He hired me as helper yesterday."

"Well, what do you know! You sure are in luck." Cesare joined Gabriello and walked beside him across the square, then along the narrow rio where, in quick succession, three little bridges led directly to the doors of fine red houses on the opposite bank.

"Is that slicker your father's?" Cesare asked, studying Gabriello's appearance with what seemed to be a more than casual interest.

"Yes. The boots too. The outfit's a little too big for me, but it keeps me warm."

"The slicker would just fit me. I am at least as tall as your father was. A pity I have nothing to swap for it. I've been saving up for a slicker for ever so long, but the cheapest are five thousand lire."

"Eight thousand!" Gabriello amended. "If you look in the stores, of course. But I've heard that you can pick up slickers in the pawnshop quite cheap. Silvio got his there."

"Say, that is an idea." Cesare slapped Gabriello gratefully on the shoulders. "Here I am shivering my head off day after day, and maybe I can buy the stuff for a song at the pawnshop. . . . Come along, you deserve a treat for thinking of that." Cesare drew Gabriello toward the nearest coffee bar. "You haven't had anything to warm you up yet, I bet."

"No, it was too early for breakfast. Besides, I thought I'd have coffee with Uncle Beppe before we go out on the lagoon."

"Well, you can always have a second." Even at this early hour, the small coffee bar was open and had a number of fishermen and truck farmers from the islands in the lagoon standing at its counter.

"But I have no money. . . ." Gabriello hung back at the door.

"No nonsense, come along. That tip about the pawn-shop is worth a cup of coffee. Besides, I had a good day yesterday."

"Two coffees," he called to the barman. He reached for a basket of fresh crescent-shaped rolls and pushed it toward Gabriello. "Here, dig in."

"What a good fellow Cesare is," Gabriello thought, looking sideways along the bar at his friend. Cesare was a head taller than the sturdiest of the fishermen who stood beside him at the counter. And how manfully he sipped his coffee and cast a shrewd glance over all the men in the place. Did Cesare ever feel unsure of himself, not knowing whether he was acting properly? Gabriello felt terribly young as this question shot into his mind. He wished he had not thought of it. He couldn't afford to feel uncertain; he had Mother to take care of.

"Well, let's go. We can walk together as far as the vegetable market. Your uncle lives somewhere around there, doesn't he?"

"Yes, near the Campo delle Beccarie. Just back of the bridge. I hope he is up already, so that we can start right out."

"You seem to look forward to this fishing business." Cesare laughed, and gazed down at his young friend with just a touch of good-natured mockery.

"And how! Why, I'll be on the water all day again, just the way it used to be with Father. Imagine, old Zanze has tried to put a flea in Mother's ear that I ought to go to work in a glass factory on Murano."

"Nonsense! You don't belong in any glass factory!" Cesare spat emphatically from the Rialto Bridge, which they had just climbed, down into the Grand Canal.

Abruptly he paused, eyed Gabriello curiously, and asked: "What have you done with your father's fine new gondola? People in the Arsenal were saying it's a total wreck."

"Well, not exactly. But it's badly rammed, right in the middle. Ernesto has it in his gondola shed. Yesterday I thought perhaps I would ask Trevisan, the carpenter, for his big transport barge, so that the gondola can be taken to the San Trovaso yard. Not for repair yet, of course. That would cost too much. But if they kept it at the yard, it would not rot to pieces. Storing it shouldn't cost a fortune."

"Hm. Listen, Gabriello, don't take the gondola to San Trovaso. Everything is high-class and expensive there. Take it to the yard on the Rio dei Mendicanti. They are much cheaper. Besides, I know a fellow there. I'll put in a word for you with him, so that they'll store your gondola on reasonable terms. . . . Where do you think you're going!" Cesare suddenly bellowed. He rubbed his head and gave a vigorous poke at a young man walking along with a large box full of lobsters which he tried to balance over the heads of the passers-by. "My head isn't made of wood." He turned to Gabriello again. "From San Pietro's Island, of course. That's the kind of clumsy idiot they have over there. Well, here we part. So long. Let me know when you're ready to take the gondola to the yard." Cesare gave Gabriello a comradely pat on the back and with his long arms thrust his way through the farmers from the islands, the fishermen and the porters who were clogging the *Erberia,* the city's wholesale market. Dozens of vegetable, fruit and fish barges rocked side by side and one behind the other in the dark canal, while their owners, shivering in the cold morning air, waited for their turn to unload.

Gabriello watched Cesare until he had reached the barges. 'It was a break for me, running into him on the square,' he thought. 'He treated me just as though I were sixteen. It's funny, he hardly ever used to notice me.'

As Gabriello trudged on toward the Campo delle Beccarie, his thoughts lingered on Cesare. Cesare was the strongest of all the boys around Arsenal Square. The others admired and feared him. His father had not returned from the war; no one knew what had become of him. After the war, Cesare's mother had died also. From grief, people said. Since then Cesare had been living with his grandmother, a sour old woman who had scarcely spoken a word for years. Their house was one of the most decrepit in the neighborhood. Cesare had been fending for himself for ever so long; he worked at the vegetable market, helping to unload boxes and crates. People said he was good to his grandmother and provided for her.

Meanwhile Gabriello had reached the Beccarie Bridge. He passed a marketwoman who was setting out her boxes of vegetables and apples and stringing up a few braids of garlic under a wretched piece of ancient canvas. The barbershop on the left was still closed; an old woman was hobbling toward it, bowed down by the weight of two straw shopping bags full of coal. The sign of a tavern called "The Good Friend" squeaked and swayed in the morning breeze. At the top of the narrow alley lay a heap of garbage deposited there for the city garbage scow—it would be right in front of Uncle Beppe's door. All the other houses on the street had put out their standard tall metal garbage cans.

Light glimmered through the cracks in the battered front door. Gabriello pounded on the door with his boots, and shouted: "Hey, Uncle, open up. It's me, Gabriello!"

"So early?" a voice inside replied. Then his uncle coughed, cleared his throat, shuffled to the door, and opened it. "Why, I'll be!" he exclaimed, blinking at Gabriello out of red-rimmed eyes. "You look spanking. I

certainly have got myself a fine boy. Come, the coffee is
hot, and there's some bread left. Or have you had your
breakfast already?"

"Yes, but I'll gladly have a bit more." Gabriello entered and looked around the dark, cellar-like room whose
two barred windows opened on the Rio delle Beccarie.
What a hole! A riddled mattress with a few rags on it

served as bed. In the middle of the room was a rusty iron table, like those that stood outside cheap cafés. On this was a wine bottle serving as a holder for a burning candle; in front of it, two rusted garden chairs. In one corner was a worm-eaten chest. Along the walls hung old clothes, various-sized pieces of burlap, fishing lines, two types of net. In a nook lay two old oars, a wooden tub with a lid for storing shellfish, a few fishbaskets and buckets, and a charcoal stove which Uncle usually took with him in the boat. And the boxes on the floor—boxes of all sizes, thrown here, there and everywhere, and among them straw-covered bottles, pots and pans, a spirit stove, Uncle's ancient scales, a hammer, tongs, and other tools—an incredible confusion of stuff and junk. The stone flagstones of the floor were greasy with old filth.

'Well, this is a good beginning,' Gabriello thought. 'I hope he hasn't let the boat go to wrack and ruin this way. If only it isn't leaky.' He looked around for a hook to hang his coat on, while Uncle reached for the pot on top of the spirit stove and poured its black brew into two cups. From one of the boxes he produced a loaf of bread, a knife, and a tin can filled with sugar.

"Would you like a little canned milk in your coffee?" Uncle Beppe asked. He pushed a half-rusted can of evaporated milk toward Gabriello, who had sat down opposite him in the garden chair. "You can even have wine if you wish. I'm well stocked. How do you like my den? Not bad, eh? The things here are all stuff I picked up and fixed to suit me." Uncle Beppe's eyes roved with obvious satisfaction over the chaos in the room. Then he moved his chair a little closer to Gabriello's and asked eagerly: "Tell me, what's the weather like? Cloudy? Foggy? Drizzly? Is the sky high or low? South wind?"

"I don't know." Gabriello stirred the brew in his cup with a tin spoon. "When I left the house it was dark, cold and damp. No south wind anyway. As for the sky—I really didn't notice."

"That is a mistake, my son, a grave mistake. In the future you must watch the sky closely. Weather is all-important to a fisherman. He depends on the weather. That is why the first thing a fisherman does in the morning is bend his head back, look at the sky and sniff like a bloodhound. To be a proper fisherman you have to be plenty sharp where weather's concerned. You have to be able to predict it at least a day in advance. Come on, let's go outside and sniff." Uncle Beppe drew Gabriello out into the long open courtyard, and looked up at the sky between the wash hanging on lines all across the yard. "Cirrus clouds, light breeze. . .fish smell from the fish market weak. . . . We'll have decent weather, my boy. Let's get started. Fetch the oars, the shellfish net and the dragnet. . . ."

"But we aren't going to take only the shellfish net and the dragnet, are we?" Gabriello objected. "We may as well take the lines also."

"Greenhorn! Here you are going out fishing for the first time and you start making suggestions to a seasoned old fisherman!" Uncle burst into bleating laughter. But then he said: "Well, if it gives you pleasure, take the lines too."

Gabriello handed his uncle the tackle, baskets and burlap, and Uncle Beppe stowed them away in the dory.

"Bring the charcoal stove, too," Uncle Beppe ordered. "If the weather stays good, we'll fry ourselves some fish out there. Put the bread into the bag, and tuck the bottle of wine under your arm. Meanwhile I'll fasten the shellfish tub to the dory."

"Aren't you going to wear your slicker, Uncle?" Gabriello asked. "You yourself said yesterday that it is cold on the lagoon in the morning."

"For a greenhorn like you, yes. An old sea-lion like me

goes out without a slicker in weather like this. A couple
of shirts, a wadded jacket over them and a pair of boots—
that does me." Uncle Beppe limped back to the door and
locked it with a rusty padlock. Then he said: "So, my boy,
now we can start. You'd better row up the rio by yourself.
Rowing is one thing you know how to do, or you wouldn't
be Ludovico's son. . . ."

Before he could say another word Gabriello had
leaped back to the rear, taken the long oar in his hand,
fitted it into the oarlock, and leaned forward. And now
the dory, under the regular strokes of his oar, moved forward as lightly as a gondola.

"Aha, I call that rowing. *Bene!*" Uncle Beppe's eyes
shone with unconcealed admiration.

"Hey there, Signor Beppe, you've got yourself a smart
oarsman!" Over the heads of the two a window had flown
open, and out poked a head bristling with curlers: the
proprietress of The Good Friend Restaurant.

"Yes, indeed, Signora Amalia! Old Beppe Padoan can
look forward to better days now. This is my late nephew
Ludovico's boy. He's taken pity on his lonely old uncle
and is going to help him fish from now on."

Signora Amalia smiled down at Gabriello, who had
politely rowed the dory under her window. "Well, if
you're both going out on the lagoon, bring me back
around twenty pounds of mussels, before eleven, if possible. You should easily catch that much in a few hours.
And any crabs you pick up with them I can use, too. I'm
going to be having twenty-five for lunch this noon. If I
buy the mussels from you, I need not go to the fish market, and I can be sure of getting fresh goods."

"It's a deal. Twenty pounds of mussels will be delivered
at eleven sharp to The Good Friend Restaurant. And a
few pounds of crabs also. But what will you pay for a
pound of mussels, Signora Amalia?"

"Oh, I guess ninety lire is the market price."

"Ninety lire? Signora Amalia, overnight your memory seems to have gone back on you! Ninety lire for a pound of mussels when mussels are selling at the fish market for between a hundred and ten and a hundred and twenty lire per pound. If you insist upon this price, Signora Amalia, to my great regret I must refuse your order."

"Oh, come now, since when have mussels been selling at a hundred and twenty lire at the fish market? But to meet you halfway, let us say one hundred lire even. That is a good price for a wholesale purchase."

"One hundred lire? For perfectly fresh mussels! Do you hear that, Gabriello? One hundred lire for absolutely fresh mussels? I can scarcely believe my ears."

"Well, all right, I'll give you a hundred and five. But not a centesimo more. That is my top offer, Signor Beppe."

"Well, Signora Amalia, it certainly is not a generous price. But since it is for you, and since we are neighbors after all. . . . At eleven sharp the twenty pounds of mussels will be here. Goodbye for now, and a pleasant morning to you."

"And don't forget the crabs," Signora Amalia called after them.

"The crabs will cost you a hundred and fifty lire!" Uncle Beppe shouted back. But they were already out of earshot.

"Did you see mussels at the fish market for one hundred and twenty lire yesterday?" Gabriello asked. "All I saw were at a hundred, and a single basket at a hundred and ten."

"Oh, Gabriello, what a greenhorn you are in business." Uncle Beppe bleated his high-pitched laugh. "Naturally no one paid a hundred and twenty lire for mussels, not yesterday or the day before or the day before that. But you always have to use your imagination a little in business dealings, my boy. Keep that in mind and never forget it. You can always go lower than your first price, but never higher. That is why you must set the price you ask first a good bit higher than the one you hope to receive. Remember that once and for all, or you will never succeed in business.... But look sharp now, we're in the Grand Canal." Uncle Beppe stood up, seized the second oar, fitted it into the oarlock, and croaked in his hoarse, carrying voice: "Staaa."

"Why, Uncle, you're still pretty good at rowing yourself!" Gabriello exclaimed with admiration.

"Mouth shut and eyes open, Gabriello. In all this traffic we can't afford to talk. Watch that motorboat! Keep left! And look over there, at that speeding hellcat. Going much too fast, as usual, and not a police boat in sight. The cops are never around where they're needed." Uncle Beppe spat angrily into the canal and rowed grimly on past vegetable, fish and coal barges, motorboats, and a gondola crowded with sightseers visiting the market. Through all the traffic he steered up the canal toward the Rio di San Felice.

When they reached the rio, he lifted the oar out of the oarlock, sat down on the thwart and grunted to Gabriello: "You can manage it up the rio by yourself."

Gabriello glanced at the two-story houses crowned with curious chimney pots and at the pretty little bridges which led from one narrow alley to the next. It was a lovely, quiet district. On the water of the rio floated golden autumn leaves from a tree in an inner courtyard, whose branches hung over the wall. Except for a white-haired fisherwoman who was rowing toward the Grand Canal in a dory filled with boxes of lagoon fish and white cuttlefish, the entire rio was deserted. Emerging into the lagoon, they heard again the tee-deeee and the chug of the ships which ran between the Fondamente Nuove, San Michele and Murano. But on the whole there was little traffic in the lagoon, and on the Laguna Morta—the

stagnant lagoon—to the left of San Michele, they were the only fishermen.

"So, here we are," Uncle Beppe said. "Now lift your oar for a moment." Uncle Beppe let the shellfish net slide into the shallow water of the lagoon. This net was shaped like a sack and attached to a rectangular frame of iron. It was meant to be dragged along behind the dory at the end of a long rope fastened to the stern.

Now Uncle Beppe returned to the bow of the dory, set the second oar into the oarlock, and called to Gabriello: "And now let's go, my boy, my pet. *Forza, forza!*"

It was hard work. The water in the Laguna Morta was barely a foot and a half deep, and the net had already caught on something at the bottom. They had to strain every muscle to make the dory move forward at all. "Wait a moment," Gabriello called out to his uncle. "I must take off this coat. I'm beginning to broil."

"Sure enough, sure enough, my boy, I told you so. I've been wondering how long you could stand rowing in that outfit. But now let's go on. I'll be sadly mistaken if the net isn't half full already. Let's take a look."

Uncle Beppe laid his oar aside, and thrust two wooden poles through a pair of rings on the outside of the dory, anchoring it firmly in the sand. Then he spread out a piece of burlap, grasped the rope of the net, and drew it slowly, carefully, toward himself. When the iron frame of the net came in sight, the old man chortled gleefully.

"Look, look at that! What a catch! You're bringing me luck, my boy. It's a long while since I've brought a catch like this out of the lagoon. On to the burlap with them, out with the poles, and let's keep going. We seem to have run into a fine shellfish bank here."

As Gabriello rowed with all his strength, he glanced again and again at the tumbled confusion of mussels and crabs on the bottom of the dory. The brown crabs, active on their thin legs, were working their way out from among the mussels. They would have to go into a fish pail, or they would be escaping over the side of the dory. There, one was already climbing the wall. "Hey, you, down with you!" Gabriello shouted, knocking the little crab down with the oar.

"What is all the fuss about back there?" Uncle Beppe called.

"One of the crabs was trying to escape. We'd better put those fellows in a safe place as soon as we can."

"We can't bother about that until we have enough mussels. They are what count now. One crab more or less doesn't matter.... You mustn't bother about such trifles —that isn't the way for a real fisherman."

Three times they drew in the shellfish net. By then the dory was so full of mussels and crabs that Uncle Beppe said: "There, that's enough. This will make a whole basketful for beautiful Amalia. Now it's high time for a good drink from the bottle." Uncle Beppe pulled the bottle toward him, uncorked it, and drank greedily. "Ah, that's good," he sighed deeply. He wiped his hand over the mouth of the bottle and held it out to Gabriello.

"No, thank you, Uncle. I am terribly thirsty, but I'm not used to wine...."

"Well, how about our making a little fire and frying the few fish that wandered into the net." Uncle Beppe plunged his hands into the heap of clams and crabs and produced several small pink fish. Then he blinked up at the sun, which had just worked its way out of the morning mist and the filmy clouds, and observed: "I don't think it's more than half past nine yet. We can afford a little rest before we return."

Uncle Beppe cleaned and salted the fish. Running his boot along the bottom of the boat, he shoved the heap of mussels and crabs toward the stern of the dory. Then he stuffed chips of wood and charcoal into the stove, and lit the fire. When it was blazing merrily, he placed the grill over the flame and spread the fish on the grill. Soon the air was filled with such a luscious odor of broiled fish that Gabriello's mouth watered and his stomach contracted with hunger.

"There, they're ready, dig in. Put your fish on the bread. But be careful you don't burn your hands. You're going to need them for rowing. . . . Well, how does it taste?" The old man grinned over at Gabriello, who bit ecstatically into his fish sandwich.

"Marvelous. I feel as though I hadn't eaten for days."

"That's the sea air. Eat hearty. And now's the time to wet your whistle. On a full stomach the wine won't do you any harm. . . . As soon as you're finished, we must sort out the catch. Or wait, let's do it this way. You do the rowing on the way back, and keep beyond the stakes, in the deep water for awhile, so that the mussels in the tub are thoroughly watered. We want to bring perfectly fresh goods to our friend Amalia. At a hundred and five lire a pound she has a right to quality. While you're rowing, I'll select the best ones for her." Uncle Beppe busied himself with the catch, placing the fine, big mus-

sels in the tub floating alongside the dory, and the crabs
into pails filled with sea water. The sand and seaweed,
the smaller mussels and crabs, and the debris that had
come in with the net, he shoveled over the gunwale of
the dory back into the lagoon, using for the purpose the
deep wooden scoop which was also employed in fishing
for small squid.

Long after sunset, Gabriello trotted, happy and dead
tired, through the dark, poorly illuminated streets of
Venice toward home.

He and Uncle Beppe had delivered to the proprietress
of the restaurant some twenty-four pounds of mussels
and seven pounds of crabs, all fresh and absolutely first-
class. So pleased was she over the excellent quality of
the merchandise that Signora Amalia had not even hag-
gled; she had laid on the table three thousand five hundred lire and even given Uncle Beppe a glass of wine
and Gabriello a hundred lire tip. And when they returned
to the dory, Uncle Beppe had said: "Let's share equally;
you've earned it." He had handed Gabriello one thousand
seven hundred and fifty lire. One thousand seven hundred and fifty lire! And besides that there were the hundred lire from Signora Amalia. For that sum Mother
would have to work eight hours a day for nearly three
days! The Saints be thanked that his father's mates had
not had any work for him at the gondola stand. He never
could have earned so much in a single day, working for
them. He decided that he would not go to the gondoliers'
stand again before the time came for his gondolier's examination, unless his father's mates urgently needed
him. Then, of course, he would not refuse; that was clear.
But otherwise, during the six years he must wait until
the examination, he would stay with Uncle Beppe. Fishing was in any case the best preparation for the profession
of gondolier. The famous Ernesto Pollo, the dean of the

gondoliers of Venice, who in his youth had won the race five times, was the son of a fisherman from Burano. Old Beppe knew a great deal about fishing and rowing. Just as much as the great gondoliers, perhaps. Who could say, perhaps in his youth Uncle Beppe would have been able to win the gondoliers' race if he had wanted to. But he had not cared to try. He had told Gabriello about that during the afternoon, while they were out hunting *cape lunghe* and *vongole* during the ebb tide. [*Cape lunghe* are narrow-shaped shellfish, about the length of a finger, mother-of-pearl in color. *Vongole* are small gray and blue shellfish which inhabitants of the Adriatic coast like to eat with rice.] What counted, as far as he was concerned, Uncle Beppe had said, was not fame, but independence. "All my life I've tried to do or not to do whatever I liked. That's why I have never married." And that, Gabriello thought, was probably why he felt so comfortable in that impossible den of his.

The old man certainly was a queer character, Gabriello thought. Muttering half to himself, often breaking into a high chuckle, he had talked about his life during the afternoon out on the sandbars which had suddenly risen out of the sea at low tide. These were really tiny islands, which you could ford only if you were wearing high boots. The sandbars swarmed with *cape lunghe* and *vongole*. The old man tramped over the sand, dragging his collecting sack behind him, mumbling his stories out of the corners of his mouth. Sometimes he also spoke of the curious behavior of these amusing shellfish, the *cape lunghe*. As soon as the water receded, they took fright. They dug down into the wet sand, leaving holes behind all over the sandbar. Then he had only to reach down into the hole and pull out a *capa lunga*. The *vongole* lay scattered about on top of the sand or just a little below the surface. Gathering them was merely a matter of picking them up.

When it turned dark, Uncle Beppe had grown silent. With weary movements—or was he being only deliberate?—he had fastened a lantern to the gunwale, and with the shallow wooden scoop in his hand had leaned over the stern. As soon as one of the foolish, light-hungry squid came undulating up, Uncle Beppe made a quick dip into the water and—plop—the creature plumped into the bottom of the dory. In a short time he had caught five fat squid. Gabriello, however, had been little more than half awake during all this. He was barely able to keep the oars going. His hands burned, and twinges of pain ran through the muscles of his shoulders from the unaccustomed exertion. He did not begin waking up again until Uncle Beppe put him ashore at the mouth of the Rio di Santa Giustina. There he handed up to Gabriello a small bag full of *cape lunghe, vongole,* and two squid, saying: "Take this to your mother. She can use it to make a good pot of fish and rice." To think that old Zanze had called this man a lazy good-for-nothing!

For Gabriello, this had been the first happy day since his father's death. On his way home he noticed a fruit-shop still open. Should he bring his mother a bunch of grapes? It had been such a fine day; Mother ought to have some pleasure out of it, too, he thought.

He had passed the shop, but turned back and bought two pounds of fine grapes. While the shopkeeper was easing the grapes carefully into a bag, a familiar fragrance struck Gabriello's nostrils. 'Why, roasted chestnuts! Shall I get some for the twins?' "Will you please give me half a pound of hot chestnuts too." He could not help being extravagant; this was the first time he had ever had money of his own in his pocket.

Holding Uncle Beppe's bag in one hand, and the grapes in the other, feeling the pleasant warmth of the chestnuts in his coat pocket, he tramped jauntily along until the chalky white neon light from the ground-floor windows of a building caught his attention. 'What's this, are they still working?' He went up to one of the open windows and looked in. A wave of intense heat struck him in the face. It took him a moment to recognize the curious humming sound as the singing of the young girls who sat at two tables running the length of a middle-sized room. Each of them had a small, green-framed windowpane protecting her face and chest from the heat of the sharp blue flames which shot like a dragon's fiery breath from metal pipes fastened to the table. Each of the girls was holding a long, dark glass rod in the glow of the flames, and a thin metal needle with which she artfully teased the melting, red-hot tip of the rod, which was then thrust into sand for cooling. In a few moments a lovely colored glass bead was lifted into the light. The foreman of the beadshop leaned over a counter, carefully selecting and arranging the beads.

How skillful the girls were. They knew their craft. But what frightful heat! And in this killing heat they were singing! It must be as hot as this in the glass factories of Murano. Similar work, after all—this was a small glass factory. So old Zanze wanted to send him into this searing heat, into such choking air!

Why did his thoughts keep coming back to her and her ideas? Abruptly, Gabriello turned away from the beadmakers and tramped on toward the Arsenal.

"Are you home already? Is it so late?" Confused, Mother looked up from her embroidery.

"Why, Mother, it's already half past eight." Gabriello went up to his mother and kissed her.

"Half past eight? *Madonna mia,* here I've been sitting over this embroidery without even noticing the time. I'll warm up our supper right away."

"Yes, yes, there's lots of polenta left," the twins called from the next room, and since food was being talked of, they promptly appeared in the kitchen. "You weren't home for supper and there's so-o-o much left. But what have you got there?"

"Here, you twirps, take these and have a treat." Gabriello tossed the bagful of chestnuts to the twins. Then he

arranged the grapes on a big plate, put the plate on a chair, and moved it alongside his mother. "And these are for you, Mammina!"

"Why, Gabriello, what extravagance. Such beautiful grapes."

"Enjoy them. Do you know what I earned today? Here, look." Gabriello took a number of banknotes from his pocket and laid them on the chair beside the grapes.

"What? A thousand seven hundred lire? Why, that simply isn't possible." Mother stared in amazement at the thousand lire note, the five hundred and the two hundreds.

"Don't strain your eyes, Mammina!" Gabriello laughed happily. "It's true: seventeen hundred lire. In fact there were eighteen hundred and fifty, but I spent a hundred and fifty for the grapes and the chestnuts."

"But where did you get all this money?"

"From Uncle Beppe, of course. Where else? And a hundred lire as a tip from Signora Amalia, who runs The Good Friend Restaurant. We had an extra good day today. Just think, we sold mussels and crabs to Signora Amalia for thirty-five hundred lire. That was just our morning's catch in the lagoon. And then Uncle Beppe behaved like a prince and went halves with me. Oh, and here, he gave me this bag to bring along, too."

"I would never have thought it of Beppe."

"Yes, I think we have been very much mistaken about Uncle Beppe. He is a wonderful person. Believe me, he is. . . . Hey, you two, let up on the chestnuts for a minute and make yourselves useful. Set the table. Don't forget the bread and the polenta."

The twins nudged each other, and Pia giggled. "He says it just like Papa. Copycat."

"But the chestnuts were nice," Angelina whispered. "And now we're going to have *cape lunghe* and *vongole* too!"

Meanwhile, Mother was scrubbing the shellfish at the sink. She put them in a saucepan and set the pan on the fire. While waiting for the shells to open, she chopped garlic and parsley, fried them with a little oil, and shook the open mussels out on the small side table. With the help of the twins, she extracted the white "worms" of the *cape lunghe* and the tiny snails from the *vongole*, stirred them in with the garlic and parsley, added spices —and in a few minutes the finest of fried-fish dishes was ready.

"Yum, is that good!" The twins ladled a second portion over the polenta on their plates. "May we have a little wine with it?"

"You two? Wine?" Gabriello exclaimed. "Take water, as I do."

"Just a few drops."

"Oh well, as far as I'm concerned you may have a few drops, to celebrate. Give me your glasses."

"What holiday is it today?" Pia asked. "Nobody said anything about a holiday. There aren't any flags out on the square."

"Gabriello means, to celebrate his first day with Uncle Beppe," Mother explained to the twins. "And that he was able to bring home so much money."

"Oooo, that," Pia and Angelina chirped. They then turned eagerly to the rest of their meal, and to making plans for the next day.

Mother and Gabriello talked until late that night about the future, which all at once seemed to be far rosier than they had dared to hope.

If you enjoyed this tale of a little Italian boy in the fabulous city of Venice, you will certainly like Confetti for Cortorelli, *the story of a boy in Sicily, by David Fletcher, also published by Pantheon.*

The Sesemann House Is Haunted

BY JOHANNA SPYRI

Translated by Helen B. Dole

Illustrations by William Sharp

> When little Heidi is forced to leave the free-
> dom of her Swiss mountain life and the
> companionship of her beloved grandfather
> to live in town as the companion of a rich
> invalid child, she finds the change almost
> more than she can bear.

FOR several days Fräulein Rottenmeier had been going about the house, for the most part, in silence and wrapped in thought. If at dusk she went from one room to another, or through the long corridor, she often looked around her and into the corners, giving a quick glance behind now and then, as if she thought some one might be coming softly after her and, unnoticed, pull her dress. She went alone into the living rooms only. If she had something to do on the upper floor where the hand-somely furnished guest rooms were situated, or down-stairs in the great mysterious hall, in which every step gave a resounding echo, and the old senators, with their big white collars, looked down from the walls so sternly and steadily with their big eyes, she would pretend there was something to carry up or down, and she would summon Tinette and tell her she must come with her.

From Heidi, by Johanna Spyri.

Tinette did exactly the same; if she had any work to do upstairs or down, she would call Sebastian and tell him he was to go with her, for she might have something to carry which she could not manage alone. Strange to say, Sebastian did precisely the same; if he was sent to the remote part of the house, he called up Johann and directed him to accompany him, for fear he could not bring what was needed. Each one followed the other quite willingly, although there was really nothing to be carried, and each might have gone alone; but it seemed as if the companion always thought he might soon need the other for the same service. While this was going on upstairs, the cook, who had been in the house for many years, stood below, deep in thought among her pots, and shook her head and sighed:—

"That I should live to see this!"

For some time there had been something strange and uncanny going on in the Sesemann house. Every morning when the servants came down the house door stood wide open, but no one was to be seen anywhere about who could give any account of the matter. The first few times when this happened all the chambers and rooms of the house were anxiously searched to see what had been stolen, for they thought a thief had broken into the house in the night and had escaped with his booty; but such was not the case; not a single thing in the whole house was missing.

At night the door was not only double locked, but also a wooden bar was put across; it made no difference, in the morning the door stood wide open; and no matter how early the servants in their excitement came down, there stood the door open; yet everything round about was wrapped in deep sleep, and the doors and windows in all the other houses were still firmly fastened.

At last Johann and Sebastian took courage, and, at Fräulein Rottenmeier's urgent request, prepared to

spend the night below in the room adjoining the great
hall, to see what would happen.

Fräulein Rottenmeier got out some of Herr Sesemann's weapons and gave them to Sebastian.

The two men sat down on the appointed evening, and
after being at first very talkative they became rather
sleepy; whereupon they both leaned back in their chairs
and were silent. When the old tower clock struck twelve,
Sebastian grew bold and called to his companion; but he
was not easy to waken; as often as Sebastian called to
him he would turn his head from one side of the chair
back to the other and go to sleep again. Sebastian now
listened eagerly, for he was wide awake again. It was
as still as a mouse everywhere; even in the street there
was no sound to be heard. Sebastian did not go to sleep
again, for it seemed to him uncanny in the deep stillness, and he called Johann in a subdued voice and shook
him a little from time to time. Finally, when it had struck

one o'clock, Johann woke up and realized why he was sitting in a chair and not lying in his bed. Suddenly he began to be very brave and called out:—

"Now, Sebastian, we must go out and see how things are; you needn't be afraid. Come after me."

Johann opened wide the room door, which had been left ajar, and stepped outside. At the same moment a sharp gust of air blew in from the open house door and put out the light which Johann held in his hand. He rushed back, almost threw Sebastian, who was standing behind him, backward into the room, then dragged him along, closed the door, and in feverish haste turned the key as far as it would go. Then he pulled out his matchbox and made a light again. Sebastian did not know just what had happened, for, standing behind the broad-shouldered Johann, he had not so plainly felt the draft of air. But when they could see each other by the light, Sebastian cried out from fright, for Johann was deadly pale and trembled like an aspen leaf.

"What is the matter? What was outside there?" asked Sebastian anxiously.

"The door was as wide open as it could be," gasped Johann, "and there was a white form on the steps; you see, Sebastian, it came up the steps, disappeared, and was gone."

Cold shivers ran down Sebastian's back. Then they sat down very close together and did not stir again until it was morning and people began to be moving in the street. Then they went out together, closed the open door, and went upstairs to tell Fräulein Rottenmeier about their experience. The lady was quite ready to talk, for the expectation of what might happen had kept her from sleeping. As soon as she learned what had occurred she sat down and wrote such a letter to Herr Sesemann as he had never received before. In it she said that her fingers were paralyzed with fright. Herr Sesemann must

immediately come home, for the most unheard-of things
had happened there. Then she told him what had taken
place; how the door was found wide open every morning, and in consequence no one in the house was any
longer sure of his life, and that no one could tell what
horrible results might follow this mysterious occurrence.
Herr Sesemann replied by return mail that it was impossible for him to leave his business so suddenly to
come home. The ghost story was very strange, and he
hoped it was all past. Meanwhile, if there should be any
further trouble, Fräulein Rottenmeier might write to
Frau Sesemann and ask her to come to Frankfurt to their
assistance; his mother would surely dispel the ghosts in
a very short space of time, and after that they would
never again venture to disturb his house.

Fräulein Rottenmeier was not pleased with the tone
of this letter; the matter had made too little impression
on him. She wrote immediately to Frau Sesemann, but
she did not get any more satisfaction from this direction,
and the reply contained some very sarcastic remarks.
Frau Sesemann wrote that she did not think it worth
while for her to travel from Holstein to Frankfurt because Rottenmeier saw ghosts. Moreover, a ghost had
never been seen in the Sesemann house, and if there was
one wandering around there now, it could be nothing
but a living being, and Rottenmeier ought to be able to
come to an understanding with it; if not, she should
call the night watchman to her aid.

But Fräulein Rottenmeier was determined not to
spend her days any longer in terror, and she knew how
to help herself. Until then she had told the children
nothing about the appearance of a ghost, lest they should
be afraid to stay alone a single moment day or night, and
that might have very uncomfortable consequences for
her. Now she went straight to the library, where the two
were sitting together, and in a suppressed voice told

them how a strange being appeared every night. Immediately Klara screamed out that she would not stay alone another moment, that her papa must come home, and Fräulein Rottenmeier must sleep in her room, and Heidi ought not to be alone either, or the ghost might come to her and do her some harm. She wanted them all to stay in the same room and to have a light burning all night, and Tinette must sleep near, and Sebastian and Johann must come down and spend the night in the hall, in order to scream and frighten away the ghost if it should come up on the stairs.

Klara was very much excited, and Fräulein Rottenmeier had the greatest difficulty to quiet her. She promised to write to her papa immediately, and to put her bed in Klara's room, and never to leave her alone again. They could not all sleep in the same room, but if Adelheid was afraid, Tinette must put up a couch in her room. But Heidi was more afraid of Tinette than of ghosts, for she had never even heard of such things, and she insisted that she was not afraid and preferred to remain alone in her room.

Hereupon Fräulein Rottenmeier flew to her writing table and wrote to Herr Sesemann how the mysterious proceedings which were repeated every night in his house had so affected his daughter's delicate constitution that the most serious consequences were to be anticipated. Examples were known of sudden epileptic seizures, or attacks of St. Vitus's dance, in similar cases, and his daughter was liable to any such misfortune if the house were not relieved from this state of terror.

This had some effect. Two days later Herr Sesemann was standing at his door and rang so violently that everyone in the house came hurrying down, and each gazed at the other, for they believed nothing less than that the ghost was most impudently playing his evil tricks even in the daytime. Sebastian, on the floor above, cautiously peered out through a half-opened shutter; and just at that instant there was another ring at the bell, and this time so imperatively that no doubt was left in any one's mind that it was a human hand behind the summons.

Sebastian had recognized the hand, dashed through the room, flew headfirst downstairs, but landed on his feet at the bottom and flung the front door open. Herr Sesemann did not stop to talk with him, but went immediately up to his daughter's room. Klara received her papa with a cry of joy, and when he saw her looking so cheerful and unchanged, his face, which had looked very stern, softened, and his expression grew more and more pleasant, as he heard from his daughter's own lips that she was as well as usual, and that she was perfectly delighted to have him at home again, and that she was most grateful to the ghost that was haunting the house, because it had caused her papa to come home.

"And what further pranks has the ghost been up to, Fräulein Rottenmeier?" asked Herr Sesemann with a comical expression in the corners of his mouth.

"Indeed, Herr Sesemann," replied that lady with solemnity, "it is no laughing matter. I have no doubt at all that by to-morrow Herr Sesemann will find it serious enough; for what is going on in this house signifies that something terrible must have happened here in days gone by and have been kept secret."

"Well, I know nothing about it," observed Herr Sesemann, "but I must beg of you not to harbor any suspicions of my most honorable ancestors. And now call Sebastian into the dining room; I wish to talk with him alone."

Herr Sesemann went into the dining room, and Sebastian made his appearance. Herr Sesemann had not failed to observe that Sebastian and Fräulein Rotten-

meier were not the best of friends; so he had his suspicions.

"Come here, Sebastian," said he, beckoning the servant
to enter. "Now tell me honestly, have you not your own
self been playing the part of a ghost in order to plague
Fräulein Rottenmeier a little? Tell me!"

"No, on my word; you must not think any such thing;
I myself have not felt at all comfortable about the matter," replied Sebastian with unmistakable frankness.

"Well, if that is the case, I will show you and the brave
Johann to-morrow how ghosts look by daylight. Shame
upon you, Sebastian! a strong young fellow like you running away from ghosts! Now go at once to my old friend,
Dr. Classen; give him my compliments, and tell him he
must come here without fail to-night at nine o'clock. I
have come home from Paris on purpose to consult him. It
is such a serious matter that he must spend the night
with me; he must make his arrangements accordingly.
Do you understand, Sebastian?"

"Yes, indeed; yes, indeed! Herr Sesemann may be sure
that I shall do as he says."

Sebastian left the room, and Herr Sesemann returned
to his little daughter to quiet her fears about the appari-
tion which he was going that very day to put in its true
light.

Punctually at nine o'clock, when the children had
gone to sleep and Fräulein Rottenmeier had retired, the
doctor appeared, showing still under his gray hair a very
fresh face and two bright, kind twinkling eyes. He
looked somewhat anxious, but as his friend greeted him,
broke out into a hearty laugh and said, clapping him on
the shoulder:—

"Well, well, for one who needs to be watched with, you
look tolerably hearty, old friend."

"Have patience, my dear doctor," replied Herr Sese-

mann; "the one you have to watch with will look worse when we have caught him."

"What! a sick person in the house and one that must be caught?"

"Far worse, doctor, far worse. A ghost in the house; the house is haunted!"

The doctor laughed aloud.

"A fine state of affairs, doctor!" continued Herr Sesemann. "It's a shame that my friend Rottenmeier cannot enjoy it. She is convinced that a former Sesemann is wandering about here and expiating some dreadful deed."

"How did she find out about it?" asked the doctor, still very much amused.

Herr Sesemann now told his friend about the whole proceeding, and added that, in order to be prepared for whatever might happen, he had left two well-loaded revolvers where they were to watch; for either the affair was a very undesirable joke, which possibly some of the servants' acquaintances were playing, in order to frighten the people in the house during the master's absence—in that case a little scare, such as a good shot into the air, could not be unwholesome—or else it was a case of thieves, who had taken this means to make them think they were ghosts, in order to be safer later on, as no one would dare to venture forth; if this were so, a good weapon might not come amiss.

During this explanation the gentlemen had gone downstairs and entered the same room where Johann and Sebastian had watched. On the table lay the two revolvers, and two brightly lighted candelabra stood in the centre, for Herr Sesemann did not care to await the ghost in a dim light.

The door was now partly shut, so that too much light need not shine out into the hall to frighten away the ghost. Then the gentlemen seated themselves comfortably in their easy-chairs and began to talk about all sorts of things, now and then taking a little refreshment, and so the clock struck twelve before they were aware of it.

"The ghost has spied us out and is not coming to-night at all," said the doctor.

"Have patience; it may come at one o'clock," replied his friend.

They went on with their talking. It struck one. It was perfectly still all about; even on the street there was no sound to be heard. Suddenly the doctor lifted his finger:—

"Sh, Sesemann! don't you hear something?"

They both listened. They heard the bar softly but quite distinctly pushed back, the key turned twice in the lock, and the door was opened. Herr Sesemann reached after the revolver.

"You are not afraid?" said the doctor, rising.

"It is better to be cautious," whispered Herr Sesemann, seizing the candelabrum with three candles in his left hand, and the revolver in his right, and followed the doctor, who had preceded likewise provided with lights and a revolver. They stepped out into the corridor.

Through the wide-open door the pale moonlight came in and lighted up a white form, which stood motionless on the threshold.

"Who is there?" the doctor thundered forth, so that it echoed through the entire length of the corridor, and both gentlemen, with lights and weapons, went toward the figure. It turned around and gave a little scream. There stood Heidi, with bare feet, in her white nightclothes, looking bewildered at the bright lights and the firearms, and shivering and trembling from head to foot like a little leaf in the wind. The gentlemen looked at each other in the greatest astonishment.

"I really believe, Sesemann, that it is your little water-carrier," said the doctor.

"Child, what does this mean?" asked Herr Sesemann. "What are you going to do? Why have you come down here?"

White as snow from fright, Heidi stood there and said, scarcely able to make a sound:—"I don't know."

Then the doctor stepped forward:—

"Sesemann, the case belongs to my domain; go and sit down in your easy-chair in there for a while. I will first of all take the child back where she belongs."

Whereupon he laid his revolver on the floor, took the trembling child by the hand, as a father would, and went upstairs with her.

"Don't be afraid, don't be afraid," he said kindly, as they went up; "only be very quiet; there is no harm done, so never mind."

When they were in Heidi's room the doctor placed his light on the table, took Heidi in his arms, laid her in her bed and covered her up carefully. He sat down in a chair by the bed and waited until she was somewhat calmer and did not tremble in every limb. Then he took Heidi's hand and said soothingly:—

"There, now everything is all right; now tell me where you wanted to go."

"I didn't want to go anywhere," asserted Heidi, "I did not go down there myself; I was only there all at once."

"Indeed! and did you dream anything in the night, do you know, so that you saw and heard something very clearly?"

"Yes, every night I dream, and always the same thing. I think I am with my grandfather, and I hear the fir trees roaring outdoors, and I think, 'Now the stars are sparkling so brightly in the sky,' and I run swiftly and open the door of the hut, and it is so beautiful there! But when I wake up I am always in Frankfurt still." Heidi began to struggle and to swallow down the lump that rose in her throat.

"Hm! and do you ever have any pain anywhere? In your head or in your back?"

"Oh, no; only something presses here all the time, like a great stone."

"Hm! somewhat as if you had eaten something and then afterwards wished you could give it back again?"

"No, not like that; but so heavy, as if I must cry hard."

"Indeed! and then do you cry right out loud?"

"Oh, no, I don't dare to do that; Fräulein Rottenmeier has forbidden that."

"Then you swallow it down till another time, don't you? Really! Well, you like to stay in Frankfurt, do you not?"

"Oh, yes," she replied faintly; but it sounded as if she meant the opposite.

"Hm! and where did you live with your grandfather?"

"Always on the Alm."

"It is not particularly pleasant there, but rather dreary, is it not?"

"Oh, no; it is so lovely there, so lovely!"

Heidi could say no more; the recollection of it all, the excitement she had just passed through, and the long-restrained weeping overpowered the child; the tears rushed from her eyes in streams, and she broke into loud, passionate sobbing.

The doctor rose; he laid Heidi's head gently on the pillow and said:—

"There, now cry a little—it can do no harm—and then go to sleep, and be happy in your sleep; tomorrow everything will be all right."

Then he went downstairs.

When he was once more in the room where they had been watching, he drew the easy-chair opposite his waiting friend and explained to him, as he listened with eager expectation:—

"Sesemann, in the first place, your little protégée walks in her sleep; all unconsciously she has opened the door every night like a ghost and put all your servants into a fever of fright. In the second place, the child is wasting away from homesickness, so that she is almost reduced to a little skeleton and will soon be entirely so; something must be done for her at once! For the first evil and for the nervous excitement existing in a high degree there is but one remedy, namely, to send the child immediately back to her native mountain air; for the second there is but one medicine, and that the very same thing. So send the child home to-morrow; that is my prescription."

Herr Sesemann rose from his chair. He walked up and down the room in the greatest excitement; then he exclaimed:—

"A sleepwalker! Sick! Homesick! wasted away in my house! All this in my house! And no one noticed it or knew anything about it! And do you think, doctor, that I will send the child, who came fresh and healthy into my house, back to her grandfather miserable and wasted away? No, doctor, you cannot expect that; I can't do that; that I will never do. Take the child in hand, put her under treatment, do what you like, but make her sound and healthy, and then I will send her home if she wants to go; but first give her your aid!"

"Sesemann," replied the doctor earnestly, "think what you are doing! Her condition is no illness that can be cured with powders and pills. The child has no delicate constitution; if you send her back now to the bracing mountain air, to which she is accustomed, she will be perfectly well again; if not—you would not like to send her back beyond all help to her grandfather, or never send her back at all, would you?"

Herr Sesemann stood still in astonishment:—

"Well, if this is your advice, doctor, there is only one way; it must be followed immediately."

With these words Herr Sesemann took his friend's arm and walked about with him to talk the matter over still further. Then the doctor started to go home, for much time had passed during their conversation, and the bright morning light was coming through the house door, which was opened this time by the master of the house.

Herr Sesemann climbed the stairs in the greatest agitation and went with a firm step to Fräulein Rottenmeier's sleeping room. Here he rapped so unusually loud on the door that the good lady woke from sleep with a cry of terror. She heard Herr Sesemann's voice outside:—

"Pray hasten to come into the dining room; preparations must be immediately made for a journey."

Fräulein Rottenmeier looked at her clock; it was half past four in the morning; she had never risen at such an hour in her life before. What could have happened? Curiosity and anxious expectation made everything she touched go wrong, and she made slow progress in dressing, for she kept hunting about uneasily in her room for the things she had already put on.

Meanwhile Herr Sesemann went the entire length of the hall and furiously rang every one of the bells used to summon the different servants, so that in each respective room a terrified form jumped out of bed and hurried to dress, for one and all thought the same thing, that the ghost had seized the master of the house, and this was his call for help.

So they came down one after another, each looking more terrified than the last, and stood in surprise before the master of the house, for he was walking up and down the room, looking fresh and cheerful, and not at all as if a ghost had frightened him.

Johann was immediately dispatched to put the horses and carriage in order, to be brought round later on. Tinette was ordered to waken Heidi at once, and to make her ready to take a journey. Sebastian was ordered to hasten to the house where Heidi's aunt was at service and to bring her back. Fräulein Rottenmeier had meanwhile succeeded in getting dressed, and everything was all right except her headdress, which was on crooked, so that from a distance she looked as if her face were on backwards. Herr Sesemann ascribed her perplexing appearance to the fact that she had been awakened so early, and proceeded at once to business. He explained to the lady that she was to procure a trunk without delay, and to pack up all the things belonging to the Swiss child—Herr Sesemann usually spoke of Heidi in this way, as her name was somewhat unfamiliar to him —and also a good part of Klara's clothes, that the child might have everything that was necessary to take with her; but all must be done quickly and without stopping to deliberate.

Fräulein Rottenmeier stood as if rooted to the floor and stared at Herr Sesemann in amazement. She had expected that he was going to tell her in confidence some horrible story of his ghostly experience the night before, and she would not have been displeased to hear it now in the clear morning light; instead of that came these very prosaic and particularly inconvenient commands. She could not at once overcome her surprise. She still stood speechless, expecting something further.

But Her Sesemann had no intention of making further explanations; he let the lady stand where she was and went to his daughter's room. As he supposed, the unusual stir in the house had awakened her, and she was listening to everything and wondering what was going on.

Her father sat down by her bed and told her what the ghost really was, and that in the doctor's opinion Heidi was in a very bad condition, and that her nightly wanderings would become more extensive, and perhaps she might climb up to the roof, and that would be very dangerous. So he had decided to send the child home

at once, for he could not be responsible for her; and
Klara must be reconciled, for she could see that it could
not be otherwise.

Klara was very painfully surprised by this news, and
at first wanted to find some way out of the difficulty,
but it was of no use; her father remained firm in his
decision; but he promised to take Klara the following
year to Switzerland, if she would be reasonable now and
not grieve. So Klara yielded to what could not be helped;
she asked that Heidi's trunk should be brought into her
room and packed there, so that she might put in some
things Heidi would enjoy; and this her papa willingly
granted; indeed, he even encouraged Klara to give the
child a fine outfit.

Meanwhile Aunt Dete had arrived and stood with
great expectation in the vestibule; for to be summoned
at this unusual time must mean something extraordi-
nary. Herr Sesemann went out to her and told her how
it was with Heidi, and that he wished she would take
the child home at once, that very day. The aunt looked
very much disappointed. She had not expected such
news. She still remembered very distinctly the parting
words the uncle had spoken to her: never to come before
his eyes again; and having taken the child to him, and
then brought her away, it did not seem advisable to take
her back again. So she did not consider the matter long,
but said, with great earnestness, that unfortunately it
would be quite impossible for her to take the journey
that day, and the next day she could think of it still less,
and the day after that it would be utterly impossible on
account of the work to be done then, and after that
she would be no better able to go.

Herr Sesemann understood the aunt's excuses and
dismissed her without saying anything further. He then
summoned Sebastian and told him that he was to prepare immediately to take a journey; he was to go that

very day with the child as far as Basle, and the next day to take her home. Then he could at once return; he would have no statement to make, for a letter to the grandfather would explain everything to him.

"There is one thing more of great importance, Sebastian," said Herr Sesemann in conclusion, "and I want you to look out for it carefully. I am acquainted at the hotel in Basle, the name of which I have written down here on my card for you. Show my card there and a good room will be given you for the child; you must provide for yourself. Go first into the child's room and fasten all the windows so securely that they can be opened only with great force. When the child is in bed go and fasten the door outside, for the child wanders around in the night and might run into danger in a strange house if she went out and tried to open the house door; do you understand?"

"Aha! That was it, was it? That was it!" exclaimed Sebastian in the greatest surprise, for a great light had just been thrown on the ghosts.

"Yes, that was it! That was it! And you are a coward, and you can tell Johann that he is another, and all of you together a ridiculous set of men."

Having said this, Herr Sesemann went to his room and sat down to write a letter to the Alm-Uncle.

Sebastian stood confounded in the middle of the room and repeated over and over again to himself:—

"If only I hadn't let that coward of a Johann pull me back into the room, but had gone after the little white figure, as I undoubtedly should have done!" for now the bright sunshine distinctly lighted up every corner of the sombre room.

Meanwhile Heidi, entirely unsuspicious of what was going to happen, stood waiting in her Sunday frock, for Tinette had merely roused her from sleep, taken her clothes out of the closet and put them on hurriedly

without saying a word. She never talked with the un-
cultivated Heidi, for she considered her beneath her
notice.

Herr Sesemann walked with his letter to the dining
room, where the breakfast was already served, and
asked:—

"Where is the child?"

Heidi was called. When she approached Herr Sesemann to say "good-morning" to him, he looked into her
face inquiringly:—

"Well, what do you say to it, little one?"

Heidi looked up at him in amazement.

"You don't know anything about it even now," said
Herr Sesemann, laughing. "Well, you are going home
to-day, right away."

"Home?" repeated Heidi, unable to speak aloud, and
turned white as snow. For a little while she could hardly
get her breath, her heart was so violently affected by
the impression.

"Don't you want to know something about it?" asked
Herr Sesemann, laughing.

"Oh, yes, I do," she now was able to gasp; and she
turned a deep red.

"Good, good!" said Herr Sesemann encouragingly,
while he seated himself and motioned to Heidi to do
the same. "And now eat a hearty breakfast and then into
the carriage and away."

But Heidi could not swallow a mouthful, although
through obedience she tried to force herself to eat; she
was in such a state of excitement that she did not know
whether she was awake or dreaming, or whether she
would not suddenly awaken and be standing at the door
in her nightgown.

"Sebastian must take plenty of luncheon," said Herr
Sesemann to Fräulein Rottenmeier, who was just enter-
ing the room; "the child cannot eat, of course not. Go

in to Klara until the carriage comes," he added kindly, turning to Heidi.

This was what Heidi wished, and she ran out of the room. In the middle of Klara's room stood a huge trunk, with the cover still wide open.

"Come, Heidi, come!" Klara called out to her; "see what I have had packed for you! Come, do you like it?"

And she showed her a quantity of things, dresses and aprons, underwear and sewing materials; "and see here, Heidi," and Klara held up a basket triumphantly. Heidi peeped in and jumped high in her delight, for inside lay twelve lovely, round white rolls, all for the grandmother. The children in their glee entirely forgot that the moment had come for them to part, and when suddenly the call was heard—"The carriage is ready!"—there was no time left to be sad.

Heidi ran to her room; her beautiful book from the grandmamma must still be there; no one could have packed it; it lay under her pillow, for Heidi could not be parted from it day or night. That was laid in the basket on the bread. Then she opened her closet to see if there was anything left that had not been packed. To be sure—the old red neckerchief still lay there, for Fräulein Rottenmeier had not thought it worth packing. Heidi wrapped it around something else and laid it on top of the basket, so that the red parcel was very conspicuous. Then she put on her fine hat and left her room.

The two children had to say a speedy farewell, for Herr Sesemann was already there to take Heidi down to the carriage. Fräulein Rottenmeier stood at the head of the stairs to bid Heidi good-bye. When she noticed the strange red bundle, she took it quickly out of the basket and threw it on the floor.

"No, Adelheid," she said, still finding fault, "you cannot leave this house so; you do not need to carry off such a thing as that. Now good-bye."

After this Heidi did not dare to pick up her bundle again, but she looked beseechingly at the master of the house, as if she were having her greatest treasure taken from her.

"No, no," said Herr Sesemann in a very decided voice, "the child shall carry home whatever gives her pleasure, and if she takes away kittens or turtles we will not get excited about it, Fräulein Rottenmeier."

Heidi quickly picked up her bundle from the floor, and her eyes beamed with gratitude and pleasure.

When Heidi reached the carriage Herr Sesemann held out his hand to the child and said to her with friendly words that she must think of him and his daughter Klara. He wished her a happy journey, and Heidi thanked him very prettily for all the kindness he had shown her and finally said:—

"And I leave a thousand good-byes for the doctor, and thank him many times," for she had noticed how he had said to her the night before: "And to-morrow everything will be all right." Now it had all come true, and Heidi thought he was the cause of it.

Then the child was lifted into the carriage, and the basket and the lunch box and Sebastian followed. Herr Sesemann called out once more in a friendly voice: "A pleasant journey!" and the carriage rolled away.

Soon after, Heidi was sitting in the train and holding her basket firmly in her lap, for she would not let it out of her hands for a moment; the precious rolls for the grandmother were inside, and she had to watch them carefully and delight her eyes with a look at them every now and then. Heidi sat as still as a mouse for several hours, for now she began to realize that she was on the way home to her grandfather on the Alm, to the grandmother, and Peter, the goatherd; one thing after another came before her eyes—all that she was going to see again, and she imagined how everything would look at

home, and new thoughts kept arising in her mind; suddenly she said anxiously:—

"Sebastian, are you sure that the grandmother on the Alm is not dead?"

"No, no," said he soothingly; "we hope she's not dead. She must be still alive."

Then Heidi became absorbed again in her own thoughts; only now and then she peeped into her basket, for her greatest desire was to lay all the rolls on the grandmother's table. After some time she said again:—

"Sebastian, if we could only be perfectly sure that the grandmother is still alive."

"Yes, indeed! Yes, indeed!" replied her companion, half asleep; "she's still alive; I don't see any reason why not."

After a while Heidi's eyes also closed; after the disturbance of the previous night and the early start she was so heavy with sleep that she did not awaken until Sebastian shook her by the arm and called out to her:

"Wake up! Wake up! We must get out now, we are in Basle!"

On the following morning they journeyed for several hours more. Heidi again sat with the basket in her lap, for on no account would she give it up to Sebastian; but to-day she did not speak, for with each hour her eagerness became more intense. Then suddenly, when Heidi was not thinking about it, came the loud call—"Mayenfeld!" She jumped up from her seat, and Sebastian did the same, for he too had been surprised. Now they stood outside with the trunk, and the train was whistling farther on up the valley. Sebastian looked longingly after it, for he much preferred traveling in that safe and easy way to undertaking a journey on foot, which had to end in climbing a mountain, and might be hard and dangerous besides, in this country where everything was still half wild, as he supposed. He therefore looked carefully about him for some advice concerning the safest way to "Dörfli." Not far from the railway station stood a little wagon, drawn by a lean horse; into this a broad-shouldered man was loading several large bags, which had been brought by the train. Sebastian stepped up to him and questioned him about the way.

"All ways are safe here," was the curt reply.

Then Sebastian asked him about the best way one could go without falling over the precipices, and also how a trunk could be taken to Dörfli. The man looked at the trunk and measured it with his eyes; then he said that, if it was not too heavy, he would take it in his wagon, since he himself was going to Dörfli. So some words were exchanged and finally the two arranged that the man would take both the child and the trunk with him, and that the child could be sent from Dörfli up the Alm with some one that evening.

"I can go alone; I know the way from Dörfli up the Alm," said Heidi, for she had been listening attentively while they were making the bargain. A heavy load was taken from Sebastian's mind when he found himself so suddenly released from the prospect of climbing the mountain. He now secretly beckoned Heidi to one side and handed her a heavy roll and a letter to her grandfather, and explained to her that the roll was a present from Herr Sesemann, which must be kept in the bottom of her basket, under the bread, and that she must take care of it, so that it should not be lost, or Herr Sesemann would be frightfully cross about it, and would never get over it all his life long; the little Mamselle must surely remember this.

"I will not lose it," said Heidi assuringly, and placed the roll and the letter in the bottom of the basket. The trunk was put into the wagon and then Sebastian lifted Heidi with her basket up to the high seat, held out his hand to bid her good-bye, and once more urged her, with all sorts of signs, to keep her eyes on the contents of her basket; for the driver was near, and Sebastian was all the more cautious because he knew that he ought to go with the child himself to the end of her journey. The driver swung himself up on the seat beside Heidi, and the wagon rolled off toward the mountain, while Sebastian, glad to escape the dreaded mountain journey, sat down in the station to wait for the returning train.

The man on the wagon was the baker of Dörfli, and he was carrying home his bags of meal. He had never seen Heidi, but like everyone else in Dörfli he knew about the child that had been brought to the Alm-Uncle. Besides, he had known Heidi's parents and at once surmised that she was the much-talked-of little girl. He wondered somewhat why the child was so soon coming home again, and during the journey began to talk with Heidi:—

"You are the child who was up with the Alm-Uncle, your grandfather, aren't you?"

"Yes."

"Did you fare badly that you have already come home from so far?"

"No, I did not; no one can fare better than I did in Frankfurt."

"Why are you running home then?"

"Only because Herr Sesemann allowed me, or I should not be coming home."

"Bah! why didn't you prefer to stay there, if you were only *allowed* to come home?"

"Because I would a thousand times rather be at home with my grandfather on the Alm than do anything else in the world."

"Perhaps you'll think differently when you get up there," growled the baker; "but I wonder," he said to himself, "if she can know how it is."

Then he began to whistle and said nothing more, and Heidi looked around her and began to tremble inwardly from excitement, for she recognized the trees by the way, and over yonder stood the lofty peaks of the Falkniss Mountain looking down at her, as if they were greeting her like good old friends. And Heidi greeted them in return, and with every step forward Heidi's expectation grew more eager, and she felt as if she would have to jump down from the wagon and run with all her might until she was up there. However, she remained still and did not move, but trembled all over. As they came into Dörfli the clock was just striking five. In a moment a crowd of women and children gathered around the wagon, and two neighbors came out to it, for the child and trunk on the baker's cart had attracted the attention of all the inhabitants, and each one wanted to know where they had come from and where they were going.

When the baker had lifted Heidi down, she said quickly:—"Thank you, my grandfather will come for my trunk"; and she would have run away, but she was held fast on every side, and there was a tumult of voices, each asking something different. Heidi pressed through the crowd with such anxiety on her face that they reluctantly made room for her and let her pass, and one said to another:—"You see how frightened she is; she has every reason to be."

Then they began to tell one another how the Alm-Uncle for a year past had been worse than ever, and would not speak a word to any one, and when any one came in his way he made up a face, as if he would like to kill him; and if the child knew anything in the world about it, she would not run to the old dragon's nest. But here the baker interrupted their remarks by saying he knew more about it than all the rest, and then told them, with an air of mystery, how a gentleman had brought the child as far as Mayenfeld, parted from her in a very friendly way, and had at once, without any bargaining, paid the fare he asked, besides adding a fee; and, more than all, he could say surely that the child had been well off where she was, and that she was anxious to come back to her grandfather. This news caused great surprise and was immediately spread through all Dörfli, so that there was not a house that evening where it was not repeated that Heidi had been anxious to come back from a life of luxury to her grandfather.

Heidi ran up the mountain from Dörfli as fast as she could; but now and then she would suddenly stand still, for she quite lost her breath; the basket on her arm was heavy for her, and besides the way grew steeper and steeper the higher she went. Heidi had only one thought:—

"Will the grandmother still be sitting in the corner at her spinning wheel; has she not died in all this time?"

Now Heidi saw the hut up in the hollow on the Alm, and her heart began to throb; she ran still faster; her heart kept beating louder and louder.—Now she was up there—she could hardly open the door, she trembled so—but now!—She ran into the middle of the little room and stood there, completely out of breath and unable to speak.

"O heavens!" sounded from the corner, "our Heidi used to run in like that! Ah, if only I could have her with me once more while I live! Who has come in?"

"Here I am, grandmother; here I am, really!" exclaimed Heidi.

Rushing into the corner and into the old dame's lap, she seized her arm and her hands and snuggled up to her, and was unable to say anything more from delight. At first the grandmother was so overcome that she could not speak a word; then she began to stroke Heidi's curly hair with her hand and kept saying again and again:—

"Yes, yes, it is her hair; and it is her voice; ah, dear Lord, that thou shouldest have permitted me this!"

And two great tears of joy dropped from her blind eyes on Heidi's hand.

"Are you here, Heidi? are you really here?"

"Yes, yes, really, grandmother," said Heidi with all assurance; "but do not cry; I am very surely here again and will come to you every day and never go away again; and you won't have to eat hard bread for many days, for see, grandmother, do you see?"

And Heidi now took one roll after another out of her basket, until she had piled up all twelve in the grandmother's lap.

"O child! O child! what a blessing you have brought me!" exclaimed the grandmother, when the rolls did not come to an end, but one kept following another. "But the greatest blessing is you yourself, child!" Then she seized hold of Heidi's curly hair and stroked her hot cheeks and said again:—

"Say just a word more, child; say something more, so that I can hear you."

Heidi then told the grandmother how she had suffered, fearing that the grandmother might perhaps die
while she was away and not have the white rolls, and
that she would never, never be able to go to her.

Then Peter's mother came in, and for a moment stood
still in astonishment. Then she exclaimed:—

"Surely, it is Heidi! how can it be possible!"

Heidi rose and shook hands with her, and Brigitte
could not wonder enough at Heidi's appearance, and she
walked around the child, saying:—

"Grandmother, if you only could see what a beautiful
dress the child has on and how she looks; I hardly know
her. And does the little hat trimmed with feathers, on the
table, belong to you also? Just put it on, so I can see
how you look in it."

"No, I will not," said Heidi decidedly. "You can have
it; I don't need it any longer, I still have my own."

Whereupon Heidi opened her little red bundle and
took out her old hat, which had become still more bent
during the journey than it was before. But that troubled
Heidi little; she had never forgotten how, when she was
leaving her grandfather, he had called after her that he
never wanted to see her in a hat trimmed with feathers,
and that was why Heidi had kept her old hat so carefully, for she always thought of the time when she should
go home to him.

But Brigitte said she must not be so foolish; it was
a splendid hat, and she might sell it to the teacher's little
daughter in Dörfli, and get a good deal of money for it,
if she did not care to wear it. But Heidi was firm in her
decision and laid the hat gently in the corner behind
the grandmother, where it was entirely hidden. Then
Heidi took off her lovely dress, and she folded the red
neckerchief over her underwaist, in which she now stood
with bare arms, and then seized the grandmother's hand,
saying:—

"Now I must go home to my grandfather, but tomorrow I will come to you again; good-night, grandmother."

"Yes, come again, Heidi; come again to-morrow morning," said the grandmother; and she pressed Heidi's hand between her own and could hardly let her go.

"Why have you taken off your beautiful dress?" asked Brigitte.

"Because I would rather go to my grandfather without it, or he might not know me; you hardly knew me in it."

Brigitte went out the door with Heidi, and said a few words secretly to her:—

"You can keep on the dress, he will know you; but you must take care of yourself, for Peterli says the Alm-Uncle is always very cross now and never says a word."

Heidi said "good-night" and went on up the mountain with her basket on her arm. The evening sun shone all around on the green Alm, and now the snow field on Cäsaplana came into sight and gleamed in the distance.

Every few steps Heidi had to stand still and look around, for the high mountains were behind her as she climbed. Now a red glow fell over the grass at her feet; she turned around; there—she had forgotten the splendor, and never had seen it in her dreams like this—the rocky peaks on Falkniss flamed up to the sky, the broad snow field was all aglow, and rosy clouds were drifting high above. The grass all around on the Alm was golden; from all the crags it glimmered and gleamed down, and below, the far-reaching valley swam in a golden vapor.

Heidi stood in the midst of all this glory, and bright tears of joy and rapture ran down her cheeks, and she had to fold her hands, and, looking up to Heaven, thank the dear Lord aloud that He had brought her back home again, and that everything, everything was still so beautiful, and even more beautiful than she had thought, and that it all was hers once more. And Heidi felt so happy and so rich in the great glory that she could not find words to express her thankfulness to the dear Lord.

Not until the light all about began to fade could Heidi move away from the place. But then she ran so fast up the mountain that it was not long before she saw the boughs of the fir trees above the roof, and then the roof itself, and then the whole hut, and on the seat beside it sat her grandfather, smoking his pipe; and over the hut the old fir trees were rocking their branches and roaring in the evening wind. Then Heidi ran all the faster, and before the Alm-Uncle could really see what was coming the child rushed up to him, threw her basket on the ground, and hugged the old man. In her excitement at seeing him again she was unable to say anything, except to keep exclaiming: "Grandfather! grandfather! grandfather!"

Neither did the grandfather say anything. For the first time in many years his eyes grew moist, and he had to pass his hand over them. Then he loosened Heidi's arms from his neck, took her on his knee, and looked at her for a moment.

"So you have come home again, Heidi," he said then; "how is it? You don't look particularly fine. Did they send you away?"

"Oh, no, grandfather," Heidi now began fervently to say; "you must not think that; they were all so good— Klara and the grandmamma and Herr Sesemann. But you see, grandfather, I could hardly bear to wait any longer to come home again to you, and I often thought I should stifle, it choked me so; but I really never said anything about it, because it would be ungrateful. And then suddenly one morning Herr Sesemann called me very early; but I believe the doctor was the cause of it; but perhaps it tells all about it in the letter"—whereupon Heidi jumped down on the ground, took her letter and her roll out of the basket and laid them both in her grandfather's hand.

"That belongs to you," he said, laying the roll beside

him on the seat. Then he took the letter and read it through; without saying a word he put it into his pocket.

"Do you think you can drink milk with me still, Heidi?" he then asked, while he took the child by the hand to lead her into the hut. "But take your money with you; you can buy a bed with it, and clothes enough to last you for two or three years."

"I really don't need it, grandfather," said Heidi; "I have a bed already; and Klara packed up so many clothes for me that I shall really never need any more."

"Take it, take it, and put it in the cupboard; you will be able to use it sometime."

Heidi obeyed and skipped after her grandfather into the hut, where, delighted to see everything again, she ran into every corner and up the ladder; but there she suddenly stood still and called down, somewhat concerned:—

"Oh, grandfather, I no longer have any bed!"

"You will soon have another," sounded from below. "I didn't know that you would return; now come and get your milk!"

Heidi came down and took her seat on her high stool in the old place, and then grasped her little bowl and drank as eagerly as if she had never had anything so precious within her reach before, and when she put down her bowl, with a deep breath, she said:—

"There is nothing in all the world so good as our milk, grandfather."

A shrill whistle sounded outside. Heidi shot out the door like lightning. There was the whole flock of goats, skipping, jumping, and leaping down from the heights above, and Peter in their midst. When he saw Heidi he stood perfectly still, as if rooted to the spot, and stared at her speechless. Heidi called out: "Good-evening, Peter!" and rushed in among the goats. "Schwänli! Bärli! Do you know me still?"

The goats must have recognized her voice, for they rubbed their heads against her and began to bleat passionately for joy, and Heidi called them all by name, one after the other, and they all ran like wild creatures in confusion and crowded around her. The impatient Distelfinck jumped high into the air and over two other goats, in order to get near her at once, and the timid Schneehöpli gave the big Türk a very determined thrust and pushed him aside, so that he stood looking much amazed at the impudence, and raised his beard in the air to show that it was he.

Heidi was beside herself with joy to see all her old companions once more; she threw her arms around the little affectionate Schneehöpli again and again, stroked the violent Distelfinck, and was pushed and jolted hither and thither by the fond, trusting goats until she came quite near to Peter, who remained standing in the same place.

"Come down, Peter, and say good-evening to me!" Heidi called to him.

"Are you really back again?" he finally managed to say in his astonishment; and then he came forward and took Heidi's hand, which she had been offering him for some time, and asked, as he always did when he was returning home at evening:—

"Will you come with me again to-morrow?"

"No, not to-morrow, but the day after, perhaps; for to-morrow I must go to the grandmother's."

"It is good to have you back again," said Peter, making all sorts of wry faces from huge delight; then he started homeward; but he had never before had such difficulty with his goats, for when he had at last, with coaxing and threatening, succeeded in collecting them about him, and Heidi had walked away with one arm around Schwänli's and the other about Bärli's neck, they all with one accord turned around again and ran after the three. Heidi had to go into the shed with her two goats and shut the door, or Peter would never have succeeded in getting away with his flock.

When the child came back into the hut she found her bed already made up again, wonderfully high and fragrant, for the hay had not been in long, and the grandfather had very carefully spread the clean linen sheet over it. Heidi lay down on it with great delight and had a refreshing sleep, such as she had not enjoyed for a whole long year. During the night her grandfather left his couch at least ten times, climbed the ladder and listened carefully to see if Heidi was still asleep and was not restless, and looked at the window where the moon used to shine in on Heidi's bed, to see if the hay he had stuffed into it was still there, for the moon should be kept out henceforth. But Heidi slept right on and wandered about no longer, for her great, hungry, longing was satisfied; she had seen all the mountains and cliffs in the evening glow again, she had heard the fir trees roaring, she was at home again on the Alm.

Heidi *was first published in 1880. Attractive editions are published by McKay, illustrated by Jessie Wilcox Smith; and by Lippincott, illustrated by Agnes Tait.*

Christophilos and the Pascal Lamb

BY JOICE M. NANKIVELL

Illustrations by Panos Ghikas

The people in Pyrgos call their tiny village in Greece, "the world." When they say, "the world knows," they mean everybody in the village knows. When they say "the sun has teeth," they mean that the sun is strong enough to bite after the winter. Christophilos, his mother, and his grandmother, whom he calls Yaryar, like almost everyone in Pyrgos, are very poor. There are many tales of Christophilos. Some people say they are only legends. But the people who live in "the world" know they are true.

IT was the time of the year when fishermen paint their boats. Some of them could afford paint, but most of them couldn't, and those who had no money for paint stood along the shore, or sat in cafés on the sea front and said it was too early to paint the boats.

The octopuses in the sea, and the hens in the village were preparing to lay their spring eggs. Of course an octopus's egg is only of importance to an octopus; but in their way they are just as fussy over them as hens are.

Yaryar said it was not the time of year to shed one's clothes, although the sun had teeth, and Christophilos's neighbor said that even a donkey knew that, and that is why they drop their coats so slowly.

Everything in the world knew it was spring. White herons mated along the shore, and dolphins wheeled in the sea near the tower. The sun drew so much color out of the sky and dropped it into the sea that men paused on their way to work to admire the brilliant, glistening waves.

It was the Easter fast, and everybody ate dry bread and olives, and young green garlic, and weeds from the fields. Only the babies drank milk. The whole village prepared for Easter.

Houses were whitewashed inside and out, and those who could not afford to buy whitewash stole it from their neighbors. Every man kept a careful watch on his lime pit. Yaryar even whitewashed the big cobblestones in the floor, so that it looked very clean indeed.

On calm days boats stole out to fish for octopuses, and when the afternoon breeze came up and spoiled the fishing you could hear the flap, flap, slap, slap of octopuses being beaten along the shore. And you could see a long line of men rubbing, and stroking, and beating them, until they were tender enough for the pot. Octopus is neither fish nor meat, and can be eaten all the year round, even in the Easter fast.

Octopus poles on either side of the boats were hung with long, lank octopuses drying in the sun, and by day and night the smell of them hung over the village.

One day the swifts came back to the tower, helter-skelter, from the lands they had wintered in, and there began a great clamor and the rush of wings up and down the chutes outside the top of the tower. The swifts built their nests in the chutes, but the swallows flew into the tower and stuck their nests all over the big, old wooden beams. They passed in and out of the windows and arrow holes as they had done for hundreds and hundreds of years.

The world climbed up and down the stairs twice a
day to church; the old people, and the young people, and
the women with babies. They sighed as they climbed
because the tower was so high, and the stairs so steep,
and the old people felt it was such a labor that their
hearts must really break; but they all went.

The men of the village walked among their herds
each day and poked the baby goats in the ribs to see
which was the fattest because every household had to

kill a fine fat kid for Easter. The mother of Christophilos
had only she-goats, and she thought it terrible to kill a
little she-goat for eating.

Yaryar said, "Change the she-goat for a little he-goat,
and kill that."

"Who would give away a good she-goat for a he-goat?"
asked Christophilos's mother. "Only a fool would do
that. I will kill Mavroula, the wild pig."

This shocked everyone very much indeed, because
the world knew that Mavroula, the wild pig, had been
suckled by a dog, and they believed that her flesh had
become the same as a dog's. To eat dog's flesh is shame-
ful but to eat it at Easter would be terrible. The boys
called, "Dog eater!" after Christophilos, as he walked
through the village, and at last he felt it was more than
he could bear. But his mother was a very determined
woman, and the more people cried, "Dog eater!" the
more she intended to kill Mavroula.

Yaryar cried for two whole days, and then said she
would pass Easter fasting unless she could eat with the
neighbors, for never in all her life had she done anything
so sinful as to eat dog's meat.

Easter is a very joyous occasion, and everyone should
eat lambs, because lambs are young and joyful. That
has been the custom from very old times indeed.

The lamb must be killed on the threshold of the house
at midday, the day before Easter Sunday, and it must
be roasted in the great village oven at night while everyone is at the Easter Service. It must be finished when
the guns go off, and the people shout to each other,
"Christ has risen! Truly He has risen!" And all the children crack colored Easter eggs.

The old tower becomes lively and wonderful at Easter,
blazing with candles. Up and down the stairs, and on
the landings, and in the big empty rooms. Everyone
holds a candle, and sometimes two. Big fat brown can-

dles made of beeswax and big fat white candles made of tallow. They take the holy fire from the priest on Easter night, and then carry their candles home through the village in procession, sheltering the lights with their hands.

They laugh and drop candle grease over each other, and if a candle blows out, a dozen offer light to it, so that each house has its own portion of holy fire for the year.

Then the lambs are eaten with great rejoicing, even if they are only goats. But how could anyone rejoice over a wild pig that has been suckled by a dog?

Christophilos spoke to the priest about it, but the priest was only thinking of Easter, and he said, "Speak to me afterwards, boy," and he got off his chair and limped about his room. Christophilos knew that after Easter would be too late.

When he went home he found his mother angry and red in the face. She stood in the middle of the room talking fast and loud, and Yaryar crouched on her heels spinning wool with a hand spindle.

"I carry more brushwood to the village oven than any other woman, and I've always done so," cried Christophilos's mother as he came in, "and now the women dare say that I cannot roast Mavroula, the wild pig, in the oven! We'll see who's who when the time comes! If necessary I will cook her on a spit over charcoal in the village square!"

"Is it wise to go against the world—" began Yaryar, but Christophilos's mother stamped her foot, and cried, "Na!" which is a term of great contempt. Then she turned on Christophilos.

"Are you a little goat, that you play!" she cried. "Go to the forest with the pig and feed her there!"

"It's going to rain," said Yaryar. "See how low the swallows are flying."

"Rain, or no rain the pig must go to the forest," she cried.

Christophilos took Mavroula out of the house. She trotted briskly along beside him on her toe-tips, running on ahead and grunting back at him, nosing everything out of curiosity. He used to be proud of her following him, because everyone used to say, "There goes Christophilos and his wild pig." They nodded their heads and told strangers how he caught her himself when she was very small. Now they all cried, "Dog eater!" after him, and he felt terribly ashamed.

He found a choice spot for Mavroula, and drove the

peg of her rope into the ground, and she began to enjoy herself grunting and rooting as all pigs do.

Christophilos thought how good it would be if she broke her rope and ran off and became wild again; but he didn't dare to let her go because of his mother's anger. Then he heard a monk singing along the forest road and he was singing an old song to keep the devil off his path. He walked very fast, leading a mule loaded with wine, and the wine was in pigskins, tied with thongs of leather round the neck and four legs. The legs stuck out fat and funny, and the wine churned in the skins and made them wabble as the mule walked.

"Ho, Christophilos!" cried the monk, and at that moment the mule stepped on a small stone, which slipped under its shoe.

"There!" cried the monk, "that is because I stopped singing for protection against the devil!" He made a funny face at Christophilos, and dropped the rope of the mule's halter, which was plastered with blue beads for luck and had a knot of garlic plaited into it against the evil eye.

Christophilos ran to help the monk because he was naturally a helpful boy; and because the monk was old and stout and breathed heavily when he stooped. Christophilos picked up the mule's foot and held it between his knees. The monk pulled a long, hooked knife out of his pocket under his gown, and between them they got out the stone.

While they worked, Mavroula, who was exceedingly inquisitive, sniffed at the calves of the monk's great legs. The monk was very pleased with Christophilos, and very interested in Mavroula, and he wanted to know how Christophilos had caught her. Christophilos told him everything. He even told him how they must eat Mavroula when the dear Christ had risen, and everyone else was joyfully eating lamb.

"But," said the monk, "that is a sin. She has been suckled by a dog. You must let her go to the forest again."

Then he suddenly remembered his grapes, and how the wild pigs came each summer and spoilt the vineyards in spite of a guard of eighty monks with stout sticks, and tin cans to beat them off with, and in spite of blazing bonfires, and a great deal of fuss and noise.

"No, that won't do at all," he said quickly. "There are too many wild pigs!" Then he saw Christophilos's sad face, and he cried, "I have it! I am going to sell my wine in the town of Errisos, and I have a spare sack to bring things back to the monastery in. I will carry Mavroula off in it, and sell her for you in the market, and I will buy a fat Easter lamb with the money!"

"A lamb!" cried Christophilos, "but that would be wonderful! No one in our village eats lamb, because we have only goats."

So they tied Mavroula in the sack and hung her among the sacks of wine, and she squealed and yelled as the monk hurried her through the village, but Christophilos's mother never guessed it was Mavroula when she saw the monk leading the mule past her house. But when Christophilos went home and told her what had happened, she was very angry indeed, so angry that she took a stick and Christophilos into the yard, meaning to beat him where the world could see, but the neighbor looked over the fence and cried out, "You will hurt him for all his life if you beat him for that!" And Christophilos's mother threw down the stick and started to quarrel with the neighbor instead, which was what he wanted.

The next morning the monk came riding back, and he had sold the wine, and Mavroula, the wild pig, and he had a fine, fat lamb on the saddle in front of him.

When she saw the lamb, and the great crowd of villagers following the mule, the mother of Christophilos was proud and happy because no one else had a lamb.

She cried, "See what comes of being a virtuous, hard-working woman!" and she ran out of the house, and helped the monk off the mule and thanked him. She tied the lamb near the front door where all the world could see it; and the world came, and poked it in the ribs and said with a fine lamb it was. The children brought him flowers and grass to eat, and some brought him raisins, for he was the only lamb in the village.

There are many more stories about Christophilos in Tales of Chistophilos *and its sequel,* Again Christophilos, *both published by Houghton Mifflin Company.*

Wild Elephant Raid

BY WILLIS LINDQUIST

Illustrations by Nicolas Mordvinoff

At one time the mighty elephant Majda Koom had been as a playfellow to the boy Haji, who rode everywhere on the great animal's head. But now Majda Koom leads a herd of wild elephants and is known as a killer. The men of the village say he must die.

For a time he dozed, trying to sleep so that he would be well rested for his long journey through the jungle.

Presently, something brought him out of his sleep. He was suddenly wide awake, and he could not understand why. He sat up.

"What is it?" Ket Kay asked.

"I don't know. Did you hear anything?"

"There was nothing to hear."

That was odd, Haji thought. He knew only that his keen senses had brought him a warning. He listened, turning his head this way and that.

Somewhere in the paddy a porcupine called softly to its mate. Frogs and crickets were singing their usual songs to the starry heavens. But Haji knew these sounds would not have awakened him.

Perhaps it was not a sound at all. He tested the cool night breeze coming down from the jungled hills, and his sensitive nostrils caught a familiar smell, like the spicy fragrance of crushed grasses.

"Elephants!" he whispered. "A big herd, and very close, too, or I couldn't smell them."

"Do you think Majda Koom—"

"Look!" Haji pointed to a dark shape moving into the paddy.

Other shapes followed. Like ghostly shadows they came, large elephants and small, slipping quietly out from the fringe of the jungle to feast on the precious rice.

Ket Kay grabbed Haji's arm so hard it hurt. "All our rice will be eaten. The soldiers will not be here until tomorrow. What can we do?"

"I don't know," Haji said. He had hoped to find the elephants in the jungle, before they reached the rice fields. Even the tame animals from the elephant camp would be hard to manage if they got in a rice field.

The whole margin of the jungle now was alive with shadowy motion. On they came, without making a sound. Haji had never seen such a large herd. He bent forward, trying to locate Majda Koom.

"Quick!" Ket Kay said. "Ring the bell of Majda Koom!"

An elephant hungry for rice would pay no attention to a bell, Haji knew. But he rang the bell just the same, more to please Ket Kay than anything else.

The voice of the bell brought the boys in the other watchtowers to life. They saw the elephants and began shouting and banging gongs and throwing stones to frighten away the herd. The hail of stones and the noise merely annoyed the elephants.

Haji did not like this. If the boys made the elephants angry there would be bad trouble. Stones and noise were not going to stop a mighty herd.

But one of the stones must have found its mark, for suddenly, above the din, came a scream and a crash. A watchtower disappeared at the end of the field. There were more screams from the boys, and more crashes.

"It's Majda Koom," cried Haji. "They made him angry with their stones. Now he's charging the towers!"

In frozen horror, the boys watched.

"We'll all be killed," cried Ket Kay. "Now he's coming this way! Do something, Haji. Stop him!"

What could he do? Down went the towers, one by one. Boys leaped for their lives as the bamboo frames of the towers exploded beneath them. Haji couldn't think. He couldn't move. Was there nothing that could stop that furious charge?

Down the line of towers rushed the enraged elephant. He smacked into the tower next to theirs and over it went with a sickening crash.

"Here he comes!" screamed Ket Kay.

"Jump aside when he rams," Haji told him. "Jump that way. No harm will come if you hide in the rice and leave him alone."

In his haste to get ready for the leap, Ket Kay accidentally kicked the wooden elephant bell from the platform. Not that it mattered. It could not help them now.

Haji had no thought of saving himself. The mighty beast would soon pass under the platform as he rammed their tower. He had to be stopped if the rice fields and the village were to be saved. But how?

He had only seconds to think, for rushing at them out of the night came the giant elephant, trumpeting with rage.

Only one thing could stop him now—fear! If he could be frightened somehow, his fear would spread through the entire elephant herd like wildfire. They would scatter in panic and never come back.

"I have to try to scare him," Haji thought. His heart hammered as he braced himself. There was still hope, still a chance, if he could do it right. If he failed, he would die.

He waited till the elephant was almost beneath him. Then, with the savage snarl of a tiger breaking from his lips, he jumped.

Nimble as a cat he twisted in mid-air and came down where he wanted to land—squarely on the back of the huge elephant.

Majda Koom was taken completely by surprise. His screams of terror filled the night. He turned in sudden panic and bolted for the jungle, as if ten tigers were clawing his back.

Haji clung desperately with fingers and toes. With all the power of his lungs, he kept snarling like a royal tiger making a kill.

He could hear the frightened trumpeting of the other elephants. Panic spread through the big herd. They had seen their great leader frightened off by some mysterious attack, and now they scattered and fled from the unknown danger.

Haji saw them disappearing into the jungle far to the left of him. A tight smile came to his lips. He had won. His plan had worked. The village and rice fields were

saved, and none of them would ever return, for elephants never came back to a place where they had been badly frightened.

But Haji had little time to be pleased with himself. The wild, swaying ride took all his attention and strength. Now he had to find a way to escape from Majda Koom— if he could. It wouldn't be easy.

He did not think he could hang on the broad back for long. His fingers were not strong enough to dig into the rough hide. There was nothing to which he could hold. One slip would bring sudden death, for if he fell, the desperate beast would wheel instantly and trample him into the earth in a few seconds.

When they were deep in the jungle, Majda Koom slackened his pace suddenly. Haji caught his breath. The battle for his life was just beginning.

Without warning, the great trunk lashed back at him. It whipped so close to his face he could feel the wind of it. Again and again Majda struck out with his trunk, mighty blows that could have crushed the skull of a tiger. But Haji knew how far back an elephant could reach with its trunk and stayed clear.

Then Majda abruptly changed his method of attack. Tossing his mighty head, he reared, went up and over on his back to crush the unknown thing beneath him, just as See Po had killed the tiger.

Haji was not to be caught so easily. He jumped aside at the last moment.

With a rumble of disgust, the big tusker rolled over on its side. As it made to rise, Haji sprang up on a huge hind knee and vaulted to the broad back again.

"Tah! Tah! Stand up! Stand up!" he shouted. "I am not a tiger. I am Haji."

Now that they were alone in the jungle, Haji began to hope that somehow, by his actions and words, he could make Majda Koom recognize him.

"If I had not lost your bell in the rice field," he said, "you would soon remember me."

The sound of his voice seemed only to anger the beast. It went off through the brush and made for the river. Soon it was splashing out through the shallows.

"Ay, big brother," said Haji. "What you need is a bath in the river. Perhaps it will cool your temper."

The big bull made a rumbling answer in his throat and plowed deeper and deeper into the river, until at last the muddy water closed over the elephant completely. Soon the water was up to Haji's neck. Then he had to swim. All he could see of Majda, who was walking on the bottom, was the tip of the trunk, held above water for breathing.

It reminded Haji of the water game they had played so often together. He looked at the tip of the trunk only a few feet ahead of him. To play the game he had only to swim over, grab the trunk, and pull it below the surface. Did Majda Koom want him to play the game now? Was the animal testing him to find out if he really was the boy Haji?

There was no way of being sure. Haji was afraid to go near. How could he be certain the trunk would not coil about him and drag him down to an awful death?

Slowly the tip of the trunk moved toward the far shore. Once it stopped and waved from side to side, as if inviting Haji to grab it.

Then suddenly the trunk disappeared altogether. Haji knew what that meant. It was the trick of a killer elephant!

In the muddy water an elephant could turn unseen below the surface and drag down a swimmer in a matter of moments. Haji took no chances. He dived, found the elephant's tail, and hung on. So long as he could hang onto the tail and hold his breath he was safe enough.

Twice he had to kick up to the surface for air, and dive for the tail again. But when Majda Koom emerged on the far bank of the river, Haji was once again perched on his back.

Again the mighty elephant had failed to get rid of him. But the battle was far from over. With a bellow of rage as big as six tiger roars, Majda Koom rammed into the thickest of the jungle to brush the pesky man-thing from his back.

It was what Haji had most dreaded. He would be helpless against such an attack. A terrible fear gripped him as they smashed headlong through snarled entanglements that lashed and tore at his body.

Though he flattened down, it did not help him. There was no protection against the scraping jungle. Branches clubbed him. Twigs jabbed into his flesh like hot needles. Thorns ripped the length of his back till he cried out in pain. No one could take such bruising punishment for long.

Again and again he screamed for Majda to stop.

Tears blinded him. Dizziness and pain took the strength from his body. His fingers grew numb. The end was near, he knew, for he couldn't hold on much longer. Death would come quickly and take away the pain. He was thankful for that.

Just when he thought he would have to give up, a strange thing happened. The terrible punishment ceased as quickly as it had begun. They were in the open now, rushing through milky morning mists. It was almost too good to be true.

Cautiously, Haji raised his head to look in front of them. Too late he saw the branch—a low branch coming at him like a swinging club.

It struck with a solid jolt. Stars burst in his head. The world spun and dipped and turned on edge, so that he couldn't tell up from down. It began to grow dark. For

a terrible instant he hung on, fighting the swirling gray-
ness that was closing over him.

But it closed down just the same. He went limp. He
could feel his fingers lose their hold. He was slipping. . .
slipping. . .sliding off into space. . .falling down, down,
down into a bottomless pit of darkness.

It seemed like a long and restless sleep. And when he
opened his eyes at last, the sun was lacing down through
leafy bowers in the roof of the Burma jungle. How peaceful it was! Flies buzzed around him. Birds were chattering.

Nothing seemed quite real at first. It felt good to rest.
But after a time, he remembered his fall from the elephant's back. His arms and legs felt as stiff as sticks, and
his head hurt where the branch had struck him.

Slowly, he tested his arms, then his legs. He could
move them. He felt of his head. There was a lump on
the top. That was all. There was nothing to worry about.
He could get up and go home as soon as he had rested.

For a time, he tried to sleep. Then, suddenly, all the
little lazy sounds of the jungle morning were shattered
by the loud flopping of elephant ears.

Haji sat up with a start. His eyes went wide.

Only a few feet away stood the mighty Majda Koom,
swaying gently back and forth, as elephants usually do.
Majda stopped swaying. They looked at each other.

For an endless moment, Haji forgot to breathe. He
had not been trampled—not yet—but he knew that was
not the miracle it seemed. When he had fallen and hit
the ground, he had lain there in a lifeless heap—and
elephants rarely attacked anything that did not move
or show some sign of life.

But now! Now that he had moved, what would the
elephant do? Had it waited to kill him? Or had it touched
and smelled of his body and recognized him?

As if in answer, Majda reached slowly out with his long trunk. He touched Haji's chest gently as he had done so many times before, and made the small whistling sounds of a happy elephant.

A cry broke from Haji's lips. With both hands he caught the trunk and laid his cheek against it. Majda Koom knew him and loved him still!

Two years, two long years of waiting and hoping—and now it was over. They were back together again. Haji knew his father had been right. An elephant's eyes were not very sharp at a distance. All Majda had needed was a close look at him, and to touch and smell of him.

Late the following afternoon, with Haji riding proudly

on the mighty head of his tusker, they entered the elephant camp. In a moment, the entire camp was in an uproar. People came running from all directions, and among them were Ket Kay and several others from the village.

"I said you would bring him here!" cried Ket Kay. "They did not believe me, but I knew it. We told how you saved the village. They did not want to believe that either."

Byoo, Haji's young friend from the elephant camp, stared. "We believe it now," he said. "It is Majda Koom. No one but Haji could have brought him back."

The villagers from Chinwa pressed through the crowd and one of them said, "The elders have sent us to take you back to the village for a day. They wish to honor you."

Oo Yan, the chief of the oozies, was nodding his head. "It is well," he said. "For one day he may go. But you will remind your elders that this boy is one of the elephant people. He belongs here with us."

At a word from Haji, the great tusker lowered him to the ground with his trunk. Haji turned to face Thakin Jensen and the amazed oozies. Thakin Jensen still acted as if he could hardly believe what he saw.

Oo Yan stepped forward and placed a hand warmly on Haji's shoulder. "If our faith in you has been small, my son, you have at last opened our eyes. You have done what our best oozies could not do."

Ket Kay's dark eyes sparkled. "I knew he would do it. I knew it! Was there ever anyone so brave?"

Slowly a smile grew on Thakin Jensen's lips. "Many are brave," he said. "What this boy Haji has done took far more than courage. It took love—the kind of love that a great oozie has for his elephant."

Thakin Jensen turned to Oo Yan. "Majda Koom will need careful watching for a time. See that no one handles him but this boy, and make sure the boy is properly trained as an oozie."

The oozies smiled and nodded. The wrinkled one said, "Truly this boy is the son of his father. He will make a good oozie."

Oo Yan seemed more pleased than anyone. He raised his hands for silence. "Hail! Hail to the new oozie of Majda Koom!"

Loudly and long, they hailed him.

Haji could not keep the painful lump from swelling in his throat, or the tears from his eyes. He stepped back and, resting one of his hands on a great curved tusk of his elephant, stood proudly.

Then a smile broke upon his lips, for he heard the best hail of all. It came from the great beast beside him—the happy whistling sounds of the lord of all elephants.

Willis Lindquist has also written Call of the White Fox *(published by Whittlesey House), a story of the friendship between an Eskimo boy and a wild fox cub.*

Snow Treasure

BY MARIE McSWIGAN

Illustrations by Mary Reardon

> During World War II, in the early days of
> the occupation of Norway, a group of brave
> children played an important part in saving
> their country's gold. Under the leadership of
> twelve-year-old Peter they used their sleds
> to smuggle the gold past the very noses of
> the Nazi soldiers. This story is based on an
> actual happening.

THE next night saw Norway blacked out from one end
to the other. Over a thousand miles and not a light.
Windows were draped in black and people were cautioned not to allow so much as a candle ray to show
outside their houses.

That was the night of April eighth.

Throughout the country was the feeling of impend-
ing evil. It was as if some unknown terror would come
out of the deep shadows.

Children who were old enough to know, cried themselves to sleep. But it was not alone they who were
afraid. The grown-ups, too, saw fright in the black of
night.

The air raid shelters were hastily finished. Big blocks
of ice served the purpose of sand bags in other countries.

In the houses were strange preparations. For what,—

no one could tell clearly. Hunting rifles were brought
out and cleaned, though this was often unnecessary in
that land of great hunters. Ancient pistols came out of
hiding places and clumsy fowling pieces were lifted
down from pegs above doors.

Peter would have liked to go out to see what Riswyk
looked like without a light anywhere. But that was impossible. Even though there was not yet a war, his
father was leaving that night to join the regiment to
which his class in military college belonged. Peter could
not go out on his last night home.

"You're the man of the house, Peter," his father told
him. "You must look after your mother and the little
ones."

Peter had expected to do this without being told.

"What about the gold?" he asked his father.

"Uncle Victor will tell you what to do. You may not
need to do anything at all. There may be no trouble
after all."

"But if there is? If there's a war?"

"You must wait for Uncle Victor. He'll tell you all you
need to know. And though I know I don't have to warn
you, not a word to anyone about what you're doing. If
any stranger addresses you, you're to be deaf, dumb and
blind. But you're not to talk."

"When do you suppose we'll start?"

"When Uncle Victor gives the word."

Peter thought this a most unsatisfactory answer. But
he could see no good in asking further. If his father
knew anything, clearly he wasn't going to tell.

Some of the men of Riswyk had already left town.
Nanson, the sail-maker, had gone and Michael Berg's
father and many more. Mr. Anders, the schoolmaster,
too. With him away, that day had been a holiday as
would be the morrow and every other day. But what

was the good of a holiday like that? No one wanted to play. They tried all the games they knew but no one seemed to enjoy any of them. Peter called a meeting of the Defense Club. The air raid drill wasn't very exciting. For although they could blow a warning whistle, they had no one to give them the "All Clear" signal when to come out.

Helga and some of the girls thought it would be fun to play at being Red Cross nurses. But when they picked Bunny for the first air raid victim, he kicked and screamed so they had to let him go, even though his legs were supposed to be shot away.

But the long day dragged through somehow and now it was night. But what a different night, different from any Peter had ever lived through. He didn't know but what he would rather have a toothache.

After supper his father seemed to be waiting for some message. It never came. He kept taking his watch out to see the time although there were clocks everywhere you could look. His train did not go until midnight and the sleigh to take him to the station would not come for hours yet.

Peter peeped out of the window, careful that no light showed outside. There was nothing but darkness. There wasn't even a sound in this terrifying void. The world seemed to have come to an end at Peter's house. Life could not be possible in the blackness beyond.

When the hour finally came for Mr. Lundstrom to leave, they all tried to be cheerful. Peter's mother even started to make a little joke. Old Per Garson shuffled in for the bags and then the door closed and blotted out Peter's father in the black of the outside.

Mrs. Lundstrom turned to Peter in a flood of tears.

He tried to comfort her but there was little he could say.

"You've me, Mother. I'll not let anything happen to you. Father said I was to look after you and Lovisa and Bunny and I will."

She smiled when she spoke. "I know, Peter. I'm being foolish. After all, I *do* have you."

Four hours after that, German parachute troops landed in Norway, and through all the ports clear into the Arctic Circle, soldiers and marines poured out of merchant ships in the harbors. There were even grey clad Nazi soldiers on the beach at Riswyk Fiord. It was Uncle Victor who brought the news in the morning.

"On your sleds, children," he directed. "There's not a day to lose."

"Aren't you in danger, Uncle Victor?" Peter asked. "Couldn't they take you prisoner?"

They were in the living room of Peter's home. Mrs. Lundstrom had taken Lovisa and Bunny and had gone to get some of the other children who were to help.

"Per Garson's on the watch. He'll tell me if anyone comes and I'll slip out the back and down the slope. They'll be good skiers to catch me."

"But they could shoot."

Uncle Victor only shrugged.

"Do you know where the British and French have laid their mines?" Peter hoped the answer would be yes. Otherwise what would be the use of taking the gold out of the cave if Uncle Victor couldn't sail away with it?

"Only partly."

"Well, why do we take the gold down the mountain if you can't sail away? I should think it'd be safer where it is."

"Peter, it's not right you should question anyone in authority," his uncle spoke irritably. "In military school you'll learn to do as you're told without asking why. But I'll tell you why it's important for you children to be seen on your sleds today. In the future, however, you're not to question."

"Yes, Uncle Victor," Peter spoke meekly. "You can't sail the *Cleng Peerson* out of the Snake till you know where the mines are laid. But you can load her and have her ready to leave the minute you learn where they are. Is that the reason?"

"Not at all, Peter," his uncle answered. "The reason you must be on your sleds today near the fiord is to accustom the Germans to seeing you there. If they see you today and every day, they won't suspect anything unusual. But if, all at once, you started going in the direction of the Snake, they'd be stupid geese not to know something was going on."

Peter hadn't thought of that. How smart Uncle Victor was!

"Now about the mines," his uncle went on. "By the time the gold is loaded we'll know all we need to know about them. You don't suppose my fishermen can't find out anything they want to, about our coast, do you? Remember, Peter, we're Norwegians and we're as much at home in the water as we are on land. This is our country and these are our waters and there's no foreign power that can keep us from using what's always belonged to us."

Victor Lundstrom thought he heard a noise. But it was not the heavy tread of marching men but the light quick steps of children, those who were to be seen on their sleds either around the town or down at the Snake. Today, only four of them would take gold to the Snake but after that there would be many more. Mrs. Lundstrom had gone first for Michael and Helga; and here they were, and Lovisa was with them.

"Now we can get started," Uncle Victor spoke. "Listen carefully while I tell you what you're to do. I may have to leave any minute so pay attention. If there's anything I miss, Fru Lundstrom or Per Garson will tell you."

There wasn't a sound from any of the four.

"What I'm going to say is of the gravest importance. On you, to an extent, depends the welfare of your country. If you do what you're told and do it right, you'll be helping countless Norwegians,—not only the soldiers in the army but the people at home."

Eyes were bright at this mention of a chance to help their country.

"If you children win out, the enemy that today has invaded a peace-loving, unoffending country, will have less gold and so, fewer guns and less ammunition and food. Also, fewer opportunities to use our wealth to bring suffering and death to our people," he went on.

"Peter will take you to a place where we've hidden thirteen tons of gold bullion—money, you know, that's not been made into coins. Now, you are to take that bullion from its hiding place to the Snake where it will be loaded on my boat and taken to America to be kept safe for Norway.

"Here is what you do. Peter will take you to the hiding place. After that it's up to you. You'll have to find your own way back there later. What is more, you'll have to show the other children. So watch how you get there. Now in Riswyk School there are thirty-eight pupils, we think, old enough for this. These will divide into teams of nine, a captain and a squad of eight."

"That leaves two over," Peter spoke.

"Right," his uncle answered. "You and Michael will each have ten. Your mother has made up the teams. You four are captains and you must take the ones assigned to you, and no quarreling. And if any differences arise, Peter's the one to settle them. You must do as he says. Of course your teams will split up on the way. You'll go in twos and threes. For if they counted nine and ten each time, they'd know something was up."

He stopped for a minute and then went on. "It's getting late and I've something very important to tell you. And that is, under no circumstances must you speak one word to a stranger. Not a syllable. Not so much as yes or no or good-day. Understand?"

The four of them nodded.

"Now today Peter will take you to the cave where we hid the gold. Per Garson will go along to load each sled. You'll each be given seventy-five pounds of bullion, that's over eighty thousand kroner, twenty thousand United States dollars. It will be packed in flat bricks and each of you will take four bricks. These you'll sit on or lie on when you ride 'bellygrinder.'

"When you get to the Snake this afternoon you're to look for a place where there are two fallen trees. They are pretty well buried under the snow, but you'll find them because you're Norwegians. You know such things. Between these trees you're to bury your bricks in the snow. Over the top of each pile you'll build a snowman. When I come out at night with Rolls, my mate, I'll only have to find the snowmen."

This was even better than playing pirates, Peter decided.

"Now about the return trip. You start back up the mountain to the Holms' farm where you'll spend the night. They have room for dozens. The girls will stay in the house and the boys in the barn. You will get a warm supper and breakfast next day. Then you'll come back here. But it won't matter if you are late because you are to rest that day and start back to the Snake the next day. The way we've planned it is for two teams to go one day and the two others the next. That will give you a day to rest up, or almost a day."

Per Garson stuck his head in the door.

"Jan from the sailyard comes," he said. "He thinks the Germans are starting up the mountain."

Uncle Victor jumped up.

"Oh, Uncle Victor, don't let them get you," Lovisa moaned.

He slipped out of the room and through the kitchen to the outside. They could hear the whiz of his skis on the hard snow.

"Well, what are we waiting for?" Michael asked. "You know the way to this cave or whatever it is." He turned to Peter. "What's wrong with going there and getting this thing started?"

Uncle Victor had left because he had been warned the Germans were on their way to Riswyk. Per Garson had shown him out and the children were alone in the room. They could hear nothing after the sound of his skis had died away.

"Right," Peter jumped up. "We're supposed to be seen near the beach today so we'll have to get started. But first there's something we should do before we begin any of this. I think we ought to make a pact we'll never tell anything if we're caught."

"We won't get caught," Michael spoke.

"But if we are?"

"Bah!" he shook his crew-cut hair.

"I still think we should make a pact we won't tell one word about what we're doing, about taking gold to the Snake."

"We'd hardly do that after what your Uncle Victor said about not so much as a word to strangers." Helga Thomsen was scornful that Peter thought such a promise necessary.

"But if we're tortured? If they try to make us tell, and torture us if we don't?" Michael's eyes shone with excitement. "What if they threaten to pull out our tongues if we don't tell?"

"Not if our tongues were to be pulled out would we tell!" Helga shook her black curls.

"There'd be little sense in that if they really wanted us to talk." Lovisa could always see the funny side.

"Then you wouldn't mind swearing?" Peter ignored Lovisa's interruption. "If you're sure you wouldn't tell, you wouldn't mind pledging yourselves."

"Certainly I wouldn't mind swearing," Helga answered. "No matter how I was tortured, I'd not say a word."

Peter went to the fireplace and climbed on a chair to bring down a sword his ancestors had used in wars against the Swedes, hundreds of years before. He drew off its dried leather cover.

"Swear on this then. Hands on the blade."

"I swear." Helga put her hand on the wide blade and Lovisa and Michael put theirs beside hers.

"I swear." Lovisa's blue eyes were round.

"I swear I'll have my tongue pulled out. I'll be tortured with a red hot poker, and I'll have my head on a pole before I'll say a single word." Michael spoke excitedly.

"And I the same." Peter put back the sword. "Now we'd better be off to the cave for our loads. It's just us today. Tomorrow or the next day we will take the others."

"Should we make them swear, too?" Michael asked.

"What's the use? They'll know they're not to talk to strangers."

"But maybe we should make them swear."

"After what Uncle Victor said in school? About obeying without a question? I guess not." Peter had great faith in his uncle. When he gave a command it was obeyed. "Come on. Let's be going."

"Beat you to the sleds," Helga spoke.

There was a scramble for the door. On the way, but-

tons were done up and zippers made magic silver seams
down the fronts of wind breakers that had been loosened
when the children came indoors.

"Per Garson," Peter remembered. "He's to be at the
cave to load the sleds."

He ran to the kitchen to look for him. He was not
there. Peter opened the kitchen door. Outside on the
snow he saw a strange sight.

Per Garson was racing madly around and around on
skis. Old and bent, he was nevertheless skiing with the
grace of an Olympic entrant. He swooped and sailed.
He would loop and then would take off in a jump. Peter
thought he had lost his senses. Then he saw there was a
design in the crazy pattern he was making in the snow.

"He's covering Uncle Victor's tracks," he guessed. For
Per had already been down the slope and had made cat-
steps all the way down to the hollow at its base.

"We're going now, Per Garson," he called.

"Ja, I go, too." He made a mad leap and landed exactly
at Peter's side. "I see you by the woods. You know how
to go? Sure?" Then he gave a solemn wink, his old eyes
screwed in his brown wrinkled face.

Peter had not the least doubt where to go. He told
Per Garson so.

"Is good. I see you there." He gave another long leap
and began a long swift flight through the churned snow.

Peter raced around to the front to get his sled.

"What'd you do if you met a German right here?"
Michael tried to frighten the girls.

"I'd do just what I'm doing now." Helga's eyes flashed.
"I'd go on without so much as a look at him," she sniffed.

They all knew the way to Thor's Rock, so Peter found
he wasn't much needed as a guide. Never mind. After
they got there he'd have to show them how to go around
the wall of snow into the cave.

They trudged through the woods taking all possible

short cuts. When they got to Thor's Rock and the place where the cave had been, Peter got the surprise of his life.

There was no cave.

Peter was sure he had not been mistaken. But here was Thor's Rock and there was no cave anywhere that he could see.

There had been a high wall of snow in front of it, he remembered. But look as he would, all he could see were young pines.

"Ole said it was where the rock curved so you could stand in a heavy rain and not get wet. That's here," he told the others. But for all they searched they could find neither wall nor cave.

It was Lovisa who spied Per Garson's brown face framed in the branches of a young fir.

"You said you could get here without help," he teased Peter when they came close. "It's here all the time."

"There weren't any trees the other night." Peter felt ashamed. He had been so sure he knew just where to find the cave but he had to be shown after all.

"These we fixed to make it seem more real," Per Garson explained. When Peter looked again he saw that a strip of evergreens made a narrow corridor in front of the wall.

"You made it since the night I was here—since the night before last?"

"Ja. Ole and some others. They came yesterday and finished before the blackout."

Peter was still unbelieving. But sure enough, behind the trees was the wall of snow and back of that the cave. Per Garson led them around shrubbery to the entrance.

"Shouldn't someone stand guard over the door in case the Germans come?" Helga asked. "I'll do it."

"Is no need, I think," Per Garson answered. "Still,—is no harm to watch. Spies are everywhere."

So Helga posted herself behind the tree where Per

Garson had been waiting and the others went into the cave.

There was a strange kind of white light inside. Peter thought it might be like being in one of the sepulchres of the Bible. For the strong sunlight was cut down by the wall in front of the doorway and a pearly beam fell on the sides and floor.

Per Garson went at once to the end where a stack of brown bricks rose up like a garden wall.

"Gold," Peter whispered to Michael.

"That? Gold?" Peter agreed with Michael that it was hard to believe that each of those brown bricks was money enough to buy an airplane.

Per Garson began lifting down the bricks.

He laid four of them, side by side, on Peter's sled. Then he went to the far side of the cave to a pile of rough brown sacks like potato sacks,—the bags that had covered the bricks on their journey to the cave. He carried one of these to Peter's sled. He folded it twice and laid it over the rectangle of bricks.

"Next the rope." He produced a new clothesline and with it began lashing the sack and bricks to the sled. Over and over went the rope. Then he drew out a long knife and cut the clothesline.

"We could help you, Per Garson," Peter suggested. "Then we could start sooner."

"Na, this must be done right."

"We could do it right."

"Na. Na. Your Uncle Victor holds me to blame if anything goes wrong. He says we can't have the rope coming loose and the bricks falling in the snow. One time for that and the Germans would have our gold."

They watched him take down more bricks for the next sled. Then more for the next and the next. For an old man he worked quickly. With each sled, the same procedure. First the bricks, then the sack folded twice, then the clothesline.

"Now you tell Helga to come here. I think we can be safe these few minutes."

Michael went to get Helga. She had seen nothing more than a few squirrels.

"Now I show you how to untie the rope," Per Garson announced. "When you get to the Snake you first look for a pair of trees that are fallen and covered with snow. They're 'bout two hundred feet apart. Be sure you find them for that's the place your uncle thinks is safest. Now you untie the knots. And so. And so!"

"Can you do it? Try." He laced the bricks onto the sled again and Peter tried to untie them. He was clumsy at first. Instead of openings he made knots. But after a time he learned how to untie the rope.

When it came Helga's turn she gave one quick pull and the rope was dangling from her hand.

"Good. You learn things fast," Per Garson praised.

Each of them had to prove he knew how to unload the sleds. Michael was slower than Peter to learn. He tried again and again and each time succeeded only in making the knots tighter.

"Never mind." Peter was anxious to get started. I'll untie his for him."

"Na, he'll have to know. Next time he'll have to show his team."

The lesson went on and after a time Michael learned the trick.

"And can you show the others?"

Michael felt he could.

"All right, then. Off with you. You bring back the ropes and sacks. These we need again," Per Garson instructed. "For your pockets, here." He handed each a flat parcel. "Your lunch. For supper you go to Holms' farm where you'll get plenty good hot meal."

He led the way to the opening. "Now I think it's time you go."

Soon would come the moment the four children dreaded—the first German sentry.

Per Garson said the Nazis were on their way to the town but the children had not seen them.

The rest of the morning had been spent pulling the heavy sleds through the woods. They had to go almost all the way back to Riswyk before they could begin to toboggan down the mountain.

What would happen?

What if the Nazis refused to allow them to go on?

What if, somehow, they suspected and began to search the sleds?

Peter wouldn't let himself think of what might happen. He made up stories about the four of them. They were Vikings and their sleds were Viking boats. They were sailing the seas. They would go far, far away. The very nearest they would go would be to America.

"Peter, I'm hungry. Let's eat," Michael proposed when they were barely out of the woods. But Peter had wanted to get a start on the long ride down the mountain. When Michael repeated his request a little later he agreed.

It's an idea, he thought. It would postpone their first brush with the sentinels.

"Girls, we eat," Michael yelled.

They pulled up on a bank beside the road. Their sleds in a cluster, they sat munching the dark bread, dried fish, cheese and cold meat.

"Come on, Michael. Race you to the look-out." Peter wiped his mouth on the back of his mitten.

The look-out was where Peter and Michael, Helga and Lovisa had seen Uncle Victor the day he had so strangely returned to Norway. But now, when the four companions reached that point, it was not to be the scene of a snow battle and all the fun that went with it. Instead there were solemnness and silence, and Lovisa's blue eyes were round with fright.

The look-out today revealed an entirely different sight and one to strike fear into the stoutest.

A German freighter was at anchor in the fiord. Steaming up, she might be about to sail. On the beach that lay between the Atlantic Ocean and Riswyk Fiord, there were hundreds of grey clad soldiers and there were others on the narrow strip of land between the big fiord and the small one they called the Snake. They were unloading enormous supplies because the snow was covered with bales, boxes, crates and drums. Rifles were stacked in neat rows, and up and down the beach in front of the fishing pier, sentries were goose-stepping while their companions worked.

"Whew!" Peter drew off his cap to wipe his forehead.

And now Lovisa was not the only one to be afraid. Fear looked out of all eyes.

It was Helga who made them brave again.

"I'm not afraid of any goose-step!" She shook the curls that hung like sausages from under her hood. "What's there to be afraid of?"

"Come on, then." Peter straightened his shoulders. He drew his sled away from the others. "Let's go."

"Look!" Michael could not take his eyes off the beach. "Soldiers marching right up our sled track. How'll we get down?"

They turned back to the sight below. Michael was right. A company of men had started up the only road that led from the sea to the mountain.

"We could hide till they passed," Lovisa urged.

"Or go down over the rocks," Michael suggested.

"But what'd we do with our sleds? We couldn't take them down that way," Peter replied.

"We'll have to meet them sometime," Helga said. "It might as well be now as later."

"Right," Peter answered. "Uncle Victor said they were to see us today on our sleds. If we sail right into them they'll see us for sure. Come on. Keep to the side and try not to spill any of 'em for that'd be bad for us."

He fell face down on his sled. With a shove he began the descent to the beach.

The Germans were a long way off. The road made several turns in the miles between the look-out and the shore below and only from the look-out could any part of the road be seen. So there was no way to tell if the Germans would turn off before they met them.

"Maybe they're not coming all the way," Peter told himself. "Maybe they'll turn aside."

But when he rounded the slope's last bend he had no such hope. Directly in front was a company of grey-clad, goose-stepping soldiers. Even on the glassy surface their legs swung out straight as rods.

Peter had no way to stop himself and now he found he was headed right into the middle of them. He let out a war whoop, a warning he was coming. But the Germans were directly in his path. He didn't see how he could avoid knocking them down like ten pins.

He was going to spill them, all right, try as he might not to. It was the worst possible thing, he knew. Near at hand these grim grey marching soldiers towered like giants to the boy on his sled.

Down he flew, faster, faster.

At one hundred yards he swerved toward the bank to avoid knocking down a whole row of men.

A voice was barking a command in German and the company took three steps to the side and out of Peter's path.

His swerve drove him into the bank and stopped him as he had not dared to hope. But he had already passed the first of the troops. Only their quick side march had saved a collision.

He raised his eyes from the snow. He was looking into the smiling face of a German infantry captain.

"I turn my men aside." He spoke in Norwegian. "It is not right that we spoil your sledding. When I was a boy I liked nothing better than sledding."

The blood rushed out of Peter's head. He was certainly dizzy. He closed his eyes. When he opened them again he was looking up the slope at the heels of the last row of German goose-steppers.

Michael and the girls joined him on the bank.

"Well, what do you know about that?" Michael was open-eyed with wonder.

"He turned his whole company aside!" Lovisa found it equally hard to believe.

Peter sat up. "If he hadn't, I would have plowed right into 'em. I might have broken my sled and the bricks would have spilled, maybe."

"The least that could have happened would have been to make them angry." Helga spoke thoughtfully.

"We've been lucky, I guess," Peter admitted.

"I told you there was nothing to be afraid of." Helga shook her curls. "When they turn out for you like that they can't be so terrible. Come on. We've got to get to the Snake."

There were more German soldiers to pass before they could make the bend into the farther fiord they called the Snake. To these they would likewise have to come close.

Nearest were the sentries that patrolled between the stacked rifles and the road down from the mountains. The sleds would pass within a few feet of where they walked.

"If Uncle Victor wants them to see us today he gets what he wants," Lovisa pointed out. "They'd have to be blind to miss us."

"Uncle Victor didn't know it would be as bad as this," Peter grumbled. "He didn't say they'd be marching on the road."

"Well, we got past them, didn't we? Come on. Peter, let me go first," Helga begged. "It would look even less suspicious if a girl went first."

But Peter was head of the Defense Club and it was for him to lead them wherever they had to go. No matter what would happen, he must go first. But he was still frightened enough to want Helga to take the lead.

On their sleds again, and the last mile before they would turn the bend by the cliff that hid the entrance to the Snake.

The sentries were taking their stiff-kneed walks beside the rifles. The other Germans went on with their work of unloading the supplies. Nobody so much as looked at the children on their sleds.

What if the sentries were to stop them? Peter asked himself. What if they wouldn't let them pass?

The captain had been friendly because he himself used to like to toboggan, and anyway it was not his job to be on watch as it was these guards'.

But when he went directly in front of the first sentry, he saw only a blank face. There was not so much as a look to show if he was pleased or displeased.

Beyond the sentry Peter saw some soldiers dragging a heavy tarpaulin over the snow. One of them looked in his direction. Under the round cap and fringe of yellow hair he saw the bluest eyes he had ever seen in his life. They seemed to say that he, too, would like to be sled-riding.

Another sentry was stepping up the line over the churned snow and beyond him, another. Like the first one, they had only blank looks to give the children. None of them so much as lifted a finger to stop them.

So they were going to be allowed to go on!

Uncle Victor had been right when he said that no one would suspect boys and girls on their sleds.

Peter breathed a sigh of relief and dug his heels into the snow for a fresh start.

The cliff that hid the Snake was just ahead. Beyond it they would be safe from curious eyes. That day, anyway, would be won.

The sleds would have to be dragged the rest of the way as the ground was level. But it wasn't far to go, after the cliff was passed. There only remained to find the two fallen trees and to bury the gold and build the snowmen.

In the Snake, Peter stopped to get his breath. His sled was terribly, terribly heavy. He hadn't noticed how heavy it was when he pulled it through the woods from the cave. Now it was a fearful load.

The others were close on his heels. They, too, seemed tired. Even Helga crept along, dragging her crushing load of gold.

"But where's Uncle Victor's boat?" Peter searched both sides of the stream with his eyes. There was no boat on the black water.

"The trees!" Lovisa's eyes fell on a flat stretch that was closed in at two ends by long ridges of snow.

"Here's one of them." She poked her arm to the elbow into the crusted white. Then she ran through the deep untrodden stretch. "And here," she called, "is the other."

The four of them began burrowing in the snow. Four pits were made and into each went the brown covered bricks. Then four snowmen rose over the bricks. Each stood guard over a mound of gold worth more than eighty thousand kroner—twenty thousand dollars. So, between the trees, eighty thousand dollars in gold bullion lay buried in the snow.

"We've done it!" Peter exulted. "We passed them and they never guessed."

"Dumb stupid things." Helga's lips curled in scorn.

"We did it! We did it!" Lovisa thumped Helga on the back and then threw her arms around Peter.

And now none of them was tired. They pounded one another's backs and shoulders. They joined hands and circled around and around Peter's snowman.

"And the captain turned aside his troops because he didn't want to spoil our sled track!" Helga burst out laughing. "Oh, if he only knew!" Tears ran out of her eyes. Weak from laughter she could no longer stand and fell helplessly in the snow.

In roars the others fell down beside her.

"He said when he was a boy, there was nothing he liked better than sledding!" Peter choked with mirth. "He likes sledding and so do we."

"Oh, if he only knew!"

Peter would have liked to tell Uncle Victor about the events of that day. But Uncle Victor and his boat were nowhere to be seen.

It was strange, for Peter knew the *Cleng Peerson* was somewhere in the Snake. But look where he would, all he could see was the black rushing water, the bobbing ice cakes and the snow that covered ground and trees alike.

It was getting late. They had to get to the Holms' farm before the blackout. It was three miles up the road from the beach. They'd have to hurry.

It was twilight by the time the little band turned into the farmyard. Here, they were on familiar ground.

They'd passed the German sentries a second time. Again they saw the friendly captain who had turned aside his soldiers. He was returning with his troops and he greeted them.

"Did you have a good sled ride?" he asked in excellent Norwegian.

Peter was sorry he wasn't allowed to answer him.

At the farm kitchen Michael pounded on the door.

"Who is it?" a frightened voice called out.

When Michael gave their names there was a scuffle inside. They had to be recognized before the door would be opened.

"But come in, come in," the farmwife called. And Peter thought that for all the sadness of that terrible day, there was still a cheerfulness about the good brown face. That they had succeeded in carrying the gold past the Nazi sentries seemed to bring hope for Norway.

"You had no trouble?" Her husband came out of a dim corner.

Their supper was even now being dished into great earthenware bowls. Peter thought he had never smelled anything so good. Nor had he seen anything for a long time as pleasant as the flickering dancing light from the fire and from the candles on the dresser and great long kitchen table.

"First they eat, Papa. Then they talk." Fru Holm and her servant bustled back and forth between the fire and the table. "Draw up now and eat, you brave children. You must be famished."

Great steaming dishes dotted the red and white checkered cloth,—meat, potatoes, dumplings, cabbage. On the table were also many cold foods, dried herrings, pickled eggs, mackerel and great round sheets of the hard rye *knackebrod*. Also huge mounds of iced cookies.

The children fell upon the food like puppies around a basin of milk. It disappeared like snow when brought into the house. Fru Holm and Marie, the servant, were kept busy walking back and forth between the table and the stove refilling the bowls. Herr Holm sat in a rocking chair, his pipe between his teeth.

"So you got through all right?" The rough old farmer could not wait to hear their story.

"Papa, let them eat," his wife kept urging. "When Marie and I are washing up you shall hear."

"Ja. Ja. Eat your fill." He rocked contentedly. "It's wonderful that we have boys and girls like these who can trick the Germans and not get caught." He chuckled.

"Shhhh, Papa. Spies everywhere," Fru Holm cautioned. "Could be even here."

Peter drew a long sigh of satisfaction. Never before had he felt so content. The warm food sent a glow to every part of his body.

"We fooled them, all right," he boasted. "They even turned out of our way. The captain said they didn't want to spoil our sledding."

With that, the four of them went into spasms of laughter. The tears rolled down Lovisa's face. Michael had to hold his stomach after all that food.

"But what is so funny?" their host inquired. "Tell us so we can laugh, too. You fooled them, but what is funny?"

The four of them started talking at once. But they kept interrupting themselves to laugh. They started to tell of Peter's ride down the mountain, head on in the path of the German army corps. Then they all had to stop because they were choking. So it was some time before poor Herr Holm could make out what had happened. But when he learned of the politeness of the captain whose only fear was that he might spoil their sled track, he, too, shouted with laughter.

Marie McSwigan received both the Junior Scholastic Magazine Gold Seal and the Pacific Northwest Young Readers' Choice Award for Snow Treasure. She has also written Juan of Manila (Dutton), based on the story of a Filipino boy who broadcast resistance messages during the Japanese occupation of the Philippines.

A Picnic on the Island

BY HILDA VAN STOCKUM

Illustrations by the author

> Paddy the Piper has come home to help his mother, Mrs. O'Flaherty, celebrate her birthday. All the O'Sullivans, big and little, are to share in the fun of an Irish holiday.

FRANCIE and Liam adored Paddy the Piper. As soon as they awoke the next morning they were out of their beds and into their breeches, in the hope of meeting him. Paddy was so accustomed to be out in the open air that he never could stay long indoors and would be roaming about before the cocks crowed. Sure enough, there he was at the well, drawing water for his mother.

Francie gave a whoop and Paddy looked up.

"Is it Cuchulinn and Finn I'm seeing?" he cried, and went to meet them, a bucket in each hand. It was his joke to call the twins by the names of those ancient warriors. He said they had the same spirit entirely.

The twins hurled themselves at him; Liam nearly fell into one of the buckets and spilled half the water over him.

"Well, what have ye been doing since I came here last? Have ye been using the scissors again?" Paddy remembered ruefully the holes they had cut into his hat on the last occasion.

"If it's the same to you, I'd rather keep me other clothes the way they are, though the ventilation in me hat has been a great comfort on hot days!" The twins blushed. They remembered how angry Mother had been and how Paddy had pleaded for them, saying that it was holes he'd been pining for secretly ever since he got the hat.

"I'll give ye a new one as soon as I'm grown," Cuchulinn promised him. "I'm going to be a policeman."

"Well, you'll have to grow a lot then," Paddy remarked, looking down at Francie. "I meself tried for that high honor and they told me no one under six feet would do."

"Do ye think they'd mind me foot?" asked Francie anxiously. Paddy's eyes softened.

"The greatest of men," he said, "were men who had something wrong with them and conquered it. There was a poet once who could not write down his own poems because he was blind, and a musician who could not hear his own pieces because he was deaf. Far away in a country over the sea one day, a babe was born and it was so deformed that people around wanted to kill it in mercy. But the angels protected it and it grew into a saint of great wisdom whom all men flocked to see."

"It's a policeman I'll be," Francie argued stubbornly, not attracted by scholarship or saintliness.

"I, too," echoed Liam.

"Well, who knows?" Paddy agreed cheerfully. "Maybe you'll be holding me up yet and asking me, have I a license for walking the roads; and when I don't show one, ye'll be locking me up for not watching me steps and knocking the motorcars to smithereens."

The twins laughed heartily at this notion, but they didn't laugh long for Clementine poked her nose around the corner of Mrs. O'Flaherty's cottage and rolled her eyes. She was devoured with jealousy for Paddy and would try to butt him whenever he came near. This time she pranced along the road with threatening motions of her head and the twins fled with a scream, hiding themselves behind Paddy's back.

Paddy laughed. "Arra, policemen, ye're not afraid of a cow, are ye?"

"She may be a cow," said a timid voice behind his back, "but it's a bull's look she gave us!" Paddy grinned.

"Watch what I do to her," he said, taking a blowpipe from his pocket and stuffing a wad of paper into it. He blew up his cheeks, and the next minute the paper ball flew through the air, and landed on Clementine's nose. She sneezed and capered, shaking her head and squinting down to see if her nose was still there; then she jumped around and galloped off with a comical look of dismay, her tail in the air. The twins emerged cautiously from behind Paddy's back, gleefully watching the cow's flying heels while they made a show of helping to pick up the buckets.

"Your tea is wetted!" cried Mrs. O'Flaherty from the door of her cottage, the curlpapers still in her hair. "You'd better come in and have a sup!" Paddy's quick legs soon reached the door, but he wasn't allowed to go through. The twins had fastened themselves to him like leeches and would not let go.

"Ye'll not sneak away when we turn our backs?" they

begged. "Ye'll not run off on us like ye did last time? Ye'll stay awhile?" Paddy laughed and drew his little friends into the kitchen.

"Here, Mother, here's two more wanting me to take the day off. What do you say to that now?"

Mrs. O'Flaherty planted her hands on her hips and regarded her son gravely. "I say it would be a shame for you to leave your old mother to have a birthday all by herself. It's not as if I had any other children." Her voice grew husky and she turned her head away. The twins

made ready to run, for they hated to see a grownup crying, but Paddy gave his mother a kiss that sounded like a cork popping out of a bottle and she smiled again.

"Sure, and I wouldn't desert ye today, Mother!" he said. "Didn't I miss a grand wedding down at Kilgarvan only for the pleasure of being with ye! I have a plan that'll make a day of it yet, you'll see!" And he winked mysteriously. The twins were all agog to pry the secret out of him, but though he lured them on with sly grimaces and fascinating whispers they could get nothing out

of him, and down the road they heard their mother calling them to breakfast, so they had to give up.

"Paddy is planning to do something today," Liam announced importantly, when two plates of stirabout had
taken away his first hunger.

"What?" asked Michael eagerly. Liam looked at Francie, who returned his glance.

"I can't tell," he said.

"Ah, come along!"

"No, it's a secret."

"A fine secret it is when Paddy lets it out to the likes of
you! It's boasting ye are!"

Liam looked hurt, and Francie said "Pooh!"

"Sure, he wouldn't share his secrets with little boys,"
Brigid remarked. "They don't know a thing." She watched
out of the corners of her eyes, waiting for the twins to
blurt out everything; but Francie was unmoved.

"Paddy knows we wouldn't tell," he said calmly, snatching another slice of bread. "Not if you pulled our nails
out one by one, we wouldn't." He shut his mouth grimly.
Mother put her hands to her ears.

"Bless the boy, where does he get those bloodthirsty
ideas!"

"I don't get them anywhere," Francie said scornfully.
"They come to me natural." His mother shivered and the
others laughed.

"Well, I'm going to find out Paddy's secret!" cried
Michael impatiently. "If he told it to them he'll tell it to
me!" Dashing down his spoon he made for the door.

"Wait for me!" cried Brigid, hurriedly swallowing her
tea. Of course the twins wouldn't be left behind, so the
four of them burst into Mrs. O'Flaherty's kitchen and
surprised Paddy in the act of devouring his last piece
of bacon.

"They say you've told them a plan you have and they

say it's a secret!" began Michael indignantly, pointing to Liam. Liam blushed but Paddy kept a grave face.

"That's right," he said. "That's about the size of it. I'm glad to hear they've not broken their promise." Liam's face lit up but mean old Paddy went on. "Now I've changed me mind and ye may let out me grand secret if ye like." The twins looked at each other and remained mute. Paddy took pity on them.

"Well, I see ye don't know how to begin," he said, laughing a little to one side of his mouth. "I know someone who'll be able to do it better. Mother!" He called and Mrs. O'Flaherty hurried from the bedroom, dressed in her Sunday-best. "Tell them the news, will ye?" Mrs. O'Flaherty's face beamed.

"We're going on a picnic!" she said. "We'll be out for the day and all of you are welcome. I was just on me way to ask your mother."

"Hurray!" cried the children. The twins quite forgot they had pretended to know all the time and exulted openly.

Father and Mother O'Sullivan were delighted to accept the invitation. There was no work to be done that day that couldn't be done as well tomorrow, and it was long since they had been on a regular holiday. They were to go in Mr. O'Sullivan's boat, and row to one of the islands where they'd make a fire and roast potatoes and cook the fish they would catch. The day couldn't be finer and everyone felt in high spirits.

First the food and fishing tackle had to be packed and Brigid was instructed to wash the ears of the twins. Their howls mingled with the excited barking of Bran and the sad lowing of the poor cow Clementine, who had to be left behind, as she was inclined to get sick in a boat. Mrs. O'Flaherty hated leaving her behind and she went down to the Murphys' to ask them if they would keep an eye on her.

"Her heart'll be broke if she sees me go. She's that jealous of me son she'd eat him if she could, bless her heart," she explained. "If ye send someone around now and again to see if she's got something to drink and to speak a friendly word to her I'll be much obliged."

The Murphys promised, and so, with a lump in her throat, Mrs. O'Flaherty parted from her pet. Clementine stuck her head out over the lower half of her stable door and mooed tragically when she saw the happy party go off without her. Three times her mistress turned to wave to her, then the bushes at the bend of the road swallowed her up. Clementine gave a sniff and settled down on the straw for a lonely chew.

Bran, of course, was allowed to come; he jumped, barked, romped, tailwagged, and goggled his delight. He and the twins ran up and down the road whilst the others came behind slowly, laden with nets and oars and pans and packages.

Father's boat was beached in a small inlet of the bay, where pine trees soughed dolefully and brown weeds trailed down into the water from the pebbly shore. It was a nice roomy boat, and the packages and pans could be stowed away safely in a dry spot under the front seat. When they had all climbed in, Father and Paddy each took an oar and softly the boat glided between weed-laden stones and towering pines out into the bay. There the water surged more strongly, the boat rocked, and a breeze blew the locks of the children into their eyes.

"Mm! How the wind smells!" cried Brigid, sniffing up the snappy sea air and licking the salt from her lips. The water sparkled in the sun, overhead seagulls screeched and circled darting down now and again to snatch up a fish, their wings cutting the air like silver scythes. Steadily the boat made its way, the waves gurgling and lapping against the bottom, the oars creaking and sighing as they swung to and fro. The morning light shone on the faces of the women, who sat back in their seats with contented smiles, glad to have a day off.

When they were well out into the bay, Father and Paddy put out the nets. While they worked, the twins fished in the water with their fingers, trying to catch pieces of floating seaweed, till their mother told them to leave off or they'd fall in. Bran behaved very well; he sat in a huddle in the middle of the boat and felt too unsafe to dare move a paw. When the nets were spread Paddy and Father took the oars up again and they rippled on.

At last the boat arrived at the largest island in the bay, where they moored it to a stone. They all scrambled out and the children ran around the island, exploring it and peeping around rocks whilst the men hauled up their catch. It wasn't a large haul, but there were enough mackerel for a good meal, and they set to cleaning them.

Meanwhile Brigid and Michael went looking for sticks to build a fire and the twins romped on the long, waving grass with Bran. Under a small, crooked, windswept tree where Mother built an oven, she and Mrs. O'Flaherty kept a fire of pine cones and straw until the children came back with armfuls of wood. Then the potatoes were washed and dropped into a pan of sea water, whilst Mother put on the kettle with fresh water she had brought for the tea. Meanwhile the children slipped down to the pebbly beach to bathe. It was such lovely warm weather that Mother made no objections, though she warned them not to stay too long in the water, and she called out to Paddy to keep an eye on them on account of the currents.

The water was too cold for the children to venture far; they preferred to race around in the surf, sending fountains of spray into the blue air; or they urged Bran to fetch a stick they'd thrown in, and watched him sneeze and snort as he dived through the billows to retrieve it. Their laughter rang out clearly, causing Mother and Mrs. O'Flaherty to smile to themselves as they laid out the tin plates and spread butter on thick slices of bread.

At last the men clambered up the rocky slope with the clean fish, and as soon as the seafood sputtered on the skillet its lovely smell coaxed the children out of the water. They slipped back into their clothes, with chattering teeth. Smoothing their wet locks, they ran to get

warm and flopped breathlessly down on the grass under the pine tree, where a delicious meal awaited them.

"Here's to me darling Mother and may she live long!" said Paddy, lifting up his mug of tea. The children promptly cheered, saying they wished that Mrs. O'Flaherty had a birthday every day.

"God forgive ye, then I'd be old too soon!" chuckled Mrs. O'Flaherty, whose face shone with pleasure. They all felt lazy after the good food, and stretched themselves full length on the grass.

"Will ye be staying long, Paddy?" asked Michael. Paddy gave his nose a rub until it shone like a berry.

"I'll have to be leaving tomorrow," he said, with a guilty glance at his mother. "I'm going to the fair in Bantry to fill up me bag and then I'll be taking the bus to Cork!"

"So ye're going to the fair, Paddy?" said Father, taking a puff at his pipe. "Faith, we'll be together then, I'm going there meself with some eggs."

"Oh, Father, take us with you!" begged the children. "We love the fair."

"Maybe I will and maybe I won't," promised Father. "Hold yer whisht now, for I want to talk to Paddy. What's the hurry on ye that ye're leaving us so soon?"

"It's the poems the children found," explained Paddy. "They're shouting to come out into the world. Is it meself will keep them prisoner after the long years of waiting they had, under the cold wet sand? Sure, ye can't blame me if me feet are itching to be on their way to Dublin."

"What do ye plan to do with them?" asked Father.

"Sell them, if I can," said Paddy briefly. "The money belongs to the children, of course, but I don't know if the poems will be worth anything. I'd be willing to pay for having them published; they seem that valuable to me."

"Would ye get money, real money for them?" asked Brigid excitedly. "And would it belong to us entirely?"

"Hush, hush!" said Paddy. "Don't you go fancying things now. There's too much good in the world that's certain, to go worrying about what isn't certain. It's the fine fish you're after eating that ye should be thinking about and the warm sun on your skin and all the lovely days that roll like apples into your lap."

"Bedad, you're right, Paddy," Father agreed, blowing out a cloud of smoke. "We do be thinking of what might happen when we ought to be thankful for the good we've got."

Mother nodded silently over her knitting, a slow smile coming and going on her face.

"Tell us a story, Paddy," begged Francie, who was getting restless among all these sleepy people. Even Bran sat dozing near the fire and Liam had put his head in Mother's lap and looked as though he didn't want to get up ever.

"Yes, yes, do tell us a story!" the others echoed. Paddy was nothing loath. Accustomed to the open air he seemed to need as little rest as the wild animals.

"Here goes," he said, settling himself more comfortably and tilting his hat against the sun. "In the days long ago, before Saint Patrick banished the snakes, there were giants in Ireland so big that they could swallow an ox whole. They were strong but they were just like any other body in their hearts. So when a Connemara giant, called Fergus McGrath, who was champion of all Ireland, heard of another stronger giant in Donegal he grew pale with jealousy, just as you or I would. He was getting old and there had been no need for him to fight for such a long time that he had gotten out of practice.

" 'Must I fight this new giant and prove I am stronger?' he asked of his little wife, his voice quavering as he said it. His wife said nothing as she sat by the fire with her knitting. She knew he was not what he had been, but she didn't mind that. She set no store by muscular strength. 'What's strength to a woman's wit?' she'd say. She just sat and knitted and counted stitches till her husband stamped out of the house in a rage.

"Well, the other giant—Donal was his name—was like a young bull, bursting to test his mettle. He had heard of Fergus McGrath's fame and he said it was all put up. He didn't believe it.

" 'I'm going to find out meself if he'll stand up in a fight,' he said, and he meant it. When Fergus heard this he quaked so the house shook.

" 'Must I fight him?' he asked of his wife, but his wife kept on knitting and counting stitches. Suddenly there was a big bang on the door and when Fergus peeped through the window he saw a man twice the size of himself waiting to be let in.

" 'It's Donal!' he cried, running around in a circle like a dog that's mad. 'It's not meself that'll knock the likes of him down! Ochone! Me reputation is ruined!' And he burst into tears. Then his wife saw that she must put by her knitting. 'Go to bed,' she said, 'and don't say a word. Leave it all to me!' Before the visitor knocked the second time she had lifted the latch.

" 'How are ye, ma'am?' the giant said. 'I'm Donal O'Ma-

honey from Donegal.' He tugged at his forelock, for he
didn't carry a hat and he had been taught manners by
his mother. 'Is Fergus McGrath at home?'

" 'He is not,' said the missus. 'But you're welcome all the
same and he may be in any minute now. Sit ye down and
make yourself comfortable.' So Donal scraped his boots
on the threshold and went in. 'What might you be wanting of himself now?' asked Mrs. McGrath. 'It's not often
we have visitors in these parts.'

" 'Have ye never heard him speak of me?' asked Donal
in a disappointed voice. Mrs. McGrath pretended to
think deeply. She wrinkled her forehead.

" 'No,' she said, 'unless you be the man that promised
to call for the old suit he's grown out of.'

" 'How can I be him?' cried Donal with flashing eyes,
pushing out his chest. 'Sure, ye can't have looked at me
properly, ma'am, or ye wouldn't be saying such a thing.'
Mrs. McGrath took up her knitting again and settled herself beside the fire.

" 'It is true,' she said, glancing at him. 'The old suit
would not fit you; you're too narrow in the shoulders.'
Donal snorted, but awe crept into his eyes.

" 'Well, if so, it's your husband'll find a smaller man can
beat him.' Donal puffed himself up with pride until he
was a formidable sight. Fergus peered through the curtains of the press-bed and groaned.

" 'What's that?' asked Donal, who had sharp ears. 'Did
I hear a man's voice?'

" 'No,' said Mrs. McGrath, dropping a stitch. 'It's only
me wee babe has the colic.'

" 'Oh!' And Donal sank back in his chair. 'Will your
husband be here soon?' he asked.

" 'He will, so. He has only gone out to the woods to
root out some trees,' she said and, as she noticed the rumbling of thunder in the distance, she put up a finger. 'Do
ye hear them falling? He has the wood nearly plowed up

now. He pulls the trees out like radishes. "Why don't you use a hatchet?" says I to him often and often. "What for," says he, "when this way is simpler and saves trouble in the end?" So I let him be; he must have his own way in everything. Mrs. McGrath shook her head. 'It's terrible to be wedded to a man with a temper,' she went on with a sigh.

"Donal's cheeks paled and he began to fidget on his chair. 'What's the matter?' asked Mrs. McGrath. 'Aren't ye comfortable? Come, take a cake. They're me husband's favorite.' She handed him a stale dog biscuit. Donal took a bite and broke two teeth.

"'Thank ye,' said he, putting the biscuit down. 'I'm not fond of sweets.'

"'I'm sorry to hear it,' said Mrs. McGrath. 'If I had known you were coming I'd have made you something heartier; but me husband likes soft food.'

"'Do ye think he'll be here soon?' asked Donal hastily, with a timid glance at the door.

"'He'll be here as soon as he has loaded the trees on his back,' said the missus. 'Come and have a look at me babe to while away the time. He's a bit puny; all his brothers were handsome fellows, but he, being the last and a trifle sickly, he's not much to look at for a six months' child. Still, have a peep.' And she led her visitor to the bed where her husband was lying and pulled the covers from his terrified face. When Donal saw the huge bearded fellow and heard he was only a six months' infant, he put a hand to his head.

" 'If so, what'll the father be like!' he thought, and terror came over him like a whirlwind. 'Don't let me keep ye any longer, ma'am!' he said to Mrs. McGrath. 'I don't think I'll wait for your husband after all!' and he ran to the door, stumbling over a pitchfork.

" 'Och! I'm sorry now,' murmured Mrs. McGrath picking it up. 'Me husband *will* leave his pocket combs lying about. . . .' Donal didn't listen. He ran out of the door and down the road and up hill and down hill all the way until he reached his mother's kitchen, where he fell gasping on a chair and asked for a glass of water. Fergus crawled cautiously out of his bed.

" 'Is he gone?' said he. His wife had taken up her knitting and paid no attention to him.

" 'What's strength to a woman's wit?' she thought."

"Oh, Paddy, that's a lovely story!" cried Brigid. "I never heard that one before!" Paddy grinned and chewed some grass.

"It's very old and very Irish," he said. "It's the kind of story that is told from father to son around firesides in the West and everyone changes it a little. Most of our stories come that way. They are not dead tales, lying forgotten in a book on a dusty shelf. No, they live on the tongues of people and they grow and change like all live things."

"But Fergus wasn't truly Irish," said Francie, who had listened wide-eyed. "He was a coward."

"We're all cowards," Paddy explained, "when we meet something that's too strong for us."

"I'm not!" said Francie, setting his jaw. The others laughed.

"Did Donal find out about Fergus later?" asked Liam.

"Oh, no," said Paddy, "Donal was so frightened, he never again put the tip of his nose outside Donegal, and Fergus remained champion till he died."

"I'm glad," sighed Liam.

Bran had finished his afternoon nap and barked impatiently. He tugged at Francie's shirt, his eyes begging for a rollicking romp. The twins were ready for it, for their legs felt prickly from sitting, and soon the dog and the little boys tumbled out of sight, their mother's warning ringing in their ears: "Don't go too near the water!"

The older people sat around and talked a little longer but Michael and Brigid wandered off to the shore, where they found mussels on the rocks. They gathered as many as Brigid's apron would hold and then they found a jellyfish dithering on the seaweed, with long rosy tentacles flopping in all directions and blue veins running across its glassy body. They poked it with a stick and turned it over, looking with interest at its belly. When the shadows began to slant long across the grass, they went back to the others. They found their mother and Mrs. O'Flaherty busy packing up.

"Here, you help carry these down to the boat," Mother told Michael as soon as she saw him, and she shoved a parcel into his arms. "It's time to go."

"What am I to do with these?" asked Brigid, showing the contents of her apron.

"Bless your heart, where did you find so many mussels? Put them in this basket; they'll make a fine soup tomorrow!" Michael was already scrambling down to the boat, but on his way he met Father and Paddy, who came running back, looking worried.

"Did ye play with the boat, Michael?" shouted Father. "What have ye done with it?"

"I didn't touch it," said Michael indignantly. "We've not been near the place. We were on the other side of the island all the time!"

"Well, it's gone," Paddy explained quietly. He stood in his shirtsleeves with his thumbs tucked in the armholes of his waistcoat. He had wound a string of seaweed round his hat and he looked so funny that Michael would have laughed, if the news had not been so terrible.

"Gone?" he stammered, looking at the place where the boat had been moored. Only strands of seaweed floated on the empty waves which caught the amber glow of the late sky. "Gone. . . ." He looked around helplessly. It suddenly dawned on him that they were on an island and that they couldn't get off unless they had a boat. Pictures of a clammy night spent in the open, frosty breezes nipping toes and fingers, and a pale, indifferent moon looking down on huddled prisoners, flashed through his mind. "But we must find it," he cried. "It can't have gone far."

"What's the matter?" asked Brigid, who had followed him and was climbing the rocks with a load of pans that clattered at each movement.

"The boat is gone!" shouted Michael. "We've got to find it!" He put down his burden, and started running off like a goat, Paddy after him. Father chose the opposite direction and Brigid joined him, putting her small hand into his large hairy one.

"Perhaps the twins went out in it," she suggested. "I haven't seen them for a long while."

"Begob!" Father stood still and frowned. "Maybe you're right!" An anxious look wrinkled his face.

"Here, I must go to Mother and find out what happened to the lads." He turned about and leaped up the hill in great strides, Brigid clinging breathlessly to his coat. "Mother!" he shouted, as soon as they caught sight of the women under the tree. "Mother! Where are the twins?"

Mother came running to them. "The twins?" she gasped. "I thought they were with you. . . . I haven't had me eye on them since they went off with their dog, God preserve us. Has anything happened to them?" She looked around wildly.

"I fear they may have gone in the boat," said Father, his voice trembling. "It's disappeared."

"Oh, why, why didn't ye keep an eye on them!" cried Mother fiercely, turning on poor Brigid, who flushed scarlet, the tears welling up in her eyes.

"Didn't ye know the scamps would be up to mischief?" But when Brigid burst out weeping she kissed her hurriedly. "Hush, it's me own fault entirely. I'm their mother that suckled them and should have known better than to lift me eyes off them a minute. There, there, don't take on, Mother didn't mean it. Hush, there's no time to be lost, we must be up and after them for fear they'll . . ." Her voice trailed off, she dared not say the fearful word "drown."

Father was already pacing the island, holloing for the twins. A clump of pine trees hid the north part of the bay from view and he dashed through it. As soon as he reached the open he saw the boat rocking uncertainly in the distance, and in it two helpless little boys waved frantically to attract notice. Father didn't stop to think at all. He promptly threw off his coat and shoes and plunged into the surf, the salt stinging his eyes as he dived.

Paddy and Michael were just clambering around the bend when they saw him leap. "There is the boat!" cried Michael, who spotted it at once with his sharp young eyes. "And it isn't empty, I notice," added Paddy grimly. "I know what your father is after now." He shed his waistcoat and shirt to plunge into the water himself. "You stay here," he cried out. "There are whirlpools about. Go and tell your mother." Off he went to help Father. Mich-

ael dashed through the pines, running breathlessly till
he saw his mother.

"Mother! Hollo! Mother!" he cried. "We've seen the
boat! The twins are in it and Father and Paddy are swimming to fetch them!"

"Where, where?" cried Mother, hurriedly scanning the
horizon but unable to see the boat on account of the trees.

"Come here, I'll show you." Michael dragged his mother
through the clump of pines, followed by Brigid and Mrs.
O'Flaherty, who twisted her apron and prophesied all
sorts of dreadful things.

"There! look!" Mother flopped down on a convenient
rock with a sigh half of relief and half of concern. She
watched the two men struggling on to reach the boat
which rolled perilously with its precious cargo.

"Will they make it?" asked Brigid anxiously. It seemed
to her that her father was about to drown and she gave a
shriek every time his head dipped under.

"Oh! me son!" wailed Mrs. O'Flaherty, wringing her
hands. "The last one that's left to me—Oh! I'll see him
perish afore me naked eyes! O Saint Patrick and Saint
Brigid, protect us!" But Mother said nothing; her eyes
were glued to the boat and her lips moved soundlessly.
The boat seemed to be drifting off and one of the twins
put out an oar in an effort to stop it. This clumsy movement nearly unbalanced the boat and Father shouted
from the water between hoarse gasps: "Leave go! Sit
still. . .double-eared donkeys!" The boy dropped the oar
into the water and it drifted away.

"Now they won't be able to row back!" wailed Brigid.

"Hush!" whispered Michael. "Don't worry, Mother,
more'n you can help. Father'll settle it. . . ." His eyes followed his father's valiant efforts with admiration. In the
meantime Paddy had noticed the floating oar and, seeing
that Father was well on his way to the boat, he swerved
and struck out after the oar. Mrs. O'Flaherty was now

convinced he would be lost. She gave up wailing and started to weep, rocking herself to and fro and wiping away her copious tears with the tip of her shawl.

At last Father reached the boat. After some heaving and trying, he managed to climb in. The watchers on the shore could see the twins cling to him joyously, though the distance was too great to carry their voices. A moment later Paddy arrived with the oar and clambered in too. Then the men rowed the boat back with long and sure strokes; Mrs. O'Sullivan and Mrs. O'Flaherty fell into each other's arms with cries of relief; Michael and Brigid hurrayed at the top of their voices and waved with all their might. Soon the boat was close enough for them to hear Bran's excited barking and the unceasing chatter of the rescued twins.

"What made you do such a foolish thing after I had warned you not to be venturing near the water?" asked Mother of her youngest sprouts, when the boat had landed and everyone sat around a newly lit fire to get warm and dry again.

"Francie wanted to row," explained Liam. "He wanted to go around the island and explore."

"And then the sea would not leave hold of us," added his brother. "We didn't mean to go so far, but we couldn't get back. I think the fishes pulled us, or maybe the sea fairies did."

"No, there are currents around; you were caught in one of them," explained Father. Francie shook his head.

"They were no currents," he protested. "They were big, black monsters, and made a fountain, and then there was another fountain and another. Bran was frightened too. He barked at them, he did. Are there giants in the sea, Paddy?" he asked hopefully.

"Giants in the sea, me darling?" said Paddy, who sat so close to the fire that his toes got singed and clouds of steam fled from his soaked trousers. "Giants? 'Course there are. Why wouldn't there be? And they are specially fond of little boys like you! There are great big dragons down there, and when they sweep their tails it storms and the ships sink and fall right down their mouths and are snapped up like that." Paddy snapped his fingers.

"Arra, don't fill his head with nonsense," protested Father. "He's fanciful enough already. You saw porpoises, me lad. They come around in shoals and squirt water through their nostrils. They are big fish." Michael looked enviously at his brothers. He was a little sorry he hadn't thought of getting lost in the boat himself. Now that all had ended well it seemed a grand adventure. But the twins snuggled close to their mother.

"We thought we'd never get back," whispered Liam tremulously. "The sea growled and growled and looked so deep and dark and we shouted and shouted till we had no more noise here." He pointed to his throat. "And then there was a huge fish with prickles standing on his back. We saw him quite close with teeth like Father's wood-saw. He looked at us and well I knew he'd have liked to eat us, only he couldn't, so he swam away." Father shuddered and Mother pressed her boys close to her heart.

"A shark!" muttered Paddy, his face blanched. "Holy saints!" They were all silent for a minute, thinking of the merciful escape, not only of the boys but also of the grown men, who might easily have been attacked by the monster. Only rarely did sharks venture into the bay, so neither of the men had suspected the danger they were in. Mrs. O'Flaherty began to weep again, but Paddy wouldn't have it.

"Thanks be to God we're all back safely and it's songs we should be singing, not spilling tears!" he cried. "I'll start with a ballad." So Paddy sang:

> "Clarence McFadden, he wanted to waltz
>   But his feet weren't gaited that way.
>   He went to a teacher who looked at his feet
>   And added two pounds to his pay.
>
>   One two three,
>   Balance like me,
>   You're quite a fairy but you have your faults,
>   Your left foot is lazy
>   Your right foot is crazy
>   But don't be unaisy, I'll teach you to waltz."

Everyone joined in the chorus and laughed at the last couplet, in which Clarence gets entangled in his partner's feet and they both tumble on the floor.

"Now we'll sing *our* song!" cried Francie, eager to win some applause. So the twins stood up in the firelight, clasped each other's hand, and sang in their piercing treble:

> "Dan Dan was a funny wee man,
>   He washed his face in the frying pan,
>   His hair was like a donkey's tail,
>   And he combed it with his big toe nail."

After that they were hugged by the women, though goodness knows they had been naughty enough and didn't deserve to be made so much of!

The sun had dropped low; it was time to hurry home. The breeze had died and the water in the bay stood like pale glass and mirrored the purple islands, the feathery yellow clouds, and the slowly winging seagulls. Stuffing the picnic things back in their place under the front seat, they all climbed into the boat. As it slowly glided off in the evening stillness, Mrs. O'Flaherty and Mother sang a wistful song about the "Minstrel Boy." Their voices rang clear across the water and seemed to express the thankfulness with which their hearts ran over. The twins dropped asleep against their mother's lap, Bran whimpered a little and then settled down quietly, and the elder children trailed their fingers in the water with drowsy content. Creak, splash, went the oars, until the boat bumped against the pebbly shore. The lovely holiday had ended.

The lovable O'Sullivans live in a delightful world where each member of the family takes part in caring for the rest. Their adventures are continued in Francie on the Run *and* Pegeen.

INDEX of Authors and Titles

ACKNOWLEDGMENTS

The publishers wish to express their appreciation to the following publishers, agents, authors, and artists who have granted permission to use material appearing in this book. Any errors or omissions are unintentional and will be corrected in future printings if notice is sent to The Crowell-Collier Publishing Company.

ABINGDON PRESS Excerpt from *Li Lun, Lad of Courage*, by Carolyn Treffinger, illustrated by Kurt Wiese, copyright 1947 by Stone and Pierce; used by permission of Abingdon Press, publishers.

THE BOBBS-MERRILL COMPANY, INC. "Ajax, the Golden Dog," from *Ajax, Golden Dog of the Australian Bush* by Mary Elwyn Patchett, illustrated by Eric Tassley, copyright 1953 by Mary Elwyn Patchett; used in the U.S. by special permission of the publishers, The Bobbs-Merrill Company, Inc.

E. P. DUTTON & COMPANY, INC. Excerpt from the book *Snow Treasure*, by Marie McSwigan, illustrated by Mary Reardon, copyright 1942 by E. P. Dutton & Company, Inc.; reprinted by permission of the publishers.

FOLLETT PUBLISHING COMPANY "Damasi's Party," from *Thirty-One Brothers and Sisters* by Reba Paeff Mirsky, illustrated by W. T. Mais, copyright 1952 by Reba Paeff Mirsky; reprinted by permission of Follett Publishing Company, Chicago.

GROSSET & DUNLAP, INC. Illustrations by William Sharp for "The Sesemann House is Haunted," from *Heidi* by Johanna Spyri; reproduced from Illustrated Junior Library by permission of Grosset & Dunlap, Inc.

HARCOURT, BRACE & WORLD, INC. "Chúcaro," from *Chúcaro, Wild Pony of the Pampa*, by Francis Kalnay, illustrations by Julian de Miskey, copyright 1958 by Francis Kalnay; used by permission of Harcourt, Brace & World, Inc.

HARPER & BROTHERS Excerpt from *The Wheel on the School*, by Meindert DeJong, illustrated by Maurice Sendak, copyright 1954 by Meindert DeJong; reproduced by permission of the publishers, Harper & Brothers.

HOUGHTON MIFFLIN COMPANY "Christophilos and the Pascal Lamb," from Joice M. Nankivell's *Tales of Christophilos*, illustrated by Panos Ghikas, copyright 1954 by Joice M. Loch and Panos Ghikas; "Tomas Is Lost," from Elizabeth Kent Tarshis' *The Village That Learned to Read*, illustrated by Harold Haydon, copyright 1941 by Elizabeth Kent Tarshis; reprinted by permission of and arrangement with Houghton Mifflin Company, the authorized publishers.

LONGMANS, GREEN AND COMPANY, INC. Excerpt from *Gift of the Forest*, by R. Lal Singh and Eloise Lownsbery, illustrated by Anne Vaughan, copyright 1942 by Longmans, Green and Co., Inc.

LOTHROP, LEE & SHEPARD CO., INC. Excerpt from *Eskimo Boy* by Pipaluk Freuchen, illustrated by Ingrid Vang Nyman, copyright 1951 by Lothrop, Lee & Shepard Co., Inc.; reprinted by permission of Lothrop, Lee & Shepard Co., Inc.

LUTTERWORTH PRESS For permission to reprint in Canada "Ajax, the Golden Dog," from *Ajax the Warrior* (American title, *Ajax, Golden Dog of the Australian Bush*), by Mary Elwyn Patchett, illustrated by Eric Tassley.

THE MACMILLAN COMPANY Excerpt from *The Saucepan Journey* by Edith Unnerstad, translated by James Harker, illustrated by Louis Slobodkin, copyright 1951 by The Macmillan Company; used by permission of The Macmillan Company.

McGRAW-HILL BOOK COMPANY, INC. "Wild Elephant Raid," from *Burma Boy*, by Willis Lindquist, pictures by Nicolas Mordvinoff, copyright 1952, 1953 by Willis Lindquist and Nicolas Mordrinoff; reprinted with permission of Whittlesey House, a division of McGraw-Hill Book Company, Inc.

WILLIAM MORRIS AGENCY, INC. "Ajax, the Golden Dog," from *Ajax, Golden Dog of the Australian Bush* by Mary Elwyn Patchett, illustrated by Eric Tassley; reprinted in Canada by permission of William Morris Agency, Inc.

HAROLD OBER ASSOCIATES INCORPORATED *The Big Wave*, by Pearl S. Buck, copyright 1947 by The Curtis Publishing Company; reprinted by permission of Harold Ober Associates, Incorporated.

L. C. PAGE & COMPANY "Anne's Confession," from *Anne of Green Gables*, by L. M. Montgomery, copyright 1908 by L. C. Page and Company, 1935 by Lucy M. MacDonald; used by permission of L. C. Page & Company, a subsidiary of Farrar, Straus and Cudahy, Inc.

PANTHEON BOOKS INC. Excerpt from *The Son of the Gondolier*, by Elsa Steinmann, illustrated by Johannes Gruger, translated by Richard and Clara Winston, copyright 1958 by Pantheon Books, Inc.; published by Pantheon Books Inc.

THE VIKING PRESS, INC. "A Picnic on the Island," from *The Cottage at Bantry Bay*, by Hilda Van Stockum, illustrated by the author, copyright 1938 by Hilda Van Stockum; reprinted by permission of The Viking Press, Inc.